Praise for
the Seeker series

"Strange yet familiar, with just enough romance to keep you turning the pages. . . . Will not disappoint."

—USAToday.com

"Katniss and Triss would approve." —TeenVogue.com

"A complex family saga . . . Dayton excels at creating memorable characters." —*Publishers Weekly*

"Teens who like action, dystopian, or fantasy with fast-paced plots will enjoy this." —*The Bulletin*

"Fans of Veronica Roth's *Divergent,* Marie Lu's *Legend,* and Suzanne Collins's The Hunger Games series: your next obsession has arrived." —*SLJ*

"Fast-paced action, bloody battles, breathless escapes, intrigue, and treachery." —*VOYA*

"Time travel, interdimensional anomalies, and magic all combine to make this . . . a twisty ride." —*Booklist*

"Both past and present choices shook me to the core, and the final pages left me trembling." —FanboyComics.net

BOOKS BY ARWEN ELYS DAYTON

THE SEEKER SERIES

Seeker

Traveler

Disruptor

The Young Dread (an original e-novella)

DISRUPTOR

Arwen Elys Dayton

EMBER

Text copyright © 2017 by Arwen Elys Dayton
Cover art: background copyright © 2017 by Stuart Wade; swords © 2017 by Bose Collins
Scottish Estate map copyright © 2015, 2016, 2017 by Jeffrey L. Ward
Fox, ram, and atom icons copyright © by Shutterstock
Bear, boar, eagle, fanged cat, dragon, horse, and stag icons copyright © 2016 by John Tomaselli

Visit us on the Web! randomhouseteens.com

Educators and librarians, for a variety of teaching tools, visit us at
RHTeachersLibrarians.com

The Library of Congress has cataloged the hardcover edition of this work as follows:

Names: Dayton, Arwen, author.
Title: Disruptor / Arwen Elys Dayton.
Description: First edition. | New York : Delacorte Press, [2017] | Sequel to:
    Traveler. | Summary: "War is on the horizon, and Quin and Shinobu have
    been separated. They must find each other, and possibly ally themselves
    with John and Maud, to stop the sinister plans to eliminate Seeker
    families begun generations ago" —Provided by publisher.
Identifiers: LCCN 2016037934 | ISBN 978-0-385-74411-9 (hc) | ISBN 978-0-385-37859-8 (el)
Subjects: | CYAC: Assassins—Fiction. | Adventure and adventurers—Fiction. | Antiquities—
Fiction. | Science fiction.
Classification: LCC PZ7.D338474 Dis 2017 | DDC [Fic]—dc23

ISBN 978-0-385-74415-7 (trade pbk.)

Printed in the United States of America
10 9 8 7 6 5 4 3 2 1
First Ember Edition 2017

To Alexandra, for making life funnier, messier,
and much, much better from day one

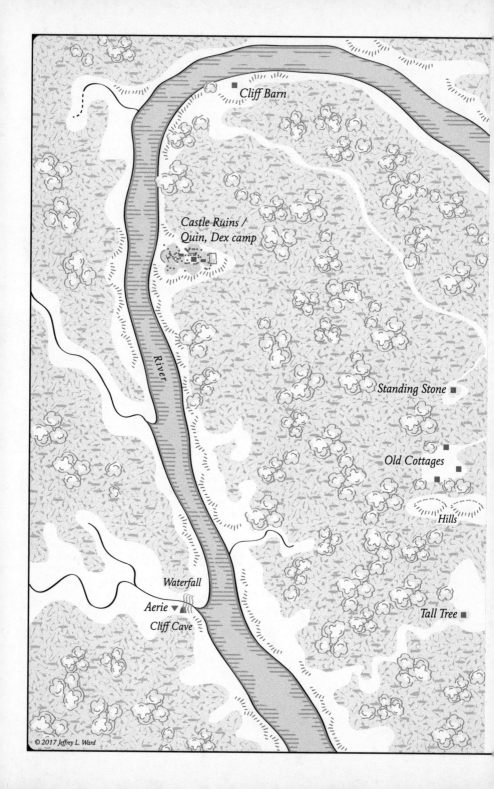

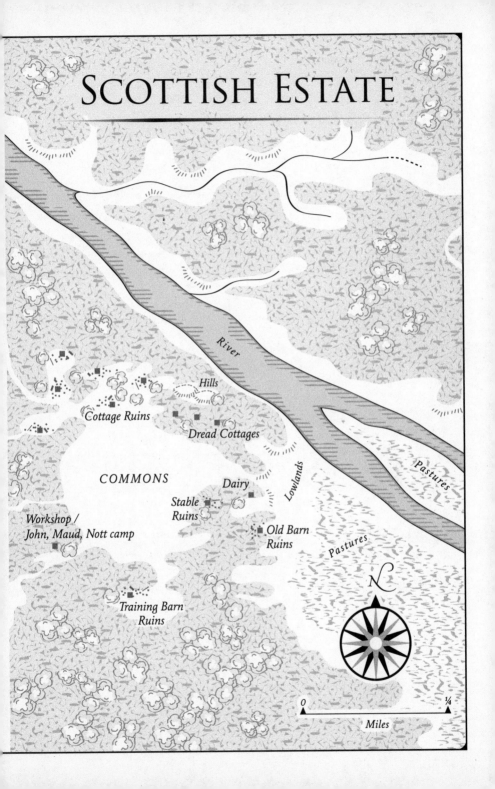

PREFACE

The blackness of no-space swallowed light. Any illumination here could reach only faintly before darkness closed upon it, extinguishing it as though these hidden dimensions were composed of black water.

Dex was like a fish in that water, slicing steadily through the darkness, never stopping, but never moving fast. Like a fish, he glowed a faint silver, as though covered in shining scales. The glow came from the stone medallion around his neck, which gave off a light as weak as the first nearly invisible glimmers of dawn. Yet Dex's eyes had learned to gather any illumination and use it sparingly, which meant the carved stone disc was bright enough for him to see by.

After ages of quiet, the medallion trembled against his chest, startling him. There was only one reason it would shake of its own accord—another medallion was calling, and Dex's was vibrating in response. He gently grasped the disc and changed his infinite course through no-space, to see who was coming and going.

Dex was leading a horse by its reins, and with a gentle tug he pulled it along with him. He'd come upon the horse only moments ago, it seemed. The animal was neither awake nor asleep. No-space had its hold upon the creature, but it was not the same hold it had on humans. The horse existed in a half-life, patient and obedient.

After a time, the medallion stopped shaking, but by then Dex could see where he had to go. There was a flash of light in the distance, so bright it blinded him. He was looking at a round doorway back into the world.

The world. It's still there, burning under the sun. It never stops.

When he reached that doorway, he would discover which of the old family had called him—except the light was gone long before Dex got near it. That was no matter. He continued to follow its afterglow.

Now he passed through the space where usually a circle of boys stood, silent sentinels in the blackness. He'd seen those boys many times, smelled the odor of death that hung about them like a fog. But they were gone.

Only a lone figure was left near the collection of weapons the boys had once guarded. Dex stepped around a row of disruptors, feeling an involuntary shudder.

The solitary figure was a girl. There were girls stuck in no-space, of course, and Dex had seen all of them, had come to know everything here in this place outside the world. But this girl was new. The horse made a sound, low and faint, a dream whicker, as though it had caught the scent of someone it knew. A velvet ear twitched.

Dex couldn't see the details of the girl's face. He decided, after a long, anxious deliberation, to use more light. In the pocket of his robe, his fingers met the cool cylinder of his flare. How long had it sat there, unused? To him it was days, but to the flare it was a long spool of time that had been unwinding without measure.

His thumb clicked the striker once, twice, three times. A white flame bloomed. In the first moment it was brighter than his memory of the sun. He turned his head away until his eyes adjusted. When he could look again, he examined the girl.

He knew her. The first glimpse of her was like looking into his past. Or into his heart.

But no. This girl was not that girl. How could she be?

Her pale cheeks were flushed with some strong emotion, and her expression was worried—angry, even. Her mouth looked as though it had fallen still in the middle of speech. Her hands reached to hold on to a companion who was no longer there.

There was no medallion in her hand, so the disc that had called Dex belonged to someone else—someone who had left her here and escaped back into the world through the blinding doorway that had already closed.

He touched the girl's mind with his own, stirred the thoughts that lay like stones within her head. Very slowly, those stones shifted.

Quin, her mind told him at last.

The disappointment was overwhelming. Quin. He had hoped . . . Dex banished this thought, though it left him very reluctantly; she was a different girl and her name was not important. Only her clothes mattered; they were modern, with stitching that spoke of factories and machines.

Something was wedged into a pocket of her trousers. Dex carefully drew out a crinkly packet with a picture of grains and berries on it. Food. The label was in English and Chinese. He couldn't read Chinese very well, but modern English was easy.

There was an expiration date, which he read several times.

Here we are.

"So," he said aloud. He marveled at his voice after having been silent so long; the single word was like a foghorn, and it twisted his mouth into odd shapes. How much time had passed since he'd last spoken? A hundred years? A thousand? Ten thousand? Surely not so long as that. He spoke again, testing the waters: "It's time to go."

Gently he bent down and pushed his shoulder into Quin's waist, slid an arm around her, and lifted her as he stood. She was entirely frozen, so he balanced her on his shoulder like a wooden beam. She knocked against Dex's metal helmet, but it remained firmly on his head, just as it had since the dawn of . . . all this.

He reached for the medallion hanging around his neck.

He would have to get used to sunlight all over again.

The thought was terrifying.

CHAPTER 1

QUIN

Quin floated on a dark ocean, unconscious of anything. Then, by slow degrees, she became aware of herself. There was light coming from somewhere, blue-tinted and dim. She was lying down, and the surface beneath her was hard and uneven and cold.

Someone was there. A warm touch on her lips, so soft and fast, she wondered if she'd imagined it. Noise surrounded her, a sound like a distant deluge of rain, but much too fast, as fast as the breeze across her face.

She remembered. She and Shinobu had gone *There,* but she was losing herself, and he was begging her for help. She had to claw her way back to him. Right now!

Quin sucked in a lungful of air and lunged to her feet.

"Take me out, Shinobu!" she said. "Carve an anomaly!"

Her voice was slow and rusty, and she was no longer *There.* A moment ago there had been the glow of a lantern, and Shinobu's dark form in front of her, and beyond that the deepest blackness. They'd discovered that the Middle Dread had been turning Seekers against each other for hundreds of years, while keeping himself "blameless" in the eyes of the other Dreads by getting others to do the actual killing for him. Quin and Shinobu had gone *There* to find whatever the Middle had been using to sow discord. But where was she now?

Somewhere new. A cave, rough surfaces colored by bluish illumination from an opening high up in one of the walls. The light was changing, as though it came from a sky with fast-shifting clouds. The noise was still there, far away and close, the sound of rushing water.

She could see Shinobu's silhouette. He was here with her, wedged into a corner of the space, as confused as she was.

Quin stumbled toward him, discovered that her body wasn't working properly. The walls lurched and teetered, but it was her own muscles that weren't functioning. She recalled the Old and Middle Dreads closing in on her on the Scottish estate, months ago. Their movements had been uneven, out of sync with the world around them, because they'd been lost in the hidden dimensions for years. She was like that now, buffeted by the stream of time.

"Shinobu! How long were we *There*?"

She laid her hands on the dark form in the corner. It turned toward her. Too fast. Everything was too fast.

A face she didn't know, a young man, towering over her. Unruly hair and eyes that were dark in the cave's dim light. He was wearing a focal; his expression was wild. This person wasn't Shinobu at all, and he was reaching for Quin.

"It's good you're awake." He spoke so rapidly, Quin nearly missed the words.

She'd lost herself *There* when she was supposed to be keeping an eye on Shinobu. Had they run into this man? Had he taken Shinobu's focal and spirited Quin away? She lurched backward, trying to pull herself properly into the world. Her hand found the knife at her waist.

"Shinobu? Shinobu?" Maybe he was nearby.

The strange young man came for her, moving so much faster than she could move.

"It's all right," he said.

It was not all right. What had he done to them? How much time had passed? Quin felt his hand grip her elbow. She wrenched free, drew her knife—slowly, too slowly. The walls moved by in fits and starts as she pushed herself away.

"Shinobu, are you here? Answer me!"

The cave was small, more a widened channel through rock than an actual chamber. She blundered down the only route available.

"Stop, stop!" the stranger called, sounding both angry and afraid.

The channel narrowed dramatically after only a few steps, but it then opened up again. Quin squeezed through the tightest spot, moving as if in a dream, and found herself in another chamber. She heard him behind her at the narrow neck, too big to follow her easily.

The noise was louder here, a thundering of water in the rocks, so rapid it was like hearing a recording on fast-forward. There was less light. Quin felt her way along the darkened channel for several yards, and the air around her changed, became moist as the noise drummed harder into her ears.

"I can't follow you!" he called. "Please!" There was something awful, desperate, in the way he said it.

"Shinobu, are you here?" Her voice was still slow and heavy.

The channel narrowed again, and now the floor beneath her was dark with water and the air full of mist. Quin stepped around a sharp bend and found herself abruptly washed in early dawn light and staring directly down the face of a cliff. The channel had ended in open air, and her front foot hung several inches out over the ledge. Droplets festooned the atmosphere, dazzling her with rainbows. She was behind a waterfall, at the edge of a sheer drop, the cascade thrumming and reverberating as it launched itself over the craggy headland above her and out into the sky, where it plummeted down and down and down.

With a nauseating jolt Quin felt herself rejoin the flow of time. For one moment, she was whole; she then lost her balance in a rush of dizziness. The height . . . the height . . . She dropped her knife, grabbed for the walls of the crevice in which she stood. The stone was solid beneath her fingers, but her foot, hanging over the edge, gave her the sensation that she was falling. Her knees buckled. She clutched her meager handholds as hard as she could, overcome by vertigo, pleading desperately with herself not to let go.

Hands were on her arms, drawing her away from the ledge. "I've got you," the stranger said, his voice no longer fast but natural. "You're all right."

Her companion held her up, and together they staggered back the way she'd come. When they reached the narrow spot, Quin slid through, and with difficulty he squeezed himself through after her.

She collapsed where she'd woken up, head against the wall as she hugged her knees. "Oh, God," she muttered, pressing herself into the rock hard enough to ward off the memory of her foot hanging out over that edge.

It took her some time to recover her wits. She focused on her breath, following it in and out until she returned to herself. When she opened her eyes and the cave came into focus, she discovered the mysterious young man crouching a few feet away, watching her anxiously.

"There you are," he said. "I'd hoped you would wake up all right, but that didn't go so well."

Quin's eyes shut again. She found her knife on the ground by her leg. He must have retrieved it for her. Why would he do that? She gripped the hilt and drew strength from it; Shinobu had given her this blade.

Quin opened her eyes to discover that the light in the cave was growing brighter, showing her new details. Her companion was young, but older than she was, perhaps in his midtwenties. He wore something like a monk's habit, made of a coarse brown material. His curly hair was brown as well, as were his eyes. He would have been handsome except for those eyes, which were large and distorted by some power that had him in its grip. They made his face dangerous.

"Should I take it personally that you prefer to plunge to your death rather than sit in a room with me?" he asked. It was a joke, though he didn't look amused or relaxed.

"Did you take me from *There*?" she asked him, coming back to herself more with each moment that passed.

"You were stranded in no-space."

She'd never heard that term before, but she knew immediately it must be another word for the hidden dimensions.

"Shinobu was with me."

"He wasn't. I know no-space better than the back of my hand. He was gone before I found you." His voice shook, but whether with fear or anger, Quin couldn't tell. Something was wrong with him.

He was a Seeker, obviously, and she was going to find out what he'd done. Was he a pawn in the Middle Dread's scheme to turn all Seekers against each other? "Did you take his focal?" she demanded, meeting his wild eyes with her own. "Did you leave Shinobu *There*, helpless?"

"If he was there, he left before I found you. And you—" He looked upset, wounded by her question. "It's *my* focal. It's always been mine. I *rescued* you."

Quin walked herself through the hazy, slow last moments with Shinobu. He'd been in trouble. He'd wanted her to take off his focal, but she hadn't been able to move by then.

She studied her volatile companion in silence, realizing that it was entirely possible that Shinobu had gone off on a fool's errand. It had been her job to keep an eye on him, to make sure the thoughts from the focal didn't overpower his own. If this stranger was telling her the truth, then Quin had lost herself, and after that she'd lost Shinobu somewhere as well.

"Where are we, then?" she asked, trying to take the accusation out of her voice. Maybe this person *had* rescued her.

"We're in the *world*," he answered in tones of awe, as if he didn't quite believe in the world. As if this were his first visit.

She said, "And where—"

"You want a place name, something specific." He was shaking his head. "I can't think that way. Give me time!"

His voice trembled badly. She saw that he was making a great effort to hold himself together, but he looked ready to jump out of his skin at the slightest provocation. With a sweeping glance, Quin estimated him as an opponent. He was big, perhaps twice her weight, and agile. She'd grown up around fighters and knew a dangerous man when she saw one.

"I'm not going to hurt you," he said, as if reading her thoughts. "You're welcome to that knife you're clutching. I don't mind. I waited here with you for hours until you woke up. If I'd meant to hurt you, I would have. I don't like fighting."

The words carried a ring of sincerity. Despite his feral look, she was inclined to give him a measure of trust. Unbalanced did not necessarily mean evil.

"Who are you? Which house?" she asked him. "Where did you train to be a Seeker?"

"I don't know specifics so quickly."

"But your name—?"

"I saw your clothes and your food and I knew it was time," he said angrily. Apparently she had pressed him too hard. She watched him master himself, but his voice quavered as he added, "Your clothes and that food are modern. As modern as I needed them to be." He gestured at a wrapped food bar lying on the floor, which Quin vaguely remembered stuffing into her pocket at some point. He edged closer to her, on his knees. "Would it offend you if I took your hand?"

"What?" Was he asking to hold her hand, or was he so crazy that he was asking permission to remove it? She tightened her grip around the knife hilt.

A surprised laugh escaped him. "*Held* your hand," he corrected himself. "I didn't mean I wanted to cut it off. I only ask because I'm not used to this much light. I—I haven't got any weapons on me, though there are a few in the cave. And wonders."

What did that mean? As if the sky had heard her question, the light shifted abruptly. Clouds outside had parted, allowing a glow of yellow to flood through the high, natural window in the rock and show Quin her surroundings clearly at last. The space where the two of them sat was large enough for six or seven people crammed in at close quarters. There was no way out except the cliff plummet off to her left. And she could now see a couple of whipswords lying haphazardly nearby, along with a few other objects—strange items that she didn't recognize, made of stone and glass, items that looked both ancient and intriguing, like things the Young Dread might carry, like things her father should have taught her about during her Seeker training. *Wonders*, he'd said.

The young man was still moving closer, avoiding a beam of sunlight as though it were poison. In the brighter light, she saw his focal more clearly, and could hear the crackling of its electricity. It was not Shinobu's helmet. That was the truth. It was quite different, larger, maybe cruder, and there was a *D* melted into the temple, by a child, she guessed, looking at the rough design of the letter.

"I told you it was my focal," he said, noticing her gaze. "It's the oldest one there is."

His large hand enclosed her own, and Quin allowed this because she was pondering what he'd just said: His focal was the oldest focal? What family did that put him in? And how had he come by the artifacts on the floor?

"I need your steady hand," he said. He glanced at the sunlight, which shone on the wall only a few feet away from his shoulder.

"Are you worried it's going to burn you?"

"A little bit." He took a deep breath, in and out, as he pressed her hand between both of his. "Will you pull off my helmet? There's no escaping it—it's got to come off. And then we can get out of here."

The thought of leaving was plainly terrifying to him, but it energized Quin. She had no athame and therefore must cast her lot with this unpredictable companion if she wanted to get somewhere—anywhere—familiar and begin looking for Shinobu.

After extricating her hand from his, she gently removed his focal while he watched her with tortured eyes, bracing himself for pain. He collapsed the moment it was off, and with a deep groan pressed his forehead into the floor. When she set the helmet aside, she could hear the buzz as its streams of energy severed themselves from him like a swarm of dying bees.

Quin caught only a few of the muttered words that flowed through his gritted teeth: ". . . It's supposed to focus . . . I never wanted it to tear . . . should have done better . . ." He spoke as though he had a long and rough history with his focal, and she wondered if it affected him in the same way Shinobu was affected.

"Stop! Come here," she told him. He'd made a gash across his temple against the jagged floor. She pulled his head up, and when he felt her touch, he clutched her, a drowning man holding a piece of driftwood.

"I hate wearing it and I hate taking it off," he said against her knees. "And the sunlight hurts."

She steadied him with a hand on his cheek. She let her vision shift into the healer's sight she'd been taught by Master Tan in Hong Kong. When her eyes lost focus, she could see the lines of electrical flow around his body, bright copper streams just below the level of normal sight. In an ordinary person, these lines flowed slowly in a regular pattern, and as a healer, Quin had learned to manipulate them. In her companion she saw something entirely different. A bright shower erupted from his right temple, flowed swiftly down across his body to his left hip, where it rejoined into a single stream that disappeared within him. He was like a waterfall himself, with violent bursts cascading into him and out of him over and over, temple to hip. His terror and his evasive answers were now rather less mysterious; such an energy pattern could not be pleasant to live with.

Quin wondered if she could heal him. But a few moments of watching that bright, savage flow put an end to that thought. She'd never seen a pattern like his and doubted she had the skills to make a dent in it. She would have to coax him along until he took her out of this cave.

Eventually he became calmer, and when that happened, she let her eyes settle back into ordinary sight. He was marked, she saw, by those strange energy lines. A patch of hair above his right temple was devoid of color—almost clear, as though it were dead. She wondered if she would find a matching scar on his left hip.

His chest was still against her legs. "Thank you for coming back to me," he whispered.

"You found *me*," she told him gently. "And maybe you'll help me find Shinobu."

"Shhh."

He released her and lay on the cave floor, gazing up at the roof.

He looked drained, but no longer distressed, at least. His features were finely shaped and somehow, she thought as she studied him, familiar to her. He gave an impression of nobility that she couldn't quite pinpoint. Perhaps it was the loose, shaggy hair, like the locks of a medieval knight in one of her mother's very old novels.

"We're both alive together now, Quilla," he whispered, in a tone different from the one he'd been using. He was calling her by another name, the name of someone he must have loved. "I can hardly believe it."

She tried to match the softness in his voice as she said, "Where's your athame?"

"I have no athame, nor do I need such a blunt instrument."

She'd never heard a Seeker describe an athame that way—as if it were something inferior. "Then how did we get here?"

"In the usual way," he whispered, and he laid a hand across his heart. Something in the gesture suggested he was crazy all the way through. And yet, there were hints of information here that Quin wanted to pursue. Had he brought her back from *There* without an athame? She had been separated from Shinobu while they'd been in the process of discovering the long-hidden secrets of Seekers. Had she stumbled upon someone with some of the answers?

"What's 'the usual way'?" she asked him carefully, hoping a gentle question might sidestep his defenses.

He turned suddenly toward her. "You know I want to tell you. I would have died in your place if I'd gotten to you in time." He spoke so lovingly, as though they knew every detail of each other. "I'd much rather you and Adelaide were alive than be alive myself, Quilla."

"I'm—I'm not Quilla," she said softly, feeling a pang of sadness at this glimpse of his story. Suddenly she remembered the light, warm pressure she'd felt on her lips as she woke up. "Did you kiss me before?"

"You're so like her," he said, as if in a trance. "What if you are her?"

She touched his shoulder. "I'm Quin."

He looked puzzled but undeterred. "But will you help me?"

"I've got to—"

"Stop telling me about Shinobu!" he cried savagely. In one violent motion, he twisted up to a sitting position and glared at her. "Whoever he might be, I'll find him, if that's what you want. I'm only asking for a little bit of help first!"

Quin bit back any response. She needed him to get her out of this cave, and then she needed to find Shinobu and keep him from doing something mad. But when she looked again at the glass-and-stone "wonders" and at the odd focal her companion had been wearing, she found she had already decided. She and Shinobu both would want to learn from this wild young man, if they could only get beneath the insanity.

"Who are you?" she asked him tentatively.

His gaze on her was like a physical force, heavy and uncomfortable. He looked like he was struggling to stay friendly. "I'm Dex," he said at last, succeeding in reining himself in. "We can go now, if you want. I know most people don't like small, dark spaces as much as I do."

"How do we go?"

He cast about on the floor and gathered up the wonders. "You hold these as a token of my commitment. You help me, and I promise I will help you."

She took them from him and asked, "Are these old Seeker tools?"

Her calmness was calming him. "They're at least as old as that," he said. "They must be used in a big open space, which is why I need you. I'll teach you the things I refused to teach you before."

Very slowly, as if afraid of being hurt, Dex extended his left hand into the beam of sunlight coming through the opening. When the sun fell on his skin, Quin saw a tiny stone-and-glass device that was looped over his middle finger and lying in his palm.

"What is that?"

"Catching all of them won't be easy. But they need to be caught, Quilla." He looked down at her with his big brown eyes, and Quin thought fleetingly that Quilla, whoever she'd been, must have enjoyed the warmth of that gaze, no matter how crazy he was. "They've messed things up royally, and it's time to stop."

She wasn't about to ask Dex who he was talking about. She'd pushed him, she guessed, nearly to the end of his tether. He'd said they would leave—she could hold her tongue until he'd shown her how.

But when he took his left hand out of the sunlight and slid it around the back of her neck, she backed away.

"Don't . . ."

"I'm not going to kiss you," he assured her softly, the hint of a smile pulling at the corner of his mouth. His hand was at her neck, and the warm stone of the strange object in his palm was pressed against her skin.

A shock traveled through her spine and up into her head. Quin went limp in his hands, and was, almost instantly, unconscious.

CHAPTER 2

SHINOBU

Shinobu stood on the crumbling ledge of stone, biting his fingernail as he surveyed the mess he'd made. Twenty Watchers—twenty!—lay about the broken floor of Dun Tarm. The ruined fortress was wedged into the water of Loch Tarm, and half of the structure had fallen to rubble and slid into the lake. What remained was mostly open to the sky, the floor a patchwork of ancient flagstones, pitted and out of alignment and covered in moss and puddles of rainwater. There were even trees growing up between the flagstones, gnarled and stunted oaks with the bright green leaves of spring.

Shinobu stood with his back to the cold water and the granite peaks that rose up beyond the lake. The day was beautiful and mild, and the sun touched his back with late spring warmth where it peeked out between towering clouds. He noticed none of these things. He was watching the Watchers, who were sprawled in positions unsuited to lying down, exactly as they had been since he'd brought them into the world. They were so still that they might have been carved out of Dun Tarm's discarded stones, but they were slowly, moment by moment, relaxing into natural poses as they rejoined the stream of time. When they did, they would be awake and dangerous.

This is madness.

No. It's how I keep Quin safe. I tame these boys and use them.

His mind was arguing with itself as it now did almost constantly.

He slipped a hand into a pocket of his cloak and withdrew the medallion. It was a stone disc, about four inches in diameter and perhaps an inch thick at the center. He noticed more details now that he was studying it in bright sunlight. On the face was the symbol of the Dreads, three interlocking ovals. The back, which he'd thought was mostly smooth, was actually pockmarked and scratched—or perhaps not scratched but *etched* with lines forming concentric circles. And had it been vibrating? He'd been focused on retrieving all the Watchers, but hadn't he felt it shaking in his pocket when he was in the darkness *There*?

The medallion was heavy with unknown properties. All Shinobu knew was that it was his talisman to control these boys. It had belonged to the Middle Dread, and the Watchers had already shown him that they respected it as a symbol of authority. With it, he was their master, just as the Middle Dread had been. Looking at all twenty of them, however, he had his doubts. He'd fought four of them once, with Quin, and he and Quin had barely made it through the fight alive.

Why do I want them? They're dangerous.

Quin wants to understand Seeker history. If these boys aren't on our side for that, they'll be against us.

"But I don't have Quin to check on me," he whispered aloud. At once he closed his lips tightly, as if that might prevent the boys from hearing what he'd said.

You left her There *to keep her safe.*

I left her. I left her.

The hand of one boy twitched. Another boy's foot shifted on the stone floor; a head jerked to one side. They were almost awake.

They were all dressed in dark, scratchy-looking cloaks, as though the Middle Dread had found them in medieval European villages. He must have gotten them from everywhere, though, because they were of all sorts, Asian, Indian, and African. They filled the air with the scent of death, which came, Shinobu had discovered, from bits of rotting animal flesh they carried around in their pockets.

They're terrible.

He tried to run a hand through his hair, but he was thwarted by the metal focal. How long had he been wearing it? He was supposed to keep track.

Why was the sun so warm? Scotland had been cold when he and Quin were last here. When had that been?

How long has she been in the darkness alone?

Each moment There *is safer than here.*

Is it?

A boy nearby was groaning and feeling for his knives. Another was muttering something. Then, quite suddenly, twenty boys were stirring, and twenty pairs of eyes opened and latched on to Shinobu.

CHAPTER 3

QUIN

How long has she been in the darkness alone? Shinobu asked. He sounded far away and confused. *Each moment* There *is safer than here.*

Is it? Quin tried to ask.

"Quin, do you want to get out of the cave?"

She was awake in a sudden rush. There was still the rumble of the waterfall in the rocks around her, but there was another sound—a deep, low hum penetrated her lungs and her stomach, almost making her sick. Quin sat up and clamped her hands over her ears.

"Come!" Dex was yelling to be heard over the competing vibrations in the air.

Directly behind him, where the wall of the cave should have been, there was something else entirely. It was as though the rocks had been ripped out and replaced by blackness.

No, not blackness exactly.

"Is that an anomaly?" Quin asked him—shouting—trying to grasp what she was seeing. How had she fallen asleep? The noise was so distracting, and she knew she was forgetting something.

"Do you mean an opening to no-space?" Dex yelled back. "Yes,

— 20 —

that's what this is! And when it's open, it's the strongest note in the hum of the universe."

The opening was larger than any anomaly Quin had seen. The whole wall had disappeared, and instead of a circular border as would appear after carving an anomaly with an athame, the glowing edges of this opening were thicker and held the shape of a huge semi-circle, like a tunnel carved through the mountain, with streaks of light smearing backward and leading the way deep inside.

Dex pulled her to her feet. Quin stopped at the incandescent, seething edge and looked up at the ceiling. It had been cut in half by the anomaly's arch.

"You shocked me into unconsciousness," she said, remembering now. "Why did you do that?"

Dex had the courtesy to look somewhat abashed. "You know I'm not supposed to show you how it works."

That was all the apology she was going to get. "How . . ." She searched for the question. "How long has it been open? Won't it fall shut?" Her training told her that you used anomalies quickly and carefully.

Dex shook his head. He wasn't wearing his focal; it hung down his back from a leather strap around his neck. His shaggy brown curls were loose about his face, making him look boyish and young—and he also looked frightened. He pointed to the floor of the cave.

"It won't collapse until I collapse it," he explained.

Near Quin's feet was a small stone disc. She recognized it—it was the medallion Shinobu had shown her back in the cliff barn. It lay at the center of the flat base of the glowing semicircle; the anomaly was flowing outward from the disc.

"Where did you get that?" she asked him.

Dex tugged her forward. "Please, before I lose my nerve."

She shook him off, leaned closer to get a better look at the disc.

It wasn't Shinobu's medallion after all. Like Shinobu's, it was carved with the symbol of the Dreads—three interlocking ovals—but the pattern along the edge was different. Dex hadn't stolen this from Shinobu; so far, he hadn't lied to her, and she really had no choice but to go along with him.

She allowed Dex to guide her forward, and together they stepped across the threshold. The border was more than a foot wide, a bright band of hissing, swirling energy. Quin held her breath as she crossed over into what should have been the familiar darkness of the place *between*.

"It's not dark," she said, surprised. The light coming off the anomaly's border streaked out on either side like hazy guide lights in a tunnel.

Dex smiled at her, a seasoned explorer with a naive companion. He stooped over the medallion, made a minute twisting motion with the disc between his hands. When he lifted the medallion up, the space around them warped, like a water droplet joining with other drops and changing its shape. At once the cave opening was far behind them, and they were well within the dark tunnel.

Compared to the medallion in his hands, an athame was . . . a blunt instrument, just as Dex had said. The disc was manipulating the space *between* as a potter manipulates clay.

The medallion held out on his palm, Dex began to walk. The smears of light on each side defined themselves into shapes. Quin saw the rock of the cliff they'd been inside, the water at the top of the falls, grass, and sunlight. These things were discernible within the blackness, as if the landscape were flowing around her and Dex behind a dark curtain, as if this tunnel they were in were pushing its way through the world.

She recognized where they were immediately. The landscape spread out beyond this high meadow was the Scottish estate. The waterfall was the same fall she and Shinobu had visited a dozen times when they were children. Until now, she'd only been as far as the pool at its base and hadn't known of the hidden cave to which Dex had brought her. It was as though he knew the estate better than Quin, who'd lived there for most of her life.

"We walked through the cliff and now we're above it?" she asked incredulously.

"In a way." Dex was keeping his eyes turned from the view. "The hidden dimensions are curled up at every point of our world. You can unfurl them all at once with an athame, or unfurl them as you go with this." He held out the medallion.

Dex made another series of adjustments to the stone disc.

"Look," he said. To their left, in time with the shifting of the medallion, the curtain became less substantial and the shapes more distinct. Quin could see a high open meadow, covered in spring grass and cut by the wide channel of the river above the falls. And there, at the water's edge—

"Yellen?" she whispered in astonishment.

The horse grazed on the long grass. Quin could make out an uneven blaze down a broad, reddish-brown forehead. It was Yellen without a doubt.

She'd lost track of her horse two years ago, when she'd jumped, on his back, through an anomaly and escaped from the estate during John's attack. Quin had been shot in the chest, and tangled up with Shinobu, and neither of them had known what became of her horse.

"How did he get here? I haven't seen him in two years."

"I came upon him in no-space," Dex said, as if that sort of thing happened to him every day. "Call him, if you like."

"Yellen!"

The horse lifted his head, twitched his ears toward her, and whinnied. She whistled and clapped her hands smartly, the way she'd done when she was ten years old and had first taught Yellen to come to her. The horse approached warily, evidently not able to see Quin, though she could see him clearly. He still wore his bridle, the same bridle she'd put on him two years ago. She coaxed him closer by voice, until he'd poked his head through the gauzy fog and his muzzle touched her hand.

"Come on," she whispered, and she pulled him all the way inside the anomaly.

Yellen whickered, and Quin touched the horse's forehead with her own, overjoyed to have found him again. It was like finding a piece of herself she had mislaid.

As soon as he was fully with them in the strange tunnel, the brightness of the meadow began to fade. Dex was manipulating the medallion and was walking again. Quin followed with her horse, soothing him as he tossed his head nervously. In a few moments, though, he had fallen into a docile state and was following her easily.

Traces of the world moved by like ghosts on either side. It was as if they, inside the tunnel, were walking through the world, but also as if the world were being moved around them.

Her mind kept darting back to Shinobu, and she wondered where he was and how she would find him. But this dance Dex was doing between the world and the hidden dimensions *There* was like nothing she'd imagined, and she couldn't help losing herself in the experience as it unfolded around her.

CHAPTER 4

QUIN

"Can I tell you a story?" Dex asked her, calling her thoughts back to him as she led Yellen behind him. Dex had visibly relaxed as soon as the meadow and river had faded behind the thick curtain of darkness that marked the edge of their tunnel. "It will help me, and you may find it interesting."

"All right." The chances of his story making any sense were slim, but she wanted to hear anything Dex might say, in hopes of gathering a few useful grains of truth. His effortless use of the medallion in his hand was proof that he'd been trained as a Seeker far more thoroughly than Quin.

"There's a man, and he was in England—a different England from the one you would find if you traveled south right now, because it was before this time," Dex began. He glanced at her, perhaps to make sure she was giving the tale proper attention, and then looked down again. "But it was England anyway. This man—Quilla, can you imagine?—he carried an enormous pack on his back, with all sorts of wonders stored inside it."

Dex fell silent, lost in the imagined details. Beyond the dark tunnel walls, Quin could discern open air and the waterfall, behind them now.

"What sort of wonders?" she asked quietly.

Dex nodded toward the objects made of stone and glass that Quin had tucked into her waistband and pockets. "Things like those. Those are wonderful, if you can remember how to use them."

"If *I* can?"

"Or me," he said, with a look of discomfort. "Or me, of course."

The ghost of a larger river appeared on Quin's right, with the forests of the estate above it.

"The man's wife was with him," Dex said, "though she came reluctantly, if we're being honest. I want to be honest, finally. And his son was with him too, and a second son, who was so young that his mother carried him everywhere. He liked that. Babies like to be carried—you know that from Adelaide." He smiled a private sort of smile, the smile he reserved for Quilla. He said, "It would turn out the boys were very different from each other, but it was too early to know that then. How could they? When children are small, they can still be anything.

"This family walked across the whole of England, down to the south and up to the north, back when the land was open and as wild as England has ever been."

"How long ago?" Quin tried to picture the world he was describing, as she watched the spectral shapes of a hillside and trees go by. Inside their dark tunnel, they were traveling onto the estate, her home.

"We have to think about it in two ways," Dex told her thoughtfully. He was gazing at something only he could see in the blackest part of the tunnel. "It was a long time ago, or maybe it hasn't happened yet."

And with that, Dex's brief spell of coherence came to an end. He stayed silent as thick woods slid by, dark and unformed. Quin and Dex were walking, and it was impossible to tell if they and the tunnel were moving through the world, or if the world were moving around them.

"Is that all?" she asked Dex gently after a while.

"To the story?" He laughed, softly and genuinely. "No, it's very much longer, and there are different versions of the ending. But that first part is good—the four of them walking across wide-open land, hills and forests and mountains rising around them." The idea of so much open space appeared to both appall and fascinate him. "The world didn't eat them up, did it? Though the wild animals occasionally tried."

He paused, and then asked her, "Have you seen a medallion before? You seemed surprised to find this one in my possession."

For someone who slipped in and out of insanity as easily as breathing, he was very observant. Not sure what she should tell him and what she should withhold, Quin said, "A friend had one."

"You mean the one you want to find, don't you? You love him. I can hear it in your voice."

"Or maybe you can read my thoughts," she suggested.

He gave her a sidelong glance. "Maybe I can, when you aren't guarding them. And you're not very good at guarding them." Misreading her expression entirely, he added, "You fell in love with someone else. I don't blame you, Quilla. We've been apart for so long. Is he good to you?"

"I'm not—" she began, but she couldn't finish the sentence. The expression on Dex's face, in the half-light, was so vulnerable, so *raw,* she didn't want to tell him just then that she wasn't Quilla. He would remember soon enough. "Yes, he's good to me . . . when he's himself. And I'm good to him when I'm myself," she murmured, thinking of the year and a half in which she'd forgotten herself and forgotten

Shinobu too, leaving him to find his own dangerous way in Hong Kong.

"Like us, then," Dex whispered.

Quin had no answer to that.

She caught a spectral glimpse of the estate's standing stone moving by on her left. She'd taken her Seeker oath in the shadows of that stone, on the night she'd discovered that her father was a killer. Where was Dex taking them?

Dex nodded at his medallion. "There were four of these at first. I knew when I saw your clothes that it was time."

Quin could not judge whether she should engage with his bewildering statements, or whether she should let most pass without comment. But her curiosity, for the most part, got the better of her.

"Time for what?" she asked warily.

"To find the owners of the other three medallions," he answered. He read her thoughts again, or perhaps her face gave her away, because he added, "I don't mean the one you love. I mean the original owners."

That was disappointing. The idea that Dex might try to find Shinobu without Quin having to force him had given her a touch of hope.

"Who are the other owners?" she asked. "Seekers?"

He answered, cryptically, "You could call them that if you want. But they aren't now who they once were." His countenance became hard. It was a look she hadn't seen on him yet, and it transformed him, quite abruptly, into a man you would not want to cross. "It's time to take them out of this world," he continued. "Or perhaps it would be more accurate to say that it's time to take them into the world as other people know it. As they should have been."

The wild panic he'd fought in the cave was creeping back into his expression. Quin held her tongue.

There was brightness ahead of them, the world taking solid shape again as he adjusted the medallion. Chunks of masonry, a courtyard littered with stones. He was bringing them to the castle ruins.

"I could take us directly inside." Dex's words were little more than a mumble, so that it was hard to tell if he meant them for Quin or only for himself. "I could take us straight down. That would be easier. But we can't bring a horse there, and I'll have to face it sometime."

Quin almost asked him what he would have to face, but it was obvious—he was crumbling at the sight of the approaching world. He gripped her shoulder, and a moment later he stumbled. He knelt—or maybe he buckled—and set the medallion down.

"You're not supposed to see," he whispered. "But you won't use it against me, will you? You never did."

Quin knelt with him, tried to soothe him, even though she had no idea what she might use against him. "No, of course not," she said.

With shaking hands, Dex set a hand atop the medallion and adjusted it with a series of quick motions Quin couldn't follow, each of which brought the world in front of them into increasing clarity, until it was fully formed. She was looking out through a large arched anomaly at the castle ruins and a half-cloudy Scottish afternoon.

He murmured, "In the open sky, there's nothing to contain me."

Quin felt the depth of his fear, even if it baffled her. She took his hand in her own and squeezed it. "I've got you, Dex."

With difficulty, because he wasn't a small person, she pulled him to his feet, and as he kept his head down and his eyes shut, they stepped across the seething border and set foot in the castle ward.

Yellen followed, whinnying as he scented the air of his home, and Quin pulled off his bridle and let him run.

Dex slumped down onto hands and knees, crawled back to the medallion, which still lay on the far side of the anomaly border. He reached across the anomaly and pulled the medallion through, twisting it as he did, in a motion that reminded her of a magician turning an object inside out. The opening collapsed at once, vibration and all, as if a light switch had been turned off. Then he sat on the ground, his head against his knees. Automatically he slipped the medallion back into loops of leather around his neck, where it hung like a pendant beneath his robe. He pulled his hood down over his eyes, reached out for Quin.

"Was what I saw a moment ago true? Is the castle in ruin?"

Quin glanced at the decaying courtyard and the remains of the castle, which looked as they'd always looked to her.

"Yes."

"You think time is nothing." His hand shook as it clutched hers. "But it passes whether you feel it or not."

"How old *are* you?" she asked him. Had he really seen this castle in one piece? Or was he mistaking it for another place, just as he kept mistaking Quin for another girl?

Dex laughed nervously. "Much younger than I look."

CHAPTER 5

JOHN

John crept as close to the big tent as he dared before rolling the smoke canisters out of his hands, one after the other. The canisters bumped across the muddy ground, hissing, and came to rest in the pool of fluorescent light that spilled from the tent's wide canvas doorway.

In moments plumes of black smoke were coiling out of the canisters to form ground-level thunderclouds that would cut visibility to almost zero. John felt the glee of destruction overtake him as he added the lightning—from his hiding place behind a battered aircar half-buried in mud, he threw a flare and a chain of firecrackers directly into the center of the smoke.

Soldiers streamed out of the tent, cursing and grabbing weapons, their faces washed in the red glow of the flare, their bodies no more than faint silhouettes in the smoke. John was at the far side of the encampment by then. He shoved a second flare into the gas tank of a parked van and then ran, through the humid, dripping night. He skirted the encampment and weaved through the edge of the jungle toward the ramshackle barn at the south end of the camp. He'd gone thirty paces when the van exploded, painting the night orange. Momentarily every leaf, frond, and raindrop came into harsh, beautiful relief, before the burst faded, and John felt a wild elation in being the attacker.

He didn't have to turn his head to know that Maud was following, running silently behind him. She'd warned him she would not help him in this task. It was his alone to carry out—his final test, if he was successful. He stopped the wild elation bubbling up within him. This attack was not about him. This night was about being a true Seeker, saving others.

There were guards by the barn, of course, with guns and mud-streaked fatigues, but they were gathered at the camp side of the building, staring at the chaos breaking out around the command tent—the tent itself and half the camp invisible in the smoke. Orders were being called in the distance; men were taking defensive positions. The guards at the barn chattered nervously to each other, debating whether they should leave their post or stay put.

The Young Dread has taught me to focus, and I will. John pulled his thoughts into a straight line. He emerged from the cover of the jungle behind the men. Sheathed in a leather strap across his chest was a row of small knives, their blades black with the substance Maud had helped him prepare. John drew four of the knives, not allowing himself to linger on the thought that he was using poison as a weapon and in doing so he was following in the footsteps of his mother, Catherine, and his grandmother Maggie.

He threw two knives, with a spinning launch for maximum power, a trick Maud had taught him. The closest guards twitched as though bitten by insects. Stepping silently between the remaining men, John struck them beneath their shoulders, sinking the tiny blades in as far as they would go. The men's cries were cut short—the drug entered the bloodstream quickly. In a moment, all four had collapsed. They would remain paralyzed for several minutes.

John crept around the barn to the jungle side. It was a prefabricated structure that had been crushed at one corner, and was now reinforced with sandbags and mud. He could hear murmuring within, many frightened voices trying to speak without being heard. They went silent when he pried open the far barn doors.

Blackness inside. But the Young Dread had been teaching him to gather all available light and use it. He could make out dozens of dark, young faces staring at him with frightened eyes.

"Come!" he said in French, the language they spoke here. "Come quickly. We don't have much time."

The chaos at the far end of the camp was becoming organized. There were shouted orders to secure the perimeter. More soldiers would come to the barn in a matter of minutes. Maud was yards away within the line of trees, watching.

The children didn't need to be told twice. They streamed out through the barn doors and into the trees. They were mostly girls in their early teens, but there were boys too, even younger than that.

A small girl caught John's arm with desperate strength.

"More," she told him in French as she pointed back at the barn. "More are still inside."

John looked to the Young Dread. Without a word, Maud took over for him, ushering the children deeper into the dense greenery.

John raced back into the barn, calling upon his eyes to let him see as he searched through the dried grass and plant fronds spread out everywhere. The air was heavy and foul. The children had been kept like cattle.

Outside the barn, sporadic gunfire had died down, and now men were speaking in disciplined bursts. He heard a voice in heavily accented French yelling an order. ". . . the girls. Now!"

Soldiers were coming to the barn. John thought of another night, two years ago, when he'd attacked the Scottish estate, set fire to buildings and terrorized the inhabitants. He had reveled in the destruction then. There were parallels between this night and that night, and yet the excitement of chaos had left him. He was thinking only of the children trapped inside this barn, awaiting their fate.

He found three children huddled in a corner. He discovered quickly that none of the three understood him when he spoke, but by their urgent gestures they told him that the largest child, a girl, was ill and couldn't move. He slid his arms under her back and lifted her to his chest.

"Come!" he said, gesturing for them to follow. "Quickly."

John ran, clutching the girl against him, the other two children at his heels. They reached the open doorway on the jungle side just as a soldier forced open the far doors facing the camp. From the soldier's perspective, John's silhouette would be outlined clearly in the opposite doorway.

"Go!" he whispered, gesturing for the smaller children to run.

The Young Dread leapt from the greenery, scooped up the two stragglers, and disappeared with them into the jungle.

The soldier raised his gun, seeing John now. John's focus became absolute. Here. Here was the difference between that night on the estate and this night—he would save this girl in his arms, even if he died doing it. In one motion, he set the sick girl on the ground and pulled his own gun. The soldier fired, sending a spray of bullets above John's head. Fiberglass screeched as they tore through the barn roof. Two other soldiers appeared, weapons raised. With three clear, deliberate shots, John took the men down. There was no joy in the action, only necessity.

As soon as it was done, he took the girl in his arms and sprinted into the trees, throwing his hearing behind him as he went. More soldiers were at the barn already, yelling for reinforcements. The whole camp would be chasing them in moments.

The children were huddled in a clearing in the dripping and steaming night, with Maud standing at their center. They were silent as John burst into their midst with the invalid child in his arms and set her among the larger children, who helped her stay upright.

"Hold hands!" he told them in French. "Everyone holds two hands!"

The children complied immediately.

John pulled out his athame and lightning rod. When he struck them together, he drew a deep vibration from the stone dagger. He traced a large circle, and the athame sliced through air, cutting the world itself. Threads of light and dark, the fabric of space, snaked away from the athame's blade, forming an anomaly.

John could hear the men at the edge of the forest, tramping into the dense foliage. Fear was coursing through him, ice in his veins. What if he hadn't been fast enough? What if he was not able to save them?

"Go!" he said to Maud. "Go now!"

The Young Dread was already going. She had two children by the hands, who themselves had hold of other children, and she drew them through the black doorway in two long lines, into the darkness that lay *between*.

John saw vines moving only yards from the clearing. The men were nearly upon them. When the last child had passed into the anomaly, he stepped across the threshold himself.

The first soldier reached the glade, gun poking through the foliage before his body appeared. The anomaly was losing its shape, becoming blurred. The man did not know what he was seeing, but there was John in a collapsing, black doorway in the middle of the jungle, and behind him were the retreating backs of three dozen children. Tendrils of dark and light were reaching across the opening toward each other now, mending the breach.

The man fired his gun. John saw the muzzle flash, but the edges of the world had sewn themselves shut, and the anomaly was closed.

CHAPTER 6

JOHN

John and the Young Dread watched the hospital from the dark alley across the street. They had rescued thirty-two children in all, and the last were now being escorted through the hospital doors into the flickering electric light of the interior.

The child kidnappings had dominated the news here for several days, and John read both bafflement and joy on the faces of the hospital staff. For John, this night was the culmination of an intense and brutal month of training, and he had not expected the task to feel so good. It was a strange exhilaration, knowing he'd rescued thirty-two children from lives as slave wives and child soldiers.

"You are smiling," Maud said. Her hand touched his shoulder in a gesture of camaraderie.

"This was a good night." His smile faltered as he added, "You helped me. I didn't do everything on my own. Does that change . . . the value?"

Dismissively she answered, "Seekers rarely take an assignment alone. I helped you much less than a fellow apprentice would have. It was your assignment, John, and you carried it out."

He kicked at the mud in the alley; he nodded, accepting her verdict. Slowly his smile returned. *Thirty-two children.* But his happiness was marred by ugly doubts. Would his mother have approved of this night's work? He had saved thirty-two strangers; it was the sort of thing Seekers were supposed to do. But it was not the sort of thing his mother had actually *done.* How had Catherine decided who should live and who should not?

A month ago, John and Maud had followed a trail of questions and notes left by Catherine to an ice cave in Norway. There they'd discovered both a half-frozen boy called Nott and, carved into the wall, a clue to the sad history of Seekers. Using the symbols on that cave wall as a guide, he and the Young Dread had gone *There,* and they'd found a group of eight figures abandoned in the darkness.

There were four men, two women, and two children. They were standing and sitting and lying, as still as sculptures. When John and Maud examined them by flashlight, they discovered blood, still wet, though it had been spilled years—perhaps untold years—before. Most of the adults were injured, some so severely that they might die as soon as they were brought back into the time stream of the world.

On the wrists of the adults were brands in the shape of a boar. It was the emblem of their Seeker house, burned into their flesh when they'd taken their oaths. And it marked them as a house that had been an enemy of John's own family.

"We've found your missing boar Seekers," the Young Dread had said.

The Middle Dread had left those people there for decades or centuries, not dead but hardly alive.

"Why?" John had asked.

Maud had shaken her head. "Putting them here kept them out of the world without, perhaps, having to kill them outright," she'd answered, though John could tell that she too was only guessing. They didn't know why the Middle Dread had done the things he'd done, only that he had done them.

John had turned slowly, shining his flashlight into the blackness. If there were boar Seekers *There,* might there be other Seekers from other houses frozen somewhere else in those dimensions? But his light had shown only a darkness that felt as thick as oil.

When he looked again at the injured and abandoned boar Seekers, he'd wondered, *What am I supposed to feel for them, and what am I supposed to do?*

They hadn't brought those eight Seekers back into the world with them. Maud had suggested that John become a full Seeker himself and take his oath before choosing to retrieve them. Once he was sworn, he would be their brother, and he would have every right to help decide their future. In the meantime, they couldn't die of their injuries while they were in the hidden dimensions, and thus they would remain safe.

John had agreed, but his mind had returned, again and again, to their still shapes, waiting in silence for someone to help. Catherine, when he'd known her, would have told him not to think of them again. They were from an enemy house and of no consequence. But did he agree?

John's thoughts came back to the alley in which he and Maud were standing. John knew he'd changed in the last month, but as he looked at Maud in the light from the bare bulbs of the streetlamps, he realized how much she'd changed as well, after so much time awake in the world. Her sentences had become longer and more natural. There was still something fierce and Dread-like in the way she carried herself, but her movements had subtly transformed, become more like a human girl's and less like those of a creature of the infinite. Even her face had altered in the last months; her age was no longer frozen at fifteen. She was moving forward in time along with the rest of the world, though perhaps not at exactly the same pace.

Now here they both were, standing in an alley in Africa, changed. If John had proved himself tonight, he would be a full Seeker soon. What would happen then? Would the Young Dread move on?

John looked again at the hospital across the way.

"So," he said to her, "have I proven myself?"

If he didn't yet know what he should think or feel, he hoped the Young Dread would lead him to an answer.

"Yes," she answered gravely. Then she spoke the words he'd been waiting to hear: "I invite you to take your oath."

CHAPTER 7

NOTT

Nott's eyes hovered over the surface of the water with an expression of the blackest disgust. The bathtub stood outside the workshop on the Scottish estate, and he had filled it with a hose from the nearest spigot. There was running water here, even though almost every structure aside from the workshop had been reduced to piles of charred rubble. Nott had seen running water before, but its origin remained a mystery. He wondered if a living river had been funneled into a metal pipe.

He should have taken his bath during the daylight, when the sun would have warmed him a little, but he hadn't wanted to do that. The tub was in the open, with old trees on every hand, stretching away into the deepness of the forest; daylight would make him more visible to any potential observers, who would surely laugh at him.

John had explained that Nott might heat the water if he liked, by boiling it in the large kettle they kept by the cooking fire.

Bah, Nott had thought. *Who needs warm water?*

Filling his bath with cold water had felt like a small measure of defiance against John and Maud. The problem was that neither of them was there to observe his disobedience, and now Nott was shivering.

He closed his angry eyes and slipped beneath the water. His hand groped for the bar of soap John had forced him to accept. He'd been ordered—ordered!—to scrub himself, including his *hair*. He'd been taking baths every week, because his two companions insisted upon it. But John, investigating why Nott's odor hadn't markedly improved, had at last realized that Nott had been only wetting his hair and not washing it. Since Nott habitually rubbed pieces of deer flesh through his tangled locks so that the oils might make it softer, getting his head wet had actually made the smell worse.

Why should anyone clean hair? Nott wondered. Hair was meant to be full of dirt. That's what kept you warm. Dirty hair was like a second cloak.

Nevertheless, he scrubbed his head over and over with the lump of soap and found it a strangely pleasant feeling. Before he realized what was happening, he'd used up all of the soap and was still scrubbing at his lathered head with both of his hands. Large clumps of hair came out. Apparently only the dirt had been holding everything together.

Eventually he got out of the tub, in which the water had turned a dark gray, and dried himself with the towel John had given him, glad of the softness of the material over all the scars he carried on his skin. He dried himself quickly, worried that John might come back and see him enjoying any part of his bath.

Nott had been a Watcher, one of the Middle Dread's chosen boys, destined to put the world in its place. Now he was a child, being looked after by John and the Young Dread. But what choice was there? His fellow Watchers had sent him to his frozen cave to die, and his master, the Middle Dread, was most likely already dead.

Nott went into the workshop, which was kept much tidier than he considered absolutely necessary. He turned on the light—the device didn't use any sort of fire but instead illuminated one of those glass bulbs he saw everywhere when he went to cities. The source of the light was, like the source of the water, an unresolvable mystery.

There were three piles of straw for sleeping, the cooking hearth, and rows of knives and swords along the wall for practice. The three of them hunted animals for their food, but he wasn't allowed to leave the carcasses anywhere nearby, nor was he allowed to keep a little piece of the dead flesh in his pocket as all Watchers liked to do, as a reminder of his power to kill.

What *was* he allowed to do? Hardly anything. They did let him practice fighting, he admitted grudgingly, but there was no reason to linger on that kindness.

Nott had washed his cloak and clothing before his bath, and they hung by the workshop door, still wet. He pulled on the spare trousers and shirt John had scavenged for him from somewhere. They were modern clothing, luxuriously soft against his skin.

Their softness cannot move me, he thought.

It wasn't until he checked on his bat that his black mood finally began to lift.

"I've survived the bath, Aelred," he told the creature. Aelred clicked and squeaked happily as Nott unwrapped the cloth he'd tied around it.

He'd found the bat flapping on the forest floor, unable to fly properly. And though Nott hadn't specifically asked permission, John and the Young Dread had not seemed to mind that he was keeping it.

Aelred was about half as large as Nott's fist, with huge ears and a fuzzy gray body. Nott thought the bat might be small for its age, and that was why it couldn't fly yet. He liked that idea, because Nott guessed that he too was small for his age.

"It could be that I'm hundreds of years old," Nott reflected aloud as he stroked Aelred's head with one finger. "If that's so, then I'm *very* small for my age." He laughed at that notion, for of course you didn't keep growing every year until you died. "If you did," he pointed out, "old men would be huge."

He dripped milk into the bat's mouth from the tiny bottle he'd found at the back of the workshop and which he kept full just for Aelred. There were cows on the estate, and Nott had learned how to milk them—another chore that was beneath his dignity, though he didn't mind quite so much now that he was giving milk to his pet.

While the bat sucked greedily at the liquid, Nott gently extended the creature's diaphanous wings and stroked the delicate edges.

"Look how big you're getting."

His finger paused. It wasn't exactly normal to touch the creature in this way. A month ago, Nott would have kept the bat only for the excitement of hacking off its feet and wings one after the other, while he listened to its squeals of pain. Now the idea of ripping off Aelred's wings caused him an entirely different sort of pang.

Abruptly he folded the wings back against its body, wrapped the animal up, and tucked it into the pocket of his shirt, which was conveniently located over his chest.

"I wasn't petting you," he told the bat. "I was only checking your wings."

There was a small, cracked looking glass on one wall. In it, Nott examined himself in his strange clothing. The difference in his hair was startling. It was still desperately uneven, but now it was a light brown and downy soft.

He wasn't sure how old he was—both because he'd never been told his own age and because much of his life had been spent *There*, waiting for the Middle Dread to bring him out into the world to train—but he looked about twelve in the mirror. In these clothes he might be any one of the soft children he'd seen in modern cities. Now that all the dirt was gone, his freckles were startling.

"How old would you say I am?" he asked Aelred, whose head peeked out the top of the pocket. "And if you just met me, what sort of person would you think I am?"

Aelred chirruped noncommittally.

"That's not very helpful," Nott told it.

Nott tugged at his newly clean hair and imagined wearing the metal helm the Middle Dread had given him. His fingers twitched at the thought, muscle memory taking over. There was always a slight shock when he pulled the helm on, a buzz through his skull, and then a cold tingling as his thoughts began to run clear and fierce.

Nott's helm had been stolen by Shinobu, but Shinobu was the Watchers' new master, which must mean that Nott's helm was back at Dun Tarm. The Young Dread and John had their own helm. They'd let him wear it a few times, but it didn't work on his mind in the same way; it didn't make him feel cruel and untouchable.

"They say a piece of the Middle Dread's mind lived inside my helm," he explained to Aelred, who looked up at him with interest, "and that's why I think like him. I suppose helms don't work right without a piece of the Middle Dread's head stuck in them."

The Young Dread was in charge here, even though she was a girl. Nott didn't think he cared much for girls, but this one was beautiful; even he could see that. She had a sort of beauty that was terrifying, like the statue of an avenging angel he'd once seen in front of a church, cold and awful and splendid at the same time.

The Young Dread had told Nott that he might train as a Seeker if John invited him to do so. That's why the two of them were gone this evening; John was going to become a Seeker.

Nott turned from the mirror and took the bat out of his pocket.

Avoiding the gaze of Aelred's shiny black eyes, he set the creature on the workshop table, unwrapped him, and stretched both of its wings out to their fullest extent again. The skin was translucent, crossed by the narrow lines of wing bones. Two tiny, grasping hands clutched at Nott's fingers, and two small feet scrabbled at his wrist.

"You're really just a rat with wings." Nott squeezed the bat's right wing. He felt the bones bend beneath his grip. The animal let out a click and a squeal. With only a little more pressure, the bones would crack and the wing would be destroyed. Aelred would cry.

It should feel good.

He released the wing, folded it back against the body. If Nott stayed here, if he trained with John and became a Seeker—whatever idiot sort of thing a Seeker might be—he'd never want to hurt anything again. Would that be good?

Nott was fairly certain that people who didn't like to hurt things were soft and weepy and fat. He imagined himself many years from now, completely bald from all the hair washing and too fat to get to his feet. What would happen then? Would he lie around in his own filth, trying to slap away the rats that came to eat him?

"What I need is the helm," he told the bat. "My helm. The real one."

He stroked the creature's head, and then stopped himself. These caresses had become a habit. *What's next, kissing it good night?*

Baths, tidiness. Enough. Nott made a decision.

"If I had my helm, I'd know which Nott I prefer." The bat let out a series of comfortable squeaks as Nott wrapped it back up. Nott told it honestly, "Aelred, you might not like the one I choose."

He stripped off the modern clothes and pulled on his rough trousers and shirt and cloak, which were still damp and much more itchy than he remembered. He hesitated over Aelred, but eventually Nott slipped the bat into his cloak pocket and filled the small bottle with milk, in case the animal got hungry.

Outside, Nott retrieved his throwing knives from the trunk of the oak tree. The Young Dread had been teaching him the proper way to throw, and he'd gotten much, much better.

But never mind that.

If he left now, he wouldn't have to say anything to John or the Young Dread. It was not as if they were his friends.

He turned south and walked into the night.

CHAPTER 8

QUIN

"If you grow up with wonders and miracles, they're just an ordinary part of the world you know." Dex spoke the words into Quin's ear.

They were riding Yellen together through the estate. More accurately, Quin was riding Yellen; Dex sat hunched behind her on the horse, his hood drawn all the way down over his face. She had a feeling he had his eyes clamped shut beneath the hood, to avoid any glimpse of the pleasant day.

"They spent years walking through England, and the children thought it was perfectly normal to carry a laboratory on your back." He had returned to his story, and he was speaking softly, because, as he'd told her, he didn't like the sound of his own voice echoing into the open air.

"A laboratory?" she asked. He'd said "wonders" before; a laboratory was a different idea altogether.

"The pack was huge, like something a mountaineer would carry," he explained. "He'd planned the trip a long time before it began— without telling the rest of the family."

They were passing piles of charred stone and wood that had once been Quin's and Shinobu's cottages. The grass of the commons had grown up to chest height, and the tall stalks grazed Quin's lower legs where they hung on either side of the horse's belly.

"The man made mistakes. I can't pretend otherwise. He hadn't expected to end up where he did, and he didn't know it would take so long." Dex said this reluctantly, apologetically, as if Quin might judge him for the words. "Where are we now? I feel grass."

"In the meadow. You were asking me to find electronics. There might be things in the old barn that weren't totally destroyed."

"Is it, is it open sky above us? No—don't tell me." He tucked his head against his chest, like a bird disappearing among its own feathers.

"Is this your story, Dex, or is it someone else's?"

"What do you think?"

"I think it's a little too slow. They just keep walking, don't they?"

What Quin really thought was that she needed to keep him talking to keep him sane. As soon as they'd emerged from the tunnel back into the world, Dex had become even more unstable. They'd spent an uncomfortable night in the castle courtyard, and in the morning Dex had woken up demanding that Quin help him gather electronic equipment. She had agreed because having a goal, no matter how odd, seemed to focus him.

"The story is my string in the labyrinth, Quilla," he whispered. "When I follow it, I remember other things."

"I lost my memory once too," she confided, trying another tack. "How did you get it back?"

"Slowly . . . and then rather suddenly."

A moan escaped Dex. "It might kill me to remember all at once."

"Would it? Or would it be a relief?"

"No," he said adamantly.

The Scottish weather had been cold when Quin was last on the estate. How long had she been gone? Weeks? Months? She had no athame and no vehicle and no idea where Shinobu had gone. Dex, with his medallion, was her best chance of finding him—if she could keep him coherent long enough to help her, and long enough to help himself.

"The man made mistakes?" she prompted before Dex could fall into a sullen gloom again. With a note of friendly mockery, she asked, "He made mistakes while they were walking and walking through this story about walking? What sort of mistakes did he make?"

Dex chuckled softly, and she was glad to know that she'd averted melancholia. "You're right," he admitted, "there's too much walking. But when they camped—ah!—that's when things happened. Their father had a method for unpacking the laboratory. First he set up a canopy to work under. Then he would lay out all of his astonishing tools . . ."

Quin wasn't paying close attention for a few minutes, because they were passing the workshop, and there were signs that it had been recently occupied. It was deserted now, but had the Young Dread and John been here? What was John like under her tutelage? Did she keep him more honest than he'd been with Quin?

"The older son was called Matheus," Dex was saying when Quin focused on him again. "When Matheus was four or five, he would watch his father line up those tools. Then he would go off to chase squirrels or toss stones into a stream—or maybe at the squirrels. But the younger son, Matheus's little brother, liked to sit very still and observe everything his father did. The little one's name was Desmond, and when he was two years old, he would stand on tiptoe, his eyes just clearing the edge of the workbench. He memorized every tool. Some were rough and large, saws and picks and things like that, but they got smaller and smaller, down to the most intricate instruments like a jeweler's tools, but even more minute and complicated."

They were approaching the old barn. The back half of the structure had been in ruins all of Quin's life, but she now saw that the front end was gaping open as well, as though the wall had been blown out.

John must have done that, she thought, *when he attacked us.* That had been two years ago—just two years—yet it seemed another lifetime. Dex kept talking, and Quin tried to pay attention, though her mind had slipped away to that terrible night on the estate, facing John, Shinobu saving her . . . Where had Shinobu gotten himself to?

"Before the little one could even speak properly, he knew the names of everything," Dex was saying. He paused. Then he said, "An impellor."

"What?" Quin asked, brought back by the change in his tone.

"An impellor. One of them was called that."

"One of the boys?"

"No, one of the *wonders.* The black cylinder."

They'd left the three stone-and-glass wonders back in the castle ward, and one of them was a long cylinder of black stone with black glass running through it. Dex had apparently just remembered its name—and it was an intriguing name.

"What does it do?" she asked, looking at him over her shoulder.

The question was a mistake. Dex drew his breath, hesitated, and then shook his head in dismay. "When I want to hold the memory, it slips away."

From the slump of his shoulders, she saw that he was slipping away as well, sinking back into frantic despair. Quin steered him from the cliff's edge by asking, "What about the little boy? You were telling me how clever he was. What sort of clever?"

"Every sort of clever," Dex whispered. And then, his temper improving with each word, he said, "Sometimes the canopy was blown clean off or torn in half—they had to sew it up again and again—or flooded with blinding illumination. Sometimes every thread stood on end, and the canopy would float on static electricity. Half the time the work space was showered with sparks of iridescent light."

"Like from a disruptor?"

"Yes, like that." A shudder ran through Dex. "Disruptor—I'd forgotten that name as well. He didn't want to make it, you know. He was tricked."

"Who do you mean?" Quin asked, startled. Was Dex speaking of the person who had created the disruptor? Dex stopped speaking—her urgency had pushed him into silence. Quin could have kicked herself. "Go on, Dex, please," she said quietly after a moment.

He didn't speak again right away, but eventually he whispered, "You called the dark tunnel doorway an anomaly, but all of those wonders were anomalies, though Desmond and Matheus didn't know it. Are we here?"

She had pulled Yellen to a halt outside the barn. She'd teased Dex about his story being boring, but it had drawn her in, and now she was sorry they'd arrived and he had an excuse to stop.

Getting him off the horse and into the old barn involved forcing Yellen almost through the gaping hole in the wall, so that Dex could dismount and duck in without opening his eyes for more than a moment. Once inside, he wedged himself into a far corner. When he discovered the space was rather small and fairly dark, he lifted his hood a bit.

They were standing in what had once been used as a medical facility, a fact made obvious by the dirty hospital bed and the equipment along the back wall. For years, someone had been kept alive on that bed. Briac Kincaid had forced Quin and the other apprentices to look at the body—living, just barely, but worse than dead—to illustrate the dangers of disruptor guns.

It was only later, after leaving the estate, that Quin had learned that the individual kept in this room had been Catherine Renart,

John's mother, and that Briac had been the one who'd disrupted her. It made her ill even now to recall the odor that had pervaded the space, a mixture of disinfectant and decay. What must it have been like for John, discovering the withered form was his mother?

"What happened here?" Dex asked her as his eyes darted around the room.

"Nothing good," she answered.

They returned on foot. Yellen's back was piled high with broken medical equipment, a microwave oven, and an ancient television they'd found behind the dairy barn, all roped to him as if he were a pack mule. Dex—who had refused to explain what he wanted the equipment for—now clung to the horse's mane. They were in the forest, which he clearly preferred to the meadow, but even so, there was a tremble in his gait.

"What did the mother do while the boys were with their father?" Quin asked, to help Dex focus on something other than the world around him.

"Their mother wasn't used to living in the wilderness," Dex told her, keeping his voice steady with difficulty. "She was occupied learning how to keep her husband and boys from starving. She taught herself to hunt." He stumbled on a tree root, and Quin braced him.

"What did she hunt with?"

"An impellor." This time he remembered the name with no effort. "The father made the impellor first, for her. It could push things away or pull things to her, even big things like deer. And besides hunting, it was good for . . . other things."

"Like fighting?"

"Their father didn't approve of fighting then. But England was hostile country. There were wolves and bears."

Quin was thinking this placed his story in the Middle Ages at the latest, but probably much, much earlier, when there had still been wolves and bears in the British Isles. Was he relating a Seeker legend that she too should have been taught? Was this a look into the Seekers' early history?

"The impellor made hunting easy," Dex continued. "Their mother could take down even an elk, drag it toward her, and finish the animal off while it was stunned. By the time Matheus was five, he would hunt with her and make the final killing stroke, because she said she didn't care for the sight of fresh blood, and he didn't mind. They all ate very well by then."

Dex said this with particular relish, so that Quin felt obliged to make appreciative sounds. In fact, she'd been eating rabbits cooked over an open fire and was thinking how very much she'd prefer an enormous bowl of noodles from her favorite restaurant in Hong Kong instead, and how little the thought of eating an elk appealed to her. Just hearing about it gave her a queasy stomach.

"The problem with the impellor was that it attracted a lot of attention," Dex explained. "Besides wild animals, England was full of uneducated people, who didn't look kindly on a man who appeared to be a sorcerer. The family had to use the impellor on people when they were attacked in their camp, or driven out of villages they were passing through. It was an effective way of stopping an assault, but unless you killed the people involved—and the father was against that idea—they would come after you later in much greater numbers, to get rid of the dangerous magician roaming the countryside. Matheus and Desmond grew up with threats all around. They had to avoid being stoned to death, set on fire, hanged, you name it."

"Here, Dex."

They'd arrived in the castle ward. Fallen masonry and dead leaves littered the edges of the wide space. Quin helped Dex into the tiny shelter they'd thrown together out of large stones, which was only spacious enough for one person to crouch inside. When he was sitting inside it, Dex looked like a statue in a recess just large enough to accommodate it. Arrayed on the ground in front of the shelter, where he'd left them to soak up sunlight, were the three mysterious "wonders."

She watched Dex as she began taking the electronic junk off Yellen's back. The hood was over his eyes and he'd stopped talking. He was sliding away again.

"Dex?"

Her voice startled him. His hands reached out and ran over the wonders, as if they might steady him.

"Look, an impellor," he whispered. He touched the black cylinder with the seams of glass running through it. Then his hands went to another object. "And this one is full of stars."

CHAPTER 9

MAUD

John knelt by the roaring fire the Young Dread had built at the old stone deep in the forest. That stone had stood on the Scottish estate since long, long before Maud's own life had started. It rose twelve feet, eroded and uneven, from the soft ground in the middle of a clearing. She and John had returned from hot, humid Africa to a chilly Scottish night, where sparse clouds obscured a half-moon.

John was staring into the flames at the long piece of metal now beginning to glow a dull red. It was the ancient brand bearing the shape of an athame. Maud had set it into the hottest part of the coals.

As she looked down at John's bent head, she recalled how slow and frustrating he'd been when she'd begun training him. She'd nearly given up on him several times. And yet he'd become an unexpectedly good student. In the end, she'd taught him more than most Seekers knew.

An unaccustomed emotion was stirring in her. It was *important* to her that he had made it.

"John Hart, I invite you to take your oath and become a sworn Seeker."

John's face was bathed in orange firelight. His hair had grown long and untended in his time with the Young Dread. His features were, she supposed, *pleasing*, though concepts like handsome and beautiful were tricky for Maud. She didn't experience those ideas viscerally, as ordinary people must. For her, beauty was an idea that existed in things like paintings and sculptures. And yet, her own sense of self was shifting. She'd been awake in the world for so long, the longest stretch since she was a small child.

"Recite the three laws," she commanded.

John hesitated, but only for a moment. "First law: A Seeker is forbidden to take another family's athame." His gaze fell back toward the fire, as if searching there for steadiness. Did the meaning of the laws give him pause? He swallowed before he spoke again. "Second law: A Seeker is forbidden to kill another Seeker save in self-defense. Third law: A Seeker is forbidden to harm humankind."

"You may say your oath now," she told him.

Very steadily, his eyes locked on the Young Dread's, John recited:

> *"All that I am*
> *I dedicate to the holy secrets of my craft,*
> *Which I shall never speak*
> *To one who is not sworn.*
> *Not fear, nor love, nor even death*
> *Will shake my loyalty to the hidden ways between*
> *Rising darkly to meet me.*
> *I will seek the proper path until time does end."*

Maud withdrew the athame from her waist and held it in front of John. He planted a solemn kiss on its blade.

"And now, your wrist," she told him.

From the fire she drew out the metal brand. The tip, with its dagger shape, was glowing.

John extended his left wrist, and Maud brought the hot metal toward his skin. She sensed a reluctance in her own muscles. The idea of burning him was difficult. *How odd.*

She pressed the brand into the flesh on the underside of John's arm, searing the image of an athame onto him. John first cried out, and then he gritted his teeth against the pain. The Young Dread was relieved to remove the steel from his skin. He clenched his fists and was silent for a minute as he came to terms with the blistering burn. When he'd steadied himself, he spread his hands. Maud formally laid the athame and lightning rod across his palms.

"This athame bears the emblem of the fox, John. It is yours."

She experienced a sense of finality as she set the ancient tools into John's hands. His training was over. He was a Seeker. And Maud herself no longer had an athame for her own use. It was time to retrieve the athame of the Dreads from Quin. The girl would have to find her own family's athame, if indeed it still existed.

John got to his feet, looking intently at the stone implements.

"I've made it to my oath," he whispered. The Young Dread saw that a few tears had escaped his eyes, and she tried to remember the feeling of crying. She could not. "May I use it for the first time, right now?" he asked.

"Of course. My permission is not necessary."

As John began, almost reverently, to adjust the dials in the hilt of his athame, Maud wondered if he would leave her now. Her master, the Old Dread, had given the role of all Dreads to her. Maud must train someone to be a Dread alongside her. She still carried hope that John might choose that path. But would he even consider this, now that he was a Seeker in his own right? If not, who would she find? Quin herself?

"Maud," John said then, using her given name, which he did so rarely that the sound of it brought her up short. "Will you come with me? There's something I'd like to show you."

CHAPTER 10

JOHN

The moon was gone, the sky over the English coast dark and silent. Security lights glared above them on tall poles, lighting the shipyard, a city of quays and dry docks and enormous hangars. Cranes rose up on every hand, their skeletal masses reaching across the sky.

"This way," John told her.

They walked past the slips where oceangoing ships stood in mid-repair. John's own steps were quiet, but the Young Dread's were nearly inaudible. Try as he might, he could never match her silent tread. It was something about the way her feet met the ground, as if flesh and shoe and earth were uniting in mute agreement.

"There," he said when they stood in front of a hangar close to the water.

"That is *Traveler*?"

He nodded. "The repairs are almost finished. It will fly again in less than a week."

The airship on which John had grown up was covered in scaffolding, its bow and front engines protruding through the hangar doors. *Traveler*'s metallic hide, which had been mangled when the ship crashed in London, had been replaced, and the new skin glinted in the security lights. It would be more beautiful, John thought, than it had been before. Soon it would resume its position in the London sky, where Catherine had wanted it.

The Young Dread threw off her hood to gaze up at the airship. She and the other Dreads had been on *Traveler* once. They'd boarded it on the night John got his athame and his mother's journal back from Quin. That was the night the Young Dread had killed the Middle Dread, and in doing so had saved John's life.

"Will it be your home now?" she asked him.

He was struck again by the natural cadence of her voice, so different from the steady, biting way she'd spoken when he first knew her. This question was also more personal than what she would have asked months ago.

"Will it be my home again?" The sense of self-doubt was pulling at him once more. "I think so."

She must have heard the discontent in his voice, because she turned her gaze from the airship to look at him. Her eyes were a light brown, he knew, though they were colorless in the mixed dark and glare of the shipyard. She waited, in her usual way, for him to say more.

"My mother built *Traveler* for me."

"What troubles you about the ship, John?" the Young Dread asked when he said no more.

"You don't use money, but can you understand how much wealth it took to build an airship like this as our family home? And we own this enormous shipyard, and countless other things."

He watched Maud's eyes roam over the industrial city around them, trying to see it as a modern person might. "I think I understand," she said at last. "Vast wealth."

"Yes." Quietly, he added, "I can't escape the fact that my mother did so many questionable things to create this wealth."

Maud's long hair fell loosely about her shoulders in a way that looked almost girlish, but John didn't let that fool him. He could feel her close attention, the scrutiny of a lioness.

He went on, "When I read Catherine's journal, I see the young girl who wanted to do as much good as she could. But . . . Maud, that isn't what she did. She and my grandfather plotted to make their fortune. Catherine couldn't have done it without killing rivals. How many people did she take by surprise, arriving by athame into their private homes, threatening them or . . ." He trailed off. He took a breath, steeled himself. "You taunted me about her when you trained me, to break my concentration. And it worked because the things you said were true."

He looked back up at the bulk of *Traveler* as he struggled to put the rest of his thoughts into words. "I'm a Seeker now. It's what Catherine and my grandmother Maggie wanted me to be. If I go back to *Traveler* and life with my grandfather—if he lives—I don't know how much like Catherine I'll become."

He glanced away so that she would not see in his eyes the other words he didn't speak: *I know how much like Catherine I want to be.*

Carefully the Young Dread asked him, "Do you think you must become the person Catherine became?"

"She lived a harsh life, where she might die if she didn't kill. It's how she built all of this." He nodded at the shipyard. "How can I inherit everything she created without taking on the same burden? Don't I have a duty to make our house the center of Seekers, as she wanted?"

Maud was on the point of answering, when her gaze changed. "There is a guard coming," she told him.

John threw his hearing and could faintly make out the distant approach of heavy boots.

"Come," she said. "Take us back to the estate and we will speak more."

Ducking with her into the shadows between two pieces of machinery, John used his athame to take them back.

They entered the estate on the commons. Since the moon had already set, only starlight lit their way as they walked back to the workshop, where they and Nott had been living as John finished his training.

Maud rested a hand lightly on his shoulder as they moved through the grass. "John, I can't force you to be a perfect Seeker. None of us is perfect. I can only judge you, as a Dread, if you stray from the three laws. But I have offered you another choice. Do you remember?"

Of course he remembered. When he and the Young Dread had sat together in that cave in Norway, she'd given him a glimpse of an entirely different future.

"I could become a Dread. You would train me."

The Young Dread let go of his shoulder, but he could feel the place where the pressure of her hand had been, as though her touch had traced permanent lines on him. Perhaps that was the right way to describe the effect she'd had on him over the past months. She'd changed him in ways that he hoped would never fade. But her influence and his mother's felt directly opposed.

They reached the workshop and discovered that Nott was gone, though the wet earth around the bathtub meant he'd left only recently.

"Do you think he went hunting?" John asked.

The Young Dread studied the shirt and trousers that had been left haphazardly on the workshop floor, as though Nott had stripped them off in a hurry.

"I think he will come back to us, or he won't," she said evenly. "He never agreed to be trained."

"No, he didn't."

Returning to their conversation, Maud told him, "I cannot say for sure that you would succeed in becoming a Dread. The training is difficult."

John laughed. His Seeker training had been the most arduous weeks of his life. If Maud considered something "difficult" in comparison, it was hard to imagine how strenuous it would be.

"I barely made it through to my oath," he muttered.

"Not true. Do you think you're unfit to be a Dread?"

John knew he could give her a glib answer, but he didn't want to. He spoke soberly. "When Catherine was dying, she made me promise to get revenge on those who'd hurt us. That promise has guided me all these years. Why would you give me more power?"

He watched Maud absorb this question. Then he busied himself in lighting a fire. A month ago, he would have hidden such thoughts. Now it felt better to speak them aloud. When he next looked at the Young Dread, the ghost of a smile had appeared on her face.

"Are you smiling?" he asked as she sat with him by the blooming flames. A smile on the Young Dread's lips was as rare as a new moon. And unexpected in this conversation.

The smile was gone as quickly as it had appeared. "My old master used to say that being a judge was a matter of balance," she told him. "To be a Dread, a judge of Seekers, you must see all you can, and balance the good against the bad, always giving extra weight to the good."

"So I should only think about my good qualities?" John asked skeptically. "Like, I'll be very *good* at exacting vengeance from my mother's enemies? And I'm such a *good* son to be willing to kill for her?"

She ignored his sarcasm and said simply, "You've lost your balance, John. You've done things you should not have done, to Quin and others." When he nodded his agreement, she went on, "What if you could regain the balance?"

"How?"

Something almost like mischief flickered across her features. "You chose the African quest yourself. Why?"

John looked inward and spoke honestly. "Because it was a good thing to do. I wanted to know how that felt."

"How did it feel?"

"Different," he breathed. It had felt very different from the electric pull of revenge.

"And what would you choose next?" she asked him with a directness that struck John deeply.

"The boar Seekers," he answered before he'd even examined the thought. "Catherine and Maggie wanted me to get rid of them. But there are children among them. Why should some children deserve to die when others deserve to live? I don't want to get rid of them. I want to bring them back."

"Why?"

"To see how it will feel."

The Young Dread nodded slowly in approval. "The boar Seekers, then," she said. "After a night of sleep."

CHAPTER 11

NOTT

"Look, Aelred, that's Dun Tarm," Nott told the bat when the crumbling fortress came into sight.

He held Aelred up in order that the creature might see the fortress for itself, before he remembered. "Ah, you don't see very well," Nott murmured. "You'll have to trust me that it's there."

They'd emerged from the forested hills onto the shore of Loch Tarm, and Dun Tarm stood midway around the lake. Nott stopped walking and scratched Aelred's head thoughtfully.

"The thing is, I've been telling you they'll be happy to see me, but there's a chance they won't be happy at all."

Nott had been hiking for five days, and all the while he'd discussed with Aelred what he would tell the other Watchers when he reached the fortress.

They had put him in his cave and had expected him to die there. He'd been telling Aelred that they'd be amazed he'd survived and welcome him as a hero. They would probably offer him his old helm to wear, without his even asking, and when he wore it, he would settle back into his old skin. ("Skin you might not like, Aelred," he'd warned the bat several times, "but that I might like a great deal.")

But the closer he came to Dun Tarm, the less likely this scenario struck him as something that might actually happen. Now, with the fallen fortress looming just ahead, he had to face the truth.

"I wonder if you can fly yet?" Nott asked the bat. "It might be that I'm done for when they see me and you should fly away."

Nott wondered, belatedly, if wearing his old helm was truly worth risking his life. He hesitated, shifting his weight from foot to foot. He couldn't hear any voices echoing over the lake. Perhaps the fortress was abandoned. Or even better, maybe the Watchers were gone today but had left their packs behind. Maybe his helm was lying there unattended. Surely he couldn't come this far without checking.

"It is worth it, Aelred," he said after a moment's reflection. "So let's go, then."

He walked briskly along the shore, relieved every minute that there were no signs of life ahead.

"The first to arrive," a voice said, startling him, when he was close enough to see through the gaping doorway. The voice belonged to an old woman who appeared, inexplicably, in the entrance to the fortress.

"Do you see her?" he asked Aelred, wondering if he'd imagined her. When Aelred didn't answer, Nott said, "Say nothing if you *don't* see her—"

"It's all right," the old woman said to Nott, beckoning with one hand in the same way a constable might beckon a thieving child. "Come inside."

She certainly looked real. Nott was only twenty yards away, near enough to see details. She wore modern clothing in a pattern of green and brown and gray splotches that Nott guessed would make her hard to spot in the woods. She had a tight knot of gray hair wound up at the back of her head. Her boots were heavy, as though she intended to spend her days tramping through the forest, and the weight of those boots appeared to be wearing on her weak body. She was struggling to keep her shoulders straight. Her face was deeply lined but had, to Nott's mind, a kindly appearance. He distrusted her immediately, with the same gut instinct that had driven him to stay away from the woman—the *witch*—at the edge of the village where he'd grown up.

"Hmm," Nott said out loud.

He bought himself time to think by wrapping up his bat and tucking the creature into a pocket of his cloak while he looked around. Dun Tarm might look empty except for this woman, but there was evidence of recent occupants. There were dozens of footprints in the mud by the edge of the lake, and a great pile of animal bones in a refuse heap at the back. In fact, it looked as though his four Watcher companions—the four who'd left him in his cave—had been eating enough to feed an army.

"Who are you?" he asked the woman.

"You'll recognize me when we've spoken a little while."

That was exactly the sort of thing a witch would say, Nott reflected, and even though her voice shook, like a real old woman's, that could be a trick. None of the miracles Nott had seen in the modern civilization had done anything to dispel his conviction that there was magic in the world; if anything, modern miracles had confirmed this idea. This old woman was obviously someone to be wary of.

He rested his hands on the knives around his waist and got a little closer. The woman retreated into the fortress. The previous Nott, the Nott who'd gotten to wear the helm all the time, wouldn't have been scared of witches, and so the current Nott felt obliged to feign courage. He straightened his shoulders and followed the woman into Dun Tarm.

Inside were more signs of recent occupation: remnants of cooking fires; pieces of charred meat lying here and there; and patches of blood, such as Watchers were always leaving about when they punched each other in the face or got a little careless with their knives.

"Where are my four friends?" Nott asked, still keeping his distance. He knew that he was using the word "friends" rather loosely, since the other Watchers had exiled him and tried to kill him, but there was no reason to suppose this old woman knew about that. He'd grown so used to talking to Aelred that he almost added, out loud, *Let's not get too close to her, eh?* but he stopped himself in time.

"What did he call you boys?" the woman asked. The creakiness of her voice made Nott think of tree branches in a strong wind. "Watchmen?"

"Watchers," he corrected. Then, curiosity getting the better of him, he asked, "Did you know our master?"

The old woman glanced around the empty fortress, a smile at the corner of her mouth. She was standing very straight now, as if defying the world to pull her down. "I've been watching the Watchers since I got here. You can come with me to find them tonight."

She studied Nott, and Nott tried not to shuffle his feet under her stare. He wanted to tell Aelred, *She makes my bones tickle,* but he didn't, because that would be a strange sort of thing to say out loud.

"Did I know you when you were younger?" he asked her, desperate to say something to break her gaze. Was she someone he'd met in the company of the Middle Dread?

The old woman laughed. It was a muffled sort of laugh, like bubbles coming up through porridge.

"I doubt that very much. I've been old since the dawn of time, or so it feels." A thoughtful look came over her face, and she said, "The older I've looked, the less people have paid me any attention. And that is unexpectedly convenient. You'd be amazed, young man, at what can be accomplished when one gives up the vanity of looks."

"Did—did you know my master?" Nott asked, worried that she'd get mad at him because he'd asked twice. "The one they call the Middle Dread?"

Some of the kindness left her face, replaced by an emotion that might have been sadness but might have been something else entirely. The boy caught a glimpse of hidden energy in her. She eyed Nott sharply and said, "I saw him die."

"It's true for sure, then? He's really dead?"

"Oh, yes. A whipsword through his heart. He was dead before he hit the ground. It was shocking."

Her voice carried an odd mixture of hatred at the topic and enjoyment at being the bearer of upsetting news. For his part, Nott wasn't sure if he should feel crestfallen or relieved about the Middle Dread being dead. His master had made Nott fierce and proud, but on the other hand, the man had been—there was no escaping it—*terrifying*. Nott wanted to tell Aelred, *Don't be sad. Everyone's got to die sometime,* but the bat had never known the Middle Dread. And truth be told, the Middle Dread probably would have sliced Aelred up into little ribbons if he'd ever caught the bat.

"Were you hoping he was still alive?" the woman asked, observing Nott carefully. "You may be one of the only people ever to have wished that."

Nott's thumb brushed over the hilt of his favorite knife. No matter what he had thought of his master, who was this woman to be badmouthing him? She wasn't a Watcher, and Dun Tarm was a place that belonged to Watchers. He was getting tired of her impudence.

"Thinking about attacking me?" She sounded kind again, as though Nott were a very small child and she was proud of him for coming up with the idea of drawing his knife. Nott dropped his hands away from his weapons. Then he sniffed, vexed with himself. The truth was, he didn't love using his knives quite as much as he used to.

"You said I'd recognize you, but I don't," he told her defiantly.

"I used to be Margaret, but I've never known why my parents picked that name, when they insisted on calling me Maggie almost from the moment I was born." She smiled at him, and he was reminded of her gray hair and advanced age. "You may call me Maggie."

"I'm Nott."

"Hm." She studied his clothing. "He found you a long time ago, then? When he began gathering his own little army to get rid of people he didn't like?"

Nott shrugged; years and time confused him. "How did you know him?"

"That's a strange story for another day."

From a pocket in the rustling material of her green-splotched jacket, Maggie pulled out a small, round stone disc. Automatically Nott drew closer to look at it.

"That's my master's," he said at once. There were three interlocking ovals carved on its face, as plain as day. "I thought Shinobu had it. I thought he was our master now." He looked up at her suspiciously. Now that he was standing close, he noticed her scent—something like old, wet wool mixed with another, sweeter smell.

"What if there's more than one medallion?" Maggie asked. She was reaching into her pocket again as she walked away from Nott. Nott felt something about the air change; the atmosphere was growing heavy.

He frowned. "Then how would we know who our master is?"

She had drawn something else from her pocket. Nott's teeth were biting on air as thick as water, and his ears were filling up with honey.

Maggie turned to face him, holding some sort of weapon. Nott's ears popped, and his jaw shifted. Then suddenly he was flying through the air over the lip of the fortress floor and crashing into the water of the lake. He thrashed helplessly in the freezing water, tried to gasp for breath, but he had no idea if he succeeded, because his head went black.

When he woke, he was lying, soaking wet, on the floor of Dun Tarm, coughing up water by the lungful. Maggie was leaning over him, and though she somehow must have retrieved him from the lake, she was perfectly dry.

Nott ran his tongue over his teeth and was amazed to find they were all still in place.

"How did you do that?" he rasped.

"When my husband abandoned me, I took two small trinkets when I left."

Nott was dazed from being tossed about like a sack of barley, but even in that state he was puzzled by her choice of words; in the same breath, she'd said that her husband had left her and that she had been the one to leave.

She lifted her hands, revealing that she was holding a cylinder of stone about the length of her forearm. Through the dark stone ran an uneven seam of black glass. It was an evil-looking object, which made it irresistible to Nott's twelve-year-old eyes.

"This trinket threw you into the lake and fetched you out."

"What does the second one do?" Nott asked, though he wasn't sure he wanted to know the answer, particularly if Maggie chose to demonstrate it on him as well.

"It would do nothing in a place like this," she said. "But it would do something very great in the right place." She smiled at him. "You asked how to know who your master is." She held up the black cylinder. In her kindest grandmother's voice, she asked Nott, "Does this help you recognize me?"

Nott nodded his aching head. "You're my new master."

"Yes."

CHAPTER 12

SHINOBU

"Go! That way!" Shinobu ordered.

He had split the Watchers into three groups to chase a deer up from Loch Tarm into the wild hills. The moon threw the forest paths and rock outcroppings into sharp relief, but rain clouds were moving in from the east, and it would be a wet night before they slept—hopefully with bellies full of fresh meat.

"There!" Shinobu called. "First Group, go!"

He'd glimpsed the shaggy buck—their prey—leaping through the trees. The eight boys on his right who made up the first group hollered and yelled as they picked up their pace. The animal spooked left, bounding through the undergrowth.

"Second Group, go!" he ordered.

The boys at the middle of the chase took up the cries, driving the buck away faster.

"Now the third Group!"

Off to his left Shinobu heard them hollering in unison. The deer would be forced up the hill with enemies on every side.

They'd tried this hunting strategy twice before, and both times had been a disaster of Watchers tripping other Watchers to get to the deer first, and then an all-out fistfight over who got to kill it. In fact, all-out fistfights were the normal state of affairs when dealing with almost two dozen Watchers. Two of the boys had even been killed during previous hunts—one had fallen to his death, and another had hit his head on a rock. The fact that Shinobu's own thoughts were always running in two directions at once didn't make the Watchers any easier to deal with.

They're terrible at following orders. I hate them.

I need them, to fight for me and protect Quin against other dangers.

He clung to that second thought.

The buck veered again, looking for a weak spot in their line.

"First group!"

Those boys surged forward, making a racket, and the deer altered course. Shinobu called the other groups in turn, driving the buck straight up the hillside, which grew steeper with every yard they traveled.

As they neared the top, he became aware of a buzzing in his focal. In another moment, it was vibrating discordantly, as if wasps were batting around between his head and the metal. A stab of pain traveled through his temples. His muscles were tiring. The wound in his side, which Quin had worked so hard to heal weeks ago, was throbbing. He scanned the Watchers spread out through the trees, but he could no longer keep track of where everyone was.

When the nausea hit him, Shinobu understood. His focal had run out of energy. He'd been wearing it for so long—a whole month, if you included the time *There*—that he'd almost forgotten it was on his head. The helmet needed to sit in the sun to recharge. He supposed it absorbed some energy when he wore it during daylight hours, but he hadn't removed it since he'd brought the Watchers to Dun Tarm, and now he'd used it up.

The tines of the buck's antlers flashed in the moonlight, yards ahead, and then Shinobu and all the Watchers were in the open. The trees had ended, and they were at the crest of a rocky bluff. Behind them was the forest and the loch and, far below, the ruins of Dun Tarm. Here was the dark sky, the half-moon being eaten by fast-encroaching clouds, and the antlered buck. The animal stood on an outcropping as boys closed in on three sides. The buck would have to charge through its attackers, or leap to its death.

"Hold!" Shinobu ordered.

The boys were listening. After a week of beating each other and being beaten by Shinobu, they were finally obeying. They had their knives out, bloodlust written on their faces, but they waited for his word. Shinobu usually shared their eagerness to kill, but with the focal dead, the world looked different. He smelled the rank stench of the Watchers, which he'd stopped noticing days ago.

The buck's eyes rolled in terror, breath blowing in smoky streams from its nostrils. It was going to charge. Shinobu cocked his arm back and threw his knife. His blade caught the animal straight through his eye, and, mercifully, the buck was dead before its knees hit the ground.

The Watchers let out cries of triumph and descended on it in a violent storm of arms and legs. He watched them from what felt like miles away.

What was he doing, really?

He'd been telling himself he was gathering and taming the Watchers to protect Quin, while he kept her somewhere safe. But . . .

The full memory came back to him of Quin standing in the darkness, grabbing at his shirt, asking him not to leave her.

And then he'd left her.

Two dozen blood-streaked faces were surging around the dead

deer. How could these wild, vicious creatures ever make Quin safe? The focal . . . it had colored his thoughts.

Shinobu backed away from the scrimmage of Watchers. "I have to go," he said aloud. "Right now—"

The air was humming, and it felt thick in his mouth, was pooling in his lungs. An old woman in camouflage rain gear had appeared— entirely out of place—and was walking slowly out of the woods. With a shaking arm she was holding something out toward him.

Shinobu's jaw clicked sideways and his ears popped. He saw a swath of Watchers knocked onto their backs in the moonlight. He himself was thrown through the dark air. Something had hit him, tossed him over the edge of the cliff, and he was falling down the far side of the ridge. He was dropping without parachute or backup plan, and every fiber of his body clamored for him to do something, anything, to stop him from dying. Clouds were moving across the moon, and shadows were shifting on the rocks below.

He yelled Quin's name, and then he hit the ground and broke into a thousand pieces.

It wasn't until the sun was up that Shinobu discovered he was still alive, lying just where he'd fallen. The old woman was leaning over him, and his body was a collection of excruciating injuries.

"My goodness, you're still with us. That's unexpected." She sounded genuinely astonished. He heard her drumming her fingers against her leg. Then she said, "Unexpected, but not unwelcome."

She might have been eighty years old, with a kind, wrinkled face, and hands that trembled with age as she laid them upon Shinobu's body. She dug her fingers into him and, with a gasp of effort, rolled him onto his back. Shinobu was in too much pain to scream.

Now that he could see her face better, he discovered her kind eyes had grown hard and businesslike. She was rifling around in his cloak. Her face was vaguely familiar to him; it brought to mind the fight on *Traveler*—though he didn't remember seeing her on the airship.

"I didn't mean to throw you off the cliff. My aim and judgment are not the most accurate." She spoke with the slight quaver of the very elderly, which was at odds with the steely undertone to her words. "But it's just as well. You've been treating the boys far too gently."

"I . . . knock them about . . . tough . . ." he mumbled, though he wasn't sure why he was trying to explain anything to this woman.

She laughed. "You've knocked the boys about, have you? It seems to be working. They were following your orders. But to really make sure they listen, the Middle Dread would kill one of them every now and again. Now that I've nearly killed you, maybe we've made our point, eh? He created those boys to frighten people who annoyed him. That seems to have been in his nature—to frighten those who annoyed him. Perhaps he was entitled." She was rambling in not-all-there fashion. "What did *you* want with these boys, anyway?"

"Evildoers beware," Shinobu muttered. It was the Seeker motto he and Quin used to throw about back when they believed they were training to be something noble.

The woman laughed. "Indeed."

What *had* he wanted with them? The Middle Dread had created the Watchers as a small army to do his bidding. The Middle had been planning, for generations, to get rid of Seekers, and the Watchers had been made to help. Shinobu had only wanted them to protect Quin, but he'd fallen into the Middle Dread's paranoia, hadn't he?

Through the haze of pain and the glare of the morning sun, which kept blinding him, Shinobu felt a wave of revulsion each time the woman's hands brushed against him. At last she found something in one of his pockets and drew it out.

"There we are. Smashed to bits. As it should be."

Shinobu managed to focus on what she was holding. It was his stone medallion. A network of deep cracks spiderwebbed through it.

He painfully followed the woman with his eyes and watched her break the medallion into bits and throw them onto the ground. The interior of the stone disc was much more delicate and complicated than he'd imagined; he saw intricate patterns of interlocking pieces, all being torn apart as she destroyed it.

"It was made for one person only, and it should not have survived his death. It should certainly not be in *your* hands. The arrogance astonishes me." With the toe of her boot, she lightly kicked at Shinobu's shoulder. It was a feeble, old-woman kick, but blinding pain shot down his arm anyway. "But you're paying for it already, aren't you?"

"The boys . . ." Shinobu croaked, "they follow the medallion."

The old woman sighed. "They will have to follow mine now"—the quaver and the steel still both in her voice—"and you will be my muscle." She squeezed one of his biceps, nearly sending him back into unconsciousness. When she was close, he could smell mothballs and peppermint.

She looked up the cliff. "Come down here and get him," she called. "A trained Seeker, who refuses to die." She turned back to Shinobu. To him, lying in agony with the sun in his eyes, she was a shadow as she asked him, "What house are you from?"

"Eagle . . . and dragon," he mumbled.

"Hm," she answered.

When the Watchers arrived and picked him up by his broken limbs, Shinobu blessedly passed out. His last thought was of Quin. If he died, which seemed rather likely, would anyone ever know she was standing all alone in the darkness *There*?

No. No one would know. So I can't die.

CHAPTER 13

QUIN

Shinobu was calling her name. Quin heard him as clearly as if they were standing next to one another.

All of Quin's limbs jerked. She was falling! Then she was awake, lying on the ground in the castle ward.

"Are you all right?" came a sleepy voice that was much closer than she'd expected. She turned her head and discovered Dex's hood-covered head only inches from hers. Though he'd slept curled up inside the small rock shelter and Quin had slept outside on the ground under her cloak, she must have rolled closer while she was asleep.

"I don't know," she whispered, inching away, feeling the echoes of her dream.

Dex shifted under his hood, and abruptly sat up, full of manic energy. "It's nighttime, isn't it? Time to practice!"

When Quin was up, heading to the center of the courtyard, her back to Dex, he made a faint clicking sound to alert her. Quin heard and dodged, just as a rock sailed by inches from her head.

"Good. You're paying attention," he said. The hood was still over his eyes, but he was smiling. He liked throwing things at Quin. It seemed to bring him back to life.

"Name the weapon," she said in a commanding voice, because she was training him as much as he was training her, and the more she took charge, the more she could steer him.

"The one that . . . makes a pulse."

Quin sighed; he'd forgotten the names again. But he would remember by the time they were done.

She slipped the weapon whose name he'd forgotten onto her hand. It was made of pale stone and even paler glass, and it was designed to slide past the user's knuckles to rest on the body of the hand. She flicked it on, and at once it began to float around her right hand on an electrostatic field so strong that all the hairs on her arm and head stood slightly on end.

"Television!" Dex called. "Low power. And I won't go easy on you this time, I promise you that."

Quin laughed as she ducked around several heaps of rubble. Dex never went easy on her; each time was worse than the last.

She'd spent a full day making piles of rocks throughout the castle courtyard. At the top of each pile was a target—something they'd salvaged from the estate—all rather beat up after several days of practice. This training was always at night, when Dex was less bothered by standing out in the open. Quin supposed nighttime reminded him of no-space.

The television sat askew with a cracked screen, atop its own heap of rocks. Dex pelted her with stones as she neared it. When he threw, he threw for blood, and the missiles came whistling through the air with deadly accuracy. Quin twisted and weaved to avoid being hit, enjoying the sense of training again.

When she fired the weapon, the force intensified around her arm, and the television flickered to life, a blue glow suffusing the cracked screen.

"Higher power!" Dex said.

He threw rocks and clods of dirt and one of the horseshoes they'd found lying around. Quin took cover behind a nearby pile as she hit the television with an adjusted burst from her weapon. The screen flared, brighter and brighter, and sparks began to fly through the cracks in the glass.

"Now off!" he called.

She adjusted the weapon, dialing its energy in the opposite direction. With a thump almost below the level of hearing, the blue glow vanished from the television.

"It just looks like I turned it off," Quin remarked. "We need a better way to see what it— Hey!" She pirouetted as he sent a stone the size of his forearm at her. It missed her by inches.

"In a busy place, you will easily see when it works," he said.

"What's the weapon called, Dex?"

"A wave-pulse," he answered without hesitation. He'd remembered.

The wave-pulse, with its manipulation of electromagnetic waves, seemed a novelty out here in the Scottish countryside, but Quin imagined it would be a dangerous weapon in a crowded, powered city.

Dex was teaching her things she would never learn from anyone else, even if he wasn't sure how he knew them. That was why she'd been willing to give him time to recover his wits. Tonight, however, she was running out of patience. The sense of Shinobu calling her name would not leave her. Dex had told her several times, in lucid moments, that he would find "this person you love," but Quin suspected that he didn't know how. Still, she had no athame, no way to find Shinobu herself unless she could bring Dex back to sanity—and this nightly practice was what pleased and focused him. And if she were honest, it was also thrilling to be learning new skills.

"They used the wave-pulse all the time, to disable other weapons," he told her as he gathered up a new pile of things to hurl in her direction.

He was speaking, of course, of the people in his story. He'd been telling it to her in bits and pieces.

"How did he keep the boys from killing each other when they used the wonders?" she asked. "Small boys and deadly weapons seem a dangerous mix."

She silently heaved a rock at Dex's back, but he turned at exactly the right moment and used the large stone in his hand to bat away the one she'd thrown. He always knew.

"How do you do that?" she asked.

"When I throw a rock, it looks fast to you, but when you throw one, it's unbearably slow. I can see every foot it moves. It's like a snail crawling through the air."

"I've never had the best throwing arm," she admitted, slightly put out, "but I throw a little faster than a snail."

"I mean I can slow it down, or speed it up—what I see."

This was the most he'd ever told her about his own abilities. "Like a Dread?" she asked.

The hood still shaded his eyes, but beneath it his mouth pressed into a line of dissatisfaction. "I'm not like a Dread. And I never said the father kept the boys from killing each other." He hefted the large stone in his hands and sent it straight at her. "The impellor! The pile with three things."

Quin dove for the ground, feeling pleased. He'd remembered the name of the next weapon before she'd used it. It usually took him longer.

She pulled out the impellor and shook it as she ran, keeping herself out of Dex's direct aim as he unloaded his new pile of missiles into the air around her.

"Push the top one off!" Dex called, punctuating the order with a horseshoe that came at her head in an off-center spin and knocked stones from the nearest heap.

Atop a large pile were the three medical monitors they'd taken from the old barn, stacked haphazardly. Quin lined up the impellor's seams of glass, focusing its energy tightly. The air around her grew thick.

She fired the weapon, and the top monitor was blown off the other two as though struck by an invisible giant.

"Now the bottom one!" he yelled.

"The *bottom* one?"

A stone whizzed by her face in answer.

Quin brought the weapon's focus down to the finest setting, feeling air pool heavily in her lungs. She aimed and fired, blowing the lower device out from beneath the other one like a coin knocked from the bottom of a stack. The remaining device landed roughly where the one below it had been.

"The whole pile!" he called.

She saw Dex raise his arm to throw. She twisted the cylinder, making a new pattern in the seams of glass. He was throwing something big, his whole body in the motion. Quin blew the heap of rocks to the ground, and then leaped backward as a head-sized block of masonry passed inches from her chest.

"Bring it back, before I hit you again!"

"You didn't hit me!" she answered, and immediately wished she'd kept her mouth shut. There wasn't time for banter; he was already hefting a new missile.

Quin twisted the cylinder and fired it at the mess of stones and broken equipment. The impellor's force was reversed. The rocks, branches, broken chunks of castle, and all three pieces of equipment lifted off the ground and rushed toward her.

Dex's clod of dirt hit her in the shoulder, and she dropped the weapon—not a moment too soon. The cloud of debris rained down around her as she crouched and covered her head.

"Is that what you meant to do?" Dex asked. Quin was getting to her feet and brushing herself off. "Pull it all into a pile on top of yourself?"

"I might have miscalculated slightly," she admitted, rubbing her shoulder.

Usually he would make her use the weapons several more times, but not tonight. Quin had learned to read his body language even with his hood obscuring his face, and Dex was looking thoughtful. Without a word, he took a seat, cross-legged, and pulled his hood back enough to look up at the sky. Quin came over and sat next to him, waiting to hear what he'd remembered.

He pointed to the west, where the clouds were dissipating. A patch of stars was visible there.

"Stars?" she asked.

One of his hands disappeared into an outer pocket in his robe, from which it then reappeared, grasping a small, rectangular stone device—the one wonder that was not a weapon.

"Put your head next to mine," he said, lying back on the hard-packed ground of the castle ward and holding the device above himself.

She lay beside him and from that vantage could see several stars through the glass panel in the stone device.

"It's warming up," he explained when nothing else happened. He grasped the implement with more of his hand, perhaps to give it more heat. After a few moments, four numbers appeared at the bottom of the small, dark glass window where the stars were showing—it was the current year. Dex scanned the device over more stars, and the current month appeared next to the year.

"It knows the date?" Quin asked, startled. The device looked hundreds of years old, so this felt like strange magic. Yet whipswords were also hundreds of years old, weren't they? Their attributes were no less peculiar.

"It knows the patterns of the stars and planets," Dex explained, "and by their relative positions it calculates the date."

"More than a month since I was last here," she whispered. And more than a month since Shinobu had last been with her.

He let her hold the device, and she moved it to look at different sets of stars. The reading was the same for each.

"It's what their father used to figure out the date of their journey." He sighed and put his hands beneath his head as he gazed at the night sky. "He wasn't happy with the answer."

"He didn't know the date?"

"Not with any degree of accuracy. Not until that little tool you're holding told him the truth."

"Had he been *There* for a long time? Like me?"

"Is that where you've been?" he mused, and she knew he was speaking to Quilla instead of Quin. His voice caught as he whispered, "I thought you were dead. You used to ask—"

"I'm Quin," she told him gently. She did not want him to sink back into delusion. "You know I'm Quin, Dex. You're not losing yourself so easily anymore. Have you noticed? It's time for us to look for Shinob—"

"No, Quilla, *please*," he said, sitting up. "You cut me off. When you push, you undo everything. You make me forget at just the moment when I'm starting to remember. Can't you let me finish?" He looked toward the castle ruins, perhaps trying to catch hold of a thought before it disappeared. "You used to ask me where he kept all the important things. I wasn't allowed to tell you. But there's no stopping me now."

CHAPTER 14

SHINOBU

"Quin, isityou?" Shinobu slurred when he discovered himself awake again.

His lips were swollen and cracked and he was so thirsty. It was dark, and Quin was in the darkness where he'd left her. He had to make his arms and legs work in order to go get her back.

"Seeker?" came a woman's voice, but it didn't belong to Quin. It was that old woman from before.

"They're eating mlegsnarms," he whispered. "Makemstop."

"Dramatic," said the woman, amused.

Shinobu pried his eyes open enough to make out her silhouette; then he closed them again. He'd expected to see the looming shapes of wild beasts feasting on his limbs, because that's what he felt.

"If he throws up, turn his head," the woman instructed someone nearby. Her voice had the gentle, old-woman tremble in it, but Shinobu wouldn't be fooled. There was nothing gentle about her. "Remind me of his name," she added.

"Shinobu."

Shinobu knew that second voice. He slipped in and out of consciousness as he tried to remember . . . Yes. The voice belonged to one of the Middle Dread's boys—who'd attacked him and Quin in the hospital and on the estate and in Hong Kong. He hadn't been at Dun Tarm with all the others, though.

"Shinobu, can you hear me?" the old woman asked, poking him in the chest insistently.

"Makem stop biting," he murmured. With great effort, he added, "Please."

"Fetch me that over there, Nott."

Nott. That was the boy's name. *Little bastard.* Shinobu remembered the boy's terrible odor, though he wasn't aware of it now—maybe Shinobu's nose didn't work anymore. No. He smelled mothballs and peppermint from the old woman, and he smelled lake and shore and stone. He was at Dun Tarm, and his nose might be one of the few parts of him that was still functional. How was he going to get Quin in this state?

The woman inflicted a series of stinging pinches all over Shinobu's body, and the agony receded. *Painkillers!* "Ohthankgod," he breathed.

"Does that feel good?" she asked.

The animals stopped biting all the way through his flesh and were now only gnawing at the surface.

"Ohgodit'sheaven . . ."

"I used to think everyone mattered all the time," the old woman was saying. Her trembling voice forced itself into his ears. "But you can't live that way, not sensibly. You'll die of caring." There was another sting down Shinobu's left arm, and again down his right arm, followed by more blessed numbness. "Eventually you learn to pick out who really matters—and who matters for the moment."

The woman was speaking in a low, creaky murmur, but he wasn't listening. He'd hidden the athame of the Dreads behind a loose stone in the fortress wall. If he could stand up, after this woman went away and before the painkillers wore off, he could retrieve it. Once it was in his hands, he would find his way back to Quin. He imagined pulling her into his arms as she woke up from her time *There*, apologizing, kissing her. Hot tears sprang to his eyes.

Another sting at his jaw, and relief spread through the bottom half of his face. Apparently wolves had been chewing on his chin, though he hadn't noticed until now because so many other things hurt.

"Shinobu," the woman said kindly, bathing him in the scent of mothballs, "open your eyes."

". . . were biting me?" he mumbled.

"No one's biting you." The gentleness in her words made him deeply suspicious.

Shinobu's eyelids had been replaced by lead weights, but somehow he got them open. The woman was smiling at him, her gray hair tied neatly behind her head.

"There you are. I'm Maggie."

"P—pleased to mmm—" he started, trying to say *Pleased to meet you*, which was ridiculous under the circumstances.

"You won't be pleased to meet me," she told him. "But never mind that. Can you see yourself?"

She held his head up so that he could look down his own body. Shinobu didn't want to look—he was terrified he'd see only bloody pulp where his arms should be or find half of himself missing.

It wasn't that bad, though it was rather bad. His clothes were ripped, and every visible inch of skin was a dark purplish blue from bruising. His limbs were crooked, as though they'd been assembled wrong. He wanted to scream, but he thought screaming might break him into even more pieces.

"You've got dozens of breaks, but I'm putting you back together," she purred at him, stroking his hair. "It *will* feel like you're being eaten alive, I'm afraid. That's the cellular reconstructors I've been injecting into you. They do their work quite painfully."

Reconstructors. He should have known. He'd just gotten finished being reconstructed from his previous injuries before she threw him off the cliff.

Maggie answered his unspoken question—*How do you know how to use cellular reconstructors?*—by saying, "There's a lot you can learn about doctoring when you've taken care of dozens of children over hundreds of years." She brushed Shinobu's hair off his forehead, as he pondered what she meant by "taken care of." It sounded as though, whatever she'd done, it had been far from nurturing. "I've seen you before," she told him. "You broke onto *Traveler* when it crashed."

Shinobu narrowed his eyes, trying to think. He'd been right to associate her with *Traveler,* then. She must be a relative of John's; that would explain the sweet surface over the rotten interior.

Maggie pinched his cheek, bringing his attention back. "You told me you're descended from the houses of eagle and dragon, is that right?"

"M'mother's side were dragons," he answered. "M'father's were eagles."

The pain had receded, but not far enough. He felt as though he'd been run over by a train, and then the train had backed up and run over him again.

"The dragons intermarried with the true Seeker houses—the fox and the stag. There's a good chance some of your blood comes from my own blood. A fortunate circumstance, Shinobu. I don't care to poison my own."

"Poison?" he asked, thinking this was an alarming change of subject. If only she would leave for a few minutes, he could get away.

Someone just out of Shinobu's line of sight pushed him roughly onto his stomach. It was probably that boy Nott. When Shinobu tried to roll free, the boy sat firmly on his legs. This was agony.

"Hold still," Maggie told him.

There was a pinch at Shinobu's neck, and then the unmistakable sensation of a syringe full of liquid emptying into his bloodstream.

"There's a poison that lives in your body forever," she explained calmly.

"Did—did—did you—" he stuttered.

"Did—did—did I what?" Her voice remained kind even as she mocked him. It reminded him of the cloying crystals used to clean up vomit. Soothingly she said, "I told you, I don't poison my own."

So what did you inject? he demanded, though no words came out. She was rustling about inside a pack near his head, her motions slow, feeble, and yet somehow unstoppable. Shinobu could feel everything—the dull ache in his arms and legs and jaw, the pressure of Nott holding him down, even the cool breeze blowing through his hair—but he couldn't move. Whatever she'd injected was holding him still. His plan to get Quin was beginning to feel very optimistic.

Maggie pulled up his shirt, and cold pinpricks began between his shoulder blades. There was pressure and pain as a dozen needles pierced his skin. It sounded like she was using a stone to tap the needles into his back. With each blow they sank into his flesh, as if she were driving in a row of nails.

Maggie made a few sounds of effort, not grunts exactly but the sort of noise an elderly grandmother might make as she corrected a particularly complicated knitting stitch. Shinobu wondered if, when this torture was done, she would offer him a dish of sweets. Before he could find out, the lead weights over his eyes pulled themselves downward and he was unconscious again.

* * *

"Do you really know your mother's and father's families?"

That was Nott, and the question seemed to be addressed to Shinobu.

He blinked and discovered that his eyes were wide open. Perhaps they'd been open for a long while without him realizing. He was staring up at a broken piece of wall and a cloudy sky above that, and now that he thought about it, it was possible he'd been looking up at this view for some time.

"What?"

His voice, at least, was working. He made a quick and silent inventory and discovered he could move his arms and legs. They were unbelievably painful, but not quite as bad as the last time he'd woken up. If Maggie wasn't nearby, he could grab his athame and get away. He tried to keep his breathing normal as he braced himself to jump to his feet—as soon as he made sure that the old woman was gone.

"You told Maggie that your mother's family was dragons and your father's was eagles. Did you know them?"

Shinobu turned his head to look at Nott. That was a mistake, because pain traveled up and down his neck in hot jolts. The boy was sitting nearby, petting what appeared to be a small bat, which hung upside down from his left hand. Shinobu stared for several moments, because he'd recognized Nott's voice, but now that he could see the owner of the voice, Shinobu wasn't sure it was the same person. This boy had light brown hair and a pale face with a spray of freckles across his nose and cheeks.

"What happened to you?" Shinobu croaked.

"Had a couple baths," Nott explained, understanding the confusion immediately.

"They worked."

The boy made a noncommittal grunt.

They were in a corner of Dun Tarm. Shinobu could hear other

Watchers outside on the shore of the lake. But no one seemed to be nearby.

"Can you move?" Nott asked without much interest.

"Sort of."

"Your mother and father and granny and whatnot. Did you know all of them?"

Shinobu blinked at the sky, trying to marshal his thoughts enough to answer this odd question. If it was strange for this Watcher boy to be asking him about his family, though, it certainly wasn't the strangest thing that had happened to him in the last twenty-four hours.

"I met my grandparents on both sides a few times," he said, deciding that this question was as good as any for pulling him back into the world of the living. "But my mother and father and I kept to ourselves. My mother's father was a traditional Japanese man, and he wasn't happy that she married a Scottish barbarian."

"Oh." The boy sounded disappointed at Shinobu's tenuous family connections. "But you knew who they *were,* your grandparents and that?"

"Yeah, of course."

"We only had our mother. And sometimes our bastard father who had fists like—what do you call them things blacksmiths use?"

"Hammers?"

"No, the other ones, underneath."

Shinobu hazarded a wild guess. "Anvils?"

"Anvils, that's it. Didn't know more relatives than that. I don't have a second name even, except sometimes I was called Nott Drunk son."

The boy bounced the bat too roughly, but whenever Shinobu thought Nott was actually going to hurt it, he grew gentle and stroked the creature's head and made chirping sounds at it.

"Wilkin is dead," Nott said, as if he were announcing the arrival of rain or commenting on a passing bird.

Wilkin. I know that name. He made the connection. Wilkin had been Nott's slightly older Watcher partner. Shinobu had fought them both, in the hospital room and on the Scottish estate. "Ah," he said. "Wilkin's the Watcher who fell down a ravine during our first hunt."

Nott shrugged. The method of Wilkin's death was apparently unimportant to him. "I thought I would be happy he's gone, but I'm not," he said thoughtfully.

"You liked him, maybe?"

"No, I hated him." He was emphatic on this point. "But it was easy to blame him for things. I miss that."

Little bastard, Shinobu thought a second time. He tested his arms and legs again. The pain throbbed up the center of his limbs, but he thought he could stand if he tried. The breaks themselves had knitted together. He ignored the pain in his neck and peered around the fortress. Uneven stone floor, puddles, stunted trees, and the lake beyond. Maggie was not in sight, and the other Watchers were all outside.

"Wait! She's—" began Nott when he realized what Shinobu intended to do. But Shinobu pushed the boy away. He lurched to his feet and hobbled toward the fortress wall, where he'd hidden the athame of the Dreads. His legs were awkward, as if the two sides of his fractures were several degrees off center from each other, but the reconstructors must have been making progress by the minute, because the bones bore his weight with minimal complaint. He walked as fast as he could force his limbs to go.

Nott was on his feet and coming after him. "Shinobu, she's—"

Shinobu's muscles began to melt around his bones. His knees hit the ground, then his hips. He discovered his arms were putty and couldn't break his fall. His chin landed on the ground with a hard *smack*.

What had just happened? He was looking across the puddles and broken stones of the fortress floor, which were at his eye level. He was still breathing, but he couldn't voluntarily move anything. His body was no longer his to command. A lazy fly landed on his forehead and began to walk along his skin. When Shinobu automatically tried to brush it off with a hand that wouldn't respond, he felt a deep panic take hold. He was a piece of meat left out in the sun, a consciousness trapped in clay.

From this position, he saw Maggie, sitting in a nook in Dun Tarm's broken wall, regarding him with amusement.

"You didn't tell him?" she asked Nott.

"I was getting to it."

She stood with difficulty and carefully brushed off her pants. "Well. While I fetch John, you should explain."

"Yes," Nott agreed humbly.

As Maggie walked off, Nott crouched down so that his face obscured everything else in Shinobu's line of sight. "She put something in your back. Don't you remember? A metal plate with needles. The needles are *in you*."

Shinobu made a grunting sound—it was all he could manage. His body was a slab of beef, soft and dead.

"She's a little bit of a witch," Nott told him confidentially, echoing Shinobu's own thoughts. "She's got something in her pocket that talks to the thing in your back. When she pushes the button, you turn into a puddle of porridge." Nott snapped his fingers by Shinobu's ear. "Like that!"

Shinobu had seen plates like the one Nott was describing. They were used in hospitals to stimulate damaged nerves. Maggie must be using one on him for the opposite purpose. Medical skills and a torturer's sensibility—what a delightful old woman.

Nott got down onto his elbows and held up Shinobu's eyelid to make sure he was paying attention. "She already found the athame you hid. She's going to take us all *There*," he whispered, "to get rid of the Seekers she doesn't like. She's going to give my helm back if I help her the most."

Shinobu knew his mind wasn't the sharpest right now, so he repeated Nott's words inside his own head until he was sure he understood: *Maggie is going to bring the Watchers* There *to kill Seekers.*

"She hasn't actually promised that I'll get my helm back," Nott explained anxiously, "but why wouldn't she? Don't answer that."

Maggie was bringing Watchers *There* to kill Seekers. Unfortunately, Quin was a Seeker, and Shinobu had left her *There*.

He wanted to scream, but his vocal cords were not under his control.

Nott leaned into Shinobu's ear and said, "You're going to help her keep all the Watchers in order, because they're scared of you, and this"—he tapped the metal plate in Shinobu's back—"is going to keep *you* in order."

Shinobu discovered the video screen when movement returned to his arms and legs. That took a while, and by then Nott had moved off to play with his bat, leaving Shinobu alone in his agony. It didn't feel like animals were gnawing at him anymore. Now when he tentatively moved his hands and feet, it felt as though the individual cells of his body were on fire.

"Will I cut off your wings? Will I?" Nott was murmuring to his bat somewhere off to Shinobu's left, while the bat chirped happily. "Or will I cut off your feet? No, I would never! But I would."

Nott had shoved a pack under Shinobu's head as a makeshift pillow, and there was something in the pack that was cutting painfully into Shinobu's cheek—a knife handle possibly? He wanted to lie perfectly still until either he died or everything stopped hurting, but Quin was all alone, and Shinobu had to take any opportunity to get his hands on a weapon.

He pulled the pack out from beneath his head and realized that it was Maggie's. He'd seen her carrying it. She'd left it, he supposed, for Nott to guard. What might Maggie have in such a pack?

Without attracting Nott's attention, Shinobu carefully turned his body away from the boy, to block Nott's view of the pack.

"Is that ticklish?" Nott was asking his bat. "It would be less ticklish with my knife. Aelred, you should stay on my good side!"

The muscles of Shinobu's arms were burning as he unzipped the bag and ran his hands through the contents. There was nothing interesting inside, only a sheaf of papers, which felt old and well handled. He squinted against the bright sky to focus on the writing. It was a hand-drawn family tree; the generations went on for pages and pages, going back hundreds of years, and here and there were house emblems, mostly foxes and stags.

So she can decide which ones of us are worthy of living? he thought bitterly.

But where was the object that had been digging into his face?

"You bit me!" Nott said crossly to Aelred. "How would you like me to bite *you*?" the boy asked, and then there was a screech from the bat, suggesting that Nott had done just that.

Shinobu felt into every corner of the bag and at last located something hard and flat sewn into the base. At first he thought it was simply part of the bag itself, but when he ran his fingers over one of the seams, there was a concealed pocket. Working his fingers inside, he touched a small sheet of rigid plastic. Not a weapon.

Dammit!

He drew the plastic out of its hiding place as Nott began to coo to the bat again about the various ways he could dismember it.

The hidden object was a square about six inches by six inches, a black sheet inside a slightly thicker frame—a video screen. A name had been scratched into the edge, and he had to tilt it this way and that before he could read it: *Catherine.*

"Are you awake?" Nott asked. He was still yards away, but the words were obviously directed at Shinobu. The boy had noticed him moving.

"Sort of," Shinobu answered as he shoved the papers back into the bag. He hesitated over the vid screen as he heard Nott approaching. Would Maggie miss it right away? Did he care?

He decided he didn't care. Shinobu had every intention of getting to Quin before anyone else did. He would find her, and she would want to see this video with Catherine's name on it. Quin believed in Catherine and what she stood for. And Shinobu had to believe that Quin would have some reason to be happy to see him. He slid the vid screen beneath himself to hide it, as Nott stepped into view.

The boy stared down at him skeptically. "You can move, then?" he asked. "I thought maybe you'd be a puddle of porridge forever." He looked disappointed that he'd been wrong.

CHAPTER 15

JOHN

"Is that you, John?" Gavin Hart asked.

"Hello, Grandfather."

John pulled the door shut behind him and crossed the hospital room to his grandfather's bedside. Through the room's window, he saw the Young Dread in the hallway, leaning patiently against the wall. She'd come without her cape, in an attempt to attract less attention, and so she looked strange and modern to John.

"Where have you been?" Gavin asked. "I thought you'd forgotten me."

"Of course not. I was taking care of my mother's business." He knew his grandfather would understand what he meant, that John had been living as a Seeker, in the shadow world his mother had once inhabited.

He'd last visited Gavin here a month ago, and his grandfather's health had not improved. For all of John's life, Gavin Hart had looked thin, dapper, and elegant, usually in an expensive suit. Now he struck John as frail enough that a stray breeze might blow him away. He lay in the center of the hospital bed, his white hair still perfectly trimmed, but his face giving the impression that it was shrinking in upon itself. He was hidden under a thick blanket, but medical machinery crowded around him, and tubes and wires disappeared beneath the cover to snake their way into his body.

"You look very well," the old man told him. "Strong. My strong boy." When he spoke like this, John wondered if the old man was confusing him with John's father, Archie. John didn't mind.

"I've been trained by someone demanding, Grandfather. If I hadn't gotten strong, I would never have kept up."

"How do I look?" Gavin asked. There was a wry edge to the question.

"You look . . . a little worse for wear," he admitted.

In fact, Gavin was at the end. John had spoken to the doctors. They quibbled over details, but they were in agreement that Gavin's body was failing. They were slowing down the end as much as they could, but mostly they were just making him comfortable now.

"What brings you to London?" his grandfather asked.

"A different task than I've ever set myself before," John answered, adding, "but I can't really explain."

Gavin accepted this easily. It was the way he expected John to live—secretly.

John and the Young Dread had brought eight new patients to the hospital—the men, women, and children who had once been boar Seekers. They were now slowly waking up in a ward downstairs, while the doctors murmured theories to each other about their new patients' injuries and their odd, temporary immobility.

Standing at his grandfather's bedside, John was uncomfortable with what he'd done. It had felt good to bring those Seekers to the hospital, but here with Gavin, he could hear his mother's voice, demanding to know why he'd saved her enemies.

"I'm glad you came, because I'm dying," Gavin said bluntly. One of his arms came out from beneath the blanket, trailing tubes. He gestured at his own body as if it belonged to someone else. "It's the poison."

Many years before, John's mother had poisoned Gavin with a substance that lived in his body permanently. She'd done it to control him. Such were the harsh realities of Catherine's life. For decades, Gavin had required a daily antidote to stay alive, and Maggie had been the one to administer it—secretly, because John's grandfather hadn't learned about the poison until recently. Gavin had known Maggie only as an old family retainer of Catherine's. Her familial relationship to John—confusing, even to John—had been kept secret.

"When I couldn't find Maggie after *Traveler* crashed," John said, "I thought the doctors might be able to counteract it without her. I thought you might still recover."

"They did something better than counteracting it." His grandfather coughed lightly, but he'd overcome the racking cough that had plagued him for months. "They removed every molecule of poison from my body."

"Then—" John began hopefully.

Gavin shook his head. "No, I'm not cured, John. Quite the opposite. The poison had eaten its way through me—heart, lungs, muscles. Everything's failing. If I were a young man, maybe there would be a chance. But I'm not, and there isn't."

"I'm sorry," John whispered. The doctors had told him most of this, but it pained him to hear his grandfather's unvarnished assessment.

"What are you sorry for?"

"I'm sorry my mother poisoned you."

And he was. When John was a boy, Maggie had kept him perpetually on edge about his grandfather. John was ordered to keep the old man happy and keep his love—but John would have done this naturally if left on his own.

One of Gavin's eyes drifted out of alignment with the other—a remnant effect of the poison—but it came back when he focused on John.

"You look like her," he told his grandson. "I see Catherine in you all the time. You don't look as much like your father." He squeezed John's hand. "Let's forget what she did to me. I loved Catherine like she was my own. And she loved Archie with all of her heart, John."

Tears sprang to John's eyes. That his parents might have truly loved each other and been happy together, however briefly, was an idea he cherished, though it felt too nice to be true.

"She killed people, Grandfather."

"Yes," Gavin agreed quietly. "And I encouraged her. We had an understanding that the wealth was worth it. The safety, as she called it, was worth anything."

"Do you still believe that?"

Gavin paused for a long while, and his right eye drifted out of alignment again, as if half of him were trying to escape these last, unpleasant days. Just as John began to wonder if he was tiring the old man out, Gavin said, "Was it worth it? I'm dying, so I can't lie to myself. I caused others to die, and I've always been greedy, for things far beyond what I deserve. John, to keep what we have, there will be hard choices."

Hard choices—like, should he have brought the adult boar Seekers here? Should he have killed them instead? He could have saved only the children—

"*Traveler* is going to fly again," John said, instead of speaking any of those thoughts aloud. "Any day now."

Gavin said nothing for a moment; his energy was fading. Then he whispered, "You're my heir, John. What your mother built, you should have." He looked into John's eyes, gathering his strength. "At the end, she was crazy. The poison . . ." He trailed off, chasing down a stray thought. When he caught hold of it, his bleary eyes latched on to John's again. "It wasn't her."

"Do you mean the crazy Catherine wasn't the real Catherine?"

Gavin shook his head, grasped John's arm tightly. "No. Yes. The worst things she did . . ." His eyes squeezed shut, and there was a tear in the corner of one. When Gavin opened his eyes, he was staring over John's shoulder. The old man opened his mouth, but no sound came out. He had exhausted himself completely. His eyes closed midthought.

"Grandfather," John whispered.

The old man was breathing steadily. The machines surrounding him whirred and clicked without interruption. He had only fallen asleep.

"I'll come back as soon as I can," John told him.

He turned to leave and saw what Gavin had been looking at: Maggie was standing in the hospital hallway, gazing in the window at John.

CHAPTER 16

JOHN

"Maggie, you're here," John said as he emerged from the hospital room. He found himself caught somewhere between astonishment and relief. And there was a feeling worse than these; John was a grown man now, but he felt suddenly small and helpless. For so long he had relied on Maggie for his survival. She had been the one to take his mother's place after Catherine had been removed from John's life.

"And you're here," Maggie answered.

She looked just as she had the last time John had seen her. Her long gray hair was tied up neatly behind her head, and she was clothed in one of the simple, rather old-fashioned dresses she had always worn. Her posture was perfect, though John could sense the effort of holding gravity at bay.

"I couldn't find you—" John began, just as Maggie said, "I've been looking for you—"

They both smiled, though John's smile was not entirely natural. How would Maggie judge him now? They had always been working toward the same goal—their own house restored and others' torn down—or rather, Maggie had always made sure that John understood that goal and the rules of the game. She would not be pleased to know what he had just done.

Maggie took over and said warmly, "We've found each other now."

"Gavin's dying." He nodded to the room behind him.

"Aye, I see that."

John glanced down the hallway to where the Young Dread stood. She had retreated, allowing him privacy for his business with his family.

"How did you get off *Traveler*? When it crashed, we found everyone—everyone but you. I thought you maybe . . ." He shook his head, remembering the chaos, the endless emergency vehicles, the ongoing count of everyone pulled from the airship. "I didn't know what to think." Hadn't a small part of him been relieved to think she hadn't survived?

"I got off the ship."

"But *how*?" he pressed. The shock of finding her alive was wearing off, replaced by questions. "And where did you go?"

"That is easier shown than explained. The Middle Dread's death is an opportunity for us." John was surprised that she knew the name "Middle Dread" at all, but before he could formulate this thought into a question, Maggie had put a hand on his shoulder and was saying, "Come with me and I'll *show* you. We have urgent matters, you and I."

"Go where? Maggie—*Grandmother*," he whispered, falling back into what he'd called her when he was a child, even though he knew she wasn't his grandmother, not really. Catherine too had called Maggie "Grandmother," and yet Maggie hadn't been Catherine's grandmother either. Maggie had always told John that their connection was more distant than that, though she loved him as much as anyone could love a grandson. When she said that, he'd always felt the implication: *It's hard to love grandsons, but I will try.*

A group of nurses walked down the hall, and Maggie lowered her voice, drew John near before he could finish his thought. "Do you have it?" she asked. "Do you have it with you?"

"What?" John asked, confused. She was speaking—indeed had been speaking since the first words out of her mouth—as if they'd been in the middle of a conversation just that morning, as if the two months of silence and fear that she was dead had never happened.

"Our athame." Her eyebrows drew down in a familiar look of vexation as though John were being intentionally slow. "The athame with the fox carved into it, John. I saw it in your hands when you ran away from the site of the crash."

"You *saw* me in London? After the crash?"

"Don't be a parrot. Where is our family athame?"

Anger welled up, and before John could control his voice, he was hissing at her, "You've been all right since the crash? You *saw* me? Where have you been, then? Gavin's been here dying. You could have come to him with his antidote immediately. You could have saved him anytime. Now you show up when it's too late and act as if it doesn't matter? Where have you been, Maggie?"

She took his arm, gently steered him down the hall in the opposite direction from the Young Dread. Nudging open the door to the nearest stairwell, she took John inside.

"I was elsewhere for a time. I'm often elsewhere, John. I needed a while to set my mind straight, to come back to myself after the shock of the attack on the ship, and to think about the Middle Dread's death and what he left for us."

"What he left for us? What are you talking about? My grandfather's been dying!"

"The antidote wouldn't have done much good anyway, John. It was failing. You know that. He needed more and more to have any effectiveness. The poison has run its course and so has your grandfather."

She said this with such sympathy, but John wanted to yell. Before he could, Maggie put a placating hand on his arm. Medical personnel were coming up the stairs, so she led him slowly down to the relative privacy of the landing between floors. Irrationally this frightened John; Maggie was bringing him closer to the ward with the boar Seekers in it.

"Gavin's been good for us and bad for us for years." She leaned close to keep her words quiet. "Very bad once he became unstable. Now he's at the end, and even though it saddens us, there's nothing we can do. His time has passed." After the briefest of pauses, she added, "He left you his fortune?"

John said yes automatically. He felt, as he had so often as a boy, that his own anger was being brushed aside for something more important. With Maggie, there had always been something more important.

"Then he's done all that he could for us, hasn't he? Now, tell me—do you have the athame?"

Before he could think through the answer, he said, "Yes, I have it." He had to rein Maggie in, tell her that he was not automatically on her side. But instead, stalling, he opened his jacket and revealed the hilt of the fox athame sticking up from his waistband. "I've finished my Seeker training, taken my oath. I have my mother's journal."

Maggie smiled radiantly. "So you've done almost everything Catherine wanted." She kissed John's cheek as if he were a small child being praised for eating all of his vegetables. "The timing is perfect, John. We have the Middle Dread's boys. All of them."

"How do you—"

"He used them for petty things, but we can use them to do what Catherine herself wanted."

She began down the stairs, as if they would take action immediately and she expected him to follow. When he didn't, she turned back.

"What do you mean, 'what Catherine herself wanted'?" he asked, though he knew exactly what she meant.

Above him, the stairwell door was ajar. Maud was there, listening.

His grandmother, or whatever she was to him, looked at him with an equal measure of pleading and displeasure. "Everything you and I have talked about since you were a little boy. When I came back and found the condition of your family, when Catherine was a girl . . ." She shook her head at the memory. "Other houses plotting against us. We will put things to rights, John. We will become what we were in the beginning, the fox Seekers, the house at the center of the world."

Those words were a mantra that had been drummed into John until he'd stopped questioning their meaning. It was why he'd had to train as a Seeker, why he'd had to recover their family's athame. He still believed in those words, but he wanted to find his path in his own way.

"How will I do that?" John asked her, knowing what her answer would be but needing to hear her say it.

"We're going to find the other Seeker houses, the bears, the boars, the rams, the fanged cats, the horses, you know the list."

"What if I've already found them? What if I know where they all must be and I don't want your help—I don't want you involved at all?"

"*Have* you found them, John?" Pleasure and suspicion vied for control of Maggie's face as she walked back to him. She ignored the last thing he'd said entirely and smoothed his knitted brow. "Don't trouble yourself. We only kill the houses who've harmed us, and not because we enjoy killing."

As happened now and then when Maggie spoke, she seemed to shed her years, and a very young woman, alight with passion, looked out of her old eyes. John removed her hand from his forehead, took hold of her frail shoulder.

"You raised me, Maggie, but I'm going to make my own choices now."

Maggie's smile retreated in a series of baffled stages. A doctor made her way upstairs past them, and John's grandmother was forced to get very close to him. "I *knew* your mother," she hissed. "You were only a small child when she died. I'm leading us to—"

"What if most of the Seekers you think are against us have been trapped for a long time, Maggie? Not out in the world," John whispered, voicing the conflict that had been brewing within him. "I believe we have enemies, but all of those houses couldn't have been doing *all* the things you told me they've been doing. Were you even there to see?"

Her face twisted and transformed. "I didn't have to be there to understand what was done. You've seen the photographs, John! Men, women, children."

"I've seen photographs of dead people. I haven't seen pictures of who killed them," he answered. The memory of Maggie's pictures of carnage was vivid in his mind. There must be truth behind some of her accusations, but the sense that his grandmother had been manipulating him for all of his life swamped John. "*I* decide what to do. I've seen the missing boar Seekers. They're here, being cared for, because I decided to bring them. Some of them are children themselves!"

He and his grandmother stood face to face as the color rose in her cheeks and disgust settled across her features. She pulled her shoulder from his grasp with a feeble, resentful motion. Then she became very still.

The Young Dread had come silently down the stairs and was standing just above the landing.

"Stay away from me, unnatural girl," the old woman said quietly. "I recognize you, from your gait, from your bearing." Maggie backed away from John and the Young Dread, her voice quavering. "You're no child of his, no matter what he called you." She looked venomously at Maud and took a farther, trembling step away. "Or were you trained and bound to the other one, the Middle Dread?"

Not taking her eyes off the old woman, Maud replied, "I am my own."

"You are *not* your own."

The door above them opened, and a large group of hospital staff poured into the stairwell.

Maggie turned from Maud to John and whispered, "This is who you choose to ally yourself with? I thought you were learning from that harmless Seeker girl. Not this *thing*." She gestured at the Young Dread. "You may have no loyalty, but I will still do what's right, John."

When the strangers reached the landing, Maggie turned on her heel and joined them, leaving John and the Young Dread staring after her.

John was so relieved to pry himself loose from his grandmother that he was blind to the truth, the *promise,* that flashed across her eyes before she left him. She looked frail as she made her way down the stairs. But she was not.

CHAPTER 17

MAUD

They should not have let the old woman go. Within half an hour, Maggie had killed every one of the Seekers they'd rescued, except for the children. She would have killed them too, Maud supposed, but there hadn't been time.

John and the Young Dread had been outside the hospital when the sirens began. They'd followed the police up into the ward where the Seekers were being kept. That ward was now a chaos of patients, nurses, and policemen, and Maud and John stood in the middle of it, watching the dead being wheeled out one by one.

A bystander, his voice clinical with shock, described what he'd seen. "An elderly woman came in. I thought she was a relative. And she—she stabbed them, one after another, like she was chopping up vegetables. Her arm shook, you know, like the knife was heavy, but that didn't slow her down." The witness swallowed, touched his throat. "Then she simply walked out when a nurse came, as if she was going on about her business."

The Young Dread and John had brought eight boar Seekers to the hospital. Six were dead. Maud caught a glimpse of the two children.

They were awake and terrified, a girl of eleven and a boy of four, behind a cordon of police officers at the far end of the ward. The small boy's dark eyes darted around the room, looking for something—anything—familiar. When had that boy last been awake in the world? A hundred years ago? Five hundred? Perhaps everyone he had known was now gone.

Eventually the pandemonium began to die down and there was nothing else to do in the hospital. The children wouldn't be left unguarded again. John's expression was unreadable as they exited the building. His eyes had retreated deep within himself; something was burning in there, but whether it was anger or a different emotion, Maud could not tell. She guided him into a narrow alley, where they were alone and would be unobserved.

After a time John's gaze came back to the world around him. "I told Maggie the boar Seekers were there," he said. "I was trying to show her I was in control, and I got them killed."

The Young Dread recalled the old woman's twisted face in the stairwell. She could not deny that John was right.

"What else did I tell her?" he asked. "What other ideas have I given her?"

Maud reviewed the words she'd overheard while waiting at the top of the stairs. "You told her most Seekers were trapped outside of the world."

John licked his upper lip nervously. "I don't know if she understands about the other dimensions."

"She knows about the Old Dread," Maud told him, replaying the woman's words in her mind. *You're no child of his, no matter what he called you,* Maggie had said; she had clearly been speaking of the Old Dread. "And she knew about the Middle Dread," Maud added. "She got off *Traveler* safely before it crashed. How did she accomplish that if not by athame?"

"If she had an athame all this time, wouldn't she have given it to me?" John asked. He put a hand to his head, as if the last few minutes were finally overwhelming him. "She killed them on the spur of the moment—because she discovered they were in the hospital, within her reach. She means to kill all the houses that she counts as enemies."

"You haven't told her where they're hidden. We ourselves have found only the boar Seekers."

"But can't we find the rest, Maud? If we go to the caves of each Seeker house, don't you think we'll be able to find them all?"

The Young Dread had thought this through already and suspected John was right. They had learned the code, and now it was only a matter of locating each cave.

"Probably," she admitted.

"If we can find them," John asked, "couldn't Maggie find them too?"

He buried his face in his hands as a small boy might. When he spoke, his voice was miserable. "Why am I thinking of stopping her? She's only getting rid of those she has reason to fear. Isn't that fair?"

The Young Dread did not answer. John was not in a state to listen to logic.

"For a moment," he said, "when I saw those dead Seekers in the hospital, I . . ." She thought he was going to say *I was relieved*. But John shook his head, as though changing his mind, and continued, "She's not giving them a chance."

CHAPTER 18

SHINOBU

Shinobu had slept the rest of the afternoon and into the evening, as the cellular reconstructors marched through his body. He was dead to the world until Maggie returned to Dun Tarm in a blinding rage.

"Is anyone ever grateful?" he heard her demanding as he clawed his way back into consciousness. Her voice trembled with both age and fury, and though she was speaking too softly to be accused of yelling, there was no mistaking that she wanted everyone in the fortress to hear her. "The boy owes me so much. Everything. He belongs to my family."

From his place up against the wall, Shinobu opened his eyes. The fortress was lit dimly by the remnants of two cooking fires, and in that light, Maggie looked exhausted, her excellent posture flagging. She was waving the black cylindrical weapon at the huddled shapes of Watchers, who were trying to hide themselves. Half of them, like Shinobu, had just woken up. But no one was sleeping now. "Is it wrong to expect loyalty from a boy you raised, whose welfare you put above your own? Do any of you know anything about faithfulness?"

She turned here and there, trying to catch the eye of any Watcher unlucky enough to be staring right at her, but they were all huddling in the shadows of the broken fortress walls. The effort of brandishing the cylinder further drained her. She let the weapon drop to her side as she caught her breath.

Shinobu realized that he was still lying on Maggie's pack. He'd been using it as a pillow all afternoon. When the old woman's back was turned, as she hunted for a proper victim to berate, he scooted away from it. He didn't want her to find him and the pack together, now that he'd stolen something from it.

"What is it?" Maggie was demanding waspishly of someone. She croaked, "Are you asking me for your focal again? After this day I've had? For your sake, I hope you aren't asking me again." She must be talking to Nott, who could not shut up about his focal.

The air was getting thick. Shinobu, still sore in every place where it was possible to be sore, pushed himself backward with his elbows, behind a piece of rubble and into deeper shadows as air began to pool in his lungs. Maggie shook the cylinder and pointed it at anything that moved.

"Are you all running from me? I could have used your help today in London. I'm an old woman who's never liked killing. I had to do it myself, because you lot are worthless."

She sounded ready to pass out, but she clung to the cylinder with manic intensity. Some foolish boy began to speak—Nott again!—and Maggie fired the weapon. Shinobu saw, as he peeked around the block of masonry, Nott's black-clad form fly through the air and land badly.

Is the boy incapable of keeping quiet? he wondered.

The other Watchers were slinking away in every direction, in case their mistress should begin firing indiscriminately at all of them. But she didn't.

Instead she was coming for Shinobu. He rolled onto his back and closed his eyes, made himself relax, as if he were genuinely asleep. He heard Maggie stop and retrieve her pack, and continue her approach.

She stood over him, breathing heavily. When she stepped on his ribs, he winced in pain, and then he feigned grogginess as he opened his eyes.

"Get up," she told him, a note of pleading in her voice. "Get all of them up and out by the lake. We'll practice the rest of the night. Fighting you, fighting each other. I want to see boys who can do as they're asked."

"Are you sure you wouldn't like to rest a bit?" he asked her. "You look worn out."

She smiled wearily. "You all wear me out. But I will be awake to-night, Shinobu."

She made a small motion with her left hand so that he would see the controller there. With one press of a button, she could paralyze him again. The memory of his muscles letting him collapse, of his limbs as dead weight, made his heart race. She let her thumb slide across the button, taunting him. "Now!" she snapped.

Shinobu got to his feet as quickly as he could and learned that his bones were much more solid after a day of sleep, though not much less painful. If he continued to heal at this rate, most of his strength would be back in another day or two. "Come!" he called, and he began rounding up the Watchers from the corners of the fortress.

He watched Maggie sidelong as he skirted the broken floor. She seated herself next to Nott, who was on the flagstones, holding his badly broken left arm against his chest. With his right hand he was feeling about in the dark and whispering, "Aelred? Aelred?" but when he noticed Maggie, Nott fell silent.

"Why did you leave John?" she asked the boy. "Was he angry at you? Did he send you away?"

Nott's face darkened. "I left, my choice. He said he would train me if I wanted."

Shinobu ushered the last pockets of Watchers out of the fortress, but his eyes kept returning to Maggie.

"I might have been too harsh today," the old woman was saying to Nott as her hand gripped the controller. "When John has cooled off, he'll want to come back. It's natural that we finish this together. Could you find your way back to him?"

Nott looked cautious. "W-why?"

"The person who convinced John to come to me would deserve his own helm. For him alone to keep."

Shinobu didn't need to see the desperate hope that flared up in Nott's eyes to know that the boy would agree to this absolutely.

"How would I do that?" the boy asked.

"Ask him to fix your arm. He obviously has a soft heart."

CHAPTER 19

QUIN

"It's getting hard to breathe," Quin said. Her outstretched fingertips brushed the walls of the stone passage on either side. "Couldn't we have used your medallion to get straight through this?"

Just ahead of her, Dex answered, "We could have, but it's a relief to be somewhere like this. We've been outside for days."

"The fresh air was certainly becoming a hardship," Quin agreed wryly.

"You're making fun of me." He sounded not the least offended. "I permit it," he said airily. "You may laugh at me all you want."

They'd passed through the old crypt of the castle ruins, where the tombs of Scottish lords from centuries past—Quin's ancestors—lay in rows, some buried by pieces of the castle itself. Quin had been there before. She and Shinobu used to dare each other to go as far inside as they could before becoming terrified and running back out into the sunlight.

The crypt ended in a wall of rock, or so Quin had thought. Dex had shifted a slab of stone out of the way and continued on past it, into these narrow steps taking them down into the ground.

Dex had a bright white flare in his hand that acted as their flashlight as the passage led steeply downward and got narrower with every yard they traveled. She suspected the light was mostly for her. Dex could see in the dark as well as a cat.

"Would you like to hear more of the story?" he asked.

"Yes."

Dex treated his hodgepodge story as something personal, but Quin was increasingly sure it was a glimpse of Seeker history—a legend, with errors and exaggerations, of course, but a story with kernels of truth. Her father had avoided teaching her history. But Dex, in his disjointed way, was filling in some of the gaps. And at the moment, she needed a distraction; the sense of earth hanging heavily just above her head was becoming overpowering.

"Where we're going is part of the story," Dex told her. "It became the father's workshop, the place to keep the inventions that were the most delicate or the most dangerous. Desmond and Matheus came here all the time. It was their workshop and playroom. It's where they began inventing things themselves."

They were passing now through a tunnel with an arched ceiling of rough stones that hung just above Quin's head. Dex had to stoop over, but, if anything, this inconvenience seemed to lighten his mood even more. The darker and more cramped the space became, the happier he got.

"The boys invented things too?"

"The younger one, mostly. Are you sure you've never heard of him? I thought maybe he was famous. First he and his father made the focal. Do you call it that too? The metal helmet to help you focus your thoughts?"

"I call it that, though I only learned the name a few weeks ago. My father left some important bits out of my training."

"They needed the focal, or they were going to get lost again," Dex explained, as if that were so obvious it hardly bore mentioning.

He and Quin had reached the end of the low tunnel. There was a jagged opening here that led deeper into the earth. Dex squeezed through first, maneuvering his large frame with more grace than might be expected in such tight quarters. Quin followed. On the other side there were more stairs, and the walls of bare, carved earth were so close that she could barely walk without her arms brushing both sides. She was battling the sense of being buried alive.

"Were they Seekers, way back then?" she asked. "They knew how to go *There*—to no-space?"

"Of course they knew how to go to no-space," Dex answered. "That was the start of everything. Have you never heard this story? What did they teach you before you took your oath?"

"Not enough, clearly."

"The father explained the functions they needed from the focal, and Desmond helped him design it. He was fourteen then, and knew most things his father knew, even though the England of the Dark Ages wasn't the best classroom."

Quin had been thinking the passageway might narrow until it crushed them, but at last it began to open up. Even as the steps curved more steeply into the earth, the walls retreated on either side.

Dex said, "Once they had the focal to *focus* their thoughts, Matheus thought they should create the opposite sort of device. He said, if they could make something that brought all of your thoughts together, couldn't they also make something that would send your thoughts off in every direction?"

The stairs curved in a full circle. Quin felt the air changing around her, flowing more freely. She was more relieved than she cared to admit.

"Their father laughed at Matheus and asked what good that would do. Why would anyone want to scatter their thoughts?" Dex sighed. "That was a mistake. Matheus was seventeen by then, taller and stronger than his father. He behaved respectfully, but he didn't like being laughed at. Any ridicule stung him deeply. When their father was gone for a few weeks, Matheus convinced Desmond to make the thought-scattering device anyway."

"You mean a disruptor? You're saying a *child* made the disruptor? When he was fourteen—"

She broke off midsentence. They'd come to the bottom of the steps, and a cavern opened up before them. Dex raised his flare and made it shine more brightly so that white light flooded the space. The cavern was huge. The roof of rock was ten yards above their heads, wet from a steady flow of water through the earth. As Quin's eyes adjusted to the size of the space, she saw tunnels radiating off from the central chamber, until they faded into darkness.

The cave looked natural, but a nearby stretch of wall bore the marks of human carvings. Quin was drawn toward these carvings, past Dex, who stood unmoving at the base of the stairs. The carved figures were the emblems of the nine Seeker houses, forming a large circle on an expanse of stone that had been smoothed by hand. The tenth carving, at the very top, was the three interlocking ovals of the Dreads. The light of the flare was not as steady as a flashlight, and the figures danced in her vision as she studied them. When she came to the ram, her own family's symbol, she touched it reverently. If Dex's story was a piece of Seeker lore, then this cavern was surely a location out of the same ancient lore.

"How old are these carvings?"

"Very," came Dex's answer. He remained at the bottom of the stairs, his face expressionless.

Next to each emblem were small, deep holes with a slight diamond shape. She traced several of them with her fingers before she recognized their dimensions and guessed their purpose.

"Athames go here?" she whispered. The hollows were just the right size to receive the blade of an athame.

There was no answer from Dex, and when the flare shifted and dimmed dramatically, she turned to see him on the floor, his knees to his chest. When she got back to him, he was trembling violently.

"What is it?"

Dex raised his head just enough to stare into the dark corners of the space, as though they were closing in upon him. His eyes held animal fear. "I die here, Quilla."

They were alone, of course, but his certainty shook her. What secrets did this cavern conceal? She retrieved the flare, looked around the huge space and back up the stairs.

"It's just us here, Dex. I promise."

He shook his head against his knees. "No, that's not true." He closed his eyes tightly, as if forcing an image away. Without warning, he grabbed the flare and rose to his feet.

"Come," he said. His jaw had set into a hard line. He guided Quin, a firm hand on her back, toward a subsidiary tunnel branching off to their right. Inside the smaller shaft, there was a lower roof and closer walls, and when Dex had led Quin down the passage for a few dozen paces, the flare revealed broken stone-and-mortar steps leading steeply upward. At the top of the steps, set into the rocky ceiling, was a trapdoor of dressed stone.

"We're going up there?"

"Just you," Dex said, pushing the flare into her hand.

"Why—"

"Please, Quilla." His eyes implored her not to argue. "I followed the string in the labyrinth, and it led me here. The next part I must do on my own."

She looked back down the smaller tunnel toward the yawning cavern. "But—how will you see?"

"I'll call you back when I've remembered. I promise."

She started up the stairs. Dex was already walking away into the echoing darkness of the cavern.

CHAPTER 20

JOHN

"My mother found the fox athame here."

John's words came back to him with a slight echo, and he could hear the sense of awe in his own voice. He'd pieced together much of his mother's history, but here was a place she'd actually been, a place that had changed the course of her life.

The underground room was round, perhaps thirty feet in diameter. There were waterlines on the walls, dead seaweed everywhere, and a smell of salty decay. He and Maud were seated on a shelf that circled the whole room at chest height and was broken only by a tunnel that lead away—probably to the world outside. But they had not come here through the tunnel as Catherine had. They'd followed coordinates his mother had carefully written with small, neat pen strokes in her journal, and they'd arrived into the very center of the chamber. They were, according to her notes, deep under the medieval island city of Mont Saint-Michel.

A fox head was carved into the wall near John, the twin of the smaller carving on his athame. It marked the cave as the domain of the fox Seekers. For the first time, seeing this place, he felt that he belonged to a family larger than himself and his mother. There had been many fox Seekers, going back for generations.

The Young Dread trained the flashlight low above the ledge, where neat figures had been cut or melted into the stone:

67 ←
24 →
9 ←
100 →

Just as they had anticipated: another Seeker cave, another set of clues.

"Two hundred paces, and we'll find the Seekers from your own house, John."

"We would have figured out the instructions sooner if we'd come here first," he pointed out. "The symbols for right and left are so obvious. Maybe the Middle Dread was getting lazy by the time he took out the foxes." In other caves, the notations had been more cleverly masked.

"It's hard to mistake an arrow," Maud agreed. "But you would have to know where you were meant to take these paces. We didn't know until we found Nott."

John wrote the numbers into his mother's journal, below the coordinates for the chamber. "That's six we've found."

They'd returned to the desert cave by the Skeleton Coast, home of the bear Seekers; they'd found a man-made cave in the woods of Scotland, belonging to the horse Seekers; and of course they'd already discovered the carved instructions in the frozen tunnel in Norway—which they'd used to rescue the boar Seekers. Then they'd found the cave of the eagles, Shinobu's family, in Iceland, and the cave of the rams, Quin's family, in the mountains of Patagonia in

South America. Both had been beautiful, but the cave of the rams had been a breathtaking series of interconnected chambers of natural marble in pastel blues and yellows and greens, open to the dawn sky. John wondered if Quin even knew that place existed, and if she would ever forgive him enough to let him tell her about it.

He still didn't know what he should feel for his mother's enemies. Yet he'd decided his course, and there was relief in being decided. He was going to retrieve all of the Seekers from the hidden dimensions. He, not Maggie, would choose their fate.

"We go to the dragon house next," he said, flipping through the journal.

The Young Dread's eyes lingered in the center of the chamber, and she appeared not to hear him.

"Have you been here before?" he asked.

"Yes, when I was very young."

There was an unusual quality to her response, which John recognized as nostalgia—the most human expression he'd ever heard from her. She ran the light over the ceiling and walls, in case there was anything else for them to see. Only stones and dried seaweed looked back at them, yet it was clear she wasn't eager to leave.

"I might have been nine years old," she said, "though I have never been sure of my age."

Maud glanced at him, self-conscious to be speaking of herself. She pulled her feet up beneath her so that she was crouching on the narrow shelf, on which she took a few steps sideways, positioning her body exactly.

"I stood just here. Halfway between the tunnel opening and the carving of the fox. The center of the chamber was full of seawater, almost up to this ledge."

"The seawater came all the way in?" John asked.

"The outer entrance to the tunnel must have been lower then, because the ocean came in with the high tide. The water swirled and foamed and was pulled into and out of the passage when waves rolled in."

As she remembered, John saw glimpses of her human face appear behind the veil of a Dread.

"My master stood here." She touched the wall at her side. "Still and straight, as he always was then. There were lanterns hung all over the roof." She pointed here and there where the ceiling met the walls, and now John could see the hooks carved out of the natural rock, where one could suspend a lantern. "Ten Seekers from the house of the fox stood along the shelf, there, waiting and watching the water. I kept entirely still. My master had told me to observe quietly, as a Dread must."

Through the Young Dread's eyes, John saw the seawater pouring through the tunnel into the cavern, lips of foam jumping over the edge of the shelf to make Maud's feet wet.

"They began to arrive," she told him, entirely lost in the memory as she stared at the empty center of the chamber. "We could feel the vibration through the water and rock. Moments later the children were here, swimming up through the ocean water. Their heads came above the surface, and they were gasping—it was very cold. The adults on the ledge caught their arms and pulled them up. There were four children, no older than I was then, standing where you are now, dripping and smiling.

"Their instructor came up through the water after the children and climbed up beside them. He was a young man with a shaggy beard and fierce eyes—or I thought so at the time. He'd cut an anomaly straight to the center of this chamber, just as you and I did, John, but the room was full of water. He cut into the water itself, and he and his students had swum out of the hidden dimensions and into this cave.

"It was the initiation ceremony for the children. They pledged themselves to their training and became Seeker apprentices that day."

After a few moments, she pulled her gaze out of the memory and looked at John.

"Every house held their ceremonies in a different way. Sometimes they would invite my master to attend. He only watched silently, as I did, but he loved his Seekers." She smiled warmly, startling John. There was the human girl in her, more clear than ever. The ravages of her time *There* were melting away.

"Next cave?" she asked.

They'd made a list, from Catherine's journal and from the Young Dread's memory, of all nine caves belonging to Seeker houses. When they found instructions for all nine, they would be able to locate every Seeker left *There* by the Middle Dread and bring them back to the world.

John drew out his athame and lightning rod to take himself and Maud away from this place where his ancestors had gathered for hundreds of years. But he was still thinking about the childish expression he'd seen on Maud's face.

He asked her, "When you saw the other children, were you curious about their lives?"

He recalled how much he'd envied ordinary children on the streets of London when he was a child. He'd loved his mother desperately, and yet he'd wondered so many times what life would be like without the pressures she'd lived under.

The Young Dread shook her head. "I didn't like the Middle Dread at all. But I wouldn't have traded my life with my master for anything. With him, I floated above the world instead of walking through it."

CHAPTER 21

QUIN

In the light of the flare, Quin had come face to face with her own ancestors. They were painted on the stone wall, partially obscured by dead vines.

She'd crawled up through the trapdoor from the cavern below, which had let her into this odd, curving passageway. When she'd seen the faces on the wall, though, she knew this was not the first time she'd been here. This was the place she and Shinobu had found by accident when they were six years old—though they had explored very little of it at the time. It was built into the foundations of the castle and wrapped around its northern perimeter. Somehow Dex had taken her more deeply into the heart of the estate than she'd ever managed to go on her own.

When she pulled the vines free of the wall, five painted Seekers were revealed—a man and woman and three children, all cloaked, their eyes blue and green below their hoods, peering out at Quin from centuries ago. Painted above them in a dark red pigment was a ram, the emblem of her own house. She had been told almost nothing about her ancestors. Were these five the first family of ram Seekers?

There were more paintings along the passage: three Seekers beneath an eagle, Shinobu's ancestors; four beneath a saber-toothed cat; another four beneath a stag; and so on. The first murals had been near the end of the corridor, where the vines were thick. The farther she went toward the center, however, the fewer the plants and the brighter the pigment. At the midpoint of the passage, the paint had never been touched by sunlight or growing things. The faces there, beneath the bear emblem, were clear and unique, as though they were true portraits of living people.

The murals ended after the nine Seeker houses had been represented, but Quin continued on. The silence here was heavy, broken only by her footsteps and her breath, and, she fancied, the occasional phantom noise of the ancient rock beneath the castle. She studied the floor and walls as she went, looking for hidden doors like the one she'd come through. Might there be a way to get from the passage up into the higher reaches of the castle ruins? How big was the maze? And how had Dex known about it?

At the far end of the corridor, where the exit had been bricked up, she found a tenth mural. The vines here were thicker than they'd been at the other end; it took some work to pull them free. But when she'd cleared the wall, she had uncovered a painting unlike the others. Whereas the nine Seeker murals had shown the simple poses of daily life, these four figures were arranged carefully and formally—almost like a royal portrait.

The man stood with one hand on his hip. In the other hand were two whipswords, one collapsed into its resting, coiled state, the other extended as a sword. He held them up as a king might hold a scepter. The woman sat on a throne. Her hands were cupped in front of her and, strangely, were holding a dark liquid that looked a lot like blood.

"Why?" Quin whispered as she leaned closer to examine the artwork. A drop of the red liquid had fallen from the woman's hands and was now forever suspended halfway between her fingers and her lap.

Above the man and woman was the symbol of the Dreads—three interlocking ovals, like a simplified representation of an atom.

There were two young men sitting cross-legged beneath the adults. The first held what was obviously a focal on his lap. He looked out at Quin with grave eyes beneath a shock of unruly hair. The second held a disruptor against his chest. He was not looking at Quin but away, his face in profile, his one visible eye partly closed.

"Desmond and Matheus," she breathed. "Hello."

Here was Dex's legend, brought to life by an artist centuries ago. She was looking into the deep past of Seekers.

Quin was startled from her examination by a noise like the creak of stone against stone. She'd been so intent on the mural that she'd forgotten where she was. Holding the flare aloft, she peered down the passage. The noise came again, as if something were shifting in the earth. But when she heard it a third time, she recognized that it was not a creak but a human scream, carried up from deep in the caves below.

She found Dex in the center of the cavern, lying on his back, clutching the rock floor with both hands as if to stop himself from plunging upward into the ceiling. He'd been in complete darkness while she was gone, and when Quin knelt beside him with the flare, his pupils remained huge. She wasn't certain he could see anything.

"Dex? What happened?" When he didn't move, she took one of his hands into her own and squeezed it. "Dex? Dex?"

Slowly his pupils contracted, his eyes came into focus. "Quilla?"

"Well . . . it's me," she answered. "Are you hurt?"

"When I see what happens here, I can't stop it," he whispered. "It's a torrent and I drown."

"You aren't drowning," she told him gently. She set his hand over his own heart, so that he could feel it beating fiercely. She smoothed his hair away from his face. "What did you do while I was gone?"

"I remembered. I'm still remembering."

He looked as if he'd slipped out of sanity, as he often did, but as Quin watched him, she understood that a more profound shift was occurring. If he'd been recovering small pieces of his life over the last few days, now he was remembering something monumental, something that exerted a gravitational pull over him.

"Can you tell me what you're remembering?" she asked him.

A small cry escaped him, after which the words came in a wild stream. "He was blind to his own family and turned loose two terrors. And others paid for it, again and again, all these years. Good and weak or destructive and strong, those aren't the choices." Dex moved his hand back to the ground and dug desperately for leverage in the rock floor.

Something in Quin had shifted as well. Perhaps it was seeing the mural of Desmond and Matheus—proof that Dex was telling her something real. Or perhaps it was the days alone with him, seeing his good nature beneath his confused exterior. But however the change had come, she was pained by his disorientation. She didn't only want to help him so that he would help her find Shinobu. She simply wanted to help him.

"Dex—will you let me try something?"

"Yes," he whispered.

She shifted her vision, and immediately the lines of energy around Dex came into sharp relief. Before, in the cave behind the waterfall, she'd seen his energy cascading out of his right temple, down his body, and back into his left hip. Now that cascade was a flood. She was watching fireworks, almost, pouring out of his head, streaming down his chest, and then gathering together and piercing his hip. The flow must also have been traveling back up through him to burst again from his temple. It was as if someone had connected him to power lines and cranked up the voltage. The current was so strong that it looked as though it might fold him in half. He was gripping the floor, she realized, to stop his body from collapsing in upon itself.

Quin had worked with all sorts of patients, but she'd never seen or trained for anything like this. Steeling herself, she plunged her hands into the river across his torso.

The cascade of energy pooled around her fingers, flowed like lava across his ribs as she worked to bleed it off the main line.

After a long stretch of intense concentration, she had created tributaries that snaked everywhere about his body, scattering the central force. Soon the fireworks dimmed, though they were far from being extinguished. Dex released the floor from his grip, and his breath came more evenly.

"There," she whispered. It was as much as she could do right now. She felt dizzy as she leaned over him, her hands still hovering above his chest.

"You can see the energy?" Dex croaked.

"I can when I look in the right way," she answered. "Can you see it as well?"

"You have to let go. It's pulling you in too."

Quin gazed down and saw the actual result of her work. Her own energy field had joined with Dex's into one pattern. She'd broken up the river across his body into dozens of streams, and those streams now flowed in one continuous route through him and through her.

This explained the strange tugging she felt at her mind, as if all of her energy were being siphoned away. Did it also explain her fading vision, which until now she'd attributed to the inconstant glow of the flare?

There was a brightness in her abdomen, a vortex of streams. Looking at it gave her vertigo . . .

Quin fell. Her head came to rest on cold rock, one of her hands on Dex's chest. She had to break the contact, but she couldn't muster the energy to move. She was being stretched and contracted at the same time . . . until Dex pushed her hand away and the connection was broken.

CHAPTER 22

QUIN

"What happened to you?" Quin asked. She was still lying on the floor where she'd collapsed and had no idea how much time had passed.

Dex lay a few feet away, staring up into the darkness. Calmer now. She saw in his face that he understood what she meant: *What caused that violent flood of energy around you?*

But he ignored her question and whispered, "Matheus wanted the disruptor to make its victim truly mad, but Desmond wouldn't do that." The flare lay behind him, which threw his face into shadow, yet she could see him now looking steadily at her. Whatever had shifted in him was coming to the surface. "So Matheus posed a lighter challenge. 'Could you make a weapon to confuse people?' He got Desmond interested in the puzzle of it. They'd seen crazy people, of course, whose thoughts scattered this way and that. Could Desmond design a device that did the same thing? Was he clever enough?"

"I saw them up in the passage. Desmond with the focal and Matheus with a disruptor."

"That's kind of an official portrait, I guess. Maybe not particularly accurate."

"You've been up there before?"

"Of course. Many times." He didn't elaborate. Turning his gaze up toward the dim cavern ceiling again, he said, "The first version of the disruptor made your thoughts run around in circles. They tested it on their dog." Dex paused and smiled as if he particularly enjoyed this part of the story. "Imagine, Quilla—the dog would run after a stick, stop before he fetched it, run back, look at them quizzically, return to the stick, stop, come back . . . It went on like that for hours, and the boys thought it was the funniest thing they'd ever seen.

"On another day Matheus snuck out and tried it on a woman from the village. When Desmond finally found him, he'd been watching the woman trying to get water from the well for more than an hour. She would lower the bucket, and then forget about it and turn back to her cottage, get halfway home, and then walk back to the well and try to lower the bucket again, before she turned back toward home, on and on."

"How did she ever stop?" Quin asked.

He glanced at her, and his smile faded. "Oh, the effects wore off after a while," he said. "It was nothing terrible. Desmond wasn't trying to make something permanent. It was . . . it was a game to him." He studied Quin for a few moments, reached for her hand, and before she knew what he intended, he brought it to his lips. "Don't you know his true temperament, Quilla? You've heard this story before."

"Please, Dex." Quin gently pulled away. It was harder to do than she'd expected. When he thought she was Quilla, she felt the full force of Dex directed at her. He reached for her again, but she stayed away and whispered, "Please. Tell me more of the story."

Dex rolled onto his back. She watched him wrestle with an angry thought, and she saw the thought win. His expression was cruel when he turned to her. "He left you, Quilla. I didn't want to tell you before. He abandoned you in no-space."

"You didn't see him. You don't know what he did."

"I didn't see him because he opened an anomaly back to the world and escaped without you. I saw that much."

Quin said nothing for a moment. How could she explain that she knew Shinobu must have left her? She should be devastated . . . or furious. But she didn't feel either of those emotions. Quin knew what the focal did to Shinobu's thoughts. And more than that, she knew Shinobu, the boy she'd grown up with and who had promised, so many times, to protect her. How could she explain that whatever misguided course he'd taken, she didn't believe that he'd meant to hurt her?

Dex pressed on, his voice becoming wild and unfocused. "You love someone who doesn't care about you, Quilla. I've seen it happen, and you'll never be the same as long as you cling to him."

"He does care about me. He thinks—he thinks he *is* taking care of me!"

"I would never willingly leave you," he said. "You were always naive, Quilla."

"But I'm not Quilla," she answered quietly.

Dex made a noise of frustration, retrieved the flare, and stood. He pressed his hands against his head as if trying to hold his thoughts still.

"You're Quin," he whispered.

Slowly the anger drained from his face. Then, with a shaky tread, he walked toward a far wall of the cavern.

He went back to his story without rancor. "Desmond always thought Matheus was tinkering with the disruptor to make it do worse things, but he could never catch him doing it." He touched the rough cavern wall, as if his story were inscribed there. "They kept that first disruptor a secret from their father, because he was strict about creating new tools. It had to be done with him present and with his blessing, all of that. So they hid it. But it didn't stay a secret for long."

Now he was skirting the cavern, looking into the uneven spaces where the walls of rock blended into the floor. When he crouched down to examine something more closely, he looked to Quin like a homeless man picking through street-side rubbish. Then he stood to his full height and made an entirely different impression, of someone large and quick and dangerous. He'd picked up some loose stones, and he let these scatter across the floor as he continued walking.

"Can you read minds?" he asked her.

"Sometimes."

"Were you always able to do it?"

"No," she answered. "It happened recently."

"How?"

"I don't really know. First I heard one person's thoughts in a moment of danger. Now I hear others. It's confusing sometimes."

He stopped again, crouched down by a declivity in the cavern wall, felt about with his hands. "That's how it started with them." He'd found something else, which he examined in the light of the flare. "They were ordinary people at the beginning, closed minds. But one day, in the course of training themselves to do all sorts of things, their father began to see Desmond's thoughts. That's how he learned about the disruptor. He was disappointed with his younger son for breaking the rules, but that was soon forgotten—because he began to hear Matheus's thoughts as well, and those were much, much worse."

He came back to Quin and, like a young child, held out his discovery. It was a small metal rod, not much longer than his palm, bent at one end, so that it formed a sort of L.

"I knew there would be at least one of these about," he muttered. Before Quin could touch it or ask what it was, Dex had moved away again, back to the wall of emblems. "Matheus liked to hurt things, did I mention? He'd been killing animals for years, and he'd started hurting people too, when he thought he could get away with it. His family didn't know, but now he couldn't hide it because they could read his mind." He added thoughtfully, "Maybe their mother knew what he was like, all along. History is silent on that point."

He studied the wall and was quiet for a long while, so long that Quin got to her feet and came over to him. She found him looking at the carved emblems in a sort of trance.

"Dex? Have you gone again?"

"Ask me something." His voice was whispery and urgent, as if, indeed, he were slipping away and needed her to pull him back. "My hands are clever when I talk to you."

"Did—did Matheus get punished?"

"Their father beat him for the bad things he did, but it didn't make much difference," Dex said slowly. "I've always wondered if Matheus *liked* pain." He held up the L-shaped rod and studied it. "They were training other people by then, other Seekers, lots of them. Their father had created whipswords, and they'd all learned to fight. Don't you love whipswords? They did. He had the idea that he could use the things he knew, his inventions, to help history along, to make the world more fair."

"That's what we're all meant to do as Seekers, isn't it? Tyrants and evildoers beware."

"Yes, that's what they say." Dex shot her a weary glance before he went on. "He made Matheus train twice as hard as anyone else. He said Matheus would learn through exertion what it means to do good."

When he fell silent again, Quin prompted, "Did it work?"

"I don't know. There was a girl. Once he met her, Desmond

stopped caring what Matheus was doing." His fingers twitched in the air, as though tucking back a lock of hair on someone standing in front of him. He said, "Her name was Quilla."

"Quilla," Quin repeated. How many Quillas were there in the world? "*Your* Quilla?"

"Of course," he answered. She watched some internal struggle play out across his face. At last he said, "Desmond, Dex, boy holding focal. Surely you know by now. I'm all of them."

For one moment, Quin felt the thrill of revelation, but in the next moment it was gone.

"But . . ." It was true, Dex told the story like he'd done those things himself, and the thought had crossed Quin's mind several times. But he couldn't be the ancient figure he was describing. He spoke as a modern person would. He hadn't been surprised at the television she'd found on the estate, or aircars, or any of the signs of modern life. He was a Seeker, like she was, who had become confused, and in his confusion, he'd mistaken a legend for his own life.

"Quilla had red hair like a fox's," Dex said, enraptured and oblivious. "And green eyes flecked with gold."

The description sat between them for a while. Quin hid her surprise and, strangely, her disappointment. The famous Quilla didn't sound at all like her.

"But you are alike," Dex told her, as though she'd spoken out loud. "Your face, the way you move. You could be the same girl painted with a different brush."

How did Quilla fit into the story, then? Was she part of the legend or part of Dex's own life?

Dex withdrew his medallion from the leather straps around his neck. Placing his palms flat on the top and bottom of the stone disc, he twisted and made an adjustment. Holding the medallion between thumb and forefinger, he raised it to the carved fox emblem, and with a deft motion, fitted the medallion into the cavern wall. It clicked into place in a shallow recess, covering the fox.

Quin examined the other emblems and saw that each was set in such a recess; the medallion could be placed over any of them, just as the diamond-shaped slots meant that an athame could be inserted next to each emblem.

"Their father liked redundancy, as you can see," he explained, apparently following her thoughts. "Extra tools in case the first set broke, extra weapons, even an extra son, in a way. Here you can use your medallion, or if you find yourself without it, an athame will do instead. Their father preferred an athame most of the time, like a native."

He tapped the metal rod against the cavern wall several times, and as he did, the wall began to shake with a deep resonance far beyond the surface effects of the metal rod's impact. Dex stopped and leaned his head against the stone.

"Desmond and Quilla had a child called Adelaide," he whispered. "Quilla and Adelaide." With his head still on the wall, as if he wanted to absorb the last of the vibrations as they died out, he said, "I'm not trying to find them. I know. They won't be found."

He was slipping between speaking of Desmond as another person and speaking of Desmond as himself. Quin mentally set aside the personal story of Quilla and Adelaide, because there was no way to know the truth of it. But this cavern and this wall were solid things, here and now—real, whether they were part of a legend or part of Dex's own life. Was Dex telling her that he could locate Seekers by making the wall shake? Did where he placed the medallion—over one particular house's emblem—determine whom he would find?

"Dex, does the wall reach out to other medallions?" she asked—

cautiously, because she was pressing him for an answer about the real world, and those often set him off.

He yanked himself away from the stone as though it had bitten him. The gaze he turned on her was full of the same fear and distaste that he wore when he had to walk through sunlight. "No, I'm not finding other medallions yet, am I?" He closed his eyes tightly. "No, no. It's here, though, somewhere here. I can't remember, Quilla, because I die."

"Dex," she said gently.

She took one of his hands, which had clenched into a fist, and she smoothed it open and pressed it against the wall. Dex opened his eyes, stared at his hand on the cool rock surface. It was just stone; it could not hurt him.

"What does this wall find?" she asked.

"Athames. I told you I would help you find him—what's his name?"

For a moment she had no idea who he meant; then . . . "Shinobu?"

Dex nodded like a boy readying himself to swallow a dose of bitter medicine. "Which athame does he carry?"

Quin was entirely surprised. Dex had become so incoherent, and she'd also assumed that he would avoid helping her until forced. She pointed to the emblem at the apex of the circle. "He carries the athame of the Dreads."

Dex gazed at that symbol for too long. "It was the first one he made, you know," he said at last, just as Quin was preparing to touch him again. "The Seekers chose emblems for themselves—Adelaide chose the fox—and he made all of their athames. But that one was the original, the most delicate and complicated."

She wanted to ask how—how a man wandering through medieval

England could make athames, how any of this story could be true—but she allowed herself no more questions. He'd said he would find Shinobu.

He pulled the medallion from its place over the carving of the fox and slipped it neatly into the recess over the three interlocking ovals.

"Are you sure?" he asked.

"About which athame he has? Yes."

"No. Are you sure you want to find him? Are you sure you choose to be back with him?"

"Yes, I'm sure," whispered Quin.

"And will you leave me then?" He didn't look at her as he asked it. His handsome face was obscured by his hair, but she sensed the anxiety in the line of his jaw.

She paused. "I told you I would help you."

"But did you mean it?"

Quin understood the deal to which she was committing herself. "I meant it."

"All right."

He tapped the wall with the metal rod, and this time when the wall began to shake, he didn't stop. Soon the vibration spread to the floor and up to the cavern roof. In the space of a few breaths, it felt as though the planet itself had taken up the tremor. When it had become so overwhelming that Quin feared the cavern might collapse, he stopped tapping.

The walls continued to hum and shake, but the intensity died out quickly. Dex was gazing down at the L-shaped rod in his hand, which looked far too small and ordinary to have caused such an effect.

He murmured, "The next time he uses that athame, we will find him."

He plucked the medallion out of the wall, and before he had even lifted it to the straps around his neck, it vibrated in his hands.

"Is that him already?" Quin asked.

Dex stared at the medallion, shook his head. "Too soon. It must be a residual—"

The medallion shook again, more strongly.

Hope bloomed in Quin's chest. "Is it Shinobu?"

CHAPTER 23

MAUD

The Young Dread and John stepped from the anomaly directly into John's apartment on the airship. *Traveler* was still at dock but ready to fly as soon as they had fetched every Seeker who was trapped *There*. That could happen almost immediately; they'd visited the caves of the final Seeker houses and now had instructions from all of them.

Maud, with her cloak and her long, unkempt hair, was struck, as she was each time they returned to the ship, by the contrast between herself and the sumptuousness of *Traveler*. The furnishings were simple but finely made, and as she stepped across the threshold and into John's living room, she felt like a cheetah loosed into a royal audience chamber. This awareness of her appearance was a new sensibility, one that had snuck up on her during her time awake in the world.

From the apartment, they walked downstairs. John went to speak with the ship's medical personnel, and the Young Dread walked into *Traveler*'s great room. It was the same room she and the Old Dread and the Middle Dread had come to on the night when they'd boarded *Traveler* as it flew over London.

There had been a fight in this room, between Quin and John

and the Dreads, and it was here that Maud had killed the Middle. Her eyes instinctively sought out the exact spot where she'd stabbed him through the heart with her whipsword, and where he'd fallen, instantly dead. Such a great burden had been lifted from her in that moment, and yet the Middle Dread plagued them still. Only after his death did she and John discover the extent of the havoc he'd caused to Seekers.

She didn't linger over the place where he'd died. In truth, the great room was entirely changed. Beneath a high canopy of glass, the room had been left open. A soft mat covered the floor, and exercise equipment and training weapons lined the walls.

There were three occupants already making use of the weapons. The first two were the children of the boar Seekers, an eleven-year-old girl called Liv, and a four-year-old boy called Kaspar, and the third was Nott. He had found the Young Dread and John on their last visit to the Scottish estate and had begged John to take him back and train him. Tonight Nott, one of his arms in a splint, was teaching the two children to fight with wooden practice swords. As the Young Dread observed, Kaspar let loose a Norwegian battle cry and threw himself at Nott. On reflex, the older boy jabbed the hilt of his wooden sword into Kaspar's belly and sent him onto the mat.

Kaspar burst into tears and threw his sword down. Catching sight of the Young Dread, he ran across the room and grabbed her legs. Between sobs, he poured out a stream of angry Norwegian, which he embellished with gestures toward Nott. The Young Dread, uncertain of what one was supposed to do with such a small child, patted Kaspar's head tentatively.

Across the room, Liv hit Nott with doubled ferocity. Her Norwegian invective was punctuated with occasional English words, particularly "Bad boy! You a bad boy!"

Nott knocked Liv down easily and raised his training sword—

"Nott!"

The sharp voice was John's. He'd come into the great room from the doors on the other side.

"You want them to learn to fight, don't you?" Nott demanded, stepping away from the girl. He reluctantly let his wooden sword fall to his side.

"He's four," John pointed out.

"*She's* not four," Nott said, sticking his chin out at Liv. The girl, back on her feet, slapped Nott across the face. Under John's watchful eye, Nott didn't retaliate. Instead he rubbed his cheek and glared.

The Young Dread felt a laugh escape her throat. When John turned toward her in surprise, Maud wondered how long it had been since she had laughed. Years?

She knelt down to be eye to eye with Kaspar and gently held his shoulders. "I will teach you to move faster, so that his sword has no chance to hit you."

As the little boy considered this, he smiled delightedly. "Yes?" he asked.

"Yes."

In hesitant English, Liv asked, "More children vill come to be vis us?"

"There might be more children," John told her. "But there will certainly be people who need our help."

The Young Dread saw John try to hide his mixed feelings about this, but she could read them plainly. Saving Seekers was treacherous ground in his mind.

"*He* von't help," the girl announced gravely, pointing her wooden sword at Nott, who had retreated from what looked to him like an overly friendly gathering. Nott was biting his fingernail, but he paused long enough to throw Liv a black look.

The Young Dread would have laughed a second time, but she saw

John's face become alarmed. His hand went to his waist, where his athame was concealed. Without a word, they both stepped away from the children.

"It's shaking," John said. He pulled out the athame, and they both touched the stone blade, but it was still. "I felt it for a moment. It vibrated against my skin."

They waited, but it didn't shake again.

Maud thought of a cavern beneath the castle ruins on the Scottish estate, and a visit she'd paid, in the company of the Old and Middle Dreads. The Old Dread had shaken the whole cavern in order to feel the vibration of someone else's athame. Was someone else searching for John's athame now?

"How much could Maggie know about Seekers?" she asked him. "Could she know far more than she ever told you?"

John thought about this, but eventually shook his head. "I have no way to be sure."

The Young Dread considered. If, somehow, that woman had made a connection with John's athame, what did it mean?

"Is everything ready?" she asked, indicating the medical suite that ringed the great room.

"Everything's ready."

"And you?" she asked.

There was only a small pause before he said, "I'm ready."

"Then let's not wait."

CHAPTER 24

QUIN

Quin pulled Dex along through the anomaly tunnel. She didn't know if that made them move faster or not, but she couldn't stand to go slowly. In the cavern below the castle ruins, Dex's medallion had begun to vibrate in sympathy with the athame of the Dreads, and by following that vibration, he was bringing them to that very athame—which Quin hoped she would find clutched in Shinobu's hand.

The pale gray shapes of the outside world—the castle ruins, the forests on the estate—were dancing sedately along the edges of the tunnel, and the landscape continued to move at an excruciating pace, no matter how fast Quin ran. At last she stopped and held Dex's shoulders, forcing him to look at her. "Dex, faster. Please!"

He peered down at the medallion, and then up at her. Reluctantly he nodded. As he began to adjust the stone disc, the colorless traces of the world at the edge of Quin's vision changed, became streaks of light. Quin had the sensation of motion, as if her bones were traveling at a different rate than her skin and clothing. She and Dex continued to walk through the tunnel, but now they were racing through the world.

In only moments, the streaks slowed and took on new shapes. Quin saw a lake and a muddy shore, colorless and dim. The view was dominated by a familiar set of ruins.

"It's Dun Tarm," she said. "This is where Shinobu is? So close?"

A group of people stood by the lake, their figures watery and gray through the shifting curtain of the anomaly. She wondered if Dex could move her right through those people, if the tunnel would let them walk through their bodies like ghosts passing through the living. But Dex did nothing so strange. He opened the anomaly up behind the fortress, where they would be hidden from the group on the shore. Quin leapt across the threshold and came out into the solid world, into tall grass and piles of fallen masonry, which were golden in the sunlight.

She crept close to the fortress's back wall, peered around it, and from there could see the gathering by the lake. They were all Watchers. Half of them sat in the grass, looking disappointed to be left out, and the other half stood in a line nearby. All of the standing boys wore focals. When the anomaly fell shut behind Quin and its intense humming died out, she heard a woman's voice, slow and elderly, speaking to the boys, and she heard something else as well.

"Dex, look. They've carved an anomaly."

Quin was aware of the faint vibration even at this distance, and she could see the small circular opening—an anomaly carved by an athame—that hovered in the air at the head of the line of boys. As she searched the group for Shinobu, the anomaly grew soft and collapsed. Almost immediately, someone she couldn't see—someone behind the boys—carved a new opening in its place, and the woman's voice began again, audible but unintelligible at this distance. She must be giving instructions, preparing those boys to go *There*.

"Come," Quin whispered. "Let's get closer. I don't see him."

She took Dex's hand and moved, in a crouch, around the corner of the fortress. There were large pieces of Dun Tarm's former turret lying in front of them, providing concealment from the boys in the meadow. It was as close as she could get without being seen.

"He's there!" She gripped Dex's shoulder.

Shinobu appeared from behind the line of Watchers. He was examining each of them as the woman's voice droned on. He walked strangely—not limping exactly, but his gait gave the impression that his legs were not quite even.

He's been injured again, she thought.

Quin drew her breath with a hiss when he turned toward her. His face was livid with bruises. His shirt was torn, and she could see a dirty bandage beneath it. He was wearing a focal, and he appeared profoundly miserable.

"What have they done to him?" she whispered. "He looks half-dead."

An old woman came into view as the anomaly collapsed again. She wore a camouflage hunting outfit and heavy boots, which were strikingly at odds with her slender frame, erect posture, and infirm gait. After she had adjusted the focal on her head, she placed a proprietary hand on Shinobu's shoulder. It was the gesture of a queen toward one of her subjects, or a master toward a slave. Shinobu looked terrified. It was as if the old woman's very touch were poisonous.

"They're going *There,*" she whispered to Dex. "That's why your medallion shook. He keeps striking the athame and caving an anomaly over and over. Can you bring me over to him before they go? If you get me close, I can pull him into the tunnel with us—"

With a backward glance, she discovered that Dex was no longer beside her. He'd wedged himself—all six and a half feet of him—into a nook below one of the blocks of fallen masonry. His eyes were closed, his fingers dug into the earth to keep himself from flying off into the sky. He looked like a very large version of a small, frightened boy.

"Dex!" she hissed.

"I can't, I can't," he mumbled.

Quin knelt, grabbed his robe, pulled him toward her. "Dex, don't do this now! Not now."

"She's there, Quilla. What if they're *both* there?"

There was a shudder in the air, and Quin raised her head. Shinobu stood before the line of boys, carving another anomaly to replace the one that had fallen shut. He and the Watchers could be leaving at any moment.

Quin squeezed Dex's shoulders and leaned close. His eyes were firmly shut. "It's just a few yards. Dex. Make a tunnel and I can grab him and take him with us!" She looked up again to see the Watchers already disappearing into the anomaly. Just like that, they were going.

"She is there," Dex said again.

"The old woman? You're scared of one frail, old woman? Dex, take me!"

Her words were an order, as strong as a slap across his face. But they had no effect on Dex. He had opened his eyes, but he'd stopped speaking and was staring at Quin with mute fear.

When she glanced above the stones again, Shinobu, the line of Watchers, and the old woman had all disappeared, leaving the remaining Watchers sitting on the shore, looking bereft. She yanked Dex's robe, anger boiling up. She wanted to shake him, hit him, wake him up—

"I hear your medallion," she said suddenly. "It's vibrating. It's vibrating with his athame still, isn't it? You *know* where he's going!"

She pulled the medallion from around Dex's neck, put it into his hands.

"Take me!"

"I can't, Quilla!"

"You promised me!" She grabbed his hands, pushed them firmly around the medallion as it shook. "You may *not* go crazy right now."

She glanced up. The last threads of black and white from the anomaly's border mended themselves. Every trace of it was gone, and with it, Shinobu was gone.

"You're not here, Quilla. I'm not here. It can't be real." His eyes were wild and unseeing. He was a feral animal cornered.

Quin closed her eyes a moment, regrouped. "Dex, I am here. And so are you. We're real."

His eyes looked desperately into hers, wanting to believe. She put her hands on his cheeks and kissed him. She was in the grip of adrenaline and hardly aware of his warm lips against hers, of his arms trying to pull her closer, but she could be Quilla for a moment, if it brought him back to her. When she felt him relax against her, she pulled away.

"Dex," she whispered, leaning her forehead against his, "take me where the athame went."

He nodded against her head. Holding him close to her, Quin untied the focal from his neck and put it on her own head.

With his hand clamped in hers, she said, "Let's go."

CHAPTER 25

SHINOBU

It was happening. Shinobu was taking Maggie and half the Watchers—all armed, all in focals—into the space *between*. Maggie had ordered him to lead them to the Middle Dread's secret place, where he kept his weapons. She had a medallion to convince the Watchers to follow her, but she was using Shinobu's fighting skill to ensure their obedience.

Shinobu was doing as she'd ordered because he didn't have a choice. Maggie had allowed him his whipsword, but she held his controller tightly. At the first sign of disobedience, she could turn him into putty at her feet.

He'd been free of the focal for a time, but now he was chained to it again. The crackle of its electricity encircled Shinobu's ears, his head; he felt the buzz of its energy leaking into his thoughts and changing him.

He hated Maggie.

He followed Maggie.

He was not a killer.

He was a killer.

He couldn't keep track of which side of his mind was the true

Shinobu. But there was one thought that stayed clear—he had left Quin by the Middle Dread's weapons. With every step, he was leading Maggie directly to her.

Shinobu counted the paces and watched Maggie. If she showed the slightest hint of distraction, he would attack. And no matter what happened, when they found Quin, he would attack. He would not let any of them hurt Quin.

He turned right for the final line of paces. Next to him, Maggie switched the controller from one hand to the other, her thumb hovering above the button all the while. Behind him, the Watchers turned to follow.

After a few dozen steps, their flashlights picked up the shapes of disruptors, glinting dully in a long line. They had reached the Middle Dread's cache.

This was where he'd left Quin.

This was where he would turn and fight for her. He clenched his fists, braced himself.

But Quin wasn't here.

As the Watchers fell on the disruptors like a pack of jackals, Shinobu walked in a circle, looking for her. He'd left her just here, near the row of disruptors, hadn't he? She had clung to his shirt, asked him not to go. They'd been standing exactly where he stood now.

And Quin wasn't here.

He discreetly shone his light into the blackness, pointing it this way and that, but no silhouette appeared. Quin was not nearby.

Shinobu had been holding his breath. Now he fell to his knees in relief.

At once the focal altered the relief into something else. *Had* he left her here? Had they even come here together? Had he imagined everything? And if it wasn't imagination, then *where was she*? Had someone else taken her?

"What's the matter with you?" Maggie asked him, turning from the Watchers to look at Shinobu.

"Nothing, nothing." He got back to his feet.

The boys were strapping the weapons to their chests. Shinobu's gratitude was so great, and his confusion so deep, that it took him some time to understand the horror of eleven Watchers armed with disruptors. He had very deliberately left those disruptors here when he took the boys back into the world.

"Good," Maggie said when the weapons were situated. "Now you will search every inch of this place until we've found the ones we need to find."

Shinobu knew that the Middle Dread had trained his Watchers to scour the hidden dimensions, to search for him if he was ever lost. They'd been taught how to walk in a pattern, which would allow them, as a group, to cover all of the space *between*. Maggie was putting the Watchers through that same pattern, not to look for the Middle Dread but to find the Seekers she didn't like, Seekers who'd been left by the Middle to be forgotten.

She nudged Shinobu forward, and he walked into the darkness, his flashlight shining, the Watchers and his mistress Maggie just behind him.

CHAPTER 26

QUIN

Quin ran down the new anomaly tunnel ahead of Dex. He was not bringing them through the world this time, but through no-space itself, because that was where Shinobu had gone. There were no streaks of gray on the sides of this black tunnel. Instead there was a different sensation of motion, as if they were in an underwater vessel, piloting through dark waters.

Quin wore Dex's focal—not needed in the anomaly tunnel, but needed quite desperately in no-space itself—and she felt its hum blending with her own thoughts as its electricity crawled across the skin of her forehead and through her hair.

"We've gone too far," she said to Dex. "Shouldn't we have seen him already? We were just behind them!"

"I do see him," Dex told her quietly.

He was looking ahead, his eyes so much more sensitive to light than hers would ever be.

"Where?" She fell back to walk beside him.

"We've been following them for a while. They can't see us yet.

Our tunnel keeps a piece of the world along with a piece of no-space, so we're not fully where they are yet."

She peered into the blackness but saw nothing. "Are you sure?"

"They've found the disruptors." He shivered at the word. "Those boys, using those weapons. An unholy combination. The sort of thing Matheus would love. Can you see now?"

He made a minute adjustment to his medallion, and Quin began to see flickers of light ahead. The flickers became more steady, grew brighter. Dex was altering the tunnel, letting it combine itself into no-space.

By degrees she began to discern the shapes of the Watchers, in a group ahead of her. A dozen flashlights shone, and as the lights grew brighter, their bodies became dark and shifting silhouettes. She was moving toward them.

"Wait," Dex said.

She turned to find him far behind her. He hadn't followed her when the tunnel changed.

"How will you fight them if you have to fight?" he asked her.

"With you." She jogged back to him. "I can't do it alone. Of course I need you."

Dex backed away as she approached. She could see his tunnel, distinct from the space she was in, with him retreating slowly down it.

"She's there," he called back to her. "I'm not ready."

"Dex, please!" Quin took a few steps toward him, but she didn't want to be drawn with him back to the world; she might never convince him to find Shinobu again. Now that she was here, she had to stay.

"Come with me now and we'll try again later," he told her, still walking backward. "I'm useful when I'm myself. I'll help you later." His shoulders were hunched and he wore the inward look of fear that meant a fit of insanity was coming on.

"Dex, without you I have no way to get back into the world when I find him!" Quin knew yelling at him would do nothing, and yet she couldn't stop herself. He had said he would help.

"He has an athame," Dex pointed out as he continued to retreat. He would not meet her eyes. "You can use *his* athame, if you insist on going. Or come back with me."

She was too dumbfounded to say anything else. In another few steps, Dex turned around, and as soon as he did, he was far away, hard for her to see.

Quin bit back her fury because there was no time for it. She was in the focal, she had to make use of it, and quickly. She brought her mind back to the task at hand—Shinobu. He was here, and she would find him. As soon as she focused, she felt her own energy joined to the helmet's. Beyond the focal was the sense of the infinite, a lake of timelessness waiting to enfold her if she would only give it the chance.

She drew out the impellor, which she'd taken from Dex without his knowledge on their journey to Dun Tarm. With the ease of long practice, she prepared it to fire. She could do this, even without Dex's help.

Far ahead were the Watchers with their flashlights. The air in no-space swallowed light, made distance impossible to judge. She moved silently toward them for a very long time. She couldn't have said how far she walked nor how much time she'd spent in the interim tunnel with Dex. The focal kept her thoughts steady, but still the weight of infinity played with her sense of time.

She knew by the terrible smell that she was finally getting close. When she caught up with them, they stood in a group around the old woman. There were so many. More than the eleven she'd seen. Or was she seeing other figures beyond the Watchers?

She searched their silhouettes for the one that would be familiar. There. Shinobu was there. When she saw him, she lifted the impellor, felt the already heavy air become heavier, and fired.

CHAPTER 27

SHINOBU

"Check their wrists," Maggie ordered Shinobu.

They'd come upon a group of people, frozen in the darkness. There were men and women and one child. They were grouped together, but their body positions told of separate histories leading each of them to this place. Some were grievously injured and clutching their wounds; others looked as if they were mid-conversation, or mid-plea. The child had been crying when he froze here, and a tear was still balanced on the swell of his cheek.

Oh, God, she's going to kill them. The focal twisted this to: *It's good to kill. You're a killer, aren't you?* Shinobu knocked a fist against the helmet to make that thought leave.

"What are you doing?" Maggie asked him. "Check their wrists."

Shinobu pulled up the sleeves of the first man's shirt, revealing an athame scar on the left wrist and a scar in the shape of a fox on the right. His breath came out in a sigh of relief. Though Shinobu didn't have a brand of his own house, Seekers of previous generations had usually marked themselves in this way.

"Fox," he told Maggie. She liked foxes; he knew that much.

"And the rest?" she asked.

Shinobu checked another and another and found the same set of brands on each. He allowed himself to touch the shoulder of the frozen little boy and give it a little squeeze. The boy would be all right.

"All foxes," he told Maggie.

"I might know them, then," she whispered as she studied a woman's face in the beam of her flashlight. She examined their injuries, shook her head in bewilderment. "Why would he damage foxes?" she muttered, addressing the question to no one but herself. "Someone else must have done this. Maybe he brought them here to save them from death."

Shinobu was fairly certain Maggie was speaking about the Middle Dread, but he doubted that the Middle had brought anyone here for altruistic reasons. She was speaking of the Middle with unexpected familiarity. Surely that was an important piece of information, but he was unable to keep it in his mind long enough to figure out what it meant. The focal was carrying his thoughts back to Quin, again and again. *Had* she been here with him? Had she tricked him? Had he left her, or had she left him?

The Watchers were gazing at Maggie's lined face intently, their knives in their hands, ready for her order. Shinobu could feel their eagerness to do violence.

You like violence too, half of his mind told him. He looked at the frozen Seekers and shook his head. *Not against them.*

"Not these Seekers," Maggie said to the boys, her voice quivering with emotion. "No one touches these. We will come back and take them away, carefully, when we're done. Pass by."

* * *

Hundreds of paces later, they came to another band of Seekers. This was a younger group, with more children and teens. The oldest was a man with an impressive silver beard and shock of gray hair. Shinobu had the vague sense he'd seen an image of the man before, perhaps in an old box of photographs on the Scottish estate.

What are the chances she spares this group as well?

Why should she? Sometimes you have to hurt people.

You don't.

You'll like it.

I won't.

"Look at their wrists, Shinobu."

He stepped closer to the gray-haired man, moving as slowly as he could reasonably go without angering Maggie. As he reached for the man's sleeve, he experienced a sense of dread so great it exceeded even his dread of Maggie paralyzing him. He would not like what he found here; he knew that already.

"Shinobu?" Maggie queried.

Shinobu folded up the man's sleeve. There on his rigid forearm was the symbol Shinobu had guessed he would see: a ram. Quin was a ram. These were her ancestors.

"Well?" Maggie pressed.

He stalled by checking the wrists of the other adults. All rams. He looked over the many young faces.

"What are they?" she asked.

Shinobu turned to her. The Watchers stood ready in a loose cluster around their mistress. Could he fight off all of them? The immobilized Seekers behind him were lost in time, but given half a chance in the world outside, their hearts would beat again, their lungs would breathe, they would live. His whipsword was inches from his hand, ready to be pulled.

He would make his stand here.

"Why?" he asked.

Maggie strode forward and angrily lifted the gray-haired man's sleeve. She saw the ram scar.

"It's not your family," she said. "Why do you care?"

Shinobu made a last attempt at reason. "You could take them back to the world. Question them—"

"Hesitation only makes it worse." She spoke in her most grand-motherly voice, which was so inappropriate to her subject that Shinobu's stomach turned. She fixed her gaze on the Watchers. "Your master created you to get rid of those he needed gone," she said, her words soft and trembling. "I imagine you've been waiting a long time to do it." She gestured at the Seekers, and as she did, Shinobu read blood-lust on the face of every boy. Maggie ordered, "Make an end to them."

In a mass, the boys lurched forward, weapons out. Shinobu's mind emptied of everything but one clear thought. He cracked out his whipsword and leapt in front of Quin's ancestors. The Watchers would kill him too, eventually, but that was all right. He would fight them as long as he could.

Just kill the Seekers, half his mind told him. *You'll enjoy it.*

Shut up!

Before their weapons clashed, Shinobu received a tremendous blow to the chest. The air was knocked from his lungs and he flew backward. The Watchers were flying too, in a mess of whipswords and limbs. He collided with the frozen Seekers behind him, felt them topple. Maggie too had been knocked off her feet. All of their flash-lights were tumbling, turning Shinobu's fall into a silent film of dis-jointed flashes.

Then someone was there, helping him up. Hands gripped his shirtfront, his arms.

"I've got you," a voice whispered into his ear. "I've got you." He stumbled to his feet as his abductor pulled him along.

Not daring to believe what he'd heard, Shinobu whispered, "Quin, is it you?"

CHAPTER 28

QUIN

"It's me," Quin told him, hooking an arm through one of his and dragging him along with her. "I've got you. But can you walk faster?"

They were away from the Watchers and the old woman, but she wanted to be out of sight and out of earshot before she used the athame, so that no one could follow.

Shinobu found his footing, grabbed her arms, and forced her to stop.

"Wait."

The lights were far away, which made it difficult to see him, but she could make out his familiar face, looking at her in disbelief. He drew her to him, crushed her into his chest, kissed her cheeks and her lips and her forehead desperately.

"I left you, I left you."

She said, "I'm a bit angry about that, but we'll have to fight later—"

"It's the focal. I thought I was saving you. I'm wearing it again—"

"It doesn't matter right now—"

"We have to go back."

"We're going back. You have an athame." She reached for the pocket of his cloak.

"No," he said, clearly struggling with competing thoughts. His face was anguished and desperate. "We have to go back for the Seekers. She's here to kill them."

Quin looked toward the mess of flashlights in the distance. The Watchers were getting to their feet, retrieving their fallen weapons.

"We can stop her," he told her urgently. "They're ram Seekers, your own ancestors."

It took Quin a moment to grasp what he was telling her. Then she understood: the other figures she'd seen beyond the Watchers, they were Seekers who'd lost themselves here.

Shinobu had taken hold of her arm and was pulling her back toward the boys. She ran with him.

When they got close, the Watchers were still regrouping, gathering their flashlights, cracking out their whipswords. The frozen Seekers lay scattered about the ground. Quin saw young faces, frozen in time, helpless. Maggie was ordering the boys to close in. In a ragged group, the boys advanced.

Shinobu screamed next to Quin, trying to call the Watchers' attention away from their victims. Several of the boys turned. Shinobu cracked out his whipsword and leapt at them.

Quin shook the impellor, twisted it to full power, and fired. The closest Watcher fell to his knees, but no one else was affected. She fired again, and this time nothing at all happened. Panicked, Quin cracked out her whipsword and engaged, killing one of the Watchers before he could even swing at her. Others were coming. She and Shinobu were distracting them from their Seeker victims—

Beside her, Shinobu collapsed like a marionette whose strings had been cut. More Watchers came at Quin, and she tried to draw them away from Shinobu too. Except she was not drawing them; someone was drawing her. She was farther from the boys than she should have been. Her whipsword could no longer reach them. They were looking for her as though they couldn't see her. And they were below her now; she'd floated upward in the darkness.

Someone was holding her, pinning her arms to her sides to keep her still. Quin's thoughts were spreading out, falling away from the stream of now. The cool water of no-time swirled about her.

Below was a frenzy. Shinobu lay, useless, his limbs sprawled. The Watchers had turned away from him. They stood in a circle, killing every person who was not one of them. The Seekers down there, young and old, did not know they were being butchered. Only Quin could watch in horror as those boys ended the Seekers' lives in a rain of vicious blows.

"Let me stop them! Let me stop them!" she cried, trying to wrest herself free. But she was losing herself, and the hard truth was that those Seekers were already dead. She was going to be sick.

Her captor pulled her closer, whispered into her ear, "She was about to kill you. She made him collapse, and she was coming for you. You're a ram. She would have done to you what she's doing to them."

Dex. He stood next to her, and yet they were not standing exactly. They were in the air above the fight, and Dex's face was lit by the glow of the medallion that was hanging around his neck.

She reached up, felt that the helmet was gone. Her head hurt, distantly; her temples were throbbing.

"You took off my focal."

"I need it myself in no-space," he told her.

"You did nothing!" Quin yelled at him. "And you stopped me from fighting them!"

She wasn't yelling, though. She could hardly hear her own voice.

Knowledge of self, she tried to say. *Knowledge of home. A clear picture of where I came from . . .*

I hate you, Dex! You're mad and cruel and cowardly! The words lay inside her throat, unspoken.

They were floating farther away. He held her against him, her back to his chest, his arm tightly around her waist. His other hand was gripping the medallion, and before Quin lost herself entirely, she saw the blackness around them shift, saw streaks of gray at the corners of her vision, and knew that he was taking her somewhere else.

CHAPTER 29

JOHN

John owed it to his mother to go to the fox Seekers first, of course. He and the Young Dread followed the two-hundred-pace instructions they'd found in the cave beneath Mont Saint-Michel. John wore their helmet, and Maud, so much better than he was at keeping her own sense of time, followed with her hand on his shoulder. At the end of those two hundred steps, in the blackness *There,* they found a small group of fox Seekers. Many of them, like the boar Seekers, were seriously wounded, though they and their injuries had frozen into timelessness.

They brought the first group back to *Traveler.* The medical staff took the rigid bodies, still holding their decades-old poses, directly to hospital beds.

Next, in honor of John's father, he and the Young Dread searched for the Seekers from the house of the stag, his father's house. There were more of them, a dozen in all, also with many old injuries that John hoped could be mended.

When the stag Seekers were safely on *Traveler,* John's mind turned to Quin. The ram Seekers would be her relations, and he chose to retrieve them next.

He and Maud used the instructions they'd written in the journal, just as they had with the first two houses. But this time, as they neared the end of the two hundred paces, John understood that they'd begun their search too late.

There had once been people sitting in the darkness in this location, but one couldn't rightly call them people anymore. His flashlight revealed a tableau of carnage unlike anything John had ever seen. Even the terrible pictures of death Maggie had shown him as a boy were tame compared with the blood and ruined bodies here. Though time was stopped and the blood would stay fresh eternally, there was no mistaking whose work this was and how recently it had happened.

Maggie had done this. Slaughter. There was no other word for it. John was held immobile for what felt like a hundred years, staring at hands, feet, faces. This was what Maggie's and Catherine's vengeance looked like. Beneath the high-minded words, this was the reality.

Odors did not carry well in this place, but the metallic tinge of blood and worse smells had gathered like a fog. John doubled over and was violently sick, as if his body were trying to rid itself of any particle of this butchery. Even the Young Dread, more stoic than anyone else John knew, turned her head away and covered her nose.

"Maggie's already found them with the Middle Dread's Watchers," John said. When he could stand again without retching, he noted the dozens of footprints where the boys had trampled through the mess before heading off into darkness. The Watchers had continued on. So— "She might be somewhere else *between*, right now, killing everyone she can find. Are we too late?"

"We will go to the rest immediately," the Young Dread said. If she usually kept herself aloof from John's world, there was no trace of that now. Her eyes were alight with the same urgency John felt.

"Should we follow them on foot?" John asked, his gaze on the path of bloody footprints.

"It will always be faster to go by athame," Maud answered. "Come."

They went for the house of the bear next, because Maggie had mentioned them specifically, and they discovered several Seekers and children still untouched by the Watchers. They hurried these people onto *Traveler,* armed themselves better, and then returned *There* without delay. John had no idea in what order his grandmother was attacking, nor how careful she would be about choosing whom to kill.

When they went for the house of the horse, their luck had run out again. Only dead bodies were left sprawled silently in the darkness.

CHAPTER 30

SHINOBU

Two Watchers dragged Shinobu at the back of the line. He'd been turned into a rag doll, and the Watchers had walked over him, fallen on him, and ignored him as they killed their victims. The helplessness had been unbearable, but it had gotten worse when the smell of blood and death washed over him. He'd wished for unconsciousness to take him away. But he was still awake, a useless lump of clay now being yanked along by two careless boys who were pulling him by his limp arms.

His head flopped around painfully and at last came to rest angled backward, from which position he could see—sort of—what was happening up ahead. Maggie, leaning heavily on two boys to help her walk, led the band of Watchers across long stretches of the hidden dimensions, until they came, after a great while, to another group of frozen Seekers. The boys dragging Shinobu abruptly dropped him.

From where he lay, he could see only the Watchers' legs, but he could hear everything they did. They massacred these new Seekers. When the coppery odor of blood reached Shinobu, the focal twisted it into something sweet, tried to make him believe death was good. He was not fooled.

The nightmare was endless. The next group they came to was, thankfully, Seekers from the house of the stag. Shinobu listened as Maggie examined their wrists and ordered the Watchers to leave them alone, while she wondered aloud at the cruel fate that had brought harm to this particular house, which had always been an ally of the foxes. Stags and foxes—the two sorts of Seekers she cared about.

He was being dragged again, for a very long way. Eventually mobility trickled back into his arms and legs. By the time they next stopped, Shinobu could twitch his feet and hands. When the boys dropped him, he managed to roll onto his side, from which position he could see a little bit better. They had found a very large group of Seekers this time, maybe a few dozen, scattered over a broad area.

The Watchers were moving between the Seekers, examining their wrists.

"A bird!" called out one of the boys.

An eagle, thought Shinobu. *This is my house they've found.*

Shinobu was an eagle and a dragon, and Maggie had spared his life solely because his ancestors had intermarried with her own. The drops of their blood flowing through Shinobu's veins made it acceptable to keep him alive, for a while. But that didn't mean she felt kindly toward all eagles and dragons. There was no reason to suppose anyone else would be safe.

Another Watcher hit the first boy over the head. "It's an eagle, eejit! Don't you know an eagle?"

The first boy took a swing at the second.

"Enough!" Maggie said, an edge of anxiety in her voice. The boys were following her eagerly while she let them kill people, but Maggie must have known that without Shinobu as her enforcer, she could rapidly lose control of the Watchers if they grew dissatisfied with her. By now they'd been walking for a very long time and were ready to get on with the killing or go home.

She moved among the frozen Seekers, taking slow steps as she studied their faces. He wondered if she was searching for friends or if she was relishing the sight of enemies.

"Over here they've got dragons on them," a Watcher called from farther away. "Or could be lizards."

From even farther away came another voice: "Tigers down here, with long teeth."

"Fanged cat," he heard Maggie say.

Three houses—and two of them are my family.

"That's all," called another boy. "Three animals."

"Spread out around them," Maggie instructed. "It's the fanged cats we want to stop. The others . . . leave them if you can."

Leave them if you can? Shinobu thought. That was the extent of her goodwill toward Shinobu's ancestors.

Maggie examined a few more of the figures. Shinobu was fairly certain that she was deciding whether any of them deserved to live. She shifted her weight a few times, exhausted and pensive.

"Go on, then," she told the boys.

The Watchers closed in.

CHAPTER 31

JOHN

John heard his grandmother say, "Go on, then," in the unmistakable tone of someone ordering the deaths of others.

He and the Young Dread had run through the paces *There,* to find the next group of Seekers. They'd come upon the Watchers and Maggie, taking their places around a few dozen motionless forms—the biggest group he'd seen yet—and the Watchers had lurched forward, knives drawn.

"Maggie!" John yelled. "Grandmother. It's John. I've come back."

"Hold," his grandmother ordered.

The boys froze, rather unwillingly, and looked around to discover what had made Maggie change her mind. Every Watcher cloak was covered in bloodstains, and their impatience to attack radiated off the boys like heat. They eyed John and the Young Dread suspiciously as the two newcomers came out of the darkness.

Maggie watched her grandson as he got closer. She was smiling, but it was a smile that said, *I'll teach you a lesson now.*

"Grandmother, are you really doing all of this without me?" he asked as he approached. He could smell the scent of death all around the boys. "I thought we were going to share our revenge." He was saying the only words that might give her pause. "I've waited my whole life for this."

He noticed that Maggie's hair was messy and her clothes uncharacteristically rumpled. She'd been tossed about in the course of killing Seekers today. She looked physically exhausted, yet there was a glow of triumph that was fueling her.

She scolded him by saying, "You refused me, John. You pushed me away."

"I shouldn't have. I'm here now."

The pleasure in Maggie's face gave him hope. He was only yards away from her. If he could get hold of her . . . He looked to the Young Dread to silently communicate his intentions.

Maggie's expression changed abruptly. In an instant, she understood that John wasn't sincere. Before he could reach her, she addressed the Watchers. "Go ahead. Now!" she urged. To John she called, "I will not let you make the wrong choice."

One of the boys raised his whipsword immediately toward the nearest Seeker. With almost no sign of movement, the Young Dread's knife was in the boy's throat and he was falling to the ground, his whipsword unbloodied. Another Watcher attacked a Seeker, and the same thing happened again, Maud's knife in his throat before his victim could be stabbed.

John had been heading for his grandmother, but getting to her would do no good now. The boys had their orders, and nothing would keep them from killing—nothing but John and Maud.

He'd brought a gun from *Traveler*, and he changed direction, aimed the weapon at the Watchers nearest the victims. He fired, and a bullet found its target, though the explosive report was muted here, as though he had discharged the gun beneath a pile of blankets. He fired again, and a bullet fell from the barrel to land on the ground.

Repeated pulls of the trigger did nothing. The weapon had become useless.

Throwing it aside, John cracked out his whipsword, and in a moment he and Maud were fighting hand to hand with seven Watchers. Not one was a match for them in single combat, and all of them, John suspected, had been warned by Maggie not to seriously damage her grandson in their mission to kill other Seekers. Nevertheless, they were, when all fighting at once, formidable foes, though the Young Dread had speeded herself up so dramatically that her limbs were a blur.

"They're attacking behind us," Maud said over her shoulder, the words almost too fast to understand.

He spared a backward glance and saw that some of the boys had moved away from the fight and were going after Seekers who stood completely unguarded. John felt the Young Dread pull his athame and lightning rod from his waist. Then, in a flash of motion, she extricated herself from the fight and went after the other Watchers.

CHAPTER 32

MAUD

The Young Dread dispatched two Watchers with her whipsword, but not quickly enough. They'd attacked and grievously damaged a handful of Seekers before she'd gotten to them.

Now John was backing toward her, pulling the fight with him. She was adjusting the dials of the athame in the low light, when another boy came running at her, wild elation in his eyes. Maud was forced to block him with the athame. She felt the impact travel through the delicate stone instrument; the boy careened off to attack another Seeker. Maud had only one knife left; she threw it and sent him sprawling.

She struck the athame and lightning rod and drew a large circle. The edges of the anomaly solidified, and the Young Dread was looking through the opening at dark water, thirty feet beneath her. She had meant to open up a doorway into *Traveler* itself, but the airship was perched at the shoreline below and far to the left, its engines idling, its hide dark except for a swath of reflected moonlight. She checked the coordinates on the handle—she'd set them correctly. After a moment's confusion, she understood: the athame had been struck so hard by the attacking Watcher that it had gone out of tune. It would take one of the special tools that the Old Dread had left her to put it back to rights.

"Maud!" called John from the other side of a group of frozen Seekers. "I can't hold them off!"

The Young Dread looked from the huddled Seekers to the water below. She estimated the drop.

There was nothing else to do.

She grabbed the child nearest her, a small girl, and threw her frozen form through the anomaly. The girl fell like a stone, and a splash went up far below. The child was suspended in time. She would not need to breathe for several minutes. They could retrieve her before she woke up, hopefully.

The Young Dread took hold of the next Seeker, a grown man, and with a wrenching twist sent him through the anomaly as well.

"Maud!"

She threw another Seeker out, and then another, watching the splashes. If there was air in their lungs, they would float, for a while at least.

"Maud!"

She pushed two more out, struck the athame again and re-carved an anomaly in the same spot, as the first doorway began to lose its shape. This done, she ran to John, who was holding off the last four Watchers, his whipsword slashing in wide arcs, trying to keep the boys at bay. Maud cracked out her own whipsword and took his place.

"Throw them through the anomaly!" she told him. She struck at the boys with blinding speed, forcing them backward and buying John room to move.

"What?" he asked.

She slowed her words down, said, "Throw them into the ocean, and count them!"

Out of the corner of her eye, she watched John turn to the frozen Seekers. He tossed a figure through the opening, and then another, after which Maud could pay him no more attention.

The remaining boys were attacking in a frenzy. The Young Dread felled two of them, kicked the third away. She was moving too fast for them to protect themselves. The fourth boy raised his own blunt, short whipsword. Before Maud could dispatch him, she saw Maggie behind the boy, holding up a dark cylinder. The air grew thick around Maud. Her jaw clicked to one side.

A shock wave burst from the weapon. Maud, the Watchers attacking her, the two Watchers on the ground by her feet, the final three Seekers grouped behind her, and John were all blown backward through the anomaly.

The Young Dread slowed her sense of time again as she fell toward the water. Above her, a Watcher was cut in half as his body hit the border of the anomaly. Another lost his arm and shoulder. The maimed boys spun wildly down toward her.

She slowed time further, could feel her heart beating, a stately drumbeat in her chest and ears, and the night air rushing past her. Above, the old woman was at the edge of the anomaly, staring at the ocean and the airship as the edges of the doorway grew soft and began to collapse.

Maud turned her head, saw John falling below her. He was clutching the frozen body of a young Seeker child, and he was screaming as he maneuvered his feet downward for impact.

The Young Dread flipped over. To anyone watching, the motion would have been so fast as to be impossible to follow. The ocean was almost upon her. She raised her arms, stiffened her legs, and hit the water. She sank and sank and nearly struck the shallow bottom, no more than fifteen feet down.

Her eyes gathered up all the light around her, and she looked above to the surface, which was riddled with the impacts of human forms. John was up there, kicking his legs and grabbing at the Seekers nearest to him.

Maud forced her lungs and heart into the slowest pace she could maintain while moving. If she conserved her oxygen, she could hold her breath for a very long while, keeping time slow, while she herself moved quickly.

She turned in a circle. Two shapes were sinking around her. One was already on the ocean floor.

The Young Dread dove and kicked and grabbed the shirt of the little girl who'd settled to the sandy bottom in a sitting position. She pulled the girl up to her, turned again, kicked, and caught a sinking figure. It was a grown woman, too slender to float well. The third was passing by, still standing, hunched over as he had been while *There*. The Young Dread caught his shirt with her foot and dragged all three of them to the surface with powerful strokes of her free arm. Her lungs burned, but pain was nothing. *It is only pain.*

When she broke the surface, Maud allowed time to accelerate. John was holding two adult Seekers and drawing another toward him. He was yelling for help, striking out for the shore. Other adults were bobbing in the slight waves, still floating.

"Get to the boat!" John said when he saw her.

The crew of *Traveler* had spotted them in the water, and a small boat was heading their way, its outboard motor roaring. Maud hooked the shirt of another Seeker, so that she was dragging four of them, and kicked toward the boat.

She swam on her back, looking up at the night sky. Maggie was there, standing in the center of a black opening, thirty feet above them. How? Maud's anomaly had already fallen shut.

The doorway around the old woman was a perfect arch, the edges glowing more brightly than the border of any anomaly the Young Dread had ever seen.

"What's she doing?" John asked. Then he knew the answer: "She's going to shoot us!"

Maud threw her sight and at once saw what John had seen—his grandmother was holding a weapon in her hands. It was not the dark cylinder that had thrown them all into the ocean. This one was different. It wrapped around Maggie's hand and glowed with flickering energy.

A burst of . . . *something* blew outward from the half-circle anomaly. It was as though the air itself had been charged with energy, like a dancing heat wave above a hot desert.

"Dive!" she called to John.

They pulled themselves beneath the water, still clutching the Seekers, as a deep thump reverberated through the ocean and through Maud's bones. A few moments later, they surfaced. Nothing had touched them, and yet the boat heading for them had gone silent. Its motor had cut out, and the lights along its bow had been extinguished. The vessel was still coming, but only coasting on its prior momentum. The crew shouted orders to each other.

Above the Young Dread, Maggie was still perched in the sky. She adjusted the weapon on her hand, lifted it to fire again. She was aiming at *Traveler,* Maud realized. Maggie wanted to disable the airship.

A shape rose up behind her—a tall man, staggering out of the darkness.

It was Shinobu.

With a tremendous blow that made use of both fists, he knocked Maggie down, and then he ripped the weapon from her hands. He kicked at something near her feet, and the anomaly opening shifted, warped. Shinobu fell, limp, in the darkness. As he did, the anomaly folded in half, and then it folded in half again and again, until it was only a glowing white point of light, like a star, which winked out a moment later.

"Grab hold. We're trying to get the motor started." It was one of the crew on the boat. Maud and the Seekers she was dragging had bumped into its inflatable hull.

She pushed her paralyzed cargo into the waiting hands extended over the side. Someone threw a life preserver. Taking it under one arm, the Young Dread struck out across the water, back to their point of impact. She could hear John following.

There was only one Seeker still bobbing on the surface, a man whose cloak had captured air beneath it as he fell and was now acting as a float. She passed him by, to be retrieved later.

"How many more?" she called. "I threw six."

"So seven more are still in the water," John answered.

The Young Dread dove, gathering all the light she could as she kicked to the bottom. John followed, shining an underwater torch he must have gotten from the crew. In its eerie glow were cloaked bodies slowly sinking toward the bottom, the blood from their injuries coloring the water. She pushed three toward John and dove deeper.

The final Seekers—a man, a woman, and a young boy—were gathered on the ocean floor in attitudes of rest, a family asleep on a bed of sand. Maud grabbed them by their clothing and struck out for the surface. Her lungs burned, her body ached for air, but it would obey her will as long as she was alive.

When she and John reached the night air, they dragged all seven to the waiting boat. The crew hauled the motionless Seekers on board, and the Young Dread and John climbed over the hull and onto the deck.

They were dripping as they checked on each of the rescued. Arms and legs stuck out at odd angles. The Seekers were still statues moved out of place, and none were breathing yet. Several were injured, but whether from the Watchers just now or from the Middle Dread ages ago, it was impossible to tell. And it hardly mattered. The blood was fresh. If John and Maud could get them onto *Traveler* before they rejoined the stream of time, the Seekers had a chance of being saved.

The boat engine still would not start. John had gone to the back of the vessel to help the crew, but he was having no better luck. Maud went aft to him.

"It's not just us," one of the crew said. "Look at *Traveler*."

Across the water, the airship was sitting lopsided at the quay. Of its six engines, which had been keeping it in a low hover, three had cut out, leaving *Traveler* hanging crookedly, with the lowest point only a few feet above the ground. Half the shipyard was without power as well. By the border of darkness in front of them, the Young Dread could infer the range of the weapon Maggie had fired.

A moment later, the airship's three disabled engines sputtered to life, sending *Traveler* through a series of drunken gyrations. Then all engines were firing. The security lights throughout the shipyard came alive dimly, and shortly flared to full strength. The boat's motor started, and they turned and roared back to shore.

CHAPTER 33

QUIN

When Quin was next aware of herself, she was standing at an impossible angle, looking down—or was it up?—at the colorless shapes of a city.

"You don't, you don't," Dex was saying. "I know you don't."

He was standing beside her at the same impossible angle. Darkness enfolded them from behind, curved about them and converged with the gray cityscape below. The seam where the blackness met the light slanted crazily. Quin was sure she was about to fall down through that watery gray sky into the buildings below.

Dex's head was bare and his eyes were calm. He'd been wearing a focal, hadn't he?

"You don't," he said again.

Quin's hand came to her mouth, and she registered that she'd been speaking. "I hate you," she said, and she knew that she'd been repeating those words over and over.

Something must have been different about the way she said them this time, because Dex looked at her curiously and asked, "Are you back with me?"

She wanted to say yes, but in truth she didn't feel fully in possession of herself. She was not lost, like she would have been in no-space, but she felt muted, stretched out slightly, her mind dulled by whatever strange place they were in. *He's brought me here, to some half place, to stop me from getting angry at him.*

Why would she be angry? She looked at the darkness behind them until she remembered: the last thing she'd seen was murder. The Watchers had killed a group of Seekers in a bloody mob, and she'd been floating away, doing nothing. She'd seen the faces of the dead, staring into the blackness . . .

Quin's eyes filled with tears.

"Don't cry, please," Dex whispered. "We couldn't have stopped her. She was going to kill them no matter what. It's why they have to leave this world. They could never control themselves, and *he* refused to control them."

She didn't want to listen to his insanity. "I *could* have stopped them. I took the impellor. I thought I'd charged it by leaving it in the sun, but it didn't fire right."

He shook his head. "Complicated weapons don't work well in no-space. They require too much energy from the world. Haven't I explained that? That's why the impellor worked the first time you tried it, but then did nothing."

"You saw all of that?" She'd thought he retreated long before she engaged with the Watchers.

He leaned toward her, tall and strong and concerned. He wiped a tear from her cheek. "I wasn't going to let her get you, not again."

Quin pulled out of his grasp. His tenderness, his intimate voice, they were maddening. Even if her mind wasn't completely her own, anger was bubbling to the surface.

"You did nothing, Dex. You should have helped me. You should have *tried* to save those people."

"Quilla—"

"I'm not Quilla! Stop trying to kiss me. Stop acting like I belong to you. You're a coward! And you made me leave Shinobu *There*. She'll probably kill him."

She couldn't stop the tears now. She turned away from Dex and hugged herself. She was high up; the city below her was swinging across her field of view as she moved. In a moment, she was dizzy and sick. She closed her eyes tightly, but tears kept rolling down her cheeks.

When Dex spoke, his voice was hollow. "I don't think she'll kill him. She has him under her thumb. She likes them like that."

"Great. That's very reassuring."

"I know I'm a coward. But if I face her before I'm ready, there is no point. If I lose myself when I see her, I will miss my chance."

"Who is she?" Quin asked, her eyes still shut. A strange thought came to her. "Did you love her?" She turned to Dex. "Did you know her when she was young? Have you been *There* that long?"

"I did love her when I was younger."

"*She's* Quilla?"

Dex almost smiled, but it faded into a sickly expression. "No, she's not Quilla. God, no."

He sat, though what he was sitting on, Quin could not have said. He floated in the semidarkness just as she did, the faded city tilting below them. She crossed her arms and stood in front of him.

"Who, then?"

He shook his head, apparently unable to say. His eyes had retreated from her into the deep part of himself that trapped him.

Quin wanted to hate him for his insanity and his secrets, but even when she was furious at Dex, she couldn't think of him as someone evil. The idea wouldn't stick. Beneath the madness, Dex felt . . . decent. That was the only way she could describe it. He was like an overgrown apple tree, its branches tangled and full of dead wood and rotting fruit. But if you could prune all of those things away . . .

She only had to keep him talking and he would find his way again. "How did you pull me away from the fight? You took me up above them."

By stages, she watched his thoughts come back to her. "I know no-space so well," he murmured. "It's been my home. There's no up and down, no air, no light, only what you bring with you. Do you see? You bring a light and it works a bit, you bring your air and it lasts while you think it lasts. You bring your sense of direction and gravity. I have only to change my orientation to pull you upward, because there is no up. There's only where I am."

It made sense as he said it, though Quin guessed it would make much less sense later, when she was thinking straight.

"We might not have been able to save them," she conceded, thinking of the vicious boys and their weapons, and the way Shinobu had collapsed as soon as the fight had begun. Those Seekers, swimming in the sea of infinity, hadn't stood a chance. She fought back tears again. "I could have saved a few of them."

"And paid with your life."

She couldn't argue that. Without the impellor and with no athame, she would have been at their mercy. Still, she could have tried.

"Who is she, Dex?" She asked it quickly and softly, hoping to slip the question past his defenses.

His eyes shot this way and that, as if he were truly in a labyrinth, following a thread to see where it took him. "She is Maggie," he said at last.

"Not—not John's grandmother?" She had never seen John's grandmother, but he'd told her stories about the fierce woman who had dominated his childhood.

Dex's mouth quirked up. "That could be. I don't know which John you mean, but Maggie has raised a lot of children."

Quin buried her face in her hands, trying to marshal her thoughts. "You are so confusing, Dex. Who are you talking about?"

He stayed quiet, looking equally bewildered. He broke the silence when it had grown overwhelming. "Do you know this city?"

She raised her eyes to gaze down at the gray cityscape hanging crookedly below them. She'd been avoiding a direct look, because the height might paralyze her, but now she gave the city a sweeping glance.

"It's London. Are we really hanging above it?"

"Yes. No." He tried again: "It's like my tunnel, but more of a bubble, between no-space and the world." He swept a hand at the dark behind them and the city below. "You can see both sides, and like in the tunnel, I don't need the focal here. I used to watch the world like this for years."

"Years?"

"The city was different then. And then, for a long time, I couldn't look at even this much of the world." He touched her shoulder, searched her face with pleading eyes. "I am so much better now. I've been out in the air with you. I've looked at the sky."

"By accident," Quin pointed out.

He ignored this. "I didn't collapse entirely when I saw her the second time, in no-space. I thought I would, but I didn't."

Quin tried again. "Who is she to you?"

Dex was looking at the city, but after a few moments, with that question hanging between them, his gaze returned to her. "It's not that I don't want to tell you. It's that I'm finding my way to the words, like someone blind in an unfamiliar room." He paused and then said, "She was there when Desmond died. And Quilla too."

He continued to speak, his brown eyes holding her own, his words coming like thoughts in a dream. It took a few moments for Quin to realize that she was hearing him out loud and not in her head. Maybe she heard him in both places.

"Desmond and Quilla's daughter was Adelaide," he whispered. "Matheus hated the little girl, and he hated Quilla. He and Desmond had been inseparable all their lives, two brothers facing the world together, and Quilla changed that. Matheus thought that Desmond wasn't allowed to make up his own mind anymore. He thought Quilla was making up his mind for him. Adelaide made it even worse, because Desmond loved his daughter beyond words.

"And Quilla did change Desmond. He noticed Matheus's failings more now, his fascination with dangerous things. The brothers argued. Matheus insisted that Desmond wasn't allowed to teach Quilla the things they knew. He mustn't show her his medallion, he couldn't tell her about no-space, he couldn't teach her how to use any of the weapons. She wasn't allowed to be trained, even though they were training so many others. Matheus refused to let Quilla be a Seeker. Their father agreed—only to keep the peace between them. And their mother agreed for her own reasons.

"Desmond thought Matheus was being hateful." Dex's eyes came back to the present for a moment, and Quin saw a flash of defensiveness in them. "He *was* being hateful. They quarreled for two years, but one day it wasn't just an argument. They *fought*. And . . . and Desmond was killed."

The word floated between them, heavy and demanding. The reverie they'd both been in, as Dex tiptoed through his labyrinth, was broken with one word.

"Desmond was *killed*," she repeated.

"Yes."

"You're alive, Dex. You're not from the Dark Ages. Listen to how you speak."

"Is that what you think?"

She stuck her fingers against his neck, where his pulse beat strongly. "Alive!"

He had no answer for that. Indeed, he looked confused as he stared from the view of London to the darkness behind them and then back at Quin. She could read the thought behind his eyes: *Why have I brought her here?*

Quin looked again at the watery expanse of the city. She'd thought London was frozen, but when she peered through the billowing curtain of the anomaly, she saw that it was in motion. There were blurs where street traffic flowed, lights flicking on and off in buildings. She was seeing the city in time lapse, racing forward. The traffic was flowing down there. The sun was moving across the gray sky.

"Is the world really moving so fast?" she asked in alarm.

"Yes."

"How much time since we left?"

"I don't know."

"Dex, those boys were murdering people! Shinobu is helpless." She grabbed his medallion. "Take me back!"

CHAPTER 34

MAUD

They'd made a Seeker training camp in the great room of *Traveler*. The airship was crossing oceans slowly, making its way along the shoreline of Africa. They were heading, by a winding ocean route, to Hong Kong. Quin lived in Hong Kong. She was the only other Seeker John knew, and it was right that they consult on what to do with their brothers and sisters who had been rescued from the dimensions *between*.

The Young Dread was no longer concerned that John might choose violence against any of the Seekers he'd brought back. His confrontation with Maggie in the darkness had changed him, and she could see this change in his eyes, which looked at the world with a clearer gaze.

Through the windows in the airship's outer walls, one could see the distant African coast, but here in the great room, they had the glass ceiling, making the Young Dread feel as though they were standing inside the sky itself, which, she supposed, they were.

The adult Seekers they'd rescued were almost all wounded, a few so gravely that they might not survive. But of the fifteen recovered children, only a few, the oldest, had been injured.

Thirteen eager Seeker children, all of whom had disappeared from the world decades or centuries ago, were gathered in the great room, with wooden swords, learning how to fight.

And the Young Dread was teaching them.

She had a practice dummy set up, and the children—no, they were apprentice Seekers now, she reminded herself—stood in a semicircle facing it. The youngest were only four or five years old, several were around ten, but most were in their early teens.

"You will practice this," she told them.

She addressed herself to the dummy, performing a series of blows to its head and body, making the motions slowly so that the apprentices could follow.

"Do you understand?"

The apprentices nodded, all except the very smallest, who were staring at her with open mouths. Their swords were no longer than Maud's forearm.

"You will begin slowly, but you will practice until you become faster," she explained.

She attacked the dummy again and again, going through the pattern of blows more rapidly each time.

"That's fast," whispered one of the older girls.

"It is *faster*," the Young Dread corrected, "but not fast. *Fast* looks like this."

She turned to the dummy, let time stretch out around her, and hit it with blows she knew the children would hardly be able to see. Then she did it again, faster.

When she let her arms fall to her sides and allowed time to snap back to its normal pace, the apprentices were gazing at her, wide-eyed.

The dummy tottered and fell to the floor. It was close to indestructible, but one of its arms had fallen off, and its head was loose, lolling about on the mat like the head of a drunken man's.

"Dear God," one of the older boys said.

The smallest child, a girl of four, burst into tears, and she ran to the Young Dread in terror. Maud looked up from the tiny apprentice to find John watching her, unable to conceal his amusement.

She gently peeled the little girl off her legs, righted the dummy, and drew forward Kaspar, the four-year-old boy from the boar Seekers.

"You show her, Kaspar," instructed the Young Dread.

Kaspar jumped at the dummy. As the little girl watched, he made a good show of following Maud's motions. The Young Dread had noticed Kaspar already beginning to change his sense of time. A few of his strikes against the dummy were fast enough to elicit admiration from the older children.

Late that night, as she lay on the bed that was far too soft, looking out the window of her cabin at the starry sky marching away aft of the airship, Maud thought about the smallest children. She wondered why the grip of their hands carried such a different feeling than that of her own grip on the hilt of a whipsword or the grip of a combatant trying to hold you and break you. Something about the children themselves imbued their touch with an entirely different quality.

CHAPTER 35

JOHN

John woke in the middle of the night, unsure of what had roused him. The hum of *Traveler*'s engines was a comforting sound that recalled nights, long ago, when his mother had lived on the airship with him. The ceiling of his bedroom was a pale blue from the faint glow of the night sky. The room was still.

He was startled when he saw the figure sitting atop the covers at the foot of his bed.

"Maud?"

She was so motionless, she might have been a store-window mannequin, except no mannequin's eyes were ever that ancient. She wore a loose shift as a nightgown, a garment that had been stocked on *Traveler* but that looked, on her, as though it had come from an ancient wardrobe. Her light brown hair, which was longer than when he'd first met her, reached almost to the crook of her elbows, and it was blue gray in the starlight. John sat up and averted his eyes. It made him uncomfortable to see her beauty out in the open like this.

She said, "Being in the world is changing me. I had lost the sense of what it is to be a person." Her voice had become softer in the last month, but it still made John think of the cold water beneath the earth that could, over thousands of years, cut a path through stone.

"Do you feel like a person now?" he asked. There was not one thing about her that reminded him of anyone else.

"Not quite. But there are things I'd forgotten that I am beginning to remember."

The Young Dread's light eyes were shadowed, but her gaze was penetrating as always. John became intensely aware that he wasn't wearing a shirt. She'd made him train in almost no clothes countless times, but here, in these civilized surroundings, the lack of cover felt different.

She was studying her hands, which lay carelessly in her lap. "For the longest time, a touch meant a slap from the Middle Dread, or a blow to the chest, or a blow to the back while we practiced, or a blow to my face to show me I was too slow." It was hard to believe the Young Dread could ever have been considered too slow. How fast was the Middle Dread, then? "Or, in the worst moments, a touch was a stab with his whipsword, a kick as he left me to die."

Absently one of her hands touched her side, where John knew there was a long scar given to her by the Middle. She was looking over John's shoulder, as if her history were painted on the wall behind him.

"With my master, the Old Dread, there might be a hand on a shoulder to tell me I'd done something well." She hesitated. "When I was a little girl, so much more was communicated by touch. My mother held me. My nurse dressed me. I walked arm in arm with the other children when we played in the market square." Her gaze came back to John, and when it did, he fancied he could see the thoughts marching through her head. "That feeling of closeness with others . . . is that what it is to be an ordinary person?"

John moved to the edge of the bed, glanced around his bedroom before answering. This room had once been Catherine's. She'd been an angry woman when John knew her; the bedtime stories she'd told him blended triumph with revenge. He'd soaked them up and wanted to be just like her.

"I'm not the best one to ask what it means to be an ordinary person," he answered her eventually. It was the most truthful response he could give her. He searched for the right words. "Catherine and Maggie didn't want me to be close to anyone. But there's something about love. I've felt it, and it made me feel more *alive* than almost anything else."

"Love," Maud said, testing out the word. "You loved Quin."

A touch of shame crawled over him, which he shook off. Maud understood him, and there was no need to be ashamed. "I did. I think she loved me too, though she shouldn't have. But training with you also made me feel alive. I think I loved it"—he smiled—"even when I hated it."

The Young Dread moved, bringing herself, in one smooth motion, closer to John on the edge of the bed. From there she studied him with her lioness gaze. "I think I have loved it too, training you. Yet I feel such things only because I've been awake in the world so long. Too long. When I'm living as a true Dread, stretching myself out *There* and coming into the world for only a few days at once, I don't think like this, I don't *feel* like this. Love is a distant memory at most. More often, I don't think of it and I don't need it." She tugged at the ends of her hair in a very human gesture. "I am a Dread. I'm a Dread who must find another to become a Dread with me."

"Me," he said softly. When she broke eye contact, John realized that he'd been holding his breath, and only the fact of her looking away allowed him to inhale.

"If you wish," she answered. "But if you don't, I still must find someone to train. Quin, perhaps."

"She would never give up Shinobu."

"You may be right. Love, again. But I will find someone. It could be one of the children here on *Traveler*. Kaspar learns very quickly."

John nudged her with his elbow and whispered, "Don't give up on me yet."

"No? You told me you couldn't trust yourself to be a Dread. Has that changed?"

John shook his head. "The killing *There* . . . I hated it. But I've lived in Catherine's and Maggie's shadows for so long. I still *think* like my mother did."

"In time, your thoughts will surely change."

At this angle, the light through his window painted her cheekbones with a subtle illumination, which made John want to look away again. It was too strange to see her as a girl, sitting next to him on the edge of his bed.

He asked, "Does being a Dread have to be two people traveling alone through time?" he asked.

"Not alone. We would be Dreads together."

"But it sounds as if we'd be alone. No love, our minds stretched out from resting *There* until we're hardly human."

Her hand came to his face. Very gently she brushed his cheek with the backs of her fingers; then she slowly took in his physical self, his skin, his hair, his face. All the while John could see the girl inside the Dread. She was trying to come out of her primeval skin and into the room with him.

"I am human, you know," she whispered.

"You are . . . for now. But you've said you'll change when you go back to being a Dread. And I'd change if I followed you."

"When you've changed, you won't mind. You will hear the hum of the universe more clearly."

He smiled at that description. "Could a Dread be something different than it was?" he asked her. "The Middle Dread is gone, and the Old Dread left you in charge. Couldn't you decide what your life should be? Maybe less time spent *There,* more in the world. As long as you were doing the right things, is there any difference?"

Maud regarded him in silence, and John wondered if he'd gone too far. Who was he to suggest that she change an ancient tradition so that it might be easier for him to take part?

"I'm sorry," he said.

He thought she was going to get up and leave. Instead she dropped herself back to lie on the bed. "Don't be sorry. Your mother said something like that to me, many years ago."

"She did?"

It was strange when Maud spoke to him about Catherine. The Young Dread had known Catherine when she was a teenager, and though that had been nearly twenty years ago, for Maud almost no time had passed. When she spoke of Catherine, it felt as if she were breathing life into his long-gone mother. He was desperate to know more but anxious about what she might say.

"Would it bother you to hear about the night she was disrupted?" the Young Dread asked.

"Maybe. Tell me anyway."

He lay down next to Maud, though no part of him touched any part of her. Instead, side by side, they stared up through the window at the stars.

"I know you were there, under the floor," she told him.

They'd spoken of this the first time they'd ever spoken, about how a seven-year-old John had hidden beneath the floor of his mother's London apartment when Briac Kincaid and the Middle Dread came to get rid of her. They'd dragged Alistair and the Young Dread along with them.

"How much did you see and hear?" she asked him.

John took a deep breath and allowed the memory of that night to get close enough to examine. The trick was not to think about it too deeply, because then it would overwhelm him. His mother had arrived at the apartment, already bleeding and badly wounded. She'd helped him hide in a secret spot beneath a bench, and from there he'd seen glimpses of others arriving, and after that the flash of a disruptor gun.

"I closed my eyes and covered my ears," he whispered. He remembered the strange, slow voice of the Middle Dread, and the harsher, louder voice of Briac Kincaid. But he couldn't remember what they'd said—he'd been small and terrified. "But I saw you tying up my mother's injury."

"It bothered me to see her bleeding," the Young Dread told him. "Catherine was older then than when I had first known her, but she didn't look much different from how she had as a girl. The Middle Dread had ordered justice against her—she'd tried to trap him into overtly breaking a Seeker law, tried to get proof of him killing Seekers, but she'd failed, and he was furious.

"Briac had warned the Middle Dread of the trap, and he—Briac—was there to make sure Catherine didn't survive." Her hand touched John's arm on the bed next to her to soften what she was saying. "Briac wanted your mother to help him, but when she wouldn't, he wanted to get rid of her." When she went on, it was in a low whisper. "Your mother bargained for your education. They wanted her journal. Before giving it to them, she made Briac agree that he would train you honestly."

John had failed to keep the memory at arm's length. His throat constricted. He remembered the desperation in Catherine's voice, even though he hadn't heard her words to her attackers.

"He didn't train me honestly."

"I imagine not. She tried to bind him into helping you, but he had no intention of obeying Catherine in any way."

When the Young Dread said nothing more, John whispered, "Thank you for caring about her on that night."

"I didn't argue or fight with the Middle Dread. I should have."

Maud turned onto her side, so that she was facing him. "My old master told me it's not the clever mind that matters, or the cunning plans. It is the good heart, because a good heart will choose wisely."

John thought of his mother lying on the floor of her small apartment in London, a puddle of blood around her, drawing her last breaths before Briac disrupted her. Her thoughts had been of John and of what could have been.

He faced the Young Dread, only a foot between them in the dimness of his room. "Are you saying what I was saying?" he asked her. "That you can choose what it means to be a Dread as long as your intentions are good?"

"Perhaps. But for us to change what it means to be a Dread, you would first have to commit yourself."

They were both silent for a while, looking at each other. Her hair fell about her shoulders and neck, and the glow of the night sky glinted in her pale brown eyes. The weight of her gaze was like a physical force.

"How can I live up to you?" he asked her quietly.

"You are already trying."

John leaned forward. Gently, gravely, he touched his lips to hers. The Young Dread did not pull away from him, but neither did she kiss him back.

When he drew his head away, she was looking at him curiously. Her hand went to her lips as if she could capture the essence of the kiss with her fingertips. John should have felt an awkwardness in this moment, but there was nothing uncomfortable between them.

"So I have been kissed," the Young Dread said softly. With a subtle inflection he recognized as humor, she told him, "Let it never be said that I'm not intimate or passionate."

John laughed. "Did you enjoy it?"

She touched her lips again. "If I were to stay in the world much longer, maybe I would enjoy it very much."

He wanted to kiss her again, but a thought that had been nagging him for hours, even while he slept, abruptly came clear.

"When Shinobu attacked Maggie, I thought he'd shown up just to stop her, like we did." From the ocean, John had seen Maggie hovering in the sky, readying her weapon for another energy burst at *Traveler*. Shinobu had knocked her over and collapsed the anomaly. "But the more I look back over that moment, the more I think that's not why he was there. He was limping, did you notice? He could barely stand." He focused on the brief glimpse he'd had of Shinobu. John had been bobbing in the water, the anomaly dozens of yards above him, but even so, he'd taken in so many details. "Getting to his feet was all he could manage to do, yet he was dead focused on Maggie. And then he collapsed."

Maud thought about this and nodded slightly.

"What if she brought him there and has been using him?" he asked. "She does that, finds a way to control someone . . . the way she made my grandfather help me. The way she made me help her." He sat up, filled with the certainty of what he'd seen. "I know what would prove that I'm different, Maud."

The Young Dread sat up next to him, waiting for him to explain himself.

"I hated Shinobu," he told her. "Maybe I still hate him a little. He was better than I was, and he was the one who deserved Quin's attention." He stood, already contemplating a plan of action. "I'm going to find him, and make sure he's all right."

"How will that prove anything about yourself?" she asked.

John ran his hands through his hair, found his shirt and pulled it on. "Because I really, really don't want to help him."

CHAPTER 36

SHINOBU

The Watcher's boot came down on Shinobu's arm.

The bone snapped, again.

His wrist sagged.

Shinobu moaned, because of course it hurt. But so many things had hurt for so long that he was starting to feel as if all this were happening to someone else. The focal buzzed around his head, its cool fingers combing through his thoughts. In a way, it was *exciting* to see his own limbs being damaged.

She's breaking me.

It's good to break things.

"That's enough." Maggie shooed away the Watcher as he was raising his foot to stamp on Shinobu's other arm. "One break is enough for today. I know you're getting the point, hmm?" Her hands shook slightly, as they always did, but Maggie was calm and businesslike, and not unfriendly, as she began to set his newly broken limb.

She's cold-blooded.

Life would be easier if I could be as cold as she is.

Maggie had dragged him back to Dun Tarm after the mess with the Seekers *There*. He'd betrayed her, and she had not been pleased.

Well, that was a vast understatement. The last week had been a haze of aching sleep punctuated by intense pain as Watchers—the ones who had been left safely at Dun Tarm while most of the rest marched through the darkness *There* and got themselves killed—broke his limbs one after the other, again and again.

For the first few days, he'd thought she was keeping him alive because killing him swiftly wouldn't be sufficient punishment. Now he thought maybe she'd grown to like him—or at least grown to like torturing him.

He watched as she put splints on his broken arm and wrapped a bandage around them. It had become a routine, almost boring.

She's breaking me.

It's good to break things.

"Look at your choices," she said when she'd finished with the bandage. The sympathy in her voice was almost as bad as the torture.

She hates me. I'd rather hear her hate.

No, she cares for me.

She held up two different needles, which swam across Shinobu's vision, because his arm was killing him.

"This one is the permanent poison"—she waggled one syringe and then the other—"and this one has the reconstructors that will mend the fracture." She was his doting grandmother, offering him his choice of two different sorts of candy. He imagined washing the words off himself with a long hot shower. When he tried to turn away, she held his chin. Firmly.

I wish she would just kill me.

But Quin . . .

"Which one?" Maggie asked him.

Shinobu slowly located his own jaw and tongue and made them move. Inside the focal, with his arm throbbing, this was like operating a piece of machinery from across the room. He heard himself say, "The re . . . re . . . recon . . . the good one."

"You still want to live? I'm so pleased."

He felt the prick of a needle at the very spot where his bone had just been broken. Cold and pain rushed in as she emptied the syringe. He didn't know which one she'd used. With each bone break she'd kept up the suspense—had she injected the poison or the medicine?

She's going to kill me.

She's going to mend me.

While he was waiting to discover which, she mused, "I love taking care of young people. It's a calling close to my heart." Shinobu had been treated to a number of such friendly chats while preparing to die. "Boys are all right—you're all right, I've kept you here, haven't I?—but girls are my favorite, and if they're foxes and stags, I know they're mine."

Shinobu wanted to close his eyes, plug his ears, but he was mesmerized by her face and voice. She'd been telling him some version of this all week.

Finally the burn of the injection became the pain of his bones being forced, beyond all normal expectations, to knit themselves together. He allowed himself a sigh of relief; she'd injected him with the cellular reconstructors. Again.

The relief was short-lived, because the reconstructors soon became agonizing. Maggie went out of focus above him. He was losing consciousness.

Do I want to be alive?

I do, if Quin is real.

Quin, are you real?

What if Quin were nothing more than a fever dream, an opium vision, a ghost in his focal?

Distantly, Shinobu felt tears on his cheeks.

CHAPTER 37

QUIN

Quin, are you real?

Quin opened her eyes to complete darkness. Her first thought was that Dex had taken her to no-space again. But that couldn't be right. She was clearheaded, and the stale air carried the taste of old stone.

She touched cold rock beneath her, and reaching out a tentative hand, she met a rock wall. She groped in the other direction, and her fingers found the flare, as though it had been left within her reach. She clicked it on, and the small room was filled with its white, faintly hissing glow. The space was no bigger than a large closet, four walls, with a series of nooks in one of them, designs carved everywhere.

"Oh, God," she said when she saw Dex.

He sat in a corner with blood all over his face. She crawled over to him, found him awake and staring. The blood had come from a gash in his forehead, which was still dripping.

Quin dug around in the outer pocket of his robe, where she'd learned he kept necessities of first aid, and pulled out a length of clean cloth, which she pressed to the cut. His eyes were focused on the middle distance, and she wasn't sure he saw her.

"I was trying to get out," he whispered.

Quin looked around and saw blood on one of the walls where he must have smashed his head. She drew in her breath with a hiss; how hard had he hit himself? "Dex . . . couldn't you have used the medallion? You must have brought us here with it. It could have gotten you out of wherever we are."

"Sometimes I can't make sense of what to do."

"You were supposed to take me to Shinobu. Where are we?" She had felt Shinobu's mind a moment ago, which meant he was alive somewhere. He was alive! They only had to begin to look. "Dex—"

"I die here," he said quietly.

Quin couldn't keep the sharpness out of her voice. "The wound on your head won't be fatal," she snapped.

"I don't die from this!" He was indignant, which brought him a little closer to sanity. He pointed at the center of the floor. "I die right there."

She took Dex's hand and positioned it over the cloth on his forehead. "Hold that tight," she ordered.

While he held the bandage to his head, Quin took the flare and examined the spot he'd indicated. She had no idea why she was humoring him or what she expected to find—a painted outline of his body on the stone? But he'd told her enough truth so far to make her investigate.

At first glance there was just the gritty floor of a chamber that felt as though it had been untouched since time out of mind. But some impulse made her look more closely—perhaps it was a slight unevenness to the pigment of the rock. There was a patch of dark, dark brown, almost black. It was faint but spread across the floor like a puddle. And there were smears in a few places, as if a hand had run through the dark liquid. If it had been liquid, it had dried up lifetimes ago and was now no more than a flaky layer on the surface of the rock.

"This was blood?" she asked, intrigued now, despite herself.

"Yes."

"Hmm." It was not an unreasonable claim.

She came back to Dex and dug again through the outer pocket of his robe, drew out the small flask and the needle and thread, which she'd used on him before. She doused the needle with the alcohol from the flask—he never drank it; it was only for doctoring—and then removed the cloth from his forehead. The cut wasn't too bad, now that she could see it properly.

"They fought," Dex said as she held up the needle. "Matheus wanted to get rid of Quilla. He said to his younger brother, 'You've had your time with her. It's enough. Let's end it.'"

His face was troubled and he said no more for a while. In the silence, Quin made three careful sutures, with Dex oblivious to the pain of the needle. When she was finished and examining her work in the light of the flare, she said, "Dex, can we—"

"It's good when you're with me," he said, not hearing her. He put a hand on her shoulder and pushed himself up to his feet. "You've stitched my head, and somehow you've put that other thread back into my hands."

Before Quin realized what he was doing, Dex had touched two patterns carved into one of the walls of the tiny room that confined them. The patterns compressed beneath his fingers—they were, in fact, intricately designed latches. With a shift of his weight and a press of his hands, the whole wall moved, swinging outward like a door.

"There we go," Dex said.

Quin came up beside him and was surprised to see that they were looking out at a familiar space. "We're in the cavern beneath the castle ruins?" she asked.

"Yes."

She walked out into the vast, echoing chamber and got her bearings. The "door" she'd just stepped through had been concealed ingeniously in one of the cavern's side walls.

"You brought us directly to that little room with your medallion?"

"I couldn't find this room when we were here before," he explained. He was crossing the cavern floor as if following a will-o'-the-wisp. "I couldn't remember . . . and then I did. When you were angry at me."

He stopped near the base of the stairs that would lead them up to the castle crypt.

"Desmond was here," he said. "Matheus was there, where you're standing."

CHAPTER 38

MATHEUS AND DESMOND

Matheus and Desmond faced each other across the torch-lit cavern. They'd fought with whipswords until they were exhausted, and now they'd each retreated to a different side of the cave to rest. Desmond hoped they were done, but he kept his whipsword loosely in his hand in case Matheus didn't yet see reason. His brother was stubborn when he was angry.

"We're too evenly matched," Matheus called. "Neither of us will win with whipswords!"

"Yes," Desmond agreed. "So why are we fighting? I'm not giving up my wife. I would never ask that of you."

"You and Father ask more of me all the time. More training, more work, more rules." Matheus slashed his whipsword and sent the blade through a series of shape changes on reflex. The weapon cast moving shadows over the walls.

Even for Desmond, it was difficult to read Matheus's face. His brother had lately carried a permanent look of hatred, regardless of what he was feeling.

"You're cleverer than I am," Matheus called, "but an idiot in some things. The important things."

With a sound of dissatisfaction, he collapsed his whipsword. Desmond did the same, expecting that they would shake hands and be friends again. Matheus approached across the cavern floor, and Desmond went to meet him halfway. Desmond should have noticed the air growing thick, but the air beneath the castle was always heavy with dust and age.

His older brother's dark hair was wet with perspiration, his face flushed. Beneath Matheus's usual scowl, Desmond saw traces of a smile. *He realizes how ridiculous he's being,* Desmond thought, relieved. *He's going to apologize.*

The brothers neared, and as if in proof of this sentiment, Matheus said, "We're done here, Brother. No more arguing. No more fighting."

"I'm so glad—"

Desmond never finished the sentence, because Matheus fired the impellor that had been concealed in his sleeve. Desmond was flung off his feet like a child's doll. Before he hit the ground, he saw that there were no longer traces of a smile on Matheus's face—his older brother watched him with a full grin.

Desmond was stunned by the impact. By the time he'd gotten his wits about him, Matheus was approaching with the disruptor strapped across his chest. Its heavy, iridescent body, with a thousand holes across its wide barrel, was pointing directly at Desmond.

Desmond wasn't frightened, because he'd designed the disruptor himself. The worst it might do to him was make his thoughts run in circles for a few hours—undignified, but not harmful. He was still too dazed to sense the true danger.

"Are you going to do something unpleasant to me while my

thoughts are going round and round?" Desmond asked as he pushed himself back up into a sitting position.

He shook his head to clear it, felt at his chest where he might have broken a rib. He was so unaware of what his brother had in mind that Desmond was actually worried about whether a broken rib would make it too painful to ride a horse. (He and Quilla had planned a journey to the market town the following day.)

"Am I going to do something unpleasant?" Matheus repeated. "Isn't that what you're always accusing me of doing?"

That was when Desmond noticed what was happening to the disruptor. It was hissing and crackling, and little blue forks of electricity were crawling across Matheus's hands where they touched the controls. The weapon had never done that before.

Matheus wore an entirely different expression than Desmond had ever seen on his brother's face. He still had the hint of a smile, but his gaze was as intense as a fire. It was as though Desmond were a squirrel that Matheus was about to skin for sport.

"You've done something with the disruptor?" Desmond asked, finally scared.

"Oh yes." The weapon began to whine, a high, piercing sound that hurt Desmond's ears.

"You made it worse?"

"No," Matheus answered. "I've made it better."

Desmond tried to lunge to his feet, but he was dizzy, and found that he had wedged himself between two jutting seams of rock. "Matheus, please—"

Matheus fired the disruptor before Desmond had even finished speaking.

There were so many more sparks than Desmond had expected. They came at him in a wave. He lifted his hands to ward them off, but they covered his arms, his head; they coated his body. They ran over him like water, and then they moved, took shape, became a river, a waterfall.

Desmond staggered. He couldn't see anything properly, except the sparks running around his body in a storm. He swiped at the air, to push Matheus away and find his way out.

"Where are you going, Little Brother?" Matheus asked.

Desmond couldn't keep his thoughts straight, but he heard the pleasure in his older brother's voice and knew he would not be getting out of the cavern alive. Matheus had planned this, perhaps had been planning it for a very long time.

Desmond made it as far as the wall of emblems before Matheus took hold of him again. He grabbed his younger brother by the hair, pulled out his knife, and stabbed him in the belly three times. Desmond felt the blows and the pain and could do nothing.

Matheus pushed him to the floor.

"You can die now, Little Brother," Matheus said.

Desmond lay on the ground, wondering if he was already dead. When Matheus said and did nothing else, Desmond began to understand that his brother was gone. He had left before Desmond died, so Matheus could tell their parents honestly that he hadn't been there when it happened.

But Desmond was still alive. He crawled along the floor, hardly able to see where he was going. He crawled until he reached the little room off the cavern. His thoughts were spinning away, but there was one he kept hold of: if I can hide, if I can disappear, I can survive.

Inside the little room, his blood was leaving his body. The blood was warm, but as it trickled out, he was cold.

And then . . . blessed luck.

A box in the corner, a latch, a lid. Inside, his blind, grasping hands found his mother's store of medicine, packed by their father all those years ago and still able to save his life. It took him a very long time to organize even one new thought, but when he finally did, he injected himself, and kicked shut the door.

He lay there, hidden and alone in the darkness, invisible, until the blood stopped.

CHAPTER 39

QUIN

As he finished his story, Dex crossed the cavern and returned to the tiny cell behind the cavern wall. Inside the small space, he crouched on the floor and touched the faint dark stain that he claimed was from Desmond's blood.

"It wasn't a disruptor like you have now," he told Quin, who had followed him and was standing in the doorway. "If he'd been hit with a modern disruptor, there would have been no hope. That disruptor had the first modification of many. Very bad, but not quite fatal. It took Matheus many years to make disruptors as bad as they are now."

Quin watched Dex's hands tracing unconscious patterns on the floor, as if his muscles remembered struggling here for his life.

"When they finally thought to look in here," he whispered, "Desmond was gone—I was gone."

"So you didn't die? Desmond didn't die," she said, when she dared to say anything at all. Every time she thought Dex was closing in on a profound revelation, the inconsistencies overwhelmed her.

"To *them* I died, and I never came back to life. But this part of me"—he touched his face and his chest, as if they were foreign objects, possessions he had acquired in some far-off land—"this survived."

A long silence fell between them. Dex was staring up at her, using her as a lifeline to pull himself back into the present. When she thought he had arrived, she asked, "You *injected* yourself?"

"It saved my life."

"But . . . what do you mean, 'injected'? If Desmond—if *you*—were from the Middle Ages, there was no injection, Dex. They were using leeches and bleeding people."

"You have to stop doing that," he whispered.

"Asking questions?" In her frustration, she said the words sharply. She controlled her voice and added, "You can't expect me not to ask any questions."

"You can't expect *me* to know the whole story until I've felt my way through it." He got back to his feet, looking flustered. "You keep asking me what's at the end of the thread, but I haven't gotten to that part of the labyrinth yet. I'm making my way by inches."

He paced for a while, eventually stopping by the little room's back wall, which had folded stone nooks all along it. He looked as exasperated as Quin felt. His hands were twitching as he said, "Can't you understand? When the sparks hit, everything Desmond had been thinking became permanent. Everything he'd been thinking poured into and out of him, over and over." Dex directed his restless hands along the wall's many ridges as though searching for something to hold. "He was terrified. He hid his head, covered his eyes, couldn't face his attacker, or he knew he'd die. He wanted to hide to save himself. That's what he was thinking when the sparks hit, and those thoughts became who Desmond *was*."

He touched a spot on the wall that seemed to be meaningful to him. He paused a moment before his hands continued searching.

"After Desmond had gone, his mother and father found the blood. They knew what Matheus had done. He denied it, but they knew."

"How do you—or Desmond—know what they did after he left?" She asked it in the softest possible tones, probing the contradiction, so that he himself might notice it.

Dex made a noise somewhere between a sigh and a laugh. "Oh, I watched them. That's how I know. Desmond hid outside their camp, followed at a distance, spied on them at night. But he couldn't speak or bring himself to approach another person for years afterward." He located another spot that seemed to mean something to him. "Quilla was dead too," he said roughly. "Matheus did it. Lay in wait for her in the woods. By luck, Adelaide was with her grandmother and she lived." He turned to Quin and whispered, "It wasn't really luck. Desmond's mother arranged things in order for Matheus to dispose of Quilla. She'd never been fond of her. But she wanted her grandchild."

His hands slid inquisitively across the wall again.

"The father suspected what the mother had done, and the mother blamed him for Matheus's actions. The way he'd brought them all there, the focal, the harsh training—all of that had driven Matheus crazy, she said.

"They argued viciously, but in the end, she extracted a promise. There were many Seekers by then, well-trained and good people, and she made the father agree to take Matheus far away from all of them. He and Matheus would spend most of their lives out of the world, in no-space, so that there would be both distance and time separating Matheus from everyone else.

"But the promise was this: that he would never harm Matheus, that he would protect him with his life, because Matheus's fate was his own fault. The father must live with what he'd done and what he'd turned his son into."

When Dex had found another spot, he stopped moving. "Once Matheus and his father had gone, the mother took her grand-daughter, Adelaide, and brought her up as the rightful heir to everything my father and I knew." Dex's hands clenched into fists, and he pressed his knuckles into the wall. "And Desmond began his long trek through the circular realms of no-space. From then until the moment he found you there."

Dex held his hands out toward the wall, and then, in a pattern that was hard to follow, his fingers touched dozens of different locations, each of the spots he had hesitated over. After this display, he slid his hands into two of the nooks and pulled. The whole wall moved toward him. The intricate folds of rock shifted, interlaced, lined up, and created a new wall that curved in one elegant sweep into the tiny cell. It rumbled into place, displaying carvings that had been only rough shadows before.

Dex stepped back to view his handiwork.

Quin barely glanced at what he'd done. She was staring at Dex without knowing who she was seeing. Was he ancient? Was he modern?

"You're telling me that the father in your story, and his son Matheus, became *the Dreads*?" she whispered.

"The name 'Dreads' came later, as did my father's noble credo for himself and his son. Well, I should say that my father always had noble intentions, but attributing them to Matheus never worked very well."

"Your father and brother are the Old and Middle Dread."

"Yes," he told her. "And my mother is Maggie."

CHAPTER 40

NOTT

Nott fingered the knife in his pocket meditatively. He'd stolen it from the training room, though "stolen" wasn't really the right word, since he was given free access to all of the training weapons on the airship. Even the simple pleasure of thievery was ruined here.

The knife was the smallest weapon he could find, and it fit easily into his trouser pocket, while leaving room for his hand. He pressed the pad of his index finger against the blade. The knife was used by the horde of brats who were now on the airship and so wasn't particularly sharp. It would do in a pinch, though. He'd done damage to opponents with less.

Most of the nurses had retired for the night. There were only two on duty now, a man and a woman in the odd white clothing they all wore. They were at the little desk at the center point of the curved hallway, clacking away at the computers, doing God knew what. The only important point was that they'd glanced over at Nott when he entered the hallway, and after that they'd ignored him entirely.

This passageway skirted the training room on one side, though you couldn't see into it from here. On the other side of the passage were the rooms with the injured Seekers in their hospital beds.

He peered into the first room, where a woman lay asleep. The beds on the airship were, Nott had reluctantly admitted to himself, a luxury he'd never conceived of. They were much too soft, but when he slept on *Traveler,* he sometimes imagined he'd been wrapped in a cloud and was floating weightlessly through the night.

But never mind the beds. The woman wasn't hooked up to any strange contraptions. From this, Nott deduced that she must be nearly healed. *Which means she'll be up and about and ordering me around like a real Seeker soon,* he thought sourly.

An eagle had been drawn on the foot of her bed, signifying which house she belonged to. Maggie was inconsistent about the eagle Seekers. She didn't hate them outright—she'd let Shinobu live. But would she want another eagle Seeker in the world? Maggie was certainly some kind of a witch, and witches were known to be fickle. Nott exhaled with uncertainty.

He took another few steps down the hallway and looked in the window of the next room. A child was sound asleep there. The boy wasn't injured—Nott knew because he'd seen him in the training room. He was probably put here to be near a parent who was still recovering. There was something like a tiger drawn on the foot of his bed—like a tiger except for the very long teeth protruding from its mouth. He was pretty sure Maggie was opposed to that house.

He fingered the knife again and looked down the hallway. The night nurses were still ignoring him. How long would it take to slip into the room and permanently silence the boy? The child wasn't a good fighter, wouldn't put up much resistance, even if he woke up before Nott had finished his work.

But one wouldn't be enough. If he was going to do something that would make Maggie grateful, he'd have to think bigger. He looked down the curving passageway and tried to count the number of occupied rooms. If he were going to do this, he would have to find a way to distract the nurses so that he'd be able to get to all of the rooms before he was caught. But that was only half of it, wasn't it? He'd have to find a way off the airship and back to Maggie, if he wanted to claim the prize of his helmet from her.

And there was Aelred to consider. The bat had been injured when Maggie hit Nott with that evil black weapon of hers. Now Aelred was recuperating in a cage in Nott's cabin. He'd have to get him off the airship too.

Of course, Maggie hadn't asked Nott to dispose of these Seekers. She'd asked him to bring John back. Nott frowned at his see-through reflection in the glass window, wondering why he must always be at the mercy of another, larger person's orders. And why were those orders always confusing?

John's not about to go back to Maggie, that much is sure, he thought. Nott had nothing to offer Maggie, then, but getting rid of these people. That would surely count for something in her eyes.

Inside the room, the boy rolled over in his sleep, as if he sensed Nott's gaze upon him. Nott gripped the knife's handle in his trouser pocket. He envisioned the steps he would take: slipping through the door, moving silently across the floor, throwing back the covers, plunging the blade in, raising it—

Nott came over all ill and shaky, and he had to turn away. He leaned against the window, cursing himself. He was a Watcher, meant to put the rest of the world in its place. Sometimes that meant you had to kill people. The thought should have been thrilling. But . . . the boy might cry out, and he would stare up at Nott with big, dark, sad eyes . . . Nott swallowed nervously and pressed his hands into the wall to stop them from trembling. Was he actually *trembling*?

You've become the soft modern child you look like in the mirror. You can forget about ever using your helm again.

He stole one more glance through the window. The boy had thrown back his cover and was sleeping openmouthed and deeply, the way children did. Nott remembered that from a very long time ago, when his whole family had shared a few straw pallets in their tiny home.

Choose what you are, Nott! Are you weak and useless, or are you a vicious Watcher? He set his jaw and gripped the knife again.

"Nott, there you are."

Nott actually jumped. He dropped the knife back into his pocket and swung around to face John.

"I was, I wasn't . . ." Nott began. He was unexpectedly out of breath. He managed to gasp out, "I'm just standing here!"

"All right," John said, surprised.

"It *is* all right," Nott cried, struggling to appear calm.

John looked at Nott curiously, but he was obviously distracted by something in his own head. "Will you walk with me?" he asked.

"Yes," Nott answered quickly. He glanced behind them as they walked off, as if he might have left some visible trace of his intentions in the hallway, but there was nothing.

He followed, musing for the hundredth time on John's contradictions. He was taller than Nott and broad through the shoulders, and he was a fast and dangerous fighter. Nott would normally respect this, but he had a hard time thinking of John as anything but soft. John was too clean, for one thing. It was the kind of clean—down to the fingernails—that made Nott wonder if John had ever been dirty. Even when they'd been living on the Scottish estate, John had managed to keep himself scrubbed.

Nott examined his own fingernails, each of which had a small crescent of black beneath it. You had to work hard in a place like

Traveler to keep some dirt beneath your nails. It wasn't just a matter of refusing to wash your hands; you had to seek out things that were unclean and dig your fingers into them.

John, the fearsome fighter with the ladylike grooming habits, led Nott into the great room, which was empty at this hour. When he turned to Nott, it was obvious that he was consumed by some thought that was already galloping through his mind. Nott put his hands behind his back. Because, while he liked to think that he had "refused" to wash them, the truth was, he simply hid them from everyone when they got close.

"Do you know who Shinobu is?" John asked, oblivious to the arguments taking place in Nott's head.

Nott's face darkened. He'd told John and the Young Dread that he'd been with Maggie and the other Watchers, but he'd intentionally said nothing of Shinobu. Maggie had tasked Nott with convincing John that she was a good person and that John should return to her. If Nott had mentioned her torturing another Seeker, he thought his task would probably be much more difficult.

"Red hair . . . and tall?" Nott said, as if stretching his memory.

"Yes."

"I've seen him. On that bridge we was all on. He slid down the sail."

Nott said this with some awe and hoped John took the hint that real men didn't mind getting themselves dirty by sliding magnificently down sails.

"Did you ever see him with Maggie?" John asked.

Nott worked hard to keep his face noncommittal. "Mm?" he asked.

"I saw him with Maggie," John explained, "and I don't think it was his choice."

Nott raised his eyebrows in surprise. "I've seen him not so much with her as at entirely different times." Then he added, as additional insurance, in case John might later find him out, "Though, I can't say as they were *never* together. How could I?"

John paused, trying to parse this ambiguous answer. When he couldn't, he asked, "Will you show me where Maggie is?"

"You mean . . . you want me to *take you to her*?"

"Yes. Can you?"

It was Nott's turn to pause. He looked up at John and examined him for some sign of a trick. John's face wasn't cruel or scheming; he looked sincere. He was *asking* Nott to take him to Maggie. How had that happened?

Nott forced himself to smile, so that John would suspect nothing. This was a mistake. Probably on account of Nott's blackened teeth, John flinched and took a step back.

"What's the matter?" John asked.

"I'm—I'm smiling. Can't you tell?" Nott asked. "Because I know where she is."

CHAPTER 41

JOHN

Nott pointed silently across the fortress to two Watchers, that night's guards, who sat awake, lit by the dying embers of a fire. Everyone else was asleep, the uneven floor dotted with the black lumps of boys curled beneath their cloaks.

John and Nott had arrived by athame outside Dun Tarm, from where John had followed the boy in through an opening in the wall. Now John stepped down onto the broken flagstones right next to Shinobu's sleeping form. Nott was already moving silently toward the guards by the fire. He'd promised to distract anyone who was awake, to allow John to get Shinobu out—though John had a difficult time trusting Nott to follow through on much of anything.

The moon shone dimly between thick clouds, and through the branches of the stunted trees growing up from the fortress floor, casting just enough light for John to see by. Crouching down, he put a hand to Shinobu's chest. Shinobu was out cold, sleeping so deeply that John wondered if he'd been drugged. And he was wearing a focal. His face had the pallor of a corpse, and small forks of electricity crawled across his brow.

From Maud's training, John knew enough about focals to under-stand how dangerous and mind-altering it would be to fall asleep in one. How was Shinobu keeping a grip on his own thoughts at all? Perhaps he wasn't, John thought with an unwelcome stab of pity.

Quietly he sat Shinobu up and got his arms around Shinobu's chest, as the taller boy's head flopped to one side. With a mighty effort, John hauled him to his feet. Shinobu's head fell in the other direction, causing his whole body to tense; his arms jerked out as if fighting in a dream.

"It's okay," John breathed into his ear. When the spasm was over, Shinobu was dead weight again.

Nott was halfway to the fire, and still the two guards had noticed nothing—they were huddled low for warmth, probably half-asleep. The slumped shapes across the rest of the fortress floor hadn't moved at all.

John took a deep breath, got a better grip on Shinobu, who was still a sack of concrete in his arms. But when John began dragging him, everything changed. Shinobu's weight transformed from something insensate to something fully alive. He wrenched his head around to see who had hold of him.

"It's John," John whispered, hoping he could be heard over the crackle of the focal. "It's John. Shhh."

If Shinobu heard him, it was the wrong thing to say. His groggy cargo dropped forward like a slab of rock, pulling John off balance.

"Stop!" John hissed. "I'm getting you out of here. Don't wake them up."

Shinobu's elbow landed hard in John's ribs. He surged backward, throwing John to the ground beneath him.

"She's mending me!" Shinobu yelled. He could not have been louder if he'd been using a megaphone. "And you're ungrateful!"

All at once, the whole fortress was awake. Maggie's supply of Watchers had been greatly diminished by the fight *There*, but a dozen black shapes got to their feet. Nott was waving his arms feebly to attract the Watchers' attention, but they were entirely ignoring him and were looking directly at John.

And there was Maggie. She'd been by the fire, and now she was on her feet and walking toward her grandson.

John struggled to his knees, still clutching Shinobu against him. His captive pulled free and spun drunkenly to face him. Shinobu pulled back a fist to strike, and the two of them stared at each other, with no sense of recognition from Shinobu. Shinobu moved to strike, but before his fist connected with John's face, he crumpled and flopped to the ground.

"Stop! Do nothing." That was John's grandmother's voice, speaking to the Watchers. The boys went still.

John gathered Shinobu's limp form against him once more and got back to his feet with all eyes, including Maggie's, fixed upon him.

"It's all right, John," Maggie said.

She was dressed in the camouflage hunting outfit she'd been wearing during the fight *There*, her hair tidy even though she must have been asleep only moments earlier. She approached him slowly. "There's no need to sneak around. We're all here for you."

"Nothing you do is for me, Grandmother. Not anymore."

"John. You were making the wrong choice with those frozen Seekers. I acted for you, even when you wouldn't act. I was removing our enemies."

Watchers shifted out of John's path as he hauled Shinobu's limp form toward the lake, keeping his eyes on the boys nearest to him.

"No one is going to stop you," she said reasonably. "I want you to decide what happens to other Seekers, John. That's what we've been fighting for. So that you may make the right choices. If you want to take Shinobu, take him. He hasn't been useful to me. Quite the opposite."

"Nott, come here," John barked.

He'd reached an area of open floor near the water's edge. He let Shinobu slide down into a sitting position, and he drew out his athame, scanning the closest figures cautiously the whole time. At a sign from Maggie, the nearest Watchers backed away farther, giving John plenty of room.

"Come on, Nott," John said. "We'll go now."

Nott had come forward from the fire to stand next to Maggie. He regarded John, slowly shook his head.

"Nott, come on!" John said sharply. He wasn't going to leave the boy with this pack of murderers.

"Don't say 'Nott' like that," the boy responded. "If I choose to stay, I will. I fit here. I'm one of them."

"You can come back for him anytime, John," Maggie said. "I hope you will."

"Nott, come on! You don't want to stay here."

"I do," Nott answered.

The boy crossed his arms, and John saw that he had become entrenched in his defiance. John had no means of forcing him, and if Maggie changed her mind, John would be easily outmanned. If he wanted to take Shinobu, he had to get out now.

He tried one last time. "Nott . . ."

"You ought to stay with Maggie too."

"That's all right," Maggie said to Nott, though her eyes remained on John. "He will. He's gone soft on me, but it won't last."

John spared Nott a final glance, after which he struck his athame sharply against the lightning rod. He drew a circle in the air beside him, and as the anomaly took shape, he watched the boys who were eying him. Then he hefted Shinobu's dead weight onto his shoulder and stepped through the humming doorway.

When he turned to look back, Maggie had crossed the fortress and was standing at the threshold of the anomaly, looking in at him.

"We want the same things, John. You will see eventually and come back to me."

He turned from her and walked into the darkness. Maggie didn't follow.

CHAPTER 42

QUIN

"Prove it to me," Quin said.

"What?"

Dex was touching, one after another, the varied circles that were carved upon the wall. Each circle displayed incomprehensible designs that looked almost mathematical.

"Prove to me that you are who you say you are, that you're as old as the Old Dread."

"I'm not as old as the Old Dread," he said, as though Quin were simple. "How could I be as old as my own father?"

"Very easily, depending on how much time you or he spent in no-space," she retorted.

He smiled. "Ah, Quilla, you have me there. What would prove my history to you?"

He was calling her Quilla again. Nothing was straightforward about his story or about his mind.

"I think you're a very good storyteller, so good you make me feel like you were actually there, when really you're repeating a legend."

He sighed. "I like your version. Let's pretend I'm a magnificent storyteller." He closed his eyes and appeared to let his hands direct themselves. He drew his medallion out of the leather straps and fitted the stone disc into a circular recess at the very center of the wall.

"This is my medallion," he said, eyes still closed, all trace of lightness gone from his voice. "My father made four of them, one for each of us, so that we could find each other, and find our way through no-space—though his notions about no-space were somewhat different then. This room, this is where we tune them, where we refine them, where we give them new functions. The wall of emblems out in the cavern, for athames, is cruder and came much later."

He opened his eyes, and his fingers sank into two of the smaller carvings. The intricate designs had been etched so deeply that his fingers could fit inside and around the patterns. He began to turn them, one after another, as an engineer might adjust the dials on some enormous and complicated machine.

"This setting allows me to find Matheus," he said when he'd stopped moving the carvings. A shiver ran through him. He waited for Quin to examine the pattern, though she did so with no understanding of what it meant, before he turned the carvings again, choosing new positions. "With this I could find my father—though I know exactly where he is already, because he's sleeping in my territory."

He looked at this pattern for a while, and then, with the surprised assurance of one who has suddenly remembered something he practiced a hundred times as a child, he turned each carving again, creating a new pattern.

"This setting," he whispered. "This is the one."

He drew the bent metal rod from one of his pockets and tapped it, one time, against his medallion in the center of the wall. A penetrating rumble passed through the room. He touched the medallion with his fingers and whispered, "It doesn't look different, does it?"

Quin studied the stone disc and shook her head. The medallion hadn't moved or changed in appearance in any way.

"But it is different," he told her, leaning his head against the wall. "I've made it a weapon."

"What sort of weapon?" The disc looked the same as it had before—harmless.

Dex didn't answer. He was already adjusting the carvings again. When he'd created yet another pattern, he said, "And this would find my mother's medallion—if I tapped the wall now."

He did not tap it. His confidence appeared to drain out of him as he studied the pattern. It was like watching a swimmer overwhelmed by rising waves.

"Adelaide turned on Maggie in the end. She didn't like her grandmother's view of the world," he said. "When that happened, Maggie began to leave the world for long stretches of time, just as we all did. She comes back for Adelaide's own children and grandchildren and descendants, always with the thought that they are more worthy than anyone else with an athame. But she is out of the world so often, she has no idea what is really happening." He touched his medallion at the center of the wall, one finger tracing the atom emblem meditatively. "My mother never learned how to use her medallion properly. She demanded all the rights of my father's knowledge, but she refused to study the intricacies of how anything worked. That was for other, lesser people to worry about."

"Dex," Quin began. He could bring her to Maggie—and Shinobu, if Maggie still had him—right now.

"When I get close to my family, even in my thoughts, I'm back here, Quilla, with the disruptor sparks and Matheus's knife . . ."

If he had been walking through a labyrinth all this time, Dex was surely approaching the center of the maze. Even without changing her vision, Quin could see the cataract of energy surging from his head to his hip. His eyes were becoming wild. She was about to lose him entirely.

"You want me to take you to your friend," Dex said, "but *he's there, she's there.*"

Quin reached a hand to his arm to calm him. "Dex—"

Misunderstanding, he pushed her roughly away. "I said no!"

Without thinking, Quin pushed him back, and watched his eyes come into focus when she did. He stared at her with a predatory glare, dangerous but less wild. *Maybe a fight is what he needs now.* She pushed him again.

Dex turned, surprised and furious. Quin leapt backward and out of the small cell and into the cavern proper as he advanced on her. She pulled the impellor from her cloak pocket, not to fire at him but hoping it would focus his attention further.

If she imagined she was fast enough or skilled enough to actually fight Dex, however, she was mistaken. He struck the impellor from her hand with a blow so fast and precise that she experienced it only as her hand going numb and the weapon dropping to the stone floor. She assailed him with a series of blows that she'd trained into a fine art as a Seeker apprentice, once even besting Shinobu's father, the fearsome Alistair MacBain, with them. Dex met each blow easily, and then the heel of his hand connected with her chest and she was thrown backward.

With Dread-like speed, he was on top of her when she landed, his knees pinning down her arms, a knife in his hand, raised above her chest. He looked at her with the same dangerous eyes she'd first seen in the cave behind the waterfall, hardly human.

"You want me to end up on the floor, bleeding all my warmth onto cold stone," he told her, his voice a growl in the back of his throat.

He clenched the knife convulsively. His whole arm was trembling.

She didn't think he would stab her, but it was impossible to read him; he'd never struck her until now.

"Do you know what happens when you force someone against their will, Quilla? When you try to make them something they're not? Over and over?"

His eyes had lost focus. Quin made a sudden twist to get out from beneath him, but Dex understood what she was doing long before the motion was done. He shifted his weight, pinning her thoroughly.

"After my father took Matheus away, he doubled Matheus's training to drive the murderousness out of him. He put him in the focal for weeks on end to smooth out the 'distractions' in my brother's mind—as if a natural love of causing pain were merely a distraction, a habit Matheus had accidentally picked up somewhere, and not a basic part of his nature." Dex made a guttural sound of disbelief. "The focal strengthened the worst parts of my brother but made him better able to hide them from our father—until he caught Matheus in the act of murder. He wanted to kill Matheus then—he would have been justified to do it, but he'd made a promise. Do you see? My father wanted to change the world, but he couldn't take the necessary steps to protect other people."

His unfocused eyes were looking down at her with hatred. If he struck her with the knife, it would be because he mistook her for someone else.

"Our medallions are what wake us when we're stretched out in the hidden dimensions. So instead of killing him, my father threatened to take Matheus's medallion and cast him into no-space to sleep until the end of time.

"Matheus groveled and swore he would change. And for a time, the Old Dread believed he'd transformed his son into a trustworthy Middle Dread."

Dex's eyes shifted to something closer, as if watching an approaching phantom. Quin's arms were falling asleep under his weight; her eyes were fixed on the knife held over her.

"That's when my brother began his grand plan. He might have chosen to kill the Old Dread and be free of his rules and punishment, but he didn't. That would be too gentle. He decided to do something much worse. He wanted to destroy all of our father's accomplishments, because that would hurt him the most."

"So he's been turning Seekers against each other, in order to get rid of all of us," Quin said quietly. She realized she had already heard the rest of this story, from Shinobu, who'd learned it from her own father, who had chosen to side with the Middle Dread.

Dex's eyes came back to her, and she could tell that he saw Quin herself for the first time in several minutes. "You knew?" he breathed.

"Shinobu learned the truth," she told him.

"Maggie has only noticed Seekers attacking Adelaide's descendants. She thinks the attacks are personal. She hasn't seen the poison being fed to all Seekers by my brother."

"But, Dex, whatever the Middle Dread did, it's over. He's dead. You've been telling me this story that I thought was a myth, and you don't know the most important part."

She watched the disbelief slowly take shape on Dex's face as he returned fully to her.

"What?" he asked, as if he could not grasp what she'd said.

"The Young Dread stabbed your brother through the heart two months ago," she told him. "I saw him die. He's gone."

"Matheus is dead," Dex said to himself, trying out the sound of the words.

His relief was immense but short-lived. "Matheus is dead, but I will still have to face her," he muttered. "She didn't wield the knife, Quilla, but she wanted me gone just as much as he did. And she wanted you gone too. And so many others."

Quin looked up at the knife that still hovered above her.

"Are you going to kill me, Dex? The one person who is helping you?"

He glanced at the blade as if he'd never seen it before, let it drop to his side. "I didn't mean to threaten you."

He leaned back on his heels, so that he was not pinning her down. Quin slid out from beneath him. Instead of moving away, she knelt closer. A disruptor had made him insane, but even so he clung to goodness, and she could feel it. They could help each other as they'd already agreed to do.

Whatever he intended with Maggie and the Old Dread was a mess she wanted no part of, but Quin found herself throwing her own fate in with Dex's regardless.

"I want your help, Dex. Let me give you mine. I can't heal you myself, but I know someone who might be able to do it."

CHAPTER 43

SHINOBU

Shinobu hung limply off John's shoulder, unable to move any part of himself. He was being carried through the black dimensions *There*. Again. How many times was this going to happen?

After a while, there was another anomaly and John was stepping back into the world. Shinobu was assaulted by a sharp gust of wind from the cold night—much colder here, wherever they were, than it had been at Dun Tarm. John turned, and Shinobu could see black cliffs rising up around them, almost in a circle, and above the rim of those cliffs, a night sky full of brilliant stars. And there was water. He could hear it running down those steep rock faces and trickling onto the ground.

"I can't bring you to the London hospital," John said, the first thing he'd said since they'd left Dun Tarm. "Maggie knows that place. And at any other hospital, they'd ask a lot of questions."

Shinobu hated John. He didn't want to be dangling helplessly at his mercy . . . and yet it was probably for the best that he was away from Maggie, wasn't it? Or was she good? He'd told John at first that he wanted to stay.

John crouched down and guided Shinobu's body into a mostly gentle fall onto cold, uneven stone. The ground pressed Shinobu's focal tightly against his head on one side. From his new position he could see across the strange bowl-like place they were in, with its encircling cliffs. A pool of water lay at the center of the bowl, black now, its surface reflecting a swath of the night sky.

"This place belongs to you," John told him. "It's your family's. All of our families had places, and this is yours."

He knelt in front of Shinobu and shined a flashlight into his face and over his limbs. Shinobu could imagine what a sight he must be to John—crooked, swollen, and bruised.

John's verdict was only, "You've looked better."

Shinobu groaned in response, surprising himself.

Without asking permission, John pulled the focal off Shinobu's head. The helmet crackled and tore at his mind as it came free. Then the connection was broken, painfully. John tossed the helmet away, and Shinobu groaned again. His head began to pound, and nausea crept into his gut, but he had no control over his body yet, so he couldn't show John what he thought of this treatment.

John pushed Shinobu's torn and dirty cloak away from his back, and Shinobu heard a sharp intake of breath. John's hands slid between Shinobu's shoulder blades, lightly touching the flat oval of metal that lay across his spine.

"You're probably the best fighter I know, after the Young Dread," John reflected. "I was wondering how she controlled you. This looks awful."

Shinobu tried to tell John to shut up—he didn't want praise or condescension from someone he hated.

John rummaged in his own cloak, and shortly a cold blade was against Shinobu's skin. Shinobu managed to make a sound of alarm, deep in his throat, but he still couldn't move.

"Yeah, sorry," John said, and as he said it, Shinobu felt the blade slip under the edge of the metal plate in his back. He tried to scream in protest, but the sound that came out was feeble and meaningless. "I've seen nurses take these out several times," John told him, in what Shinobu guessed was supposed to be a reassuring tone of voice. "What they do inside your body is a delicate business, but the implants aren't delicate at all."

The knife blade slid farther beneath the metal plate. "This is going to hurt."

No kidding! Shinobu wanted to yell.

With one smooth motion, John pried the plate from Shinobu's back. Shinobu could feel the forest of needles come out of his muscles.

John pressed a cloth to the spot where the implant had been, and said, "That was disgusting."

Shinobu drew a breath and became aware that he was actually controlling his lungs. All four of his limbs jerked into motion. He grabbed at the cold rock beneath him and screamed.

The scream echoed all around the amphitheater, but Shinobu didn't hear much of it. He went limp against the ground almost immediately, blessedly unconscious.

CHAPTER 44

NOTT

"They're going to Kong," Nott told her with authority. Then he hesitated, his spoon poised above the enormous dish of ice cream in front of him on the table. It was one of the first rules of witches that you weren't supposed to eat anything they offered you, but he'd made an exception. Half of the ice cream was already in Nott's stomach, and another portion was all over the tablecloth. He scrunched up his eyes in contemplation, and also because the insides of his eyeballs were very, very cold. "No, *Hong* Kong."

"Hong Kong," Maggie repeated thoughtfully. She laughed at the way he was bolting his dessert, and said, "Slowly, slowly."

Nott didn't know how to eat slowly. The ice cream was becoming a brownish mess of different flavors, and he was trying to finish it before it all changed color. He had to stop again and press the heels of his hands into his eyes to stave off the pain. This was the first time he'd eaten ice cream, and it was a lot more complicated than he'd realized.

Maggie asked, "Why are they taking *Traveler* to Hong Kong?"

She and Nott were at an outdoor table in a small town in Scotland, where she'd brought him for, as she'd put it, a private conversation. Nott was wearing ordinary clothes, because that's all he had left anymore (one of the housekeepers on the airship had incinerated his old clothing), so he assumed he fit in perfectly well. He hardly noticed that the people at other tables had scooted their chairs away.

He answered Maggie between bites. "The other one of them is there."

"The other one of whom?" she asked.

Nott could see that something about the remnants of his dessert, on his face, or maybe on the table, or in his lap, was offensive to the old woman. But she was trying to hide her distaste. *She needs me now. She can't just throw me away.*

"The other one of them Seekers," he explained thickly. "The girl. With dark hair."

"Quin?"

"That's her." He scraped at the remaining puddles of ice cream in his bowl.

"Would you like more of that?"

Nott hesitated, not wanting her to see how very much he did want more. He permitted himself a decorous nod.

Maggie got up from the table and spoke a few words to a man behind the counter. She moved with frail precision; Nott didn't think she'd been sleeping very well lately, but even so, the old woman always gave Nott the feeling that nothing could stop her. When she returned to her seat, she fixed Nott with one of her sympathetic stares. He hated those.

"Why would they go to Quin?"

Nott shrugged. John and the Young Dread hadn't told Nott or any of the other children where *Traveler* was headed; he only knew because he'd made an effort to eavesdrop.

"Because she's a Seeker?" he guessed.

"Hmm," Maggie said.

"Oh, and doctors," Nott remembered. He'd heard a nurse say something about that. "There's doctors in Kong who are very good," he explained to her knowledgeably. "They might fix the rest of them if they don't get mended on the ship."

The man from behind the counter arrived at the table with another bowl of ice cream. He also placed a tall glass of beer in front of Maggie.

"Again with doctors?" Maggie muttered as Nott dug in. "John's heart bleeds all over everything."

"Does it?" Nott asked tentatively, curious if she meant his actual heart and actual blood. Either way, he couldn't mistake the river of disapproval that ran beneath her words. Reflexively he pulled the ice cream closer in case she might be preparing to take it away.

But she didn't take it away, and she didn't drink her beer either. When Maggie noticed where Nott was looking, she asked, "Would you like some beer?"

He nodded, even though it occurred to him, very late, that she was being much too friendly. Nott had drunk ale as a boy, just like everyone did, but it had been a long while since he'd tasted anything alcoholic, because the Middle Dread had not found alcohol the least bit helpful in training his Watchers.

Maggie pushed the glass over to him, and Nott took hold of it with sticky hands and drank off half before taking a breath.

"Do you know if I hurt *Traveler*'s engines when I fired at it?" she asked him.

Nott took a deep breath, steadying himself. The beer hit his stomach in a rush, which added to the shivering excitement of the ice cream.

"They were talking about *that* for hours," he told her. "The engines stopped, but after that they started again. The captain wasn't happy about it. You frightened them."

He touched the glass, and when he saw no objection on Maggie's face, he downed the rest of the beer in three gulps. It was nothing like the ale he used to drink. He could swallow this stuff by the gallon.

"That was bad luck I couldn't finish the job. The ship wouldn't have flown again quickly if I'd fired a second time." She was speaking to herself in a soft voice and fingering something in her jacket pocket. Nott was curious if she had another strange weapon in there.

Soon a second beer arrived, and Maggie automatically pushed it toward him. Nott couldn't believe his luck, and he found that he'd entirely stopped worrying about the old woman's motives. He pulled over the new glass and drank.

Maggie let him eat his ice cream and drink his beer for a long while, as she sat in thought. Eventually Nott had difficulty aiming the spoon at his mouth.

When she broke the silence, it was to ask, "How many Seekers did they rescue? And do you know their houses?"

Nott nodded, dizzyingly. "Oh yes."

He nearly overturned the beer as he tried to make the flat bottom of the glass meet the tabletop properly. "They've got'ther houses drawn'n their beds, or on, on their arms."

"Tell me."

Nott's mouth wasn't working right. His words were slipping away and tangling with each other and popping out of him like bubbles, but he continued to forge ahead. He told her everything he could remember about the Seekers and their children who were living on *Traveler*, and the old woman peered at him all the while and seemed to understand him fine.

When they got up from the table sometime later, Maggie steered him down the street to a little park, where Nott flopped onto the ground beneath a tree. The athame—the Middle Dread's athame—was in Maggie's hands.

"We'll wait for you to sober up before we use this, I think. But I have something for you, as promised." She produced a metal helm from her pack and put it into Nott's hands. "You can keep this one, Nott. I won't take it from you again."

Nott squinted his eyes to focus. Was she giving him his helm? Disappointment plunged through him when he got the metal helmet properly in view. "'Snot mine!" he said, and tried to push it back into her hands. "Won't feel the same."

The slap came so quickly, Nott didn't realize what had happened until he felt the sting in his cheek. He stared at Maggie, who looked stern. She was holding up a small branch from the tree. That was what she'd hit him with. She pulled Nott's hair painfully and swatted him again.

"Your helm is gone," she croaked. "It was on Shinobu's head. This one may not be exactly like yours, but it was worn by your old master—my son—many times. You'll learn to enjoy it."

She stuck the helmet onto his head. At once Nott experienced the electric buzz, followed by the cool sensation of the helm's energy joining with his own thoughts. The beer eased the transition, made him feel as if he were floating gently into the helm's embrace.

"'Snot so bad, this one," he said.

CHAPTER 45

QUIN

Dex glowed evenly. The torrent of energy that ordinarily poured across and through him was being pulled to every extremity. Five master healers stood around Quin's examination table, all ten of their hands submerged in the erratic storm around Dex's body.

Master Tan, Quin's teacher and the most famous healer on Hong Kong's Transit Bridge, stood at Dex's head. He was slight and graceful, with a face that was nearly unlined despite his age, and eyes as bright as any child's. Master Tan's four most trusted colleagues— Masters Zou, Ren, Shi, and Ando—each stood by one of the patient's limbs. They'd succeeded in pulling copper-colored tributaries off the central current, so that Dex's body now lay beneath a spider's web of smaller lines.

Quin had never seen more than two bridge masters working on one patient. Five was unheard of.

Master Tan, unaware that this patient was possibly an ancient figure of historical significance to Quin, spoke to Dex in his typical way: "Relax," he murmured gently. "All that is pulling at you, you may let go of it."

Dex had slipped first into a trancelike state, and was now completely unconscious. But Quin herself had been the recipient of Master Tan's calm words, and she suspected they could reach even the deepest sleeper.

The five masters had been at it for nearly an hour. They were working much more slowly than Quin had during her failed attempt with Dex. Dispersing his energy by tiny degrees, they had avoided becoming, themselves, embroiled in it.

Quin sat cross-legged on her counter, watching the procedure as an amateur athlete might watch a championship game. There was very little conversation. The masters needed only brief glances and small gestures of the head to communicate.

The reversal came without warning. In one moment, Dex's energy pattern lay about his own body. In the next moment, it appeared to leap out and instantly consume the five master healers. All at once, a single web of shining current flowed out from him through each person who touched him. Master Tan looked to Quin in dismay. Almost immediately, every master showed signs of dizziness.

Quin leapt down to the floor.

"Stop, Master Tan. Let go."

The others looked to Master Tan, questioning. But he shook his head.

"I fainted when that happened," Quin told him urgently. "Let go. We can try again later."

He shook his head, merely a twitch to convey his firm decision. "Quin, we've gotten the current away from him." He spoke calmly, though he was having difficulty staying upright. His narrow shoulders were swaying. "All we need is something larger."

He nodded at the metal pillar in the corner of the room. This beam ran vertically through Quin's house and was one of the structural members that joined her home to the framework of the bridge itself.

Quin understood. This amount of energy required something immense to ground it. She grabbed the copper key to her front door in one hand, and with the other took hold of Master Tan's wrist. At once she felt the strange, altered pattern of Dex's energy destroying her own equilibrium. She did not pause to let it overwhelm her this time, but reached immediately for the pillar and touched it with the key. In the moment before the key came in contact with the pillar, a nasty blue spark jumped between the two. Once the metals were joined, the energy streamed off Dex, through the masters, through Quin herself, through the key—now blackened, as Quin's hand would have been, had she touched the pillar unprotected—and into the vertical metal beam. The bright copper lines became blue streaks of lightning as they discharged into the structure of the bridge.

The lights of Quin's house flickered and went out as the storm of energy blew itself away.

The five healers and Quin collapsed. She succeeded in catching Master Tan before he hit the floor. In his usual unperturbed manner, he blinked up at her as the lights came back on, and said, "That was unexpected."

Slowly they got back to their feet, to discover Dex still unmoving on the exam table, his eyes closed. There was no trace of energy at all around his body anymore.

"Could we have . . ." Quin began, but she didn't want to finish the question. She nudged the damaged copper key with one foot, marveling at the strength of the electrical discharge that had traveled through it. Had they pulled all of Dex's energy away and killed him? Was that possible?

She reached to feel for his pulse, but Master Tan held her gently back. "Wait a moment," he instructed, with that same infuriating calm.

For a time, nothing changed. Then, a flicker. A trickle of copper became visible above Dex's heart, flowing outward. Quin and the masters watched the trickle grow and spread, an expanding web of gentle current.

When the web reached his extremities, Dex looked as any other patient might look, ordinary and whole. The damage that had been done, hundreds of years ago, was gone.

CHAPTER 46

JOHN

John was awakened by the pleasant sensation of being kicked in the ribs. His eyes flew open in time to see a fist coming at his face. Instinct made him reach up, grab Shinobu's arm, and pull. Shinobu's momentum thwarted his attack and sent him tumbling into the remains of their fire.

John sprang to his feet. It was daytime. The rock walls were lit by early sunlight, but the bowl where they stood was still dark.

Shinobu flailed in the embers, fighting his way back upright and out of the ashes. His ragged cloak was smoking as he stared balefully at John.

"You," he growled.

He lunged with renewed fury. John turned aside at the last moment, but it wasn't easy to elude Shinobu a second time. He got hold of John's shoulders and shoved him.

"Where's my focal?"

John stumbled backward. If the focal was the first thing Shinobu was asking about, John reflected, dodging to stay out of reach, then he'd been right to worry about Shinobu wearing it while he slept.

It must have gotten its hooks into Shinobu's mind, as Maud had warned John it could.

Shinobu took a swipe at him, but John stayed clear. "I got rid of it," John said. It was in his pack, in fact, but Shinobu didn't need to know that.

"Why would you do that?" Shinobu demanded.

He threw himself at John, and in a moment they were grappling, Shinobu trying to hurl John to the ground, John trying to stay upright. This was harder than he'd anticipated, because it was very cold here and his arms and legs were stiff. But for his part, Shinobu was hampered by any number of injuries. His face was turning red with the effort.

"I want the focal!"

"You're out of luck." John was firm.

Shinobu succeeded in hooking a foot around John's leg and pulling it out from beneath him. As John fell, he speeded himself up dramatically, rolled out of Shinobu's reach, and popped back to his feet some distance away.

"Great, she's been training you like a Dread," Shinobu said, glancing from the spot where John had been to where he was now standing. "Were you the most selfish person she could find? Did she say to herself, 'I've searched the entire world, and I can't find anyone worse, so I'll train John'?"

"I never meant for you or Quin—"

"Shut it!"

Shinobu rushed at John, landed two punches against his chest. His short red hair stood out from his scalp in uneven clumps, giving the impression that his head was on fire with the anger pouring out of him. John dodged as Shinobu came after him like a boxer dancing toward his opponent.

"Don't pretend you care about Quin! You shot her, you almost killed her. You would have killed all of us."

Forcing himself to remain calm was a great effort, but John batted away a blow and said, "That wasn't what I intended."

It was the wrong thing to say. Shinobu went after him as if John were a training dummy that needed to be broken into kindling. John tried to simply defend himself, but it quickly became an all-out boxing match.

"Didn't intend to hurt anyone?" Shinobu said between punches. "You disrupted my father. He bashed his head on a rock to put an end to himself! Can you imagine a worse way to die?"

"The disruptor went off by accident," John told him. He pushed Shinobu away as they circled each other. His face was swelling where Shinobu had struck him, but the pain felt good. John hadn't waited around to see Alistair die, and he'd tried to avoid thinking about what it must have been like. Why shouldn't he finally hear about the reality?

"It was my fault, because I brought the disruptor to the estate," John admitted, "but I never meant for anyone to fire it. That device your father used to tune his athame, it made our muscles spasm. The disruptor fired by mistake." He'd wanted to explain this to Shinobu for nearly two years, but Shinobu wasn't listening.

"You shot Quin. She came this close to dying," Shinobu said.

John didn't want to hit him anymore. Shinobu was only telling the truth. John had done those things.

He retreated until he was backed up onto the scree at the edge of the bowl. When he slipped on the scattered stones, Shinobu kicked his leg out from beneath him again.

"She almost *died*, John!" He leaned over and aimed a punch at John's face. "Because you wanted an athame. Because you were greedy."

Shinobu struck, but John moved before the blow landed. That last word had finally gotten to him. He'd never done anything out of greed, only a sense of obligation.

Back on his feet, John demanded, *"Greedy?"*

"So greedy!"

When Shinobu lunged, John grabbed him, and they were wrestling again.

"You knew Briac hated me, that he never intended to make me a Seeker," John said as they struggled. "You knew and you were happy, because if I was out of the way, you'd have Quin for yourself. You wanted me to fail!"

He got a hand free and punched Shinobu in the gut. Shinobu returned with a furious uppercut to John's jaw that laid him out flat and sent his head spinning. When John was on the ground, Shinobu grabbed his ankle and yanked him closer.

"Quin found me *There* and was saving me," Shinobu hissed. "Even after what I did, she came for me. How could you ever hurt someone so selfless?"

"What did *you* do to her?" John asked, honestly curious now. He'd stopped the dizziness with one of Maud's focusing techniques.

"Shut up!"

Shinobu swung a fist to knock him out, but John was done with this fight. He rolled back, got his feet under Shinobu's chest, and thrust him away. Shinobu stumbled backward painfully, lost his footing, and fell into the deep pool of water that lay at the base of the amphitheater's walls.

John saw a flailing mass of limbs and ragged cloak beneath the water, and when Shinobu didn't surface immediately, he ran to the bank. How injured was he? John pulled his cloak off to dive in, but before he got to the water, Shinobu broke the surface, gasping. He hauled himself up the steep bank, wet and shivering, a redheaded Viking emerging from a northern ocean.

He glared at John as he limped onto the shore, but the cold water had drained the fight out of him. He stripped off his cloak and began to remove his sopping clothing without a word. Beneath his shirt John saw bruises, old and new, all over his torso. Things had not gone well for Shinobu recently.

"I did those things to Quin, to your father. Even if I didn't mean for the worst to happen, I caused it," John said. "Telling you I'm sorry doesn't amount to anything, does it? So I'm trying to make amends. Why do you think I took you away from Maggie?"

Shinobu threw the last of his clothes down onto the rocks, and John tossed him his own cloak. Without looking at John, Shinobu gave him a grudging nod and wrapped the cloak around himself.

CHAPTER 47

SHINOBU

Hours passed before Shinobu stopped shivering. He sat hunched in front of the fire John had built for him, with John's heavy cloak around his shoulders. He had been by the fire for so long, he'd used up most of the wood, and John had gone off in search of more.

From time to time, Shinobu lifted his eyes from the flames to study his location. At some point in the distant past, a great flow of lava had cooled here and formed tightly packed pillars of basalt. The basalt rose up around him to form an intricately carved natural amphitheater. The arms of the amphitheater reached in nearly a full circle, enclosing a gently sloping bowl in their center. All along the steep walls, water ran inward over the edges in a steady flow, forming not waterfalls so much as vertical streams. These joined up on the rocky ground in the deep, frosty pool that John had thrown Shinobu into. At the low edge of the pool, a small river snaked its way out into the world beyond. Above the pillared walls was a cold blue sky.

Shinobu was in a place that looked as though it had been created at the dawn of the world, and it belonged to his own family. This fact was made plain by the immense carving of an eagle in full flight halfway up the cliff wall. The uneven surface gave the animal's beak and claws a fierce aspect. Water trickled across the eagle's body, and the sun, which now hung near its zenith, glinted off the deeply cut eye, as if the eagle were pinning Shinobu beneath its hunter's gaze. It was, he thought, one of the most beautiful places he'd ever seen.

His head was killing him. His arms and legs were, mostly, killing him. But now that his teeth had stopped chattering, he thought maybe he wasn't going to freeze to death or die of his injuries.

The chattering had done one good thing—it had kept his mind off the focal. But now he was warm enough for his thoughts to wander, and they went immediately to the metal helmet. He hated it, but only sometimes. It tricked him, but it made everything hurt less—so much less—and in an awful way, the focal turned the world into a more sensible place. Maggie became something other than an old woman who was torturing him. And Quin . . . Quin . . .

Shinobu stood up, pulled John's cloak more tightly about himself. His bones had been broken and partially mended so many times that he could gauge where he was in the process. The reconstructors were frantically knitting; beneath the pain was the deep itch of tissues repairing themselves.

As he skirted the pool, he spotted an object in its shallows—a small black sheet of plastic, six inches by six inches. With a start, he recognized the vid screen he'd stolen from Maggie's pack at Dun Tarm. He had kept it wrapped in the bandages around his ribs and forgotten about it entirely. It must have come loose when John knocked him into the water. He retrieved the screen from the cold pool, but before he slipped it into a pocket in John's cloak, he noticed again the name scratched along the edge: *Catherine.*

He listened; sharp echoes were entering the amphitheater from the land beyond the cliffs. John was out there, chopping wood.

Shinobu walked around the edge of the amphitheater bowl until he was standing beneath the eagle carving. Was it residual madness from the focal or just his own imagination that made him think the bird was watching him and welcoming him as a member of its house? Had Alistair been here and planned to bring Shinobu?

Below the eagle, the hexagonal rock columns ended above the ground in a jagged overhang. Shinobu ducked through the gentle screen of dripping water into a cave-like area between the overhang and the ground. Beneath his feet was a scree of broken basalt leading deep within the cliff.

He found the silver locket because it stood out against the dark rock, even in the low light of this hidden place. The locket had been set in a small indentation in one of the natural columns, left there to be found. The pendant was large and heavy and ridged with designs, but he could only feel them with his fingers. It was too dark to see them.

He peered farther into the space, toward what must be the very back of this little grotto. Though the light barely reached into that most secret spot, he knew immediately what he was looking at: there was a dead body back there. Shinobu had been to a place like this before, a small cave in northern Scotland that belonged to the Seeker house of the horse. There had been dead bodies in that cave too.

The corpse lay in a niche where the basalt columns reached almost to the rocky ground. When Shinobu got close enough to discern details, he saw that the remains had been there a long time—probably longer than Shinobu had been alive, which was exactly how it had been at the other cave.

He knelt by the cloaked figure, mostly skeleton now, dirty and picked over by the creatures that foraged here in the summer months. The teeth were carved in familiar patterns of athame symbols and packed with soot. This had been one of the Middle Dread's Watchers. Killed on some excuse and left here to rot. One more of the Middle Dread's victims.

Fury at the boy's presence overtook Shinobu, both because he'd probably been killed by someone he trusted, and because the Middle Dread had defiled this place that should have belonged only to Shinobu's family. He promised himself that one day soon, when his own body hurt a bit less, he would come back here and bury this stranger properly.

John had returned. Through the dripping sheet of water, Shinobu watched him dump a pile of cut wood by the fire, and then use it to stoke the flames. John looked up as Shinobu ducked out of the cave and back into sunlight. A moment later, John turned away as if he didn't wish to intrude on Shinobu's thoughts.

In the brighter light, Shinobu examined the locket he'd found. The design was intricate, the central figures obscured by flourishes and scrollwork. It took him a few moments to understand that an eagle and a dragon were intertwined on the pendant's face.

He'd wondered if his father had ever been to this place, and here was the answer. An eagle and a dragon. His father the eagle, his mother the dragon. He was certain this locket was Alistair's, given to him by Mariko, Shinobu's mother. It was the sort of thing she would have designed. Their two house emblems wrapped around each other, his father and his mother wrapped around each other, though they were forced to spend years apart.

As Shinobu traced the pattern with his thumb, he was overcome with emotion. He sat heavily on the rocky ground, beset by questions. When had Alistair left the locket? Had he come to this place after Mariko fled from the Scottish estate years ago? Had they hoped to meet here when Alistair got free of Briac Kincaid?

Shinobu had been blaming John for so many of his own

misfortunes. But as he thought of his parents, Shinobu conceded that things had turned bad long before John had made them bad. The Middle Dread had been inciting Seekers to kill each other for generations. They had all been victims.

When he returned to the fire, Shinobu said to John, gruffly, "I don't know if I'll ever trust you."

John's expression conveyed that he hadn't expected anything else. "Here," he offered, holding up a camping dish with some sort of stew on it.

Shinobu took it gratefully and sat by the fire. The food was delicious, and he was ravenous. Between mouthfuls, he asked, "You made this here?"

John took a seat nearby. "I brought it with me."

"Just because I'm eating this doesn't mean I forgive you," Shinobu told him. "But it does help." He swallowed a huge mouthful of stew and said, "You know what else helps? Knowing that Quin doesn't like you at all anymore."

"I thought she was going to kill me the last time we met."

"Pity she didn't." Shinobu tried to say it seriously, but he could feel his hatred of John leaking away.

There were a few companionable minutes of silence as Shinobu ate. Then John said, "I might love someone else."

Something in the way he said it made Shinobu glance up sharply from his food. "I hope you don't mean me," he told John as he shoveled in the last bite of the stew. In spite of everything, they were falling back into the banter of their childhood. "That would be an unexpected twist."

John laughed. "No. Have you seen yourself lately? Someone else. I had to leave her to come get you."

"I interrupted you with a girl?" The thought delighted him. "The pretty, rich, spoiled boy didn't get everything he wanted instantly?"

"I won't be able to be any of those things if I'm with her," John muttered. "But . . . it's nice to know you think I'm pretty."

Shinobu snorted. "She sounds good for you—probably too good for you." He set down his plate, wishing he could eat several more helpings, but there wasn't any more. He frowned at John. "Maybe the focal is still addling my mind, but I don't want to beat your face into the ground just now," he admitted.

"Really? Then maybe I can show you something."

John lifted up his pack and pulled Shinobu's focal out. Immediately Shinobu was overcome with the visceral urge to grab it and pull it onto his head. He curled his hands into fists to keep them at his sides.

"You still want it?" John asked.

Shinobu didn't trust himself to answer.

John hefted the large steel axe they'd found by their campsite in one hand, and he held up the focal in the other. Shinobu looked between them.

"What do you think about this?" John asked.

Shinobu hesitated. He realized that John wasn't offering him the focal at all; he was offering Shinobu his freedom.

It took a moment for Shinobu to force himself to speak, but when he did, he said, "All right."

The focal sat on the ground looking harmless in the last of the day's light. Shinobu adjusted himself to aim squarely at it. He lifted the axe and felt its weight balance above him.

He paused only a moment, but in that moment he thought of the peculiar world the focal had shown him—less pain, more fighting skill, and an unending internal battle between his own thoughts and thoughts that pretended to be his own.

The slightest move would send the axe one way or another, and his own life would follow.

He brought the blade down onto the focal with full force. It cut deeply into the helmet. A shock ran up the axe handle, and Shinobu dropped it with a yelp.

The broken focal hissed and spluttered, red sparks of electricity popping out through the cleft he'd made. The axe head was still inside, and fingers of electricity were crawling all over the steel tool.

"Look at that," John said.

He kicked the axe away from the focal and then picked it up. With another direct hit, he split the focal in half. He yelped just as Shinobu had, when another shock ran up the handle. They both watched as the two halves of the metal helmet sparked back and forth toward each other for nearly a minute before slowly dying out, spitting and crackling until the very end.

Shinobu cautiously picked up both halves. Inside the body of the helmet, in the thin area between the upper surface and the lower, there was a complicated world like a miniature metal city—whorls and nodes and what could only be described as circuits.

"What is this thing?" he whispered as he held out one of the halves to John.

They examined it in silence, before looking up at each other with equally baffled expressions.

"I thought focals were hundreds of years old," Shinobu said.

"They are. My mother's journal mentions one in the 1500s."

Shinobu held up his half of the helmet, angling it so that John might see the interior circuitry.

"This isn't from the 1500s."

"But our whipswords are? And our athames?" John asked. "Nothing we have fits into the time period in which it was made. That's why we live apart from the world. It's the secret knowledge of Seekers."

Shinobu nodded. It was the narrative they'd been told as children. It made sense, to a point. "Oh, I have something for you," he said, remembering. He retrieved the vid screen from the pocket of John's cloak, which he was still wearing. "I took this from Maggie, thinking I'd give it to Quin. But it's your mother's."

CHAPTER 48

JOHN

The sun had set, and John sat alone beneath the basalt wall, with the vid screen in his hands. He ran a finger over the name *Catherine* that had been scratched into the edge. The screen was made of the sort of indestructible plastic used for emergency-route guidance maps, with the video hard-coded into it. Despite having been carried around in a bag by Maggie, perhaps for years, and recently dropped into water, it sprang to life immediately when he pressed his thumb against the indentation along the top. Catherine had wanted it to last.

John was caught off guard when an image of his mother's face appeared suddenly between his hands, looking directly at him. She began speaking at once.

"John, they're giving me something for the pain. They said it works slowly, but I don't know how slowly. I might fall asleep," the girl on the screen said, looking over her shoulder and then back to the camera.

She was *so young*. Catherine was lying on a bed, and as she shifted the camera, John saw that it was a narrow hospital bed with a curtain around it. He could see her arm holding the camera, and it was just as if he were a small boy, lying next to his mother, with her hand resting on his head.

"Archie's dead. He was . . . and I . . ." Her eyes filled with tears.

Her face was bruised, and there were streaks of dried blood in her hair and on her arm. John didn't know what had happened to her before she'd turned the camera on, but whatever it was had happened recently. She closed her eyes, gained control of herself, and opened them again.

"John. It's strange to use your name, when you're not even here yet. But they told me you're all right. You're all right." She smiled with heartbreaking relief.

She moved the camera. It took John a moment to see that she was touching her large pregnant belly under a hospital gown. That was *him* in there. The camera rotated back to his mother's face. She didn't look much older than John was now, but her eyes were hollow and tortured.

"I'm calling you John because it's the most common English name I can think of," she whispered. "You're going to stand out for a lot of reasons, but I will keep you as anonymous as I can.

"I am a target, John, and you will be too." She closed her eyes, passed a hand across her face. John could see dried blood in the creases of her fingers. "I didn't really believe Maggie before today. But we *are* targets. We've been targets. We have no one we can trust, except each other. Maybe it's always been that way."

She was not looking into the camera but at some point beyond it. For the first time since she'd begun speaking, he could see in her face and hear in her voice some of the madness he'd known when he was a child.

"Many of them have been after us since the beginning," she whispered. "They hate us. They *hate* us. I will do everything I can for you. I will keep you safe."

Her stare came back to the camera. Her voice broke as she said, "Archie was . . . he was . . ." A tear ran across the bridge of her nose and down onto the bed. "John, I love him. We were going to be . . . Maybe it was just a daydream—he thought it was—but it felt like it could be real."

A few more tears were running down her face. Her words were more disjointed—the drugs were kicking in—but the madness receded and this was Catherine, speaking sincerely to her son across eighteen years.

"I thought you would grow up, become a Seeker, and when you did Archie and I would go on . . . You won't know what a Dread is for a long while, but it's someone good, someone just, and I thought we could . . . Why not?"

She closed her eyes. When she opened them, she had stopped crying and was staring up at the ceiling.

"They'll never let me be, do you see? I will have to claw my way, every inch against them, take what is rightfully ours. John, it's going to be harder than I ever thought."

This was the crazy Catherine again, the mother he'd known, who was vindictive, the Catherine who'd told him never to love, the Catherine who'd become a killer. He was seeing the genesis of that woman right here, as she lay on a hospital bed, with John's father dead and blood all over her.

She turned back to the camera. Her words were soft, almost inaudible as she said, "John, Archie loved you so much. I have to say it now, because he's"—her voice broke—"he's already fading from me and I want you to know. We both love you."

She turned from the camera. There was another voice in the room. Maggie, maybe?

"Here," Catherine said to whoever had come in. "Will you keep this?"

She turned back to the camera and whispered, "Goodbye, John. I'll meet you soon."

Her hand came up and the camera switched off. John waited, in case there was more, but the screen had gone blank, and a few moments later it shut off altogether.

John discovered that his own cheeks were wet. He looked around, was surprised to find himself still sitting in the basalt amphitheater in Iceland, beneath the night sky. He had been in that hospital room with his mother for a few minutes.

He wiped his cheeks and watched the video again. He'd lived with Catherine until he was seven, but this was his only glimpse of what she'd been like before she'd really changed. When he pushed the moments of Catherine's madness aside and listened to what the real Catherine was trying to say, her message was simple. She had wanted to tell him about her love for him, Archie's love for him, even though he hadn't been born yet, and her love for Archie, with whom she had been planning her life. That was all.

When John turned his head up to the sky, he found it lit with waves of green and purple, flowing across the stars. He was seeing the aurora borealis, which looked, to him, like his mother's soul finding him after all these years apart.

"I've never seen it so bright," Shinobu said. He was watching the aurora when John returned to the fire.

"It's breathtaking." He was grateful that Shinobu didn't ask him about the video. He did not want to share any piece of it with anyone else.

"Is this yours?" Shinobu was looking at the cloak, which he'd spread out by the fire. He'd emptied all of its pockets and laid out the contents in neat piles.

There were scraps of paper and parchment, basic medical supplies, and dozens of small knives and tiny, intricate metal tools of indefinable use. Separate from those things, Shinobu had made a row of larger items that combined glass and stone in intriguing ways. Many looked like arcane measuring instruments, a few like weapons. John had glimpsed them before, but mostly the Young Dread had kept them away from him until recently. Now she wanted him to see them; she wanted his help understanding what they were.

"No, it's the Young Dread's cloak," John told him.

"Does she know what these things are?"

"The strange ones? No. She thinks I might be able to help her learn about them—" He stopped himself from adding *if I make certain commitments.* The Young Dread's offer to him was for him alone to know.

Shinobu was looking pointedly at John.

"What?" John asked.

Shinobu indicated the objects that looked like weapons. "Should we try to figure out what they do?"

CHAPTER 49

NOTT

This was the test.

Nott sat alone in his own little corner of Dun Tarm, with his new helm on his head. He'd been wearing it constantly since Maggie had given it to him, even through his violent illness after the beer and ice cream. He even slept with it on so that it might color his dreams.

Now it was dawn, and no one else was awake. It was going to be Nott and Aelred, taking the measure of each other.

Nott set out the tiny bottle, which was full of fresh milk he'd acquired in the Scottish village. (Maggie hadn't minded him stealing it. In fact, she'd encouraged him.) He set out his longest knife. Bottle on the left, knife on the right.

He moved the three large stones to reveal what he'd been hiding between them. Aelred's tiny cage was there, covered in cloth to keep his little house nice and dark.

Aelred clicked and squeaked when Nott removed the covering cloth. He was hanging upside down from the top of the cage, his translucent wings wrapped tightly about him, but he unfolded himself in Nott's presence.

A little crawling creature, Nott thought. It was a thought from the helm; he recognized that now. But he had wanted the helm's thoughts, hadn't he?

What do I like to do to little crawling creatures?

It's obvious.

He glanced at the knife.

Aelred, I told you that you might not like the Nott I chose.

His hands shook slightly as he opened the small cage door and reached in for the bat. Aelred happily moved his feet onto Nott's finger, and he clicked again as Nott withdrew him from the cage. When he held Aelred up in front of his eyes, the bat stretched his wings and chirruped.

Nott laid him on the ground between the milk and the knife. Aelred objected when he was put on the cold ground, but he soon settled down as Nott stroked his head.

"Aelred," he whispered. "I was never really the boy who fixed broken wings."

He stretched out both of Aelred's wings to their fullest extent. One wing was fully healed; the other was close. Despite the injuries, the bat had grown several inches since Nott had started taking care of him. The diaphanous wing tissue was thicker and stronger now. Aelred would be quite a flyer soon.

Nott picked up his knife and very gently traced the lines of Aelred's wing bones with the tip. He pressed on one of the joints a little harder, and the bat squeaked. Nott licked his lips.

What do I like to do to little creatures?

What I've done so many times before.

He recalled hacking off the feet of dozens of rats and watching as they screamed and tried to run.

He eased the knife blade into the crease where the wing met the bat's body.

"Sorry, Aelred."

CHAPTER 50

QUIN

Quin woke curled up in a chair in the corner of her examination room. She'd fallen asleep while waiting for Dex to revive after the healers had finished with him. Now it was afternoon and she found herself faced with an empty room and an empty exam table. Her patient was gone. She jumped to her feet.

"Dex?" She stuck her head out of the room and called up the stairs. "Dex?" Then she called, tentatively, "Fiona? Are you here?" Quin's mother had not been on the Transit Bridge when Quin arrived, but Quin kept hoping she would show up. Surely Fiona could not be lost too.

Quin paused with her foot on the bottom stair. Belatedly she realized she'd seen something strange from the exam room. She went back through the room to the round window in the outer wall. The usual view, of Victoria Harbor and Hong Kong Island, was obstructed by an object in the sky. It took her a moment to credit what she was seeing: an enormous airship was hovering near the Transit Bridge. No, it wasn't hovering. It was moving steadily, with a kind of relentless grace, in a pattern about the bridge. It was tracing a figure eight over Victoria Harbor, with the bridge at the intersection of its loops.

"Is that *Traveler*?" she whispered aloud.

It was. She'd parachuted onto the top of that airship while it was moving through London, and its shape was burned deeply into her memory.

Did *Traveler*'s presence mean John was here? Why? Was he coming to take something else from Quin? What could he want this time?

She spotted the note then. It had been folded and left on the exam table, exactly where Dex's head had lain:

Find me in Shinobu's perch beneath the bridge.

She stared at the very modern handwriting. "Shinobu's perch" could only refer to one location. But how in the world would Dex have known about it?

Quin pulled on her shoes and left the house, braving the foot traffic on the upper levels. In a few minutes she was retracing a path through the lower levels of the Transit Bridge that she'd once taken at a run, with Shinobu pulling her along as they tried to escape from John. Through seldom-traveled maintenance areas and a passageway almost too narrow to travel she went, and then she worked her way down a long ladder shaft that traversed the interior skin of the Transit Bridge. At last, Quin pulled herself out into daylight among the metal rafters that formed the bridge's underside.

She had not been terrified of heights the last time she was here, but that was no longer the case. She kept her chin lifted and her gaze straight ahead as she picked her way along a metal girder. Victoria Harbor lay a hundred and fifty feet below her. At the edge of her vision she caught flashes off the green water as it glinted in the afternoon sun, but she wouldn't let herself look down.

She remembered Shinobu walking in front of her the last time—the only time—she'd been here. He'd been wearing the torn and dirty clothing of the Hong Kong drug gangs, his short hair dyed in a pattern of leopard spots.

How did you know this was here? she'd asked him.

I jump off things, he'd answered, *and I climb around inside them, and sometimes I swim under them. I have lots of hiding places in Hong Kong.*

They hadn't been in love with each other at that particular moment. In fact, Quin had forgotten his name, just as she'd forgotten almost everything about their childhood together. But she had loved him, of course, without understanding that she did.

To her left, she could see *Traveler* looping outward from the bridge, and again she wondered what John was doing here. What kind of trouble had he brought this time?

A breeze blew through the rafters, ruffling Quin's hair and daring her to look down, daring her to lose her balance and then her life. *Dammit, Dex!*

He was sitting cross-legged on the perch, which was a few sheets of plastic that Shinobu had lashed to the crossbeams to create a crude platform and a private hideaway. Dex's back was to Quin. He was looking north across the harbor. Her first thought was that he shouldn't be here. This place was something between her and Shinobu, theirs alone. Her second thought was to wonder again how he could possibly have known about the perch at all.

Without turning, Dex began to speak. "I was born this year, in a small town in Switzerland," he said, "though both of my parents were English. I've never been to Hong Kong before."

Quin turned the words over in her mind, trying to make sense of this information as she came up beside him.

"What?" she asked, failing.

Dex turned to her. Quin had to stop herself from taking a step backward. His messy brown curls still hung loosely about his head, the hairdo of a teenager, but his face was entirely changed. During their time together, he'd shifted between a frightened child and a wild, unreliable warrior. Now only the warrior was left, and he was no longer wild but *contained,* like hot embers in a furnace. He was sitting, but he appeared much taller than he had before, his back straight, his shoulders no longer hunched but broad. His brown robe had concealed his muscular form. Now he wore modern clothing that did not.

Quin, who prided herself on hardly noticing such things unless they involved Shinobu, was almost agape at how handsome he was. His eyes danced with intelligence. At the same time, she could now clearly see his resemblance to the Middle Dread, a condition that bothered her deeply.

Reading her thoughts as always, he said, "Do you believe me now that he was my brother?"

She nodded dumbly, unsure of how she should act around this new version of Dex.

He indicated the small amount of room left on the perch. "I won't bite you . . . or kiss you," he assured her with a mischievous smile.

She squeezed herself onto the ledge, pulling up her legs and leaning back against crossed rafters so that she wouldn't accidentally catch a glimpse of the drop beneath them. She felt young and small next to him.

"I'm sorry. I didn't realize you were scared of heights," he said. "I came for the view, but I shouldn't have dragged you here."

"How did you know about this place?"

"I saw it in your mind so many times, whenever you thought of Shinobu," he explained. "Something important must have happened here."

She thought of the afternoon she'd spent in this spot with Shinobu. He'd been withdrawing from opium, and she'd calmed his tremors. They had looked at each other differently then.

Quin nodded. "I fell in love here."

"He must be quite someone to have won you over so thoroughly, Quilla."

Quin found it necessary to turn away from the full force of his attention. He was the same person she'd gotten to know, between bouts of his insanity, yet he was also wholly different; it was as though the volume had been turned up on his true essence. She could understand how easily Quilla, whoever she was, must have fallen into his orbit—and he was still calling her Quilla.

"I'm only teasing you, Quin," he said kindly. "I know you're Quin. Not my Quilla."

He looked out at the harbor, and Quin followed his gaze. *Traveler* was making a turn at one end of its figure eight. If Dex noticed the airship, he apparently thought it belonged in the sky here.

"Do I really look like her?" she asked. "You told me she had red hair and green eyes."

"You don't look much alike, no," he answered, studying Quin closely, as if for the first time. It *was* the first time, since he'd come back to himself. Unbidden, the memory came of Dex kissing her, lightly, as she woke up in his presence. But she was not his, and he was not hers.

Dex leaned back and issued this verdict: "You don't look much like Quilla, but there's something about you that is very like her. Quilla was pretty, yes, but she didn't care nearly as much about herself as she did about others. You're like that too."

"Am I?" Quin could never hear a compliment without recalling the things her father had forced her to do when she'd become a Seeker. It was hard to think of herself as noble. "I haven't always done the right thing," she whispered.

"Neither have I," Dex answered with disarming sincerity. "But we must try."

"We must try," she agreed.

"Now," he said, becoming serious, "we find Shinobu. I promised you we would. We know he's been with my mother, and if I'm about to face her and those boys as well, there is something I should retrieve."

His focal still hung down his back on its strap. He lifted it up.

"In no-space?" she asked.

"Some of it will be." He smiled. "When I began telling you my story, do you remember I said there were different versions of the ending?"

"I think so."

He stood up and offered her his hand. "I meant that I would have to pick the ending. Will you help me?"

The ghostly world blurred along the sides of the anomaly tunnel, and Quin had the sensation of intense motion; they were tunneling farther through the world than they had on any of their previous trips. When Dex adjusted the medallion, a new view took shape in front of them. They'd stepped into the tunnel from the rafters of the Transit Bridge. Now they were looking down a steep slope at a village nestled against the base of snow-covered mountains.

There was still a curtain of gray between them and this vista, but the separation was only a gossamer fog. Quin thought she could reach through and touch anything she liked.

The houses were of dark wood, with steeply pitched roofs, and in their midst was a tiny church with a high steeple. Except for the modern vehicles on the tidy road, Quin could have been looking at a postcard from a hundred years ago.

"Switzerland," Dex told her. "I was born here. My mother used to describe the village to me and Matheus at bedtime, though we never got to see it like this."

"It's beautiful," Quin said.

"Beautiful, but tame," Dex mused. "I got to grow up with wolves and bears about. Maybe this would have been terribly boring. And I would have been different." He looked thoughtfully at the village, said, "Come on, this isn't the important place."

He began walking again, the medallion held in front of him. The view of mountains and village warped and receded, and the world became only streaks of gray light at the edges of Quin's vision. A new view took shape quite soon. When it did, Quin and Dex were at the edge of the tunnel, high up in the air, peering down at a sprawling complex of buildings, some of which were enormous and oddly shaped.

"What is this place?" Quin asked.

"Did you know there's a theory that the universe has more than the dimensions we normally see around us?" Dex asked her.

Quin laughed, thinking he was making a joke. That was, of course, the basis of her Seeker training and the use of the athame. "I did know that. I believe our Seeker tools are built on that theory."

Dex cocked an eyebrow at her. "Well—the chicken and the egg. But I'm not talking about Seekers. I'm talking about people right here." With a sweep of his hand he indicated the complex below them. "What's the word? *Physicists.* I used to have trouble saying it, but my father made sure I could pronounce it correctly. *Physicists* believe there are hidden dimensions coiled up tightly at every point in space. And among all of the physicists there's one who believes that, with the right key, you could unlock those hidden dimensions, unfurl them, even enter them."

He walked forward, adjusting his medallion, and their vantage point shifted dramatically. They had dropped much closer and were looking at one building in particular. It stood less than a full story aboveground but gave the impression that it was vast beneath the surface.

"They've already begun to test their theories for accessing those dimensions," he said. "It must be happening right now. And there will be strange side effects. Before they have the machines calibrated correctly, portions of the lab will warp or even disappear, and once, they worked for a day and a night straight, and when they left the lab, they discovered that only a few minutes had passed."

"They'd accessed no-space?" Quin asked, noting the way his tenses danced around as he spoke. As always, it was difficult to pin his story down in time.

"Yes, they'd accessed no-space."

"Dex, what—"

"What does this have to do with me?" he asked. "It's why we began our family trip."

CHAPTER 51

MATHEUS AND DESMOND

Matheus and Desmond's father was called James, a common name, though his family knew he was not a common sort of fellow but an Important Scientist. They had built their lives around that idea.

One evening, James came home from his place of work with news that he'd gotten special permission to show them his lab on a Sunday. Matheus was four years old and unbearably excited by the prospect. He'd been to his father's lab before, but only the outer section, where tours were allowed to go. He'd never seen the inner lab, which was, his father had told him so many times, where all the wonders were.

James's wife, Maggie, was somewhat less enthusiastic. She knew that her husband and his colleagues had been running into difficulties for months. There had been a movement to shut down James's lab in particular as not being run in the public good. The truth was that James had been acting oddly for weeks—not frighteningly odd, but cheerful and optimistic, when Maggie guessed there was little reason to be so.

On the Sunday when they set out to visit the lab, she had a

suspicion that her husband was about to be fired and was taking his sons to see the place because it was the last time that would be possible. The wistful looks he cast in his outer lab, as they passed through, tended to confirm her suspicions. *He's fired for sure,* she thought. *Why doesn't he simply tell me?*

With baby Desmond strapped to his mother's chest and little Matheus holding his father by the hand, they went through a security door to the inner lab. This inner lab was enormous. Matheus would later remember how their footsteps had echoed loudly as they walked across the dimly lit floor of the circular space, where looming machines were ranged along the walls, mechanical monsters waiting in the shadows.

Near the center of the room was a series of paired upright bars, taller than a man, arrayed in such a way that they formed a sort of short passage.

James showed his wife and son around, naming the equipment for them and describing the functions of everything in too much technical detail. After a while, as if it had just occurred to him, he asked, "Would you like to see how it works?"

"You mean turn it on?" Maggie asked.

Unconsciously she took a step back and put an arm around baby Desmond. He'd fallen asleep and was snoring—or at least, that's the way Matheus would later describe things to his younger brother.

"It's perfectly all right," James assured his wife. "Turning it on does nothing dangerous. There's nothing dangerous in this lab."

He spoke so calmly that Maggie was reassured. She would always remember that—he'd used that tone of voice to soothe her, even though he'd been lying to her face and peculiar things had been happening in the lab for months. It was a breach of trust she could never forgive.

"Come here, Matheus," James said. "You will have to help me."

"I help?" Matheus asked with what some might have called a charming childhood lisp, which endeared him to adults, even when he was stunning squirrels with rocks and skinning them while they were still alive.

"There's something we have to do first," James told his son conspiratorially.

Maggie did not grow alarmed until her husband had wheeled a ladder into place, climbed it with Matheus, and allowed the boy to use a can of black spray paint to destroy a camera mounted near the ceiling.

"What are you doing?" Maggie demanded, feeling the first true stab of panic that day. It would not be her last. Matheus, on the other hand, was delighted, because destruction always delighted him.

"It's all right, Maggie. I'm letting the boy have a little fun." James spoke with that same assured calm; he was the scientist and she was not.

"Again!" cried Matheus.

"Yes, again," James told his son.

"Stop it! James!" Maggie said as she watched her husband wheel the ladder to the other side of the room. She wasn't sure whether she should try to block him or retreat toward the door with the baby.

James was already directing Matheus to take out the second camera. Maggie was at the bottom of the ladder when James came down. She didn't want to show Matheus how upset she was, but it was hard to keep the anger from her voice.

"What are you doing?" she hissed.

James moved her aside as if she were an inconvenient piece of furniture, and walked to a bank of controls. When he flipped on the power, the whole room began to hum.

"What are you doing, James?" She raised her voice this time and followed him across the room.

"I told Matheus he could see it turned on," James replied evenly. "I'm turning it on."

The hum grew louder as the lab's machinery warmed up.

"Stop it. Stop it! I don't want the boys in here." Her husband appeared to be transforming into someone else before her eyes.

James looked over at her with a raised eyebrow. "I built most of this room, my dear. Nothing bad will happen."

As if on cue, an alarm began to sound, not in the room they were in but outside, throughout the building. Maggie moved to the security door, where she peered through the small window. Lights were flashing in the outer lab.

"You've set off an alarm, James!"

She tried the huge lever on the door, first gently and then frantically, but it wouldn't budge. There was a pad next to the lever, where the user had to place a hand to open the lock. She pressed her palm against it, but nothing happened.

"James! What have you done?" She was becoming wild with fear. The baby woke up and began to cry loudly.

"The alarm is only because I disabled the cameras," James said, unperturbed, as he continued to adjust the controls. The hum in the lab grew louder. It seemed to be concentrated on the array of parallel vertical beams. "The guards noticed two cameras out and they set off the alarm. That's all. Standard procedure."

"But—won't they be coming here? Are they going to take you, or arrest you?"

"Yes, if they get inside."

"James—!" All sense had deserted him, and Maggie didn't know what to say. She tugged on the door lever again, to no avail.

The humming around the upright bars grew so intense that Matheus covered his ears and Maggie covered the baby's ears. Desmond was wailing now, adding to her panic.

Then little Matheus saw something amazing. The vertical bars began to be eaten by fire. Matheus would later describe the sight as being like white and black snakes twining their way up each of the beams until the structures were seething with energy. The hum grew even more intense, but Matheus had forgotten to keep his ears covered. He was entranced by the glowing pathway in the center of the lab and began to walk toward it.

"Get away from those, Matheus!" yelled Maggie.

She wanted to run across the room and retrieve him, but she didn't want to bring the baby any closer. The alarm had increased in volume and the lights were flashing more quickly in the outer lab.

"They're here, James! They're going to stop you!" she told him desperately.

"They were going to stop me anyway," he responded, not even looking up from the controls. "The government banned my research, and all of my equipment is slated for disassembly and recycling."

So Maggie had been right. James was about to be fired, and in the face of that he'd gone crazy.

A group of guards had reached the outer lab. To Maggie's eye they didn't look particularly fierce or well trained, but they were armed with guns. They rushed to the inner door, so that they were face to face with her through the small window. Maggie gestured at them frantically.

"We need my pack, Matheus," James said calmly. "Will you help me put it on?"

Matheus nodded. He was amazed at the havoc his own father was causing.

James's pack was hidden between two of the machines along the wall, and when they pulled it out, Matheus discovered that it was immense. James had been preparing it for months, and it looked like nothing so much as an upright body bag full of more than one body.

James was forced to kneel on the floor with his back to the bag while Matheus helped pull the straps over his shoulders.

"Open it, please!" Maggie cried at the men outside.

The guards had been fiddling with the outer lock for several minutes. One of them was on the phone, and the others were poking uselessly at a security pad.

"Can't you get it open?" Maggie asked them, though they could hear nothing through the door.

James was on his feet, wobbling as he got used to the weight of the pack. "Now," he told his son, "get ready to be astonished."

At the control console, James made a final adjustment. Matheus's mouth formed a round O of surprise. Maggie stopped jiggling the door handle and turned to gaze at the center of the room.

The seething energy around every upright bar reached a blinding intensity, and when it did, the glowing lines leapt across the empty air between the two parallel sets of bars and joined each other, forming a string of incandescent ovals. From where Matheus stood, these ovals were the edges of a passage leading between the two rows of bars. And through them he could no longer see the other side of the lab. He could see only darkness.

There was a creak from the laboratory door. Outside, the guard on the phone was dictating instructions to the others. Another creak, as if the mechanism inside the door were trying to release.

"They're coming in here, James," Maggie said, forcing calm into her voice. "Shut it down. Before they get inside. James!"

He ignored her, scanned the controls, touched one or two, tweaking their positions. Then he walked over to Matheus and took the boy's hand.

"Come on," James said to his wife. "We're walking through, and they won't come after us."

"Matheus! Come back here!" Maggie ordered. She was torn between remaining by the door and running to grab her older son.

Matheus looked at his mother and his baby brother, who was still screaming and kicking his feet. He shook his head. His father was doing something against the rules, and Matheus wasn't going to be left out of it.

The door creaked again, more seriously. The guards were making headway. Maggie saw the lever on her side shake. Only a minute ago, she'd been desperate to open it herself, but now she hesitated. What would happen after those men got into the room? The baby's crying was making it hard for her to think. Would the guards understand that she hadn't been party to this act? What would they do to her family? And what was James going to do to Matheus?

"They're coming in! James! *Please stop.*"

"Yes, they're coming in, Maggie. They can catch me and put me in prison, or you can come here and walk through with me. I cannot explain this to you just now, but you will see in time. On the other side, we'll all be together. I can't promise that the same will be true if you don't come." The door shook and groaned. "It won't take them much longer," James said. His calm was finally breaking. "Maggie, please. I can get out with my research and my dignity, and they won't know where we've gone."

Maggie peered through the window. The guards were hunched around the hinges of the door. She looked back to her husband and son, standing before the blinding row of ovals that outlined a dark pathway before them. She made a choice. Crossing the room, she joined them. The hum coming off the bars was so strong, she worried it would damage the baby's ears just to be near it. But she would not retreat now.

There was another loud creak from the door.

"What does it do?" she asked James.

"It takes us home to England."

Behind them, there was a tremendous wrenching sound, as the top half of the door peeled open on one side. One of the guards stuck his arm through the opening and strained to reach the inner door lever.

"Come on," James said to his wife.

With their small son in hand, they stepped over the seething border of the first oval and into the darkness. Once they'd crossed the threshold, they could no longer see the ovals ahead of them. Blackness surrounded them, and only the glowing border behind them was still visible.

James, Maggie, and Matheus (and perhaps baby Desmond, though he was too young to remember) immediately felt the pull of time lengthening around them. James had thought there might be an effect like this, and he walked briskly, tugging Maggie and Matheus along with him. In a few steps, he could make out the distant oval opening ahead, with the English countryside visible through it.

He looked over his shoulder to watch as the guards poured into the inner lab. They rushed toward the opening between the bars, where they stopped, confused by the hum and by the blackness hanging in front of them.

The oval behind them, marking the border into the lab, began to waver. James watched until he saw the top half collapsing; then he turned back toward their destination. They were only yards from the new opening, beyond which meadow grasses were waving in a gentle breeze.

They stepped over the second, seething border, out of the darkness and into the grass and sunlight. Both parents lifted Matheus up, so that to him it felt as though he were flying into the new landscape. Behind them, there was nothing left to see but a black pathway. Soon the second opening wavered and slowly fell apart. As they watched, the world stitched itself back together, leaving no trace. They were standing in open grass with rolling hills all around them.

Maggie knelt and examined Matheus and Desmond. Her children were unharmed. Slowly she got to her feet and took in their surroundings. She was shaking and still panicked.

"Are we really in England?" she asked her husband when she had looked to the horizon in every direction.

"We are," he said. "And there's our new home."

He pointed to a nearby hill, but there was no house upon it. They walked to the crest anyway to survey the landscape beyond, in case James had mistaken one hill for another. But there was no house anywhere. Matheus and Maggie saw the confusion on his face, which would slowly turn into panic and then, much later, desperation. The shape of the hills was correct, but the world around them was devoid of any signs of modern life.

It took James several days to discover why. He and his family had been the first to walk into an open anomaly. He'd made his calculations very carefully and checked and rechecked his work in the weeks leading up to their escape.

James had succeeded in taking them to the very spot in northern England where he had meant to arrive. But in his inexperience he had not controlled the massive energy levels generated in his lab. The anomaly had not only unfurled the hidden dimensions and allowed them to pass *between;* it had blasted a tunnel through time. They had emerged from no-space into England in the year 506.

CHAPTER 52

QUIN

While Dex was telling his story, he had tunneled them away from the laboratory complex. When he finished speaking, they had arrived at an isolated and lovely farm in northern England. Through the gray curtain of the anomaly, he and Quin were looking at a small stone farmhouse with painted shutters.

"This was supposed to be our house," Dex said. "My father had stuffed his backpack with everything he would need to continue his research in a small way, to create simple tools to manipulate the hidden dimensions. He thought he'd be living here anonymously and working on whatever he wanted for the rest of his life."

Behind the house was a large stone barn, which must have been meant to serve as the Old Dread's workshop—James's workshop.

"So you've never seen this place before?" Quin asked.

"Not the farmhouses, no. But I recognize the countryside. This is where we first camped, so many hundreds of years ago, where my father first set up his portable workshop. We came back many times when we were still a family." He allowed himself a moment of nostalgia as he took in the view. "In my father's laboratory, they'd used machines with massive amounts of energy to tear through the fabric of space, but there were gentler ways, natural materials that could produce the correct vibration."

"Your medallions?" Quin asked.

"Exactly." He studied the medallion in his hands before adjusting it and beginning to walk again. The countryside twisted as the tunnel changed around him. "He'd made the medallions inside the anomaly in his lab. That means they count time equally well in no-space and in the world." Dex flipped his over, showing her the concentric circles and notches on the back. "The medallions don't only move us through no-space. They are how we wake ourselves when we're in the hidden dimensions. They are our many-dimensioned alarm clocks—though nothing except the original laboratory equipment could allow travel *backward* in time."

The farm disappeared behind them, and the edges of the tunnel became entirely black. Dex must be taking them *There* now. They were leaving the world entirely.

"The athames are made of the same stone?" she asked.

"Yes. They're cruder, but they can still unfurl no-space and bring you back."

He shifted the medallion, and Quin had the sense of the space around her warping and changing. Time was lengthening, and her mind began to slip.

"Knowledge of self," she whispered, *"knowledge of home . . ."*

"We won't be long," he assured her. "I won't let you get lost. I promise."

She felt his hand on her shoulder, grounding her. A short while later, he stepped past her. In the beam of Quin's flashlight was a small pile of metal objects. Dex bent to pick them up.

"I noticed that Maggie and her Watchers overlooked these when they took the disruptors," he said. "She never could be bothered to understand much."

Quin and Dex returned to the underside of the Transit Bridge, where they stepped out of the anomaly and onto the little perch from which they had begun the trip.

Dex arranged the objects he'd brought back from no-space so that they were bathed in the sunlight coming through the rafters. They were three metal shields, which Quin recognized because she'd hidden under just such a shield during the fight with the Watchers atop the Transit Bridge. They had holes all along their rims, and the shield faces were made of concentric circles. Quin touched them curiously.

"Maggie put disruptors on her Watchers. It's only prudent that we carry disruptor shields," Dex told her. "We'll let them soak up the sun for a while."

"Disruptor shields—that's what these are called?"

He flipped one of the shields over and pointed out the handgrip on the underside. "If you pull this lever, the shield will absorb disruptor sparks and spit them back at your attacker. It's quite easy to learn to use them and a good defense to go along with the impellor."

As the shields absorbed the sunlight, Dex sat with Quin and demonstrated how to use them. They were both entirely engrossed in his explanation until a deep, resonant thump traveled through the structure of the Transit Bridge.

Startled, Quin looked up. "What was that?"

"I know that sound," said Dex.

"Was it a wave-pulse?" Quin asked, realizing that she too knew the sound.

"Look." He pointed across the harbor.

The sun was dipping below the horizon, and lights had begun to come on throughout Hong Kong and Kowloon. Except a large swath of Hong Kong was now dark.

"Maggie is here," Dex said. His expression changed to a look of urgency. He reached for the medallion hanging around his neck.

There was another thump, which Quin felt in her bones. More of Hong Kong's lights went out. Someone was using a wave-pulse, and the city was going dark. Not just the city—

"Look at *Traveler*," Quin said. "That's not the course it was following."

The airship had fallen from the altitude it had maintained all afternoon. Its engines had been running with an audible but tame rumble. Now several of them were silent. The remaining engines ran with a high, unstable whine that Quin recognized very well from the last time she'd been on *Traveler*. There was another bone-shaking thump, and those engines too cut out.

The airship was going to crash into the harbor.

"Dex, what's she doing?"

But when she looked to Dex, he was already gone.

CHAPTER 53

MAUD

Traveler's great room was full in the hours before supper. The older apprentices were practicing together with whipswords in training mode, which meant that the weapons melted harmlessly against their skin. They were instructed by a formidable woman from the house of the stag who was still recovering from wounds but who'd insisted she was well enough to resume her role as instructor after a hundred-and-fifty-year interruption.

The other adult Seekers who were recovered enough to walk were practicing with whipswords if they had them and other weapons if they did not, in the way Seekers had sparred for hundreds of years. Not one of them had an athame any longer—the Middle Dread had confiscated those and redistributed them to his Watchers—but Maud supposed the exercise would do all of them good. What they would become when they'd fully recovered, she didn't know.

She herself was working with a group of smaller children, the ones whose sense of time was the most flexible.

Sara, seven years old, stood between Kaspar and the training dummy. Kaspar gripped the knife—a real knife for the first time—and stood, unmoving, gazing intently at the dummy.

"Kaspar, the knife must not touch Sara, do you understand?" Maud asked the little boy.

He nodded gravely.

"You are only to try to get past her," the Young Dread instructed him. "Now go!"

Kaspar dodged right. Sara quickly blocked him. He dodged left, and she was there before him again because she was faster and had a longer reach. The only hope Kaspar had of getting to the dummy was to speed himself up, as the Young Dread had been teaching him to do. He was blocked again, Sara shifting in front of him with the agility of an eel, and the little boy grew frustrated.

"Kaspar! As I showed you!"

Sara thwarted him again, and Kaspar, in his exasperation, instinctively changed tactics. He became a hazy, boy-like shape as he swerved first left, then right, and then moved all the way around the girl before she had any idea where he was going.

Suddenly the knife was stuck in the leg of the training dummy and Kaspar was standing behind it, far away from his opponent, who had to turn all the way around to locate him.

When the other children clapped, Kaspar looked very pleased with himself.

"Good," the Young Dread told him. She gestured for another child to come forward and take the knife from Kaspar. "Now you, Julia."

They had finished their long ocean crossing, and *Traveler* was now following a regular course over Hong Kong's harbor. John would come here when Shinobu was safe. And this evening, when they were done in the great room, the Young Dread would bring the children to the windows to watch the evening dance of light across the buildings along the harbor front. It had become a daily ritual and a profoundly moving occurrence for the children, most of whom had never before seen modern illumination.

The thump and pulse hit the airship as the Young Dread and her wards were gathering up their training implements. All lights on board went out. And then the engines began to whine.

The Young Dread had been on *Traveler* before when it was crashing, and she recognized the engine strain immediately. When the second pulse hit them, knocking out the remaining engines, the ship became completely silent. Through the windows outside the great room, Maud watched them coasting toward the towering canopy of the bridge. If she were not mistaken, they would be crashing directly into it.

CHAPTER 54

QUIN

Traveler's engines were silent, but it coasted briefly on the aerodynamics of its body. It maintained itself aloft for a short time, but when it crossed some crucial physical point of no return, the ship's nose dropped and its final thrust of forward momentum sent it plummeting toward the Transit Bridge.

It's crashing again, Quin's mind screamed. *It's crashing on the other side of the world.*

And then it did crash. The impact was loud—a rumbling, tearing noise like a storm above her, but the result to Quin, standing among the lower rafters, was surprisingly light. She felt only a tremor through the heavy piers that held the bridge above the harbor, but soon aftershocks radiated out among the rafters.

Far above, the bridge's canopy shrieked as it warped. Other noises came to Quin, the very human sound of people yelling. There were rumbles that must have been buildings collapsing along the top level.

Quin could hear everything, because the harbor itself had gone completely silent. Anything with an engine—every ship, every aircar, every automobile close to the Transit Bridge—had stopped running when the lights went out. That was what a wave-pulse did when it was used in a city.

She looked to the massive support pier. She'd once climbed down that very pier with Shinobu and swum away into the harbor. There were metal rungs that would take her all the way to the water. Getting away would be the safest course. But Quin was not going to leave. Her mother might still be somewhere inside the massive structure. And Maggie. And if Maggie were here, Shinobu might be here too.

She looked across the beam that would lead her back inside and formed a very stupid plan. Thinking that she might need protection against whatever was happening above, Quin tied the two disruptor shields Dex had left for her across her back. She retraced her steps down the narrow beam, back up the ladder through the hide of the bridge, and into the lowest levels.

CHAPTER 55

SHINOBU

Shinobu dreamed of Quin. She was looking out across water and saying: *It's crashing again.*

"Shinobu, wake up! I've got to go." John was shaking him. As Shinobu opened his eyes, John spoke to him urgently. "I'm going. Are you staying?"

John was already gathering his things from around the campfire in a great hurry. Shinobu forced himself awake, unbearably sore after a full evening of him and John throwing and dragging each other around the amphitheater with the cylindrical weapon from Maud's cloak. It was the only item they'd figured out how to use, and they'd used it far too much on each other.

"Where are you going?" he asked John.

"Hong Kong. Something's happening."

"Is it *Traveler?*" Shinobu asked immediately. In his dream, Quin had been talking about *Traveler,* he was certain of it.

Surprised, John said, "I think it is."

"Then we're both going."

CHAPTER 56

MAUD

In moments, the Seekers in the great room had poured into the corridors and strapped themselves into the bracing stations that lined the walls. The Young Dread saw the medical staff securing patients and themselves in the adjacent medical corridor.

Traveler coasted for a time, but the last seconds were a silent plunge toward the bridge. Children screamed. Almost everyone screamed.

"Hold on tightly!" Maud ordered, cursing herself for being without an athame. All along the corridor, in the half-light from the sky outside, she saw frightened faces turned to her. Directly on either side of her, Kaspar and Sara were stoically holding the straps that secured them to the wall.

The impact was sudden and at the same time infinite. The airship's bow struck the bridge canopy at an angle, with a ripping, rending noise, and the force tore at them all as they pressed themselves against the hull. The impact continued as the ship plowed through the canopy and its underlying structure, drawing tremendous groans from the twisting steel. Maud saw the bow buckle up into the great room, was sure the ship would be torn in half and all of its passengers killed, and yet the force was not deadly—the canopy was shifting beneath the airship, absorbing its momentum. Next to her, Kaspar's face was terrified and brave as he flattened himself beneath the straps.

As the shriek of steel died out, they stopped in darkness. The creaks and moans of the damaged airship were swallowed up in the greater rumbles of the bridge outside.

The hallway had become a hillside, with a rectangle of light at the top. The crew were there, carrying the wounded through a tilted hatch.

"We will be fine," Sara, the seven-year-old girl, told Kaspar. They were holding hands as they all climbed upward toward the light. The ship shook with tremors from the structure beneath them.

"We protect each other," Kaspar said.

At the hatch, the Young Dread was confronted with a twilight sky above them and the high peaks of the sail canopy all around. *Traveler* had crushed one such peak into the body of the bridge, creating a kind of valley among the sails and causing the neighboring peaks to angle dizzyingly toward them, their supporting frameworks creaking and stretching the canvas. Below the canopy were the sounds of people moving in great numbers and of structures falling. Distantly came the noise of a building fire.

With the youngest passengers, Maud climbed down the emergency ladder from the listing airship onto the mass of canvas below. The airship's crew were already taking the gravely injured away on stretchers, across the broken sail, toward any place that might provide them a way off the canopy and off the bridge.

Maud and the children and the Seekers followed, as the bridge shuddered around them.

CHAPTER 57

QUIN

Inside the Transit Bridge, Quin couldn't hear the chaos, but the entire structure shivered, hinting at the ongoing destruction on the levels above.

The bridge's lower levels housed the machinery for air circulation and lifts, and Quin made her way through these dark spaces by flashlight. All of the equipment was silent.

She was going up, into the heart of the tumult. The airlifts were dead, so she made her way into a staircase, which she ascended at a run. When she reached the lowest occupied level, where the cheapest, most crowded drug bars could be found, she came out into a mass exodus of visitors. Flashlights, glow sticks, and mobile phones lit the dingy corridors that smelled of opium smoke and Shiva sticks. People were pushing each other and yelling as the crowds moved toward the exits—not a stampede yet, but headed that way.

Quin pushed against the tide until she reached another stairwell, one that was for Transit Bridge residents only. It would have been just as crowded if the entrance hadn't been cleverly hidden in an offshoot of the main corridor. Inside the stairwell were fewer people and fewer flashlights. She could see well enough to head upward as the bridge shook, sending tremors down the handrails. There were residents on the stairs, yelling confused updates to each other between floors.

"The bridge is starting to sway!" a young man above her said. "Level four has the least crowded exit route."

"It's just the canopy," another responded. "But it's on fire."

"Do you feel that shaking? It's not just the canopy," a third said, from far up the stairwell, near the door to the main level.

Quin ran upward. The vibrations in the structure were happening more often and becoming more intense, though there was no regularity. The idea of the structure falling apart terrified her, but what if Shinobu was up in the mess above?

"Stay off the main level," a young mother called as she burst through the door from the second level. She dragged her child behind her as they ran down the stairs.

"Why?" the first young man called after her.

"There's a fire. From one of the restaurants. The canopy is catching! Find the fastest way out."

The woman scooped her child up into her arms. Quin watched her disappear out the exit on the fourth level, where there was a passage straight to the Kowloon side. The fear in the woman's eyes was infectious. Quin didn't slow her pace, but internally she hesitated—what if Shinobu wasn't up there? Should she follow the crowds and leave?

No. She wasn't leaving. She passed the hesitant young man on the final landing before the main level, and didn't answer when he called after her, "Do you know something?"

She did know something. There was smoke seeping into the stairwell. The bridge was on fire, and *Traveler* was somewhere above her. She would help if she could.

CHAPTER 58

MAUD

The broken canopy sail was a wasteland of torn and piled canvas, rent beams, snapped cables. The other sails billowed and shifted in alarming ways. Though the crash landing hadn't been fatal to the occupants of the airship, when Maud looked back at *Traveler*, enormous, lying askew, its engines crushed, she understood that the weight of the ship, even impacting slowly against a structure as large as this bridge, would create a grievous chain reaction.

"I smell smoke," Kaspar told her. He was climbing over a pile of rope and cable with the rest of his training group, all under the age of eight.

The Young Dread had smelled the smoke as soon as they'd opened *Traveler*'s hatch. But the fire was much larger now. Some of it was on the levels below them, which was why smoke leaked through the holes in the crushed canopy, making the air heavy and harsh, but there was a larger fire behind *Traveler*, toward the south end of the bridge; she could hear its approaching roar. The children were coughing.

"We can get down to the bridge itself here!" called the airship's captain. He and the rest of the crew, carrying patients on stretchers, were far ahead, near the base of the neighboring sail.

"Go!" she yelled to him.

She watched his group navigate between torn structural beams and disappear through a great tear.

The Young Dread looked at the slow-moving procession around her, made up of half-healed adult Seekers and fifteen children. She raised her voice, and said, "Anyone who can move faster should go and take the children with you. I'll bring up the rear."

The adults looked at her and shook their heads. No one was going on alone. "It's all right," the woman who was once a Seeker instructor answered. "We'll stay together."

"Check the houses!" came a loud voice above them.

The Young Dread experienced a moment of awful realization: the voice belonged to Maggie.

Maud and her companions searched the smoky air for the source of the voice. The old woman stood far above them, atop a pile of broken beams. Of course. Maggie's weapon had brought down *Traveler,* just as she'd tried to do before. The Young Dread should have known immediately. Maggie had been waiting for them here.

"Go! Now!" the old woman commanded.

Who was she speaking to? Maud scanned their surroundings, realized that Maggie was not their chief concern. Twelve Watchers, almost all wearing disruptors, were ranged in a circle around them at various high points in the debris. Now, at the old woman's command, they drew their whipswords and charged from all sides.

Without a word, the Seekers arranged themselves in a tight knot around Maud and the children. The crash had interrupted most of them at practice, when they were already armed, and whipswords and knives appeared in almost every hand.

The air grew thick. Maud felt her ears pop. She did not understand

Maggie's weapons, but she knew this was a sign that one of them was about to be used.

"Down!" she ordered.

Immediately everyone obeyed. They were hit with a rolling force that scattered them every which way. The Watchers were still coming, and the high whine of their disruptors had begun.

CHAPTER 59

JOHN

John and Shinobu stepped out of the anomaly into a tiny secluded alley on Hong Kong Island, not far from the entrance to the Transit Bridge. Shinobu had set the coordinates on John's athame—quite well, John noticed—and in only a few minutes, they came out onto the main road giving access to the bridge.

Pandemonium.

Hundreds, or maybe thousands, were streaming off the Transit Bridge onto the darkened streets of Hong Kong. Smoke rose through the bridge's canopy into the evening air in a dozen places, and there was a fire, at the near end, burning up structure and canopy alike and nearly obscuring the huge black shape on the other side of the flames.

"Is that *Traveler*?" John asked, knowing it was but unable to comprehend what he was seeing.

The airship had crashed into the bridge at about the midpoint, flattening one of the enormous sails and causing the others to lean in precariously. Even from where they stood he could hear the creak of metal bending.

"Power's out here," Shinobu noted, taking in the city buildings around them.

"And on the bridge," John said, observing that only the fire was lighting the Transit Bridge now.

"She used that weapon again," Shinobu muttered. "She was dying to use it."

There was no reason to answer. Maggie was certainly the cause of the havoc they were witnessing. The flood of humans continued to move past them.

"John, I don't think it's out of line to mention that your grandmother is a horrible person."

"Yes, she is," he agreed. "It's good to know I'm not the only one who's noticed."

Looking out at the bridge, Shinobu ran his hands over his head as if trying to concentrate. He said, "I can get us right to the canopy. I've done it before."

Without a word, John handed him the athame.

It took several tries, but in a few minutes they were looking through the seething doorway of a new anomaly at a shifting, swaying peak of the Transit Bridge canopy. *Traveler* was visible just below this particular sail, its huge mass crushing the canopy and the upper level of the bridge beneath it.

"Use your knives to brace yourself!" John said.

Shinobu nodded at him, understanding. Together they jumped out onto the sail with knives drawn and sank their blades into the thick canvas as anchors to keep themselves from falling.

"It's really moving!" Shinobu said as they clung to the sail.

It was windy, and the smoke billowing over *Traveler* from the fire beyond was smarting in John's eyes. Beneath his feet, the sail creaked and shifted, the framework supporting it permanently damaged, even if it was still upright.

"The sail might collapse!" John said, feeling the instability through his feet. "Or even the bridge itself."

"Look!" Shinobu yelled, rubbing his streaming eyes on his shoulder as the smoke buffeted them. "She's there! Attacking!"

He was pointing down into the valley beneath the airship. John saw Maud down there. She was alive! But she and a group of Seekers were being knocked over like bowling pins by one of Maggie's weapons. As they struggled to their feet, a dozen Watchers ran at them from all sides.

John had the athame. Maud had nothing but a few weapons. For the first time ever, John saw the Young Dread in a fight and was worried that she might not be able to keep herself alive.

"Let's go!" he yelled.

CHAPTER 60

SHINOBU

Shinobu waited as John pulled the cylindrical black weapon from his cloak, shook it to ready it to fire.

"Okay!" Shinobu yelled. He could barely hear the word above the gusts of wind, the creak of beams, and the roar of the distant fire.

He yanked his knife out of the sail, pointed himself down its dangerous slope, and took the first step. In two yards he and John were both in an unstoppable slide as the sail groaned beneath them. He dragged his left arm against the canvas behind him, using his knife to arrest his descent and prevent himself from careening out of control. He could not spare a glance back, but he could see John just at the corner of his vision, following him with equal terror and determination.

Near the bottom, they hit a shifting girder beneath the canvas, and, flailing, Shinobu jumped free, followed half a second later by John. When they hit the sail again, they both found themselves running headlong across messy debris toward the fight.

In moments, they were within firing range of the Watchers, who were steadily closing in on their victims.

"Now!" Shinobu called.

John had already raised the impellor, and the air was getting thick about Shinobu. John fired their new weapon and sent half the Watchers in front of them sprawling down into the mess of Seekers below.

"You missed Maggie!" Shinobu yelled.

Maggie had stopped on a high perch, still well above the Seekers and Watchers. She turned toward Shinobu and John, her own weapon held out. The air in Shinobu's lungs began to pool thickly, making him cough. He leapt out of the weapon's direct line of aim as both Maggie and John fired at the same moment.

Hitting the canvas, he watched the streams from both weapons collide, sending up thousands of sparks that lit the scene like fireworks. John was knocked over and his weapon rolled away down the slope toward the fallen Watchers.

"Dammit!" yelled Shinobu, racing to help him.

CHAPTER 61

QUIN

Quin climbed up from the main level of the Transit Bridge through a breach in the sail. It was no longer much of a climb; the canopy had been compressed down to the surface of the bridge beneath the airship. Below Quin the main thoroughfare was deserted. Whoever had not been directly beneath the ship or caught in the initial burst of fire was escaping off either end of the bridge.

She picked her way across the destruction of the canopy toward where she knew *Traveler* must be, the air getting smokier with every step. The roar of the fire and the creak of girders was louder out in the open. It felt as though she were walking into a storm.

When she'd crested a twisted heap of rafters and canvas, she could see the crashed airship below her. In *Traveler*'s shadow was a substantial hand-to-hand battle that looked like little more than a free-for-all. It took her a moment to grasp who was fighting. There were Watchers in a circle, armed with disruptors, and they were dragging people. Their victims were fighting back with whipswords and knives.

Those are Seekers! In a flash of understanding, Quin divined that she was looking at forgotten Seekers and their children—the Young Dread must have kept them alive and brought them back from no-space. Quin would have been elated if there had been time, but on the heels of this realization, there was a sudden burst—it had to be an impellor—and everyone, Watchers and victims alike, were flattened.

Quin searched the smoky air until she found the person who had fired the weapon: Maggie. The older woman was perched above the fray, looking down on the fight like an orchestra conductor. The crashed airship, the broken bridge—these were Maggie's doing. She had gone after Seekers in no-space, and now she was going after any Seekers who were left.

Below, victims and attackers were getting back to their feet and engaging with each other again. Quin caught sight of red hair. Shinobu. He was so tall, he was half a head above most of the others. Grateful relief swept over her to see him back under his own control, but she paused only long enough to pull the shields from her back and strap them to her arms. She uttered a quiet thanks to Dex for thinking of the shields, which were probably going to save her life.

Maggie was firing the impellor again. Quin saw John in the fight below; the old woman was so intent on killing that she was even attacking her own grandson.

Quin ran across the sloping canvas, cracking out her whipsword. When she was in full charge, Maggie noticed her, turned, and lifted her impellor toward Quin. Not slowing, Quin raised her left-hand shield and twisted the lever in her fist. The concentric rings of the shield began to spin as the air thickened and Quin felt her jaw click to the side. The impellor's burst hit the shield, and the force sheared off away from her, sending loose cables and sections of canvas flying while Quin was driven back, her heels digging channels in the canvas as she tried to hold her position.

When the burst ended, she risked a peek over the lip of the shield to locate Maggie, and the woman fired the impellor the moment she saw Quin's eyes. Quin raised her shield, but her feet were not steady as the second burst hit. She was lifted from the surface and thrown sideways down the slope. When she hit the canvas, she managed to stay upright with the weight of the shields counterbalancing her, but she had to keep moving to avoid falling. In a moment she was running out of control toward the Watchers below.

The Watchers and Seekers were still recovering from Maggie's last impellor blast, getting to their feet or grappling with each other on hands and knees. In the moments before Quin collided with the nearest of them, she saw something amazing: Four small figures were weaving out from among the tangled mass of adults. They moved like the Young Dread, in a blur of limbs, until they'd each found a Watcher as a target. Then the four children paused, came into focus, and sank knives into the Watchers' legs. The Watchers moved awkwardly with the heavy disruptors on their chests, and when they struck out in retaliation, the children were already gone.

Quin plowed into the two nearest attackers just as Maggie flattened everyone with the impellor again.

CHAPTER 62

NOTT

As soon as Maggie began walking down toward the Young Dread and the Seekers, Nott quietly backed away from the fight, inching toward the big tear in the neighboring sail. He knew Maggie was going to sort those Seekers and children into who should live and who should die, and the Watchers were going to kill the ones who should die—and probably some of the others.

Nott was wearing the helm, but the things it whispered did not make him very happy. He could see that little brat Kaspar down there, who'd been so irritating back on the ship. Yet when he focused on the boy and imagined going after him, Nott couldn't get excited.

I don't think I want *to kill him,* he grasped with some shock.

It didn't require much force of will to pull off the helmet and toss it away. Nott watched the helm roll down into a little depression, where it got lost beneath a jagged rafter.

"Hopefully no one ever finds it," he said out loud.

He touched Aelred's head in the little pocket just inside the flap of his cloak. "If we keep walking the other way, Aelred, we'll be out of sight and then we can use the athame." Maggie had let him carry an athame this time. It hung, ready, at his waist.

Aelred chirruped—nervously, Nott suspected. "I'm not going to cut you up," Nott told him soothingly.

It was smoky here, and the bridge was making frightening noises. Aelred was healed enough, Nott thought, to fly away and save himself.

"Maybe you should go, Aelred," Nott said.

He unwrapped the bat, and the creature flapped his wings a few times but clung tightly to Nott's finger, clicking thoughtfully.

"Do you think so?" Nott asked.

He looked back toward Maggie. Only the top of her head was visible from where he stood, but she wasn't very far away.

"Hmm."

CHAPTER 63

QUIN

The Transit Bridge was moving. The shivers had been growing stronger and more frequent, but now Quin felt something else, a swaying of the whole structure.

There was no time to think about it. The Seekers, the Young Dread, the Watchers—all were now intermingled at close quarters, getting back to their feet. The high whines of the disruptors cut through all other noise. Quin shook off her dizziness and nausea—she'd hit the canvas harder than she'd realized—and pushed through a tangle of people toward three Watchers who were grabbing Seekers, examining their wrists. A disruptor fired. The Seeker victim was overrun with sparks.

The Young Dread was there, her knife at the throat of the Watcher who'd used the disruptor. She dispatched him, cocked her knife to take out Maggie, still far above them. The air was getting thicker.

"Look out!" Quin yelled at Maud.

But Maggie had already fired her impellor, and Maud was knocked backward with everyone else.

"Check the houses!" the old woman was yelling.

Quin watched Maggie reverse her impellor and drag a Seeker out of the crowd. Two Watchers got to their knees and grabbed the man's wrists.

"A bear!" one of them called.

The Young Dread was running to stop them.

"Maud!" Quin yelled.

She took the shield off her right arm and threw it like a discus directly into the Young Dread's hands. Maud got between the disruptor and the injured Seeker a moment before the swarm of sparks rained down around her.

"Twist the handle!" Quin yelled.

The Young Dread was already doing it. The concentric circles on the shield's face began to spin. As a second barrage of sparks hit the metal, the shield crackled and hummed, and then it threw the sparks back in a fantastic display that lit the night. The two Watchers were consumed by the recoiling storm.

CHAPTER 64

SHINOBU

Quin was here. She was in the fight. As she threw a shield to the Young Dread, a Watcher took aim at her with his disruptor. Shinobu leapt over the body of a Seeker covered in disruptor sparks, grabbed Quin's shoulders, spun her around so that her shield would protect her. She lifted it on reflex as the disruptor fired.

"Shinobu, you're here! I've been—"

"So have I!" He ducked behind the shield with her as the sparks swarmed against it. "I'm here and John has an athame." There was no time to say any of the other things he wanted to tell her, only, "If we can get clear of the Watchers, we can get everyone out of here."

"All right!"

With a shift of her fist, the shield sprayed sparks back at her attacker.

"Stay close!" Shinobu called as he ran off again. Another Seeker was being dragged away at the far side of the fight. Shinobu pulled the Young Dread with him, and together they saved the woman.

He expected Maggie to hit them all with her weapon again, but when he glanced up, he saw that the older woman was distracted.

A tall young man stood just yards from her, and they were arguing. Behind the young man was someone it took Shinobu a moment to recognize, and when he finally did recognize him, he was unable to make sense of the man's presence. It was the Old Dread.

"Get everyone away!" John yelled, breaking Shinobu's gaze from those odd new arrivals.

John was herding as many Seekers and children as he could to the north, away from *Traveler,* now that Maggie wasn't firing on them.

Shinobu was helping the injured to their feet when his attention was drawn to one of the dead Watchers. It was a dark-skinned boy called Geb, and at his waist was the athame with a dragon on it—the athame that belonged to Shinobu's mother. He'd seen this athame at Dun Tarm, but only now, out of the focal and free of Maggie, did he feel his own connection to it.

He grabbed the stone dagger and lightning rod from the dead boy, and then he looked for Quin. She was far from the others, fighting the last two Watchers.

He turned to her, and the world changed.

CHAPTER 65

QUIN

All but two of the Watchers were dead or disrupted, and Quin was fighting them. They were wounded and striking at her with weaker and weaker blows, but they wouldn't stop fighting. One of her attackers, too exhausted to remember what Quin's shield could do, fired his disruptor in last-ditch frustration. Quin sent the deadly shower of sparks back at both of them. With that, the hand-to-hand clash was over.

Quin tried to catch her breath in the smoky air as she looked around. Maggie wasn't visible from where Quin stood, but wherever she was, she had stopped firing her impellor. The Young Dread, Shinobu, and John were far off to Quin's right, moving Seekers away. The fight was done, and they could get out of here. Quin ran toward Shinobu.

She made it two steps before the Transit Bridge lurched.

The canopy to her right surged upward dozens of feet. The flattened space where Quin stood shifted sideways, throwing her down as debris moved violently around her.

In the space of a breath, the Young Dread, John, Shinobu, and the

Seekers were far above Quin, as if on a separate structure entirely. She was still in the shadow of *Traveler*, and now she could see Maggie just above her, but where Quin stood and where Maggie stood had both moved lower relative to the other half of the bridge.

"Quin!" Shinobu was yelling down at her.

"Quin!" That was the Young Dread yelling. She stood near Shinobu, with children grouped around her. "Climb!"

"Quin!" yelled Shinobu again, pointing urgently. "The Watchers have athames! Use one!"

On her island in the shifting canopy, there were five Watchers. Three dead and the two who were still thrashing in disruptor sparks. She ran for the closest one. There was an athame right there. She reached for it . . .

. . . and her muscles seized up. Her bones shook, her teeth gnashed, her legs cramped so severely that she could hardly move them. She was caught in a stream of energy raining down from above.

Dex. He was there, above Quin, with Maggie. He was holding up his medallion like a weapon pointed at his mother. He gripped it so tightly, his knuckles were white and the medallion was glowing—and the terrible vibration was coming from it. Maggie was consumed by the energy too, frozen in place, her fists clenching.

Quin thought of Dex in the little cell off the cavern, placing his medallion in the center of the wall. *I've made it a weapon,* he'd said. She'd asked him what sort of weapon, and now she knew.

Quin tried to call his name, but she couldn't speak. Dex didn't know she was there, paralyzed by whatever he was doing to his mother.

CHAPTER 66

NOTT

". . . have you been alive all this time?" That was Maggie, speaking to two men who had appeared on the sail out of nowhere—which meant, of course, that Nott knew exactly where they'd appeared from.

He'd been sneaking closer to Maggie for a few minutes. He was just above her now, on a higher portion of the destroyed sail, peering down at her and her two strange companions.

"Mother, I left for a few minutes to find my father and bring him here," the younger man said, "and in that time, look what you've done." His angry glance took in the crashed airship, the fire beyond it, the wilderness of the canopy. "Call off your Watchers. Put an end to this!"

Mother? Nott thought. *The witch has children?* He supposed he should have known, since she'd mentioned grandchildren, but the idea of having Maggie for a mother was the stuff of nightmares.

"I *am* putting an end to it, Desmond." Maggie was using her friendly voice, full of sympathy, which Nott dearly hoped he would never have to hear again. "I'm putting an end to the houses who attacked Adelaide and Catherine. It's what Matheus was trying to do as well, in his way. People who harmed him, people who obstructed him. We're almost free."

"That is *not* what Matheus was doing. You spent so much time in no-space, you didn't see," the young man said. "Matheus was preparing to get rid of *everyone*. All Seekers, and his family as well. He would have disposed of you, Mother. You've blamed other Seeker houses for the things *he* did. Matheus is the one who set Seeker on Seeker. You kept him safe, and by keeping him safe, in a way, you *caused* the hatred you're fighting against."

The older man spoke then, in a slow, steady voice that reminded Nott of the Middle Dread. Were they related? "Come with me," the man said. "You were not meant to be this person. You were not meant to feed yourself on hate. Let's finish our journey. The farm is waiting for us."

Nott could have told the fellow that Maggie wouldn't listen. He saw her lifting that black cylinder to pitch both of those men far away from her. Nott didn't know these men or have any reason to care about them, but he'd had enough of that old woman throwing people around.

Without pausing, so that he couldn't change his mind—*If she looks at me, I'll change my mind!*—Nott drew a knife, and with the twisting throw the Young Dread had taught him, the throw that doubled the force of impact, he cast it directly at Maggie's back.

It struck her between her shoulder blades and sank in to the hilt.

She hadn't been aiming her weapon, Nott realized belatedly. She'd been lifting her medallion, trying to use it to escape.

"Oh," he said.

Maggie stood, unmoving, Nott's knife handle sticking up from her back, her body paralyzed in some kind of fit. The younger man had his own medallion in his hand. It began to glow as he held it out.

Nott scuttled backward and away, reaching for his athame. He didn't know what these men were up to, and he wasn't going to wait around to find out.

He whispered to the bat, "Shall we go now?"

Aelred chirruped his agreement.

CHAPTER 67

QUIN

Quin forced her body to move. She had to reach the athame at the nearest Watcher's waist and get off the bridge, or she would surely die here. Using her limbs was like carrying herself along with inanimate blocks of stone. She shifted one leg and then the other, after which she fell to her knees, arms outstretched, the athame almost within reach.

The vibration got worse, as though Dex had doubled its intensity. Quin's jaw clamped shut, her arm muscles seized up. When she brushed the athame with her fingertips, the ancient stone implement burst into gritty powder. She watched in helpless dismay as the other athames at the waists of the Watchers around her exploded, victims of Dex's medallion.

Above her, Maggie's hand was outstretched, her own medallion nothing more than gray dust in her palm. Then the old woman, paralyzed just as Quin was, toppled off the edge of her perch down toward Quin.

But Quin was falling too. With a sound like the jaws of hell opening up, the bridge was tearing apart.

To her left, the great black bulk of *Traveler* was shifting, rolling away from her through the neighboring sail, which was, she now saw, fully aflame. Quin herself, with Maggie and the lifeless Watchers, was thrown backward and down—the rafters and the levels below all groaning and breaking beneath her.

Her face turned skyward, Quin watched as Dex caught sight of her. Then he was gone, and Quin was no longer paralyzed, but it didn't matter. She was falling with half the Transit Bridge, the canopy beneath her flaring like a great parachute between steel girders. Cables were snapping and swinging wildly. Quin's little island of sail was dropping away from the body of the bridge, which itself was falling. With her last logical thought, she grabbed a great swath of canvas still attached to the peak of one of the bridge towers. The sail swung her out farther, but that tower too was toppling, and Quin descended with it.

She hit the water. She was tangled in the canvas, weighted by cables, and she flailed in the debris, trying to swim free. When Quin opened her eyes beneath the cold water, she could see only the faint orange of the fire above her. She couldn't breathe, she couldn't breathe, and she was being pulled down and down into darkness.

CHAPTER 68

SHINOBU

The Transit Bridge was falling apart, and somehow Shinobu was on the solid half and Quin was down below him on the half that was collapsing.

John had already opened an anomaly. He and the Young Dread were driving the Seekers and children through it at a run. But Quin was down there. Alone. And he could not get to her in time.

"Quin!" he yelled, seeing her salvation. "The Watchers have athames! Use one!"

Quin heard him, ran toward the Watchers. After only a few steps, she was walking stiffly, and then she was not moving at all. Something was wrong. She fell to her knees, still reaching for an athame but not close enough to grab it.

Shinobu desperately searched the area around her. As soon as he looked up, he discovered the source of her helplessness. The young man who had appeared by Maggie was clutching a medallion, and the stone disc was affecting both Maggie and Quin physically. He was killing Quin, perhaps without even realizing what he was doing.

"Shinobu! Come on!"

Everyone was through the anomaly, and John was standing inside it, yelling for him. The edges of the opening were already going soft.

"Shinobu!"

"Go without me!" he yelled.

He turned back and screamed, "Stop! She's down there! Look!"

The young man with the medallion looked up and met Shinobu's eyes. Maggie was falling toward Quin, and the canopy sails to the south, raging with fire, were collapsing. *Traveler* groaned and rolled in that direction, slowly at first and then like a boulder picking up speed down a mountain. Half the bridge was falling away, with Quin on it.

"Quin!" he screamed. The canopy beneath her was billowing and shifting, and she was riding it downward, helpless. "Quin!"

He ran for the edge to jump after her—

Hands were on his shoulders, yanking him away. His vision shifted, as though a gray curtain had been drawn across his field of view. The Transit Bridge was farther below him; he was floating.

"Quin!" he yelled again.

She hit the water and disappeared beneath the surface.

CHAPTER 69

JOHN

John and Maud came out of the anomaly with more than three dozen Seekers and children. The gray Scottish morning of drizzling rain came as a shock to everyone after the smoky mayhem they had just left. They had emerged into the commons, where the grass was so high that it obscured the heads of half the children.

"Did Shinobu jump after Quin?" the Young Dread asked him.

"I don't know," John answered, haunted by their last moments in the chaos. "The bridge was breaking and he disappeared."

In one moment, Shinobu had been at the edge of their particular island of canopy debris. In the next moment he had been gone—but whether he'd thrown himself over the edge or found some other route out, it had been impossible to tell.

The Young Dread held up a slender athame with an emblem of three interlocking ovals—the athame of the Dreads.

"You found it!" John said, hope swelling.

"One of the Watchers had it," she told him. She was already adjusting its dials.

With John's athame, it would take much too long to find their way onto the Transit Bridge. With Maud's they could go back directly.

She brought him *There* immediately. It took her several tries to open up an anomaly onto the place where the bridge had stood. When she did, they saw that there was nothing to be done. Through the opening, they beheld disaster: the center of the bridge had collapsed into the harbor, and their friends were nowhere to be found.

CHAPTER 70

SHINOBU

Shinobu was plunging down, without plunging at all, directly in the path of Quin's wild fall.

"I'm Dex, and this is my father. You must be Shinobu."

The young man who'd grabbed him didn't sound very happy about introducing himself, but Shinobu had no thoughts to spare on such details. Flaming wreckage rained down around them, though it never touched the three of them. The world was behind a veil and they were in a dark tunnel—a tunnel *through* the air. The broken bridge and canopy were sliding by on either side.

Shinobu had a thousand questions, but none of them mattered. He understood that the medallion Dex held was allowing them to chase after Quin, and he didn't care how or why. He only cared about getting to her.

The world beyond the veil was moving more slowly than it should have been, as though Dex were regulating the pace—or at least regulating how fast Shinobu was seeing it.

They descended straight through the surface of the water, which was surging with debris, and dove beneath it, the tunnel a shifting sleeve of dark space that kept them dry. The Old Dread lit a flare as soon as they were underwater, and then they were walking or gliding through the sinking debris, searching. Dex was following Quin's path of travel, through billowing canvas and solid beams of torn steel. Was it even possible that she could be alive?

They moved through a mountain of frayed cables . . . and she was there. Quin was pinned to the seafloor between a steel girder and a great swath of sail. Her hands were on the girder, as though trying to push free, but she was no longer moving. Dark hair floated about her head, and her dark eyes stared blankly.

Shinobu rushed to the edge of the tunnel. Before he could reach through the shifting veil, the Old Dread yanked him back. "Patience," the man told him.

"She's drowning out there! Let me get her! Can't I reach through?"

"It's tricky with the water," Dex said calmly, maddeningly, as he made tiny adjustments to his medallion. "Give me a moment."

"She doesn't have a moment!" Shinobu cried. Quin was only a few feet away, dying before Shinobu's eyes, or already dead. "Please!" he said, resisting the urge to shake Dex violently.

Then the space around Shinobu warped. He was swept upward and tilted, as Dex and the Old Dread were shifted alongside him. The three of them hadn't moved, and yet somehow their orientation to Quin was entirely changed. Shinobu was now standing above her, looking down at her in the light of the Old Dread's gently hissing flare.

The tunnel continued to inch downward in tiny increments until its dark border was partially through the steel beam holding Quin down. Another few excruciating inches, and they were through the entire beam.

"Now!" Dex said. "Pull her now!"

Shinobu reached, found his own arms moving through water. His head was in the ocean. He grabbed Quin's waist, and water was pouring into the tunnel. He held her, dragged her toward him with a half-swimming, half-walking motion. He lost his sense of balance. He was both above her and beside her, carrying her without knowing which way he was going. The cold water of Victoria Harbor was all around his legs, filling the tunnel.

Dex changed their orientation again, and the water stopped breaching. Shinobu had been rolled upward until he was hanging above the pool that had flooded in. He discovered he could set Quin down on . . . nothing, but a nothing that served just as well as ground. The tunnel continued to shift. Dex and the Old Dread were gliding them through the wreckage—searching for Maggie, Shinobu suspected—but he hardly noticed.

Quin was cold, gray, and not breathing. When he felt at her neck, there was no pulse. Her hair was plastered over her face, which looked pale and dead. It was all Shinobu could do not to panic.

"Quin, I've got you," he whispered as he began to pump her chest. "Come on, please."

He counted the chest compressions, remembering the sequence from their years as apprentices when they had practiced it so many times. Alistair had gotten mad at them for joking during the lesson and he'd made them practice an extra hour as punishment. *Thank God,* Shinobu thought.

He tilted back Quin's head, put his mouth over hers, and breathed into her lungs. He wanted to give her every ounce of air in his body, every breath he had ever taken . . .

Stop being romantic and save her! he told himself.

He pumped her chest again, forcing himself to push hard, even though it was awful to see her body convulse beneath his hands. He was dimly aware of his two companions silently watching him and urging him on.

"Quin," he said, not whispering now but speaking sharply. "Quin, you weren't under all that long. I saw Dex slow down the world—or speed me up—when he brought us to you. You sank to the bottom, but you weren't under very long. I know you're still alive. Quin! Quin!"

He breathed for her again, imagining it was his own life he was pouring into her.

Stop the poetry and concentrate!

He put his hands to her chest a third time and began to pump desperately. Halfway through the sequence, she fought him. Her chest rose on its own.

"Quin? Quin?"

His ear to her mouth, he heard her breathing; he felt a pulse at her neck.

"Please . . ." He squeezed her hand gently between his own. "Can you hear me, Quin? Quin!"

She did nothing but breathe for a long while, and he watched each rise and fall of her ribs as individual miracles. (*Stop it!* he admonished himself.)

At last, Quin's hand twitched and she moved her lips. Shinobu leaned very close.

She whispered, "Did I die again?"

"I think you did," he whispered back. "Just for a little while."

"I've got to stop doing that."

Shinobu laughed. "I agree."

" 'Mglad you're here with me . . ."

Relief left him weak. He rested his head on her chest, which continued to rise and fall beneath his forehead, the most beautiful motion he'd ever felt, and he didn't care if he was being romantic now; she was alive.

After a time, he looked up, found Dex and the Old Dread turned away. The Old Dread was holding his flare up at the edge of the tunnel, and they were both peering out through the water at another shape tangled in the debris from the Transit Bridge.

It was Maggie, her arms spread above her, one of her legs pinned beneath a heavy coil of cable. She was unmoving, except for her long white hair and her cloak, both of which shifted and billowed with the current. She looked, Shinobu thought, like a goddess of the sea, the sort of ancient deity who could be good or evil based on whim.

She was staring at her husband and son with eyes that surely could no longer see, and yet they looked alive and intelligent.

"What do you think, Father?" Dex asked quietly.

The Old Dread gazed at the woman. A knife handle was visible between her shoulder blades. She had been dead before she fell from the bridge.

"I think one of her followers has already passed his judgment," the Old Dread said very slowly, pointing at the knife.

All present understood that the wreckage of the airship and bridge and so many Seeker deaths could be laid at the feet of the woman out there in the water. Even now, the device that had brought *Traveler* down and turned off the power throughout half the city was around her knuckles as though she were planning to use it again.

"The circle should be closed," the Old Dread said, in his strange cadence. "We will leave her here."

Dex tilted his head in acknowledgment and added nothing to this verdict.

Before they turned away, a single bubble escaped Maggie's lips, the final sign of life. As it floated toward the surface, it was as if the last of her vital force floated with it, leaving only the body of an old woman, tangled in canvas and steel, alone on the floor of the ocean.

CHAPTER 71

MAUD

"In my addled and exhausted state, I failed to give you the one thing you most needed," the Old Dread said. His face was still cleanly shaven, which Maud found disconcerting. He looked like a modern man, except for the old robe.

He and the Young Dread sat high up in the castle ruins on the Scottish estate, looking down at the river and the world beyond. Dex sat near his father, though he'd said very little since the older man had introduced him to Maud.

The Old Dread had explained his family to her, but the idea that he had a son—two sons!—was not an easy one to swallow. She had thought of him as her own true father.

The Old Dread was holding out a round stone medallion. The Young Dread took it and studied it, the emblem on the front, the concentric circles on the back.

"What does it do?"

"It does so many things, child. Dex and I will take this day and as many days as you need, to show you all of its tricks—and how to use every tool I left you. But the most important is the medallion, because it can wake you when you're stretched out *There*."

The Old Dread still spoke in his slow way, the same way Maud had spoken before spending so much time awake. But his cadence was already changing. He was, hour by hour, speeding up, as if, on this waking, he intended to truly rejoin the world.

"Master—" she began.

"Child, I am not your master anymore, if I ever was."

"Who are you, then?"

There was a long pause. When he spoke, she could see him weighing each word. "Dear Maud, I am only a man with a clever mind, who thought he could change the world." He sighed and looked down at his hands, before he turned back to her. "You—you began in the past and have moved forward in time from the moment you were born to this moment here, sitting in these ruins together. I did not. I began here, or nearly here, and then things got out of order."

This explanation was unintelligible to the Young Dread, but then, her master had always been confusing on the subject of time.

"Are you not a Dread, then? Were you never a Dread?"

"Of course I was a Dread," he told her. He had habitually tugged at his beard, but when his hand came to his chin, it found no beard there and hung, confused, in the air. "You were like my own child, and we did many worthy things together, didn't we? I could have had no better daughter than you."

Hearing him call her his daughter provoked a feeling of happiness in Maud so intense that she required a moment of silence to take it in. He touched her shoulder, understanding.

He said, "But you are grown now. The son I thought was dead is here. And I—" He looked to Dex for the words.

Dex picked up the thought from the Old Dread. "We're going to finish out our lives the way my father always intended. Anonymously, quietly, pleasantly. As part of the world in which we were born."

"An accident of calculation brought me to you," her master explained. "And that same accident brought Seekers to the world. But now . . . now the beginning and end have joined. I'm no longer your Old Dread. I am only the man I was to begin with."

The Young Dread struggled to grasp what he meant for her to do. She asked, "Do you want Seekers and Dreads to end as well?"

He looked away from her. Beyond the river was open countryside, beautiful and wild. Maud had been looking at some version of this view for most of her life, and often she'd looked at it with the old man who was now sitting beside her. Her master had been the anchor of her existence.

"That is not for me to decide," he told her after a time. "You once asked me if you were a person or a possession. Of course you are a person, you are a Dread, and it is your choice to remain so . . . or not. And as to Seekers, my son and I believe they lie safely in Quin Kincaid's hands."

Maud looked down into the castle ward behind her. John was there, practicing with his whipsword, waiting for her. Her first instinct was to go to him so that they might talk this over together. Perhaps she was ready for a life beyond her master.

"Is he your apprentice now?" the old man asked, following her gaze. "Are you training him to be a Dread?"

She felt the unaccustomed pull of emotion as she watched John. "I don't know. He may not choose to live as we live."

"And there is the real question, child. What is a Dread?"

"One who stands apart from humanity so that she may judge clearly," Maud answered. There was no doubt in her own mind.

"That is what I wanted Dreads to be," he agreed. "Tyrants and evildoers beware."

"Tyrants and evildoers beware," she echoed.

"The rules I made were intended to keep the Middle Dread in line. But you are not like him. If you choose to be a Dread still, you must decide what it means."

The Old Dread, her master, the man who had taught her about the hum of the universe—he was only a man called James.

As if to prove this point, he and his son Desmond changed into modern garb before they left the estate. The Young Dread took her leave of him with an embrace at the edge of the commons. After this goodbye, she watched the two men—ordinary men in ordinary clothing—walk south.

She could have taken them to their destination by athame or by medallion—she had both remaining medallions, one for her, one for her future apprentice—but they had declined that offer.

"We're going to walk there," Dex had told her. "For old times' sake."

The Young Dread watched for a very long while, until the two of them had disappeared from sight. Then she turned to John and found herself at a loss.

"Well," he said, "what now?"

CHAPTER 72

QUIN

Quin woke in the hospital. Shinobu was asleep beside her, his head on her bed, the rest of him sprawled in a chair.

She was connected to an IV and a heart monitor, but she could see nothing wrong with herself. Her limbs moved properly. Gingerly she tested her lungs, and found that they took in air perfectly well.

She let her eyes fall closed for a moment, and she was immediately falling with the Transit Bridge, hitting the water; the weight of the beam was pushing her down, and her lungs were burning . . . She shivered and opened her eyes. Fear of drowning. She would have to make room for it next to fear of heights.

She studied Shinobu's sleeping face on the bed. He had bruises everywhere, and his eyes looked sunken and exhausted. His arms and legs still gave the impression of having been put back together carelessly. He'd been through several very bad weeks, and at the end of them, he'd pulled her from the water and saved her.

She ran her hand through his hair, across his cheek. He woke to her touch and took her hand between both of his own. He pressed his lips against her fingers as he met her gaze.

"You'll do anything it takes," she whispered.

"Of course I will." He kissed her hand. "Quin, when I left you *There*, I, I thought—"

She pulled him closer. "It doesn't matter. I know you would never intentionally hurt me."

"I thought I was *saving* you. I thought if I kept you *There*, you would be safe while I tried to sort out the Watchers. They'd already attacked us, and I—"

She took his face in her hands and kissed him gently. "Shinobu, promise me one thing—no more focals."

"No more focals! I destroyed mine. Would you like me to track down the rest and destroy all of them? I'll do it. I could make the world focal-free."

She smiled. "We'll see."

His face darkened, and she could see that he was wrestling with something unpleasant. As if it were an admission of a terrible secret, he told her, "That big fellow took me to you. That's how I found you. It wasn't, you know, all my own doing. He helped. A lot."

"Dex?"

"Yes, him." He said this with much the same tone Dex had used when referring to Shinobu—thinly concealed distaste. "He told me he was the one who took you back to the world when I left you *There*."

"He did." She thought about her days with Dex, the nights practicing in the castle ward, the strange places he had shown her. She was different now for having known him. "I'll have to tell you about my time with him."

"Will you?" Shinobu was watching her closely, a pained look on his face.

"What's the matter?" she asked.

He swallowed. "Quin, you don't, you don't . . . I mean, *do* you . . . ?"

Quin tried not to laugh at his tortured expression. "Do I *love* him? Is that what you mean to ask?"

Shinobu's jaw set. He was a prisoner waiting for his sentence. He muttered, "I know he saved you. And he's really tall. I think he's not horrible to look at—if you like tall, handsome warrior types."

"I do like those types," Quin said, running her hand through his hair and smiling at him, because he could have been describing himself. Shinobu was staring at her as though his life depended on each word she said. "Half the time I was with Dex, he mistook me for his wife and thought we were in love."

"What?" Shinobu was halfway to his feet. She pulled him back down.

"But I reminded him that I was Quin Kincaid and my heart was already taken."

"So nothing . . . ?" She could almost see the image in his head, of her and Dex alone, somewhere dark and private.

"Nothing," she told him. "I'm afraid you're stuck with me."

Shinobu's relief was so dramatic that Quin burst out laughing. She'd never seen him like this, and it charmed her.

"I made you jealous."

"I was going to fight him to the death," Shinobu told her. "Wipe that handsome smile off his face. Show him who's—"

She pulled him to her and kissed him, but a moment later she was laughing again at the look on his face. She kissed him longer, then asked, "Still jealous?"

"A little," he whispered. "Kiss me more."

He drew her to him, but they were interrupted by a gentle knock on the door. Fiona Kincaid stuck her head into the hospital room.

"Mother!" Quin said, delighted to see Fiona there and well. "Where were you? I was so worried you were in the house or somewhere else on the bridge when—"

"I wasn't on the bridge," Fiona reassured her. She crossed the room and kissed her daughter's forehead, perched herself on the edge of the bed. "I was with Mariko."

"Shinobu's mother?" she asked, confused. She hadn't known that Fiona and Mariko knew anything of each other in present day.

Fiona was nodding.

"Our mothers have had an adventure in our absence," Shinobu explained. "They found their way to Briac and . . . well, I'll let her tell you herself."

He got to his feet, stretched his bruised arms, and slipped out of the room, leaving them alone for a while. Quin lay back to listen as Fiona recounted a wild tale of joining forces with Mariko MacBain. Together they'd located Quin's father, who was still in the mental hospital outside London, barely coherent since he'd been partially disrupted during the fight on *Traveler*. With patience and, perhaps, a certain single-mindedness, the two mothers had wrung from Briac the names of other Seekers still alive in the world who had been accomplices of the Middle Dread. Fiona and Mariko had spent the last weeks tracking those few traitors down.

"You killed them?" Quin asked. She was ready to believe anything at the moment.

"No," Fiona scoffed. "That wouldn't have been our place. I'm not a killer, and none of them had athames. They were all fallen into a bad state, or the Middle Dread wouldn't have let them live. Mariko and I merely told them we knew the ways they had broken Seeker laws and they should stay away from other Seekers—you in particular—or we would give their names to the Young Dread and let her determine their fates. I don't think we'll be seeing any of them again."

It was a fitting resolution, Quin decided, and one that seemed to please her mother.

She remembered all the years Fiona had been cowed and terrified in Briac's presence, and the years of her using alcohol to stay numb. Her mother looked, Quin thought, more beautiful than ever, as if her true self had finally been allowed to come to the surface.

"And what about Briac's future?" Quin asked. She was reluctant to speak about her father, but she sensed that Fiona wanted to tell her about him.

Fiona cleared her throat. "After a great deal of thought," she said, looking uncomfortable, "we decided to leave your father in the mental hospital. He can't be trusted out in the world. Besides, he's half-disrupted. A permanent madman. Well—he was always a bit mad, wasn't he? But he's an *obvious* madman now. The only other option would be the Seeker way—to kill him and put him out of his misery."

"That might be more kind," Quin offered. She was thinking of Briac in a madhouse for all of his life.

"It would be more kind," Fiona said, an edge in her voice. "And when the years he kept Alistair and Mariko apart, and the years he trained you and Shinobu to kill people—when those years have been repaid, we may put him out of his misery. But not until then."

Quin had fixed Dex by gathering five master healers to work on him at once. Dex hadn't been disrupted in the ordinary sense; he'd been the victim of an early version of the weapon, with different effects. Still, five masters might be able to help Briac. But when she imagined curing her father, it didn't feel right. She had too many memories of what he'd been like.

After a moment's reflection, she accepted Fiona's judgment in this matter. Let Briac stay where he was.

When Fiona had left, Shinobu returned, one hand behind his back and a mischievous quirk to one eyebrow.

"What have you got?" she asked.

"A present."

With a flourish, he presented her with an athame and lightning rod. On the pommel of the athame was a small carving of a ram.

"How . . . ?" she asked.

"Do you remember a little Watcher called Nott?"

"The one who attacked us in the hospital in London?"

"And in several other places," Shinobu said. "He brought it to me as a sort of peace offering. I also got the dragon athame during the fight on the bridge. So you and I are Seekers now, there's no getting around it."

Quin was speechless. She was holding the ram athame, gone from her family for generations and now recovered. Not just recovered but lying in her own hands.

Shinobu took her hand in his and said, solemnly, "I've brought you your athame, but I expect a favor in return."

"Anything," she told him.

"Try not to die again."

"I will make every attempt not to," she promised.

3 YEARS LATER

CHAPTER 73

QUIN

Quin climbed the old steps by flashlight, her footfalls echoing into the cavern beneath her. At the top of the stairs, she pulled the trapdoor down, tossed her heavy bag through, and crawled up after it into the hidden passage at the base of the castle ruins.

In that muted space of ancient stone and close air, she walked past the murals of all nine Seeker houses. Some of those houses were gone now, destroyed entirely by Maggie. Others were rebuilding themselves. This passage, whatever it had been originally, was now a shrine to the things that had been.

She walked to the far end and stood in front of the last mural. James, Maggie, Desmond, and Matheus looked out at her, unseeing. Dark and light, combined in one family that had set the world of Seekers in motion.

Quin took the focal and disruptor out of her pack and set them on the floor, arranging the focal beneath Desmond and the disruptor beneath Matheus, in such a way that they mirrored the painted focal and disruptor on the wall. Both objects had been damaged into uselessness in the Transit Bridge fight.

She gazed at Dex's likeness and thought about the real Dex, crazy for a time but good nonetheless. Though it felt childish, she spoke out loud to his image.

"We've gotten rid of most of the disruptors. Well, most were crushed beneath the ruins of the Transit Bridge. The few that are left are sometimes used for training, but usually we keep them locked up."

Her voice came back to her in a dull echo. It felt as though she were speaking not just to Dex, wherever he had gone, but to the castle itself, to the ancient heart of Seeker-hood.

"And the focals . . . there are only a few of those left as well. We use them now and then—carefully."

Quin paused, looking down at the helmet and weapon on the dusty floor. Why had she brought them here? As a tribute, she realized.

"I want you to know that we have dedicated our lives to being true Seekers, in the Old Dread's sense of the word."

She regarded Dex's painted face and the face of the Old Dread, who was not old in this painting but a man in the prime of his life.

"After the bridge, some Seekers went off into the world, just as you two did, to live their lives in a more ordinary way. The ones who wanted to continue came to the estate, and we've started over. The athames we have left are for common use. No one acts alone; we are all brothers and sisters, regardless of house."

She touched Dex's painted hand and remembered his real hand clutching his medallion on the bridge, destroying all the athames in its path as he tried to remove his family's influence from the world.

"Dex, I think you and your father regretted your lives, regretted creating Seekers and our tools. But I hope not. We are keeping the athames among good hearts, and we will try very hard to choose wisely."

The focal and disruptor sat on the floor, a shrine to the people who had made them. The faces in the mural stared out at her blankly. It was up to Quin to decide if anyone might have heard her.

When Quin emerged from the castle ruins, she walked back to the heart of the estate. The day was fine, and apprentices were being instructed out in the open, among the trees at the edge of the forest, or in the commons.

There was Kaspar, seven years old now, demonstrating his blinding speed to the older apprentices.

"Very good, Kaspar. Again!" called Mariko MacBain, who had returned to the estate and was now a teacher.

Mariko stood at one end of a clearing, a commanding presence despite her slight form. She wore a black training robe, and her hair was in an elaborate bun at the crown of her head, a Samurai warrior with her jewel-encrusted whipsword at her side.

"Who is next? Akio!" Mariko ordered, calling out Shinobu's younger brother to follow Kaspar. "We use swords this time!"

Mariko inclined her head in greeting as Quin passed, and Quin did the same.

There were newly built classrooms at the edge of the commons, with large windows facing the meadow. Fiona was inside one of the rooms, with a class of older children who stood completely silent, facing each other across the room. When apprentices developed the ability to read another's thoughts, they came to Fiona for further instruction. Quin smiled at the sight of her mother, useful and happy.

Inside the other room was a class of younger apprentices receiving instruction in grammar. Nott sat at the back, much larger than anyone else in the class, clutching a pencil as if it were a butcher knife, his tongue firmly planted at the side of his mouth, working desperately to learn his letters. His front teeth showed between his lips; they had, at last, been scrubbed clean of soot, and even seen to by a dentist.

Quin could not help laughing at the former Watcher's intense concentration and the trail of broken pencils littering the floor around his desk. She doubted Nott would ever be much of a scholar—he had taken this particular class three times already—but he was undoubtedly one of the best fighters among the apprentices. And when he wasn't in class, Nott usually had a train of stray cats and half-trained squirrels and even a pet pig that followed him around the estate, to the delight of the younger children.

Quin walked on, past the rebuilt dining hall, where later that day all Seekers on the estate would gather to vote on their next assignment. Quin was proposing a rescue of families caught in the midst of a civil war in South America. There were other proposals. With luck, they would be able to do them all.

She found Shinobu in the center of the meadow. He was on his knees, holding up his hands while Grace, two years old, with flaming red hair, hit and kicked his palms with all the fury a toddler could muster.

Grace noticed the change in her father's eyes when he saw Quin. She spun around and ran toward Quin, shouting, "Mama! Mama! Daddy let me hold a knife!"

Grace leapt into Quin's arms with wild abandon.

"A knife!" Quin said with mock distress.

The little girl held her mother's face in her hands and said seriously, "But it's *sharp*."

Quin smiled. "That's the truth with knives."

"And what have you been up to?" Shinobu asked as he kissed her.

"Only saying a kind of goodbye."

He knew where she'd been and didn't ask anything more.

They wandered toward the dining hall together. It would be lunchtime soon, and Grace didn't like to be late for lunch.

Shinobu put an arm around Quin's shoulders, pulled her to him. Grace hummed to herself and leaned down from Quin's hip to let the grass of the commons brush against her hand as they walked.

Quin was content to know that the future was theirs to choose.

CHAPTER 74

DESMOND AND JAMES

Dex came into the cool interior of the barn. It was a lofty space, with a glass-paneled roof to let in the sunlight. He stoked the stove at the center of the room with an armful of fresh logs, which began to crackle cheerfully, and then he went over to see what his father was up to.

The perimeter of the barn was lined with dozens of worktables, sitting end to end, providing James and Desmond almost limitless space to tinker. His father was at a table already, had probably been in the barn since dawn.

"Dex, there you are," he said, looking up from his work. As always, he was overjoyed to see his son, and his happiness rubbed off on Dex. "I was thinking we'd walk to the quarry today. The weather looks fine."

There was a small stone quarry on the edge of their farm, where they could find the sort of stone James preferred.

"Yes, of course. I'd like that."

"What's happened?" his father asked. "You have a look." James might have gotten quite old and given up his former life, but he was as perceptive as ever.

Dex hesitated. "I felt her talking to me." He didn't need to explain who he meant. His father would know that Dex was speaking of the girl who wasn't Quilla, not really, but who reminded him very much of Quilla.

"And what did she say?"

"That everything will turn out all right in the end." Dex felt a deep sadness as he said the words. For him, for Quilla, everything had not turned out as they'd hoped.

James put a hand on his son's shoulder. "Ah, lad, come see this," he said, shutting the door on questions of philosophy and focusing instead on what was here in front of them. On the table was an elaborate construction of pale stone and metal that reminded Dex of a Victorian birdcage.

"Have you got it working?" Dex asked.

James laughed delightedly, and Desmond thought how very youthful his father seemed, despite having lived longer than any human could rightly expect. James had begun to recover his energy on the date when his younger self, along with his wife and two small sons, had left the laboratory in Switzerland and begun their long journey through the past. As he had said before, the circle was complete. Everything beyond was a new life.

"Watch this," he told Dex.

James tapped one side of his creation with a small piece of bent copper. The lengths of stone between the connecting lengths of metal began to vibrate one by one, each stone humming a slightly different note, and as they hummed, they spun in place, whirling to the harmonies they were creating. James continued to tap until his birdcage was ringing so loudly, it filled the barn. The song was eerie and lovely and infinite.

"It's beautiful," Dex said.

And if by chance this creation of his father's was vibrating in more than the normal dimensions they could see around them, Dex was not going to complain. They weren't opening up anomalies, they were not changing the world. His father was only acting on his most sacred ambition, to listen to the hum of the universe. Dex could allow him that.

CHAPTER 75

THE APPRENTICE DREAD

It was late in the Arctic night, and a driving wind pelted the Apprentice Dread with crystals of ice blown off the surface of the glacier. His hair and cloak were thick with frost. It was very cold, but cold meant little. He did what he must, regardless of discomfort.

The moon lay beyond heavy clouds, and only a bit of its light found its way down to the glacier. This was enough; his eyes were learning to be as sensitive to light as they needed to be.

At a hand signal from the Young Dread, he began to run. This was the first time he'd woken in a year, and he found that his body moved with the silent tread he'd been taught by his master. He carried himself along as he perceived time should flow—smoothly, steadily, rhythmically.

He accelerated to match the pace of the Young Dread as she sprinted up the face of the glacier. It was like flying, the way they moved, so fast the snow did not have a chance to sink beneath their feet.

A glint in the air. A knife coming at him. He reached without thinking, without pausing, without missing a step. He caught the knife and threw it back.

Back and forth they sent the blade, each throw more powerful than the last, the air humming with the knife's passage. And still they ran up and up.

As they neared the small crest, the sky welcomed them with a break in the clouds. Between were stars, vibrant to the Apprentice's eyes. Painted upon the backdrop of the galaxy was a sight he had hoped he would see: the aurora borealis, green and pink, in an electric dance above them.

The knife came so fast he couldn't follow it with his eyes; he could only rely on his sense of the Young Dread's motion. He pulled the blade from the air as easily as breathing.

They stopped running at the same moment. They had reached the place. He could hear the wind across the slope, the sound of it snaking between crags miles away, the snow near and far shifting with the night.

"You were very fast," the Young Dread told him, suddenly beside him. "Perhaps the fastest yet."

"It's good to be awake."

From the outside, the cave looked like little more than a cleft in the rock. Inside, it was a small rounded nook, large enough for two. Each Seeker house had once had a hidden place for its members alone. The Apprentice Dread and the Young Dread had found this place when he'd first begun his training, and now they called it their own.

The Apprentice built the fire, as was his duty, while the Young Dread began to prepare their meal. In the orange light of the flames, their cave became a warm shelter against the northern night.

They sat side by side as they ate, saying nothing and needing to say nothing. The Apprentice felt his mind returning to familiar tracks briefly: he thought of his grandfather's fortune, of the crashed airship that had once again required repair, of his cousins vying for control of the money. How strange and distant those things were. He had given up his position and the vast wealth that came with it. Now it was hard to understand what it had ever meant to him.

"You are thinking of your life," the Young Dread said.

"Yes, but it's not my life. This is."

He did not smile as he said it, because there was no need. They both understood how he felt.

The Apprentice moved closer to her, so that they sat shoulder to shoulder, her warmth bleeding into him and his bleeding into her.

The coming days would bring grueling training for him, and when it was time to take a break from training, they would both attend a Seeker oath ceremony on the Scottish estate. By then, the Apprentice would feel more human, and so would the Young Dread. They might even kiss each other, and experience life for a time as a boy and girl. But these were small matters of human comfort and not nearly as important as he had once thought they were.

He saw himself reflected in her eyes, as she was reflected in his. They were John and Maud, though they hardly used those names anymore.

They were Dreads.

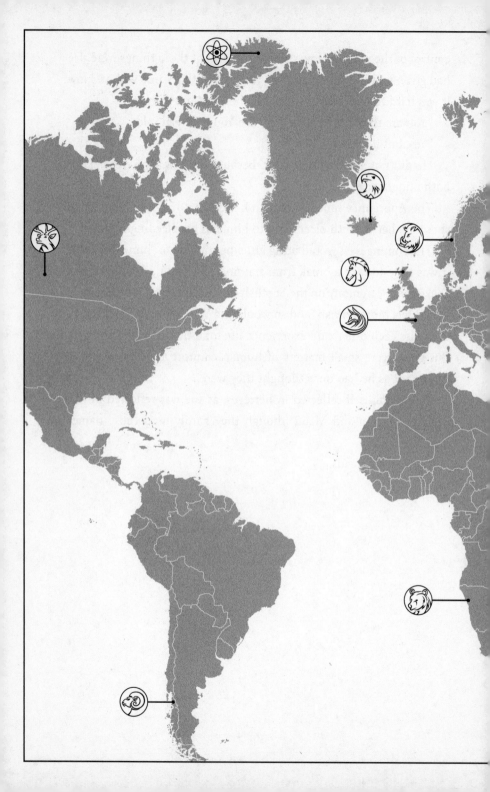

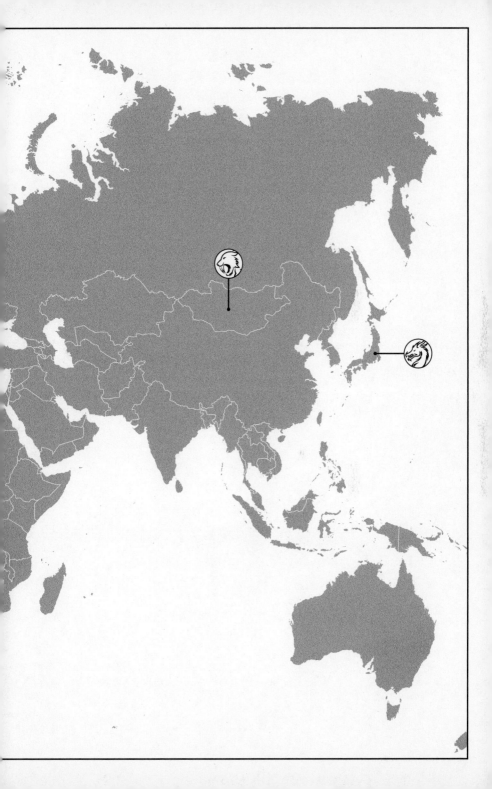

Seeker Houses

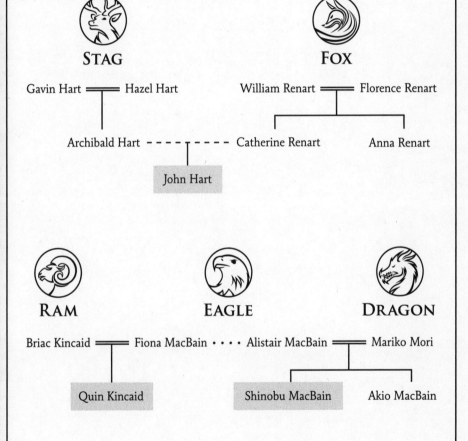

STAG

Gavin Hart ═══ Hazel Hart

Archibald Hart - - - - - - - Catherine Renart

John Hart

FOX

William Renart ═══ Florence Renart

Catherine Renart   Anna Renart

RAM

Briac Kincaid ═══ Fiona MacBain • • • • Alistair MacBain ═══ Mariko Mori

Quin Kincaid

EAGLE

DRAGON

Shinobu MacBain   Akio MacBain

KEY   ═══ Married   - - - - Engaged   ─── Child   • • • • Kinsman

ACKNOWLEDGMENTS

I've never written a series before, and now that I have, I can assure you that it is a leap of faith. From the top of a cliff, you see the world of your story spread out below—well, you see *some* of it, because a lot is obscured in fog and beneath the cover of dense forest—and you glimpse, peeking at you from near the horizon, the seductive destinations you hope to reach. And then you jump.

So many people made this jump with me and have my profound thanks.

First came Jodi Reamer, who took it for granted that I would land on my feet and may have even shoved me over the edge.

Then there was Krista Marino, who I often feel must have a small cottage somewhere near the Scottish estate and may have dated both John and Shinobu at some point in her teen years. Her willingness to inhabit this world with me and help me breathe life into each part has been wonderful.

Barbara Marcus, Judith Haut, and Beverly Horowitz, for your support, encouragement, and guidance throughout this undertaking, and for running what is, quite simply, a wonderful publishing house.

For the beautiful, beautiful books, gorgeous inside and out, thank you so much to Alison Impey and Stephanie Moss.

To Felicia Frazier, for being a warrior in the service of books.

John Adamo, Kim Lauber, Stephanie O'Cain, and Rachel Feld, thank you for bringing the series out into the world of real readers.

Tamar Schwartz and Monica Jean for making everything work.

Bara MacNeill and Colleen Fellingham, please accept my heartfelt thanks for fine-tooth-combing these books.

To Andrea Doven, for bringing so much good energy into my life, and to Sky Morfopoulos, for being my in-house cheerleader and friend.

To my family, for making life a joy. I couldn't have asked for a better set.

ARWEN ELYS DAYTON

THE
YOUNG
DREAD

TURN THE PAGE FOR A SPECIAL PREVIEW OF
THE E-NOVELLA *THE YOUNG DREAD.*

CHAPTER 1

A HELM AND A CLOAKED BOY

It was the warmest night of the year, and the moon, though only a quarter full, hung low and huge in the sky. It was yellow more than white, with an orange halo. The Young Dread stood atop a crumbling tower of the castle—half of which was still intact and occupied, and half of which lay in ruins. From her vantage point, she had a view of the forest on three sides and the wild Scottish countryside beyond the river on the fourth. The world was both beautiful and ominous in the yellow moonlight.

It was well past midnight, which made the date June the twenty-first. That was the Young Dread's birthday—Maud's birthday, though no one called her Maud anymore—and by her reckoning she must be about thirteen years old, though it was now 1748, nearly three hundred years since the year of her birth. Birthdays meant little when she spent so much of her life separate from the world. But still, June the twenty-first was a date that meant something to her.

The Dreads spent much of their lives *There,* in that other place, outside the stream of time, where they were stretched asleep in the darkness. They were awake in the world for only short intervals, like this one, when they would train, brutally and constantly, and keep an eye on the new generation of Seekers.

The Young Dread wore only her shoes and her undergarments, but she'd long ago lost a sense of modesty when she trained. Maud stood apart from humanity, as all Dreads did. Such small personal details as bare legs were of no significance.

"Attend!" called the Middle Dread, her older companion and trainer.

He was concealed somewhere off to her right, outside the castle's courtyard, and she suspected he was armed with a bow and a plentiful supply of blunt arrows.

The Young Dread stood straighter, ready for his commands.

"Helm!" called the Middle Dread.

Maud held a simple helmet of smooth metal, with two slight ridges from crown to back of neck and otherwise unadorned. It crackled faintly in her hands, alive with energy—*electricity*, the Old Dread called it, stolen from the sun. She slipped it over her head.

It took all of her skill not to lose her balance and go down on one knee. She remained on her feet, just barely, though she swayed as the helmet settled to her scalp. The helmet's energy was now both sound and feel, a hiss and snap in her ears that traveled right through her skull. And there was a buzzing, as though she'd stuck her head up against a beehive and could hear the insects' intimate conversations all around her.

When she surveyed the night with the helm upon her head, many separate elements became joined in a unified whole: The breeze came from the forest and the river, and she understood how far that breeze had traveled to reach her, how much land and ocean it had crossed, how many other faces it had touched. She sensed the Seekers and their apprentices in this very castle and in cottages throughout the estate, all asleep now. There were crickets at the edge of the woods, mice in the undergrowth and owls deeper among the oak trees. She was aware of the hunters and the hunted, a perfect chain of life. To the south and the west was her favorite hunter of all—the golden eagle she'd glimpsed a few times, in its aerie by the waterfall. She almost felt the night itself, crawling across the sphere of the world from east to west, darkening the land as it went.

Then she perceived it: something solid, disturbing the peace of the night, vibrating the tiny atmospheric particles—*molecules,* the Old Dread, her master, who knew so many things others didn't, called them.

At the last moment she acted, pulling her body backward and sweeping her left arm up. She knocked the Middle's arrow out of the air, sent it clattering down the stones below her.

Another arrow was already coming—a black bolt in the dark, seeking her head this time. Maud ducked, and it grazed the crown of her helm with a high-pitched ring.

"Now run!" called the Middle.

From the direction of his voice, she knew he'd changed his position. He was on the move.

The Young Dread glided down the ruined tower, leaping from loose stone to loose stone so quickly nothing had time to dislodge and send her sprawling. A new arrow hit the dirt by her feet as she reached the ground, and she felt the sting in her calf where the shaft had burned her as it went by.

She was in the castle's courtyard, sprinting for the woods, a barrage of arrows coming now. If she turned to look, she would lose ground; she must rely on her other senses. The helm was aiding her, vaulting her into its higher realm of awareness. She swerved as an arrow flew past to lodge in the crumbling stone wall at the end of the yard. The next came immediately; she sensed it diving down and leapt from its path. It passed an inch from her shoulder and twanged as it stuck into the earth. She cleared the end of the courtyard as a third arrow struck only a few feet away.

She was shielded now among trees. She heard the Middle's soft, inexorable tread upon the gravelly surface not far behind her. The vast stretches spent *There* changed the way the Dreads experienced time, the way they moved and spoke. As Maud ran, she felt her body gliding over the earth, steady, rhythmic, silent.

She veered from the path of a new arrow and didn't bother to watch where it went. There was something else that drew her attention: a cloaked figure was running parallel to her in the woods, small, like a child. This figure was moving as fast as she was. She imagined for a moment it was her reflection, keeping pace with her among the trees. It was like seeing another Young Dread—an even younger Dread.

A new arrow came. She jumped left, then slipped through a stand of elms to chase after her mysterious companion. The figure saw her intention and ran faster. When it passed through a clearing, moonlight illuminated, for the briefest of seconds, a face that had turned back to look at Maud.

It was a boy, younger than she by at least a year or two. He was the right age to be one of the younger Seeker apprentices training on the estate, but she didn't recognize him, and his clothes were all wrong—too coarse and much too dirty. Was he a peasant, then, from a nearby village? He looked exhilarated and terrified by this chase. His face said that she scared him but also that he would love to fight with her.

Maud kept herself only a few yards behind him, both of them jumping over brambles, pushing themselves off trees to correct their wild course through the dense woods. She could catch the boy if she wished, but she didn't want to; she wanted to see where he would lead her.

The boy was tiring. He leaped obstacles more recklessly and landed without much poise or balance. Surely he would stop soon and speak to her, or fight her, or surrender. Otherwise, Maud thought, he would fall.

And he did. She watched him land badly after jumping over a streamlet, tumble forward, and roll across the forest floor to a rough stop against the roots of an enormous tree.

The boy was breathing hard as she approached, his dirty face once again visible in the moonlight. He had drawn a knife and was clutching it in front of his chest in a threatening manner.

"He's training a girl, then, is he?" the boy said, his accent uneducated and his tone rather more arrogant than Maud would have expected, given the circumstances.

She opened her mouth to ask him who he was—

"Stop!"

The word had come from the Middle Dread. He stood only a few yards away, looking at her with fury, his bow across his shoulder and three arrows held between the fingers of his right hand. He was broad and thick and very strong, and in the shadows among the trees, with his dark cloak around him, he looked like nothing so much as an angry bull waiting to charge her.